SOMETHING TO TELL YOU

Something to Tell You

HANIF KUREISHI

faber and faber

First published in 2008
by Faber and Faber Limited
3 Queen Square London WC1N 3AU

Typeset by Faber and Faber Limited
Printed in England by Mackays of Chatham plc, Chatham, Kent

A CIP record for this book
is available from the British Library

ISBN 978-0-571-20977-4

2 4 6 8 10 9 7 5 3 1

I went down to the crossroads
Fell down on my knees

Robert Johnson

Part One

CHAPTER ONE

Secrets are my currency: I deal in them for a living. The secrets of desire, of what people really want, and of what they fear the most. The secrets of why love is difficult, sex complicated, living painful and death so close and yet placed far away. Why are pleasure and punishment closely related? How do our bodies speak? Why do we make ourselves ill? Why do you want to fail? Why is pleasure hard to bear?

A woman has just left my consulting room. Another will arrive in twenty minutes. I adjust the cushions on the analytic couch and relax in my armchair in a different silence, sipping tea, considering images, sentences and words from our conversation, as well as the joins and breaks between them.

As I do often these days, I begin to think over my work, the problems I struggle with, and how this came to be my livelihood, my vocation, my enjoyment. It is even more puzzling to me to think that my work began with a murder – today is the anniversary, but how do you mark such a thing? – followed by my first love, Ajita, going away forever.

I am a psychoanalyst. In other words, a reader of minds and signs. Sometimes I am called shrinkster, healer, detective, opener of doors, dirt digger or plain charlatan or fraud. Like a car mechanic on his back, I work with the underneath or understory: fantasies, wishes, lies, dreams, nightmares – the world beneath the world, the true words beneath the false. The weirdest intangible stuff I take seriously; I'm into places where language can't go, or where it stops – the 'indescribable' – and early in the morning too.

Giving sorrow other words, I hear of how people's desire and guilt upsets and terrorises them, the mysteries that burn a hole in the self and distort and even cripple the body, the wounds of experience, re-opened for the good of the soul as it is made over.

At the deepest level people are madder than they want to believe. You will find that they fear being eaten, and are alarmed by their desire to devour others. They also imagine, in the ordinary course of things, that they will explode, implode, dissolve or be invaded. Their daily lives are penetrated by fears that their love relations involve, among other things, the exchange of urine and faeces.

Always, before any of this began, I enjoyed gossip, an essential qualification for the job. Now I get to hear a lot of it, a river of human effluvium flowing into me, day after day, year after year. Like many modernists, Freud privileged detritus; you could call him the first artist of the 'found', making meaning out of that which is usually discarded. It is dirty work, getting closely acquainted with the human.

There is something else going on in my life now, almost an incest, and who could have predicted it? My older sister, Miriam, and my best friend, Henry, have conceived a passion for each other. All our separate existences are being altered, indeed shaken, by this unlikely liaison.

I say unlikely because these are quite different kinds of people, who you would never think of as a couple. He is a theatre and film director, a brazen intellectual whose passion is for talk, ideas, and the new. She couldn't be rougher, though she was always considered 'bright'. They have been aware of one another for years; she has sometimes accompanied me to his shows.

I guess my sister had always been waiting for me to invite her out; it took me a while to notice. Though an effort on occasion – her knees are crumbling and can't take her increasing weight – it was good for Miriam to leave the house, the kids and the neighbours. She was usually impressed and bored. She liked everything about the theatre but the plays. Her preferred part was the interval, when there was booze, cigarettes and air. I agree with her. I've seen many bad shows, but some of them had great intervals. Henry, himself, would inevitably fall asleep within fifteen minutes of the start of any play, particularly if it was directed by a friend, his furry head resting on your neck while he gurgled gently in your ear like a polluted brook.

Miriam knew Henry would never take her opinions seriously, but she wasn't afraid of him or his pomposity. It was said of Henry, and particularly of his work, that you had to praise him until you blushed, and then build from there. Miriam was not a praiser; she didn't see the need for it. She even liked to needle Henry. One time, in the foyer after an Ibsen or Molière, or maybe it was an opera, she announced that the piece was too long.

Everyone in the vicinity held their breath until he said through his grey beard, in his deep voice, 'That, I'm afraid, is exactly the time it took to get from the beginning to the end.'

'Well, they could have been closer together, that's all I'm saying,' was Miriam's reply.

Now there is something going on between the two of them – who are much closer together than before.

It occurred like this.

If Henry is not rehearsing or teaching, he strolls round to my place at lunchtime, as he did a few months ago, having rung Maria first. Maria, slow-moving, kind, easily shocked, indeed mortified – originally my cleaner but a woman I have come to rely on – prepares the food downstairs, which I like to be ready when I've finished with my last patient of the morning.

I am always glad to see Henry. In his company I can relax and do nothing important. You can say what you like, but all of us analysts go at it for long hours. I might see my first patient at 6 a.m. and not stop until one o'clock. After, I eat, make notes, walk or nap, until it's time for me to start listening again, into the early evening.

I can hear him, his voice booming from the table just outside the back door, before I am anywhere near the kitchen. His monologues are a torment for Maria, who has the misfortune to take people's words seriously.

'If only you understood me, Maria, and could see that my life is a terrible humiliation, a nothing.'

'It is not, surely? Mr Richardson, such a man as you must –'

'I am telling you I am dying of cancer and my career is a disaster.'

(She will come to me later whispering, fearfully, 'Is he really dying of cancer?'

'Not that I know.'

'Is his career a disaster?'

'There are few people more eminent.'

'Why does he say such things? What strange people they are, artists!')

He continues: 'Maria, my last two productions, the *Così*, and the version of *The Master and Margarita* in New York, bored me to death. They were successes, but not difficult enough for me. There was no struggle, no risk of annihilation. I want that!'

'No!'

'Then my son brings a woman into my flat more beautiful than Helen of Troy! I am universally hated – strangers spit in my open mouth!'

'Oh, no, no, no!'

'Just look at the newspapers. I am more hated than Tony Blair, and there's a man who is universally loathed.'

'Yes, he is terrible, everybody says, but you have not invaded anyone, or permitted them to be tortured at Guantánamo. You are loved!' There was a pause. 'Yes, you see, you know it!'

'I don't want to be loved. I want to be desired. Love is safety, but desire is foul. "Give me excess of it . . ." The awful thing is, the less one is capable of sex, the more one is capable of love, the pure thing. Nobody but you understands me. Is it too late, do you think, for me to become homosexual?'

'I don't believe it's a choice, Mr Richardson. But you must consult Dr Khan. He should be along shortly.'

The doors were open onto my little garden with its three trees and patch of grass. There were flowers on the table outside and Henry sitting at it, his stomach out front, a convenient cushion for his hands to rest on, if he wasn't scratching. On his knee was my grey cat Marcel, given to me by Miriam, a cat who wanted to smell everything, and who had to be regularly hauled from the room where I saw patients.

Having already dismissed half a bottle of good wine – 'I don't believe there's any alcohol in white!' – Henry was talking to himself, or free-associating, via Maria, who believed it was a conversation.

In the kitchen I was washing my hands. 'I want to be drunk,' I could hear him saying. 'I've wasted my life being respectable. I've reached the age when women feel safe around me! So alcohol improves my temper – everyone's temper.'

'It does? But you did tell me, when you came in, that they want you at the Paris Opera.'

'They'll take anyone. Maria, I am aware you like culture far more than I do. You are a darling of the cheap seats and every morning on the bus you read. But culture is ice creams, intervals, sponsors, critics and the same bored, over-refined queens who go to everything. There is culture, which is nothing, and there is the wasteland. Just leave London or turn on the TV and there it is. Ugly, puritanical, prurient, stupid, and people like Blair saying they don't understand modern art and our future king, Charles the Arse, rushing towards the past. Once I believed the two might overlap, the common and the high. Can you believe it? Oh Maria, I knew my life was over when I decided to take up watercolours –'

'At least you don't clean toilets for a living. Come on, try these tomatoes. Open wide and don't spit.'

'Oh, delicious. Where did you get these?'

'Tesco's. Use a napkin. It's all gone in your beard. You're attracting the flies!'

She was flapping at him. 'Thank you, mother,' he said. He looked up as I sat down. 'Jamal,' he said, 'Stop giggling and tell me: have you read the *Symposium* lately?'

'Hush, you bad man, let the doctor eat,' said Maria. 'He hasn't even put a piece of bread in his mouth yet.' I thought for a moment she was going to smack his hand. 'Dr Khan's heard enough talk this morning. He's so kind to listen to these people, when they should be chained up in the asylum. How smutty some of them are! When I open the door, even the ordinary ones like to ask me questions about the doctor. Where does he take his holidays, where has his wife gone? They get nothing from me.'

We were eating. To his credit, Henry couldn't stop talking. '"We travel with a corpse in our cargo." Ibsen is saying here that the dead – dead fathers, the living dead, in effect – are as potent, even more potent, than actually existing ones.'

I murmured, 'We are made of others.'

'How do you kill a dead father, then? Even then the guilt would be dreadful, wouldn't it?'

'Probably.'

He went on: 'Ibsen is such a realistic writer in this play. How do you symbolise the ghosts? Do you need to?' As he often did, Henry reached over to eat from my plate. 'This friendly aggression is surely a sign,' he said, holding up a bean, 'of a man who would enjoy sharing your wife?'

'Indeed. You are welcome.'

If speaking is intercourse for the dressed, Henry certainly had a good time; and these histrionic rambles at lunchtime were enjoyable and relaxing for me. When Maria was washing up and Henry and I were glancing through the sports pages, or looking at the line of gently nodding sunflowers my son Rafi had planted against the back wall of my little garden, he became less ecstatic.

'I know you don't work at lunchtime. You have your salad. You have wine. We talk rubbish, or at least I do. You just discuss Manchester United and the minds of the players and manager, then you take your walk. Hear me, though.

'You know I hate to be alone. I go mad in the silence. Luckily my boy Sam has been living at my place for nearly a year. It was a breakthrough in our relationship when he decided he couldn't bear to pay rent or bills.

That brat has had one of the finest educations his mother's money could buy.

'His childhood was dedicated to electronic devices, and as I might have told you, he's doing well in trash TV, working for a company that specialises in showing disfigurements and plastic surgery. What do they call it, car-crash television? You know what he said the other day? "Dad, don't you know? The era of high art is over."'

'You believe him?' I asked.

'What a large bite that was, torn from the middle of my existence. Everything I've believed in. How come both my children hate high culture? Lisa is a virtuoso of virtue, existing on a diet of beans and purified water. Even her dildos are organic, I'm sure. I dragged her into the Opera House one night and as we sank sighing into the velvet she became giddy and delirious, so rococo did she find it. I took a bet on how long it would be before she used the word "elitist". She had to leave at the interval. My other kid adores kitsch!'

'So?'

He went on, 'At least the boy's healthy, vigorous, and not as stupid as he'd have you believe. He comes to live with me and brings a girlfriend to stay, when she's in London. But he has other girlfriends. We go to the theatre, to a restaurant, he makes more girlfriends in front of me. You know I was considering a production, in the far unimaginable future, of *Don Giovanni.* I lie in bed in the room next to his, wearing headphones, crying for the Don, trying to see it. Most nights Sam makes love. At the beginning of the night, in the middle, and just for luck in the morning. I hear it, I overhear it. I can't escape the fluttering moans. The music of love without the terror and premature ejaculations I experienced as a young man, and indeed as a middle-aged one.

'Then I see the girls at breakfast, matching the faces to the cries. There's one, the most regular, a "writer" for fashion magazines, with this puff of screwed-up blonde hair. She wears mules and a red satin dressing gown which falls open as I am about to penetrate my egg. For one kiss from such a chick you would flood St Mark's or burn a hundred Vermeers, if there are a hundred. This,' he said, finally, 'is a kind of hell, even for a mature man like me, used to taking the blows and carrying on like a true soldier of the arts.'

'I can see that.'

He said with comical pretentiousness, as though he were me, with a patient, 'What does it make you feel?'

8

'It makes me laugh my head off.'

'I read these contemporary books to see what's happening. I wouldn't dream of buying them, the publishers send them over, and they're full of people sexing. These are irregular pleasures, my friend, involving she-men, stuff like that, and people wee-weeing on one another or wearing military fatigues, pretending to be Serb fighters, and worse. You wouldn't believe what people are up to out there. But are they really? Not that you would let on.'

'They are, they truly are,' I giggled.

'Oh Jesus. What I want,' he said, 'is some dope. I used to smoke cigarettes but gave up. My pleasures disappeared with my vices. I can't sleep and I'm sick of the pills. Can you score for me?'

'Henry, I don't need to become a dealer right now. I have a job.'

'I know, I know . . . But –'

I smiled and said, 'Come on. Let's stroll.'

We walked up the street together, him a head taller than me and a third wider. I was as neat as a clerk, with short spiky hair; I usually wore a shirt with a collar, and a jacket. He was shambling, with his T-shirt too big: he seemed untucked everywhere. As he went, bits seemed to fall from him. He wore shoes without socks, but not shorts, not today. With his arms full of books, Bosnian novelists, the notebooks of Polish theatre directors, American poets, and newspapers bought on Holland Park Avenue – *Le Monde, Corriere della Sera, El País* – he was returning to his flat by the river.

Carrying his own atmosphere with him, Henry swung around the neighbourhood like it was a village – he was brought up in a Suffolk hamlet – continually calling out across the street to someone or other, and, frequently, joining them for talk about politics and art. His solution to the fact that few people in London appeared to speak understandable English now, was to learn their language. 'The only way to get by in this 'hood is to speak Polish,' he announced recently. He also knew enough Bosnian, Czech and Portuguese to get by in the bars and shops without yelling, as well as enough of several other European languages to make his way without feeling marginalised in his own city.

I have lived on the same page of the *A-to-Z* all of my adult life. At lunchtime I liked to stroll twice around the tennis courts like the other workers. This area, between Hammersmith and Shepherd's Bush, I heard once described as 'a roundabout surrounded by misery'. Someone else suggested it might be twinned with Bogotá. Henry called it 'a great Middle Eastern city'. Certainly it had always been 'cold' there: in the seventeenth century, after the hangings at Tyburn, near Marble Arch, the bodies were brought to Shepherd's Bush Green to be displayed.

Now the area was a mixture of the pretty rich and the poor, who were mostly recent immigrants from Poland and Muslim Africa. The prosperous lived in five-storey houses, narrower, it seemed to me, than North London's Georgian houses. The poor lived in the same houses divided up into single rooms, keeping their milk and trainers fresh on the windowsill.

The newly arrived immigrants, carrying their possessions in plastic bags, often slept in the park; at night, along with the foxes, they foraged through the dustbins for food. Alcoholics and nutters begged and disputed in the street continuously; drug dealers on bikes waited on street corners. New delis, estate agents and restaurants had begun to open, also beauty parlours, which I took as a positive indication of rising house prices.

When I had more time, I liked to walk up through Shepherd's Bush market, with its rows of chauffeur-driven cars parked alongside Goldhawk Road Station. Hijabed Middle Eastern women shopped in the market, where you could buy massive bolts of vivid cloth, crocodile-skin shoes, scratchy underwear and jewellery, 'snide' CDs and DVDs, parrots and luggage, as well as illuminated 3-D pictures of Mecca and of Jesus. (One time, in the old city in Marrakech, I was asked if I'd seen anything like it before. I could only reply that I'd come all this way only to be reminded of Shepherd's Bush market.)

While no one could be happy on the Goldhawk Road, the Uxbridge Road, ten minutes away, is different. At the top of the market I'd buy a falafel and step into that wide West London street where the shops were Caribbean, Polish, Kashmiri, Somali. Along from the police station was the mosque, where, through the open door, you could see rows of shoes and men praying. Behind it was the football ground, QPR, where Rafi and I went sometimes, to be disappointed. Recently one of the shops was sprayed with gunfire. Not long ago a boy cycled past Josephine and plucked her phone from her hand. But otherwise the 'hood was remarkably calm though industrious, with most people busy with schemes and selling. I was surprised there wasn't more violence, considering how combustible the parts were.

It was my desire, so far unfulfilled, to live in luxury in the poorest and most mixed part of town. It always cheered me to walk here. This wasn't the ghetto; the ghetto was Belgravia, Knightsbridge and parts of Notting Hill. This was London as a world city.

Before we parted, Henry said, 'Jamal, you know, one of the worst things that can happen to an actor is that he gets on stage and there's no excitement, only boredom. He'd rather be anywhere else and there's still the storm scene to get through. The words and gestures are empty, and how is this not going to be communicated? I'll admit this to you, though it is hard for me to say, and I am ashamed. I have had my fair share of one-night stands. Aren't strangers' bodies terrifying! But I haven't slept with a woman properly for five years.'

'Is that all? It'll return, your appetite. You know that.'

'It's too late. Isn't it true that a person incapable of love and sex is incapable of life? Already I'm smelling of death.'

'That odour is your lunch. In fact, I suspect your appetite has already come back. That's why you're so restless.'

'If it doesn't, it's goodbye,' he said, drawing his finger across his throat. 'That's not a threat, it's a promise.'

'I'll see what I can do,' I said, 'in both matters.'

'You're a true friend.'

'Leave the entertainment to me.'

CHAPTER TWO

Early evening, and my last patient gone into the night, having endeavoured to leave me his burden.

Now someone is kicking at the front door. My son Rafi has called for me. The boy lives a couple of streets away with his mother Josephine, and comes plunging round on the scooter we bought at Argos with his PSP, trading cards and football shirts in his rucksack. He is wearing a thick gold chain around his neck, a dollar sign hanging from it. Once he told me he felt tired if he wasn't wearing the right clothes. His face is smooth and a little smudged in places, with scraps of food dotted around his mouth. His hair is razor-cropped, by his mother. We touch fists and exchange the conventional middle-class greeting, 'Yo bro – dog!'

The twelve-year-old tries to hide his head when he sees me because he's just the right height to be grabbed, but where can you hide a head? I want to kiss and hold him, the little tempest, and smell his boy flesh, pulling him to the ground and wrestling with him. His head is alive with nits, and he squints and squirms, with his father so pleased to see him, saying hopefully, 'Hello, my boy, I've missed you today, what have you been doing?'

He shoves me away. 'Piss off, don't touch me, keep away, old man – none of that!'

We're going to eat and find company, and since I've been a single man the place to do that is Miriam's.

Rafi has some juice and we exchange CDs. On the way to Miriam's, we drive past Josephine's house, the place he left earlier, slowing down. Josephine and I have been separated for eighteen months. We had stayed together because of our shared pleasure in the kid, because I feared years of TV dinners and because, at times, we liked the problem of each other. But in the end we couldn't walk down the street without her on one side, me on the other, shouting complaints across the road. 'You didn't love me!' 'You were cruel!' The usual. You don't want to hear about it, but you will, you will.

I doubted whether she'd be at home, or even that a light would be on, as she had begun to see someone. I had deduced this from the fact that a couple of weeks ago Rafi had turned up at my house wearing a new Arsenal shirt with 'Henri' on the back. He looked shifty already, and required no confirmation that no son of mine was coming in the house wearing that. We had honourable, legitimate reasons for being Manchester United fans – to be explained at length later – and he did take the shirt off, replacing it with the more respectable 'Giggs' top he'd left in his room. Neither of us mentioned the Arsenal shirt again, and there was no addition to the kit. The boy loved his father, but whether he'd have been able to resist a trip to Highbury with a strange man who fancied his mother was another matter. We would see.

We were both aware that she required him out of the way, staying with me, in order to see her boyfriend. At such times we felt homeless, abandoned. I guess we were both thinking of what she was doing, of the hope and happiness not directed at us, when she was with her new lover.

How could we not drive past, looking? When I see her in my mind, she is standing on the steps of that house, tall, unmoving and unreachable, as though she had put her self far away, where no one could touch it. We met when she was young, twenty-three, and I was maddened by my own passion and her young beauty. She was, then, virtually a teenager, and she had remained so, indifferent to most of the world's motion and fuss, as though she had seen through it all, seen through everything, until there was nothing to do or believe in.

What did preoccupy her were her 'illnesses' – cancers, tumours, diseases. Her body was in a perpetual state of crisis and breakdown. She adored doctors. A donkey with a medical degree was a stallion to her. But her passion was to frustrate them, if not to try to drive them mad, as I knew to my own cost. The hopeless search for cures was her vocation. Freud's original patients were hysterical women, and one of the first things he said about them was, 'All that is present is what might be called a symbolic relation between the cause and the pathological phenomenon, a relation such as healthy people form in dreams.' Josephine was dreaming while awake, and her adventures as a somnambulist were something else, too. During her excursions out of the house and into the night, she would smash her face against trees. Of course, when you love the unwell, you constantly have to ask yourself: do I love her, or her illness? Am I her lover or her healer?

'Okay?' I said, when he'd seen she'd already gone out.

'Yes.'

13

It was a twenty-minute drive to my older sister's. In the car Rafi pulled a silver disc from his bag and slipped it into the player. Unlike me, he is more than capable with such machines. It is Mexican hip-hop, of all things. Sam, Henry's son, records music for him; Henry brings the discs over, and Rafi and I listen to them together. ('Dad, what's a "ho"?' 'Ask your mother.') Luckily for him, Rafi was bilingual. At home, mostly, he was middle-class; on the street and at school he used his other tongue, Gangsta. His privilege was in being able to do both.

Rafi was checking his hair in the passenger mirror as we went, blowing himself kisses – 'pimp, you look hip!' – before dragging a black hood over his head. I noticed he was wearing his mother's expensive perfume again, which set off an uproar of feeling in me, but I managed to say nothing. The unlikely thing was that he and I liked the same music and, often, the same films. I wore his T-shirts, refusing to give them back; and he wore my hoodies and my Converse All-Stars which were big but not *that* big for him. I was looking forward to the time when I didn't have to buy jeans, but could take his.

Miriam lived in a rough, mainly white neighbourhood in what used to be called Middlesex – recently voted Britain's least popular county – though every place is becoming London now, the city stain spreading.

The typical figures on the street were a young man in a green bomber jacket, jeans and polished boots, followed by an under-dressed teenager with her hair scraped back – the 'Croydon face-lift' – pushing a pram. Other girls in micro-minis drift sullenly about, boys on bicycles circling them, drinking sweet vodka smashes from the bottle and tossing them into gardens. And among these binge-mingers, debtors and doggers hurried Muslim women with their heads covered, pulling their children.

Outside Miriam's detached council house Rafi hooted the horn. One of her helpful kids came out and moved their car so I could park in the front yard, next to the two charred armchairs which had sat there for months.

It was five kids she had, I think, from three different men, or was it three kids from five men? I wasn't the only one to lose count. I knew at least that the eldest two had left home: the girl was a fire officer and the guy worked at a rehearsal studio for bands; both were doing well. After the insanity of her childhood and adolescence this was what Miriam had done: got these children through, and she was proud of it.

The area was gang-ridden and political parties of the Right were well supported. Muslims, who were attacked often on the street, and whose fortunes and fears rose and fell according to the daily news, were their target.

Yet if one of the Right's candidates tried campaigning anywhere near her house, Miriam would shoot out of her chair and rush outside yelling, 'I'm a Muslim single-mother Paki mad cunt! If anyone's got any objection I'm here to hear it!' She'd be waving a cricket bat around her head, with her kids and 'assistant' Bushy dragging at her to get inside.

But no one wanted a war with Miriam. She had people's 'respect' and, often, their love. It seems funny now, but as a teenager she'd been a Hell's Angel. A month I think she lasted, before she decided the swaggering Kent boys were too straight for her. 'Builders in leather,' she called them. 'Not real bikers.' No wonder I became an intellectual.

She'd also have fist-fights in our local pubs, with both men and women. 'When I'm angry I feel at my best,' she explained to me once. Half-Indian, half-idiot she used to be called. The mongrel dog. I used to wish she'd get a good smacking, in the hope that it would turn her into someone I could like, or at least understand. It had been quite a feat, and something I was proud of, that, although we'd always seen each other, often reluctantly, in the past two years we had become close friends. I had begun to go regularly to her house.

It had taken me a long time to come to enjoy Miriam, mostly because she caused Mum such hair-tearing, brain-whirring upset. Me too, of course. I cannot forget, though, that whatever chaos she has made, here and in Pakistan, and you'll be hearing about this, it's not as bad as the crime I have committed.

I live every day with a murder. A real one. Killer, me. There; I've told you. It's out. Now everything is different. Until I put down those words, I had trusted only one other person with the information. If it got around, my career as a mind doctor might be impeded. It wouldn't be good for business.

As always, the back door to Miriam's was open. Rafi ran in and disappeared upstairs. He knew there'd be a small crowd of kids looking at the latest Xbox games or 'snide' DVDs with Thai subtitles, recorded from the screen in a Bangkok cinema. I was glad to have my son join the noise and disorder. The kids in this area, even at his age, appeared older and less naive than my son. For them, school was mainly an inconvenience.

But Miriam's kids, and Miriam herself, would never let the neighbours kick Rafi around. He'd emerge with eye-strain, both less articulate and, at the same time, full of new words like 'cuss', 'sick', 'hectic' 'deep' and, more surprisingly, 'radical', for me a word redolent with hope and joyful disruption, from which it had now become divorced. Rafi, however, would take exception to my appropriation of his words. If I were to say, for instance, 'Radical-hectic, man!', he'd murmur 'Embarrassing, sad fat bald old man nearly dead. Better hush your mouth.'

My wife Josephine had never disliked Miriam; she had, at the beginning, gone to some trouble to know her, but soon found she couldn't take too much. She did envy Miriam's 'egotism', saying, however, that Miriam 'talked and talked in the hope of finding something to say', comparing the endless stream of her conversation to the experience of having a plastic bag tightened slowly over your face.

Josephine preferred to speak through her ailments, and was suspicious and envious of the mouthy and the articulate, though she had considerable appetite for any talk of – or books about – ulcers, migraines, irritable bowel syndrome, viruses, infections and nightmares, many of which she attempted to treat with carrots, banana drinks and extreme yoga positions. She took so much aspirin I suspected she considered it to be a vitamin.

Josephine maintained she could always tell when Rafi had been to Miriam's: his language was fruitier than usual. Josephine and I had argued furiously, as parents have to, over what to put into the kid. I let him watch TV, eat what he wanted and use bad words, the more creatively the better. Familiarity with the language and its limits, I called it. For a while he referred to me only as Mr Cunty Cunt. 'What's wrong with that?' I said to Josephine. 'The "Mister" shows respect.' From her point of view, I was lax, loose, louche. What use was a father who could not prohibit? My debates with Josephine, furious and disagreeable, were over the deepest things – our ideas of what a good person was and how they would speak.

Recently I'd bought Rafi a new bike; at weekends I'd walk energetically to Barnes or Putney, and he'd cycle along with me. Or he'd persuade me to take him to a shopping mall – these were, strangely, his favourite places – or to the ice-rink at Queensway, where he'd play killing and shooting games in the arcade; sometimes we'd spin across the grey ice, screaming. I liked to watch the teenagers gossiping or playing pool, the girls dressed up, the boys watching them. I preferred my son's company to that of anyone else, but together, recently, we both felt some loneliness or absence.

'Hey, boys!' said Miriam as we came in, calling for some kid to bring us food. 'Kiss me, Jamal, little brother.' She was leaning back with her arms held out. 'No one kisses me now.'

'For fear of impalement?'

I was drawn to my sister's face but kissing it was perilous. You had to take care to mind the numerous rings and studs which pierced her eyebrows, nose, lips and chin. Parts of her face resembled a curtain rail. 'Avoid magnets,' was the only cosmetic advice I felt was applicable. I hated to think of her having to get on a plane, the airport alarms going berserk – not that piercings were likely to be a characteristic of terrorists.

In a corner of the kitchen Bushy the driver was packing cigarettes into a suitcase. All over the house there were black sacks of contraband, like a giant's droppings. Before he'd become a cabbie Bushy had been a burglar. He'd considered himself to be a 'mate' of mine ever since I told him that as a young man I myself had been torn between burglary and academia as careers. I had, in fact, even taken part in a burglary, about which I still felt ashamed.

Occasionally I ran into Bushy in the Cross Keys, a rough pub not far away where I used to drink, particularly in the long bad days before and after the separation from Josephine, when she was still lying about her affair and destroying my dream of her, though I told her repeatedly I was aware of what was going on. None of my friends could see the pub's charms, though they all found Josephine to be kind and sympathetic, a woman much exercised by my evasiveness and moods. Oddly, after the split from Josephine, it took me weeks to like music again, and I only listened to the records played in the Cross Keys.

'What's up, doc?' Bushy said. He looked about, before whispering, 'How about some Viagra? A man without Viagra inside him is no good to anyone.'

'You know I can't prescribe, Bushy. Not that a man like you would need any help.'

'I meant,' he said, 'maybe you'd fancy obtaining a bunch? I got right here a brand-new instalment of the naughty blue ones. This stuff will keep your pencil sharp for days – guaranteed, honest, straight-up pukka.'

'What's the use of a pencil without nothing to write on? You'd be wasting it on him,' called Miriam, who heard a remarkable amount for someone who liked to claim to be deaf.

'Is that right?' said Bushy, looking me over with some surprise.

'Absolutely,' I said.

'Christ,' he said. 'What is the world coming to when even a qualified doctor can't dip his wick?'

Miriam had taken her place at the long kitchen table. Here she spent much of the day and night, in a sturdy worn wooden chair from where she could reach her numerous pills, as well as her vitamins, cigarettes and dope. Without looking, she could locate her three mobile phones, a cup of tea, her address book, her tarot cards, a large box bursting with bling, several cats and dogs, as well as numerous packets of half-eaten biscuits, a dope cake, the TV changer, a calculator, a computer and a slipper she could throw – for the dogs – or use to whack either them or a kid with, if they had the misfortune to pass when she was 'going off'.

Her laptop was always on, though she mostly used it at night. The unbounded anarchy of the internet was ideal for crazies like her. She could create numerous different identities of various genders. Photographs of disembodied genitalia were exchanged with strangers, after floating in cyberspace. 'But whose balls are they?' I enquired. 'They look a little peculiar with the man's face scratched out.'

'Who cares? Those teabags are going to belong to some male, aren't they?'

I hadn't often seen her sitting there alone. One of her children might be waiting for an opportunity to speak, or there'd be at least one neighbour, usually with a baby, to whom Miriam would be giving advice, usually of a medical, legal, religious or clairvoyant nature. The table served as a kind of waiting room.

Bushy Jenkins, the minicab driver and her right-hand man, was of indeterminate age, but could only be younger than he looked – and he looked like the almost dead Dylan, not Bob, but Dylan Thomas: ruddy, cherubic, with parts of his skin the texture and colour of tobacco leaf.

I had never seen Bushy in anything but a grey suit, and I had no reason to believe he'd ever removed it to be cleaned. Perhaps he just wiped it down sometimes, as people do a kitchen surface. Bushy spent a lot of time at Miriam's, where he ate, drank, took an interest in the children, the animals and the piranha fish, and sometimes lay down on the floor to sleep, when Miriam herself 'dropped off' in the chair.

Bushy had, in fact, nowhere to live. He kept many of his possessions in his car; he stayed at Miriam's but had never had a room or bed there. I am interested in how people prepare for their dream life, for their going to bed, and how seriously they take it, lying down to make a dream. But Bushy slept on the kitchen floor, with the cats. I'd seen him, with a sack stuffed under his head, snoring.

Miriam had often claimed that Bushy was a guitar player of some originality, better and more unusual than anyone she'd heard live. However, Bushy told me – when I suggested he might relieve our sorrow with a tune – that since quitting the booze he never touched the instrument. He couldn't play sober. I said that often people couldn't do anything well if they weren't lost enough, if they couldn't feel abandoned. 'I've bin lost,' he said. 'Oh yes. And 'bandoned.'

'Your talent will return, then,' I said.

'I dunno, I dunno,' he replied. 'You really think so?'

A good deal of Bushy's chauffeuring was on behalf of Miriam and her crew. He drove Miriam – usually accompanied by a caravan of neighbours, children and animals – to her fortune teller, physiotherapist, aura reader, cigarette smuggler, veterinary surgeon, ten-pin bowling alley or tattooist. (None of her five children was allowed tattoos. I knew, though, from a passing interest in pornography – once, briefly, my profession – that Scarlett, the eldest girl, now pregnant, had a flying fish on her inner thigh.) Miriam herself, once she'd stopped cutting herself, had become a veritable illustration or mural, particularly as her size increased. 'More pictures than the Tate,' I'd say to her, after she tried to show me another fish or flag down her back.

Bushy would also deliver Miriam to what she called her 'agonies', the daytime TV shows she believed herself to be famous for appearing on. When it came to agony, she had a voluminous, flexible portfolio of complaints to exhibit. She could appear on any programme involving weight problems, drug addiction, domestic abuse, tattooing, teenagers, rape, rage, race or lesbianism – or any combination of the aforementioned.

If you wanted, and often if you didn't, she'd show you videos of the programmes. There was no way you could sneer at any of it. If I wanted to talk about the original confessionalists – those I read as a young man, such as St Augustine, Rousseau, De Quincey, Edmund Gosse – she would refer to her 'agonies' as contemporary therapy for the nation. These presenters did what I did, except it was public, for the benefit of all, not snobby, and certainly more amusing.

Most recently, 'with all this war going on', Miriam had taken up with a wise wolf. There was a sanctuary Bushy drove her to, where she sat with an old wolf, and sometimes his relatives. These animals didn't commune with just anyone, she believed. You had to have 'the spirit'. There was no doubt that she did, of all people, have the spirit.

I say that I don't know how Bushy made a living out of cab-driving, but I suppose Miriam must have paid him a percentage of her earnings. If anyone asked him, in the English manner, what he did, he would reply, 'Nuffin' without being paid'.

Miriam and I knew well enough that Bushy had something of our grandfather's 'ingenuity'; perhaps that's why we liked him. But she had it too: certainly Miriam usually had some money moving in and out. Bushy was a trusted assistant in her numerous small-time 'trades': smuggled TVs, computers, iPods, phones, cigarettes, porno, alcohol and dope, as well as the leather jackets and DVDs she obtained and sold, via him and the older children, around the neighbourhood and, mostly, in the Cross Keys.

Not long ago she bought two hundred pairs of stolen Levis from a Polish builder. Having realised they were all size 46 waist, we had to spend a weekend ripping out the labels so she could sell them as variable sizes, knowing that people at a car-boot sale wouldn't want to try them on, being dazzled, we predicted, by the low price. She'd also obtained a consignment of stolen Turgeniev vodka, for which the price was £5,000. I helped her out with a loan, and soon the local pubs and clubs were awash with the lousy stuff. People might be bleeding from the stomach, but we had made, as Miriam put it, 'a good honest profit'.

Miriam was a more capable criminal than my former pals and accomplices Wolfgang or Valentin, so much so that I liked to call her an entrepreneur, at which she scoffed. However, it was true, nevertheless, that she had spent years building up her 'business'. She knew when to sell, and who desired what. Her success had required cunning, tenacity and knowledge of others, and she kept herself, her family and several neighbours just about alive by it, quite a feat. She and the law, therefore, were not on good, or even respectful, terms. The law was naked Power, to be avoided and ignored. She liked to say she'd never appeared on any government computer, as though this liberated her.

Despite her generous description of me as a 'doctor of the soul', I wasn't so respectable that, after leaving Josephine and returning to live in the two floors of the flat I used as a consulting room, the cramped damp cellar was not already full of Bushy-delivered plastic bags containing 'hot' goods she was afraid to keep in her house, as well as rolls of bubblewrap, for which she had no room and hadn't been able to secure a buyer. I was, however, glad to be keeping my transgressions alive, even in such a lowly capacity. I would, when I got round to it, use the bubblewrap to keep Rafi's old shoes and football boots from getting damp, mementos of his fading childhood.

As a young man myself, studying movie and pop stars, I strove to make myself less nerdy, more hip. But I had always been the quiet, good, bookish one. There wasn't room for two show-offs in our household, and I believed that as long as I kept still, didn't move, there would be less trouble around me. Father hadn't protected me. He'd lived with his English wife, our mother, and us – his two half-and-half kids – for only a short time, eventually returning to the subcontinent where he'd been born, settling down in Karachi, Pakistan, which he called 'the new country'. There, briefly, he found a new wife, though much of the time he was travelling as a journalist in China, America or Mexico.

Mother and Miriam were as furiously involved with each other as any married couple. Having little choice, I had always listened to Miriam, though I had learned that when I did wish to speak I should just kick off, unintimidated and loud. As a result, Miriam and I still talk simultaneously, as though Mother, who had, after all, two ears, was still attempting to listen to us. Luckily, Mother, who was not only alive but very well, now had better things to do than pay us any attention.

Even as a teenager, usually pregnant and tripping – Janis Joplin was her heroine – Miriam had never been sullen. She believed our overheated blood made us talkative, restless and liable to fling things at people's heads. Mother had been red-haired and, at one time, bohemian. So there we were as kids, this oddball Muslim/Christian mix, and single-parented too – which was unusual then – living in a straight white neighbourhood.

Now, sighing contentedly, I sat down at my sister's table. One of the kids brought me dhal, rice and beer. 'Uncle,' they called me, respectfully. I opened the paper, in the hope of reading about others' sexual lives – politicians' in particular. I had considered taking Rafi to the cinema or to a restaurant this evening, but this was where I liked to be, the only family home I had now.

Bushy sometimes ate with me. 'I'm going to fuckin' 'ave that!' he'd cry, assailing a pork pie like a half-starved goblin who'd just emerged from underground.

But now he was at the back door with his sack, saying, 'Hey, Jamal, I had this weird dream about a guitar, a dog and a trampoline. And –'

Miriam interrupted, 'Leave off. The doctor don't do off-the-peg dreams – without being paid.'

'What's the whack then, to have a dream read? Or d'you reckon it'll be cheaper to lay off the cheese?'

'It's a good question,' I said.

'It ain't a long dream.' It had not occurred to me to charge per dream, or even for its duration. Perhaps for a satisfying interpretation I'd be rewarded with a tip. He said, 'Or do yer only do posh people?'

'Bushy, if you want, I will hear one of your dreams when I have time.'

21

'Thank you, boss, I'd be grateful. I better get some sleep, then.'

'Off you trot now, Bushy,' Miriam said.

If I was surprised by her defence of me, it was because in certain moods Miriam found my work not so much risible as ridiculous. (She had said to me that the only other man of letters she knew was the postman.) She considered my 'nutters' to be suckers, paying to hear me nod or say 'So?'

If that weren't bad enough, it was exclusively 'egotists' and the morally weak who would part with large amounts of money in order to talk, to be heard, by only me. Nevertheless, it had been Miriam who encouraged me to charge my wealthy patients more, in order that I could see others for smaller fees. I might subvert someone's deepest beliefs, but I didn't mess with the market. Most people find it unbearable that money means so much to them; they don't want what they want.

When Miriam herself decided to see an 'adviser', it was hard facts she was after: whether, for instance, a particular crystal-healer would tell her if it would rain on Sunday when she was having a car-boot sale, or whether there was 'hope' – in other words, would she get a good price for the bubblewrap and the new line of wraparound sunglasses she was hawking.

On my side, in the contemporary Freudian style, I liked to be modest. I would claim neither to predict nor even to 'cure'. Sometimes, brashly, I might use the word 'modify' or, more pompously, speak of 'enlarging the patient's capacity for pleasure by reducing inhibition'. Mostly, I believed in the efficacy of conversation – all Freud demanded of his patients was wilder words; they didn't have to live differently – as a way to expose hidden conflicts.

Nevertheless, I was told by Bushy, as though it were a secret, that Miriam 'looked up' to me. This might have been because her neighbours had started to come to me with child-care problems, eczemas, addictions, depressions, phobias. The working class were always the worst served in terms of mental health. But I was moved: at last I could impress her.

Miriam had been a terrible child, tantrummy, screaming, and absolute. A girl who claimed to be neglected but who was at the centre of the house, shoving me aside, often physically. Yet she and I had once liked each other. This was when we were children, conspiring together in the bedroom we shared until she was ten. Mother had moved downstairs, into a box room, 'the coffin' we called it. Miriam and I would play tricks on the neighbours, go scrumping for apples and roam around the fields together, looking for trouble. Our fights had always been apocalyptic, though, and she would tear wildly at my face. I bore the ruts and tears even as a teenager, which was when I started to hate her, when everything she did was too grown-up for me to participate in.

Now, in Miriam's house I seemed to serve as some sort of symbolic authority. Thankfully it was a formal role, like some presidents, and mainly involved me sitting down; at her place the world was my sofa. Until Henry, Miriam had only engaged with violent, stupid or addicted men. But here there were few actual men around, and none as bookwormy or word aware as me. Where were they? In the pub? In prison? Heaven only knows how the neighbourhood women and girls got to be perpetually pregnant. In creating a society of mothers and babies, it was as though the women believed that if they got rid of the men entirely, they would no longer need them, they would forget about them, and about sex and the confusion which accompanied it.

There were many loose adolescent boys around, in white trainers and heavily gelled, shining, thorny hair, wearing, with their acne, chains they'd obtained, no doubt, from Miriam, both of whose arms, from wrist to elbow, were covered in metal bangles. If she continued with the metal she might as well wear a suit of armour.

At times her kitchen was like a waiting room as sullen boys, secure in gangs but lacking good/bad authorities, waited to see me, a part-time, sub-urban Godfather. They'd shuffle their feet, their eyes scatting about, barely able to speak, 'Sir, if it's okay, can I tell yer, this girl's pregnant . . .' 'Mister, I done this bad thing . . .'

Miriam said to me, 'I've been speaking to Dad.'

'How is he?'

'He needs some human warmth.'

'Heaven's a lonely place, eh?'

'It can be, you know. People have the wrong idea about it.'

Having failed to reach him in this world, Miriam thought she might have more luck contacting Dad in the 'other' dimension. We had both parted from him in absurd and awful circumstances; and she still pursued his forgiveness and understanding.

Miriam was two years older than me. Before she emigrated to the far side of eccentricity, Miriam had been the intelligent one, quicker, funnier, more easily able to grasp difficult ideas, and far less nervous and reticent. The reading I hid myself in as a child she considered a waste of time. What was a book compared to experience? Mum and I would sit in the house reading together, but Miriam was more like our father, always with others, talking, kicking people in the legs, making wild dramas.

These days, however, little that was new or not mundane entered her head; she was weary. I wanted to say that I thought we should go somewhere, to the seaside or to Venice, somewhere to talk, rest and re-fill ourselves. But I was tired myself – the separation from Josephine weighed on me, how exhausting it is to hate! – and really I didn't have the energy to travel.

After I'd eaten the dhal I asked Miriam to call Rafi down. He always jumped nervously at her voice. When he appeared, he complained that he wanted to stay the night. Things could get riotous among the children even if they were quiet, they'd still be watching *Dumb and Dumber* or even *Blade 2* at four in the morning. He lived too ordered a life between me and his mother, but I wouldn't be able to pick him up from Miriam's at breakfast time. I was seeing my first patient at seven, and I wouldn't have time to pack his school bag, fill his lunch box and prepare his football gear.

Before we left I remembered to ask Miriam about the dope.

'I have a friend who needs it,' I said. 'I'm not telling you who.'

'It's Henry then. As it's him, I'll have to get up,' she said, ignoring the stuff she kept on the table in a shoebox. 'I'm not giving him this, you'd be better off smoking Marmite.'

I noticed how heavy she was, and getting heavier, as she got to her feet and moved around, holding on to the furniture as she went.

While she rummaged around in various drawers and bags, sniffing, squishing and shouting at the now absent driver, 'Bushy! Bushy – where's the decent stuff?', I informed her that Henry was considering a production of Ibsen's *Ghosts*. Years ago I'd taken Miriam to see a production of short Beckett pieces Henry had done with students. These end-of-term plays with tyro actors, which he did every couple of years, were highly considered, and packed with other directors, writers and even critics. This particular show had impressed Miriam, or at least I thought so: she'd fallen silent. 'What's Henry doing?' she'd say. 'Any more of those sad Becketts we can go and see?'

'Okay?' Having realised Bushy had left for the Cross Keys, she was holding up a piece of hash the size of a dice. 'Why does your friend want this?'

'I think Henry's discovered dissipation in his old age,' I said. 'He's taken up drinking, too. He always appreciated wine, but now it's the effect he's after.'

She asked, 'Anything else?'

'What's on your mind?'

'Does he want any pornos?' She giggled. 'Remember when you used to work in that side of things?'

'Thanks for reminding me. I wish I hadn't told you.'

'Don't you tell me everything?'

'I try not to.'

'You didn't write the films, though, did you?'

'No, not the films,' I said.

'That's where you'd have made the money. You didn't act in the pornos either, did you?'

'For God's sake, Miriam, can you see me acting, particularly without trousers?'

'Do you talk to your patients about your dodgy past?'

'No.'

'There's a lot about you they don't know.'

'They're not supposed to know. They need me to be a blank screen. As for Henry,' I went on, 'he thinks he's too old for sex and his body resembles a plate of spaghetti – or a mudslide. Among others, his son is dating a fashion writer. She walks about his flat in mules and a red satin dressing gown which falls open to expose more shimmering flimsies and worse. Imagine how terrible this is for Henry. He thinks this mule woman can only do this because she doesn't consider him to be a man but an impotent grandfather.'

'Poor guy.' Her eyes were tearing into me. 'But you like that woman too, don't you – the mule thingy? You've met her around there?'

'Yes.'

'What went on?'

I hesitated. 'You are perceptive. I invited her out. We walked together by the river one evening when Henry's son was out, stopping off at various pubs to drink whisky macs. By the end we were soused. I have to say I've never felt so strongly towards anyone before – not even Ajita. For the next week I woke up thinking about her every morning. It was a delirium, like being ducked in madness.'

'And?'

'And nothing. She didn't see me like that. Had she given me one word of hope, I'd have followed her anywhere. But I had nothing she wanted.'

'Oh, Jamal. Poor Henry, too.' She had resumed bustling about. 'If he does want any pornos, they're in your basement in a cardboard box.'

'They are?'

'Just take a couple for yourself and give some to him. You know Jordan?'

'Never been there.'

'Not the place, you cunt, the porn star. She's in some of them, with black men. You don't know who she is?'

'You mistake me for an intellectual. Late-night television's my favourite indulgence.' I went on, 'Did I tell you Henry was offered an OBE but turned it down?'

'Why did he say no?'

'The respectability of his generation is making him crazy. Once they were hippie "heads", now they're all headmasters. Blair himself is a mixture of Boy Scout and Mrs Thatcher. Henry's decided to keep the dissident flag flying.'

Miriam shut the drawer she'd been fiddling in. 'Yes or no to Her-fucking-Majesty, this stuff's not good enough for the likes of Henry. It makes you dumb, like the people around here.'

'I know you always liked him.'

'You're right. He didn't look down on me, as you did. He liked to explain what he was doing, even though I'm a fat and mad philis– . . . You know.'

'Philistine.' I said, 'He's coming for lunch next week.'

'I'll get the stuff and have it delivered to your place.' She kissed me. 'I love you so much, bro.'

On the way home Rafi played Beethoven's Ninth to me on his trembling mouth organ, which always made me laugh, though I was sure to praise the rendition. Then he did his 'conversation between an Irishman, a Jamaican and an Indian', and I almost crashed.

As we turned the corner something quick ran across the road, like a collection of brown elbows.

'A wolf!' said Rafi. 'Will it attack us?'

'It's a fox,' I said. 'There are no wolves around here, apart from the human variety.'

We were inside; as it was a warm evening, I opened the doors to the garden.

I would get Rafi into bed and then sit outside for a bit with a glass of wine and the rest of yesterday's joint. It was still light and I noticed the cats were on the back wall. Not my grey, who was on my bed with his head in my shoulder bag, but the red-collared black with a white face from next door and the local Tom tabby – gruff, up for it – with a wide head and menacing eyes. They appeared, at the moment, to be tapping one another's faces with their paws.

'Hey, Rafi, look at this. I think these cats are about to get married,' I said. 'But that wall doesn't look comfortable.'

Rafi attended to his Gameboy as well as to the scene in front of him, which was developing quickly. The cats moved down to the little lawn, a few feet from us. The Tom dug his teeth into Red's neck, threw her down and got on top of her. It didn't look promising for him, more like thrusting your fingers into a bag full of needles.

'Is it a rape?' Rafi asked.

'I'm afraid she likes it.'

'Are they happy?'

'Yes, because they've forgotten themselves, temporarily.' I pulled the door closed to give them privacy. 'They were doing it in the same place yesterday. But it is rough sex. It's wilder than you'd think in this neighbourhood.'

She was down on her back and he was on her, concentrating on thrusting, trying for a better position, pushing more while stabbing his paw into her stomach, trying to keep her in place. They spat and hissed at one another.

'Disgusting,' said Rafi, making a face. 'This new game is difficult,' he added relevantly, his toy making a tinny pop sound.

'The American poet Robert Lowell says something like, "But nature is sundrunk with sex".'

Rafi said, 'Yeah?'

'Apparently human beings are the only species that don't like to be looked at while having sex. They are, too, the only animals who bury their dead.' I added, 'Did you know the clitoris was discovered in 1559 by Columbus – this was Renald Columbus of Padua, who called it "the sweetness of Venus".'

'Yeah?'

'It's true,' I said.

'I've heard all this before, the facts of life and everything. In a book at school. D'you think I'm intelligent for my age?'

'Yes. Am I?'

'Yes.'

I said, 'That's because I read a lot as a kid.'

'Poor you, is that all there was to do?'

The cat sex went on a long time. Rafi opened the doors for a clearer view, fetched a chair and sat down, giggling and gasping. Despite his efforts, the couple were not easily disturbed. When they were done, Red frolicked on her back, celebrating, turning, stretching, while Tom Tabby sat on his haunches, watching her, before lapping at his genitals. At last the two of them strolled off together into other gardens. If they'd had hands, they'd have joined them.

Rafi wanted to ring his mother, to tell her what he'd seen. Had Rafi described the scene to her, no doubt she'd have chastised me for letting him watch, but her phone was turned off. No doubt she was attempting the same thing, at last.

When it comes to teaching the art of pleasure, parents and schools can be an obstruction, a disaster even. I looked at the boy and thought about my father, who had passed little knowledge of sex on to me, or even about the place he thought pleasure might take in someone's life. In my twenties I resented the fact he'd made no attempt to explain what I characterised then as 'the truth about sex'.

But what would I have wanted a father or, indeed, a mother to say? What did sex consist of, and what did my son have to look forward to? I remember wondering about this with Josephine one time, asking her about the variety of sexual experiences that were available, and which of them he might develop a liking for. 'As long as it's nice and loving,' she said, sweetly. Indeed; but as La Rochefoucauld remarked on ghosts and love, 'All talk of it, but none have seen it for certain.'

Her remark stopped me, briefly. I knew my son would learn that there were numerous varieties of sexual expression. Promiscuity; prostitution; pornography; perversion; phone sex; one-night stands, cruising; S&M; internet dating; sex with a wife or husband, sex with someone else's wife or husband. There was a full menu, as long as a novella. Which would appeal? Freud, the committed monogamist, began his famous *Three Essays on the Theory of Sexuality* with his thoughts about fetishism, homosexuality, exhibitionism, sadism, bestiality, anal sex, bisexuality, masochism and voyeurism. I was reminded of a joke: which way of being normal would you like to be, neurotically normal, psychotically normal or perversely normal?

Perhaps my son would, one day, prefer to be blown by a stranger in a toilet, or perhaps he would like to be spanked while being fellated by a Negro transvestite. The side circles of pleasure were manifold, and with an aesthetic edge too: there was smelling, hearing and tasting. And speaking. More than half of sex is speaking; words ignite desire; if speaking is an erotic art, what could be more erotic than a whisper? However, repetition is a love which doesn't diminish: in the Marquis de Sade's *Philosophy in the Bedroom* Mme de Saint-Ange asserts that in her twelve-year marriage her husband asked for the same thing every day: that she suck his cock while shitting in his mouth.

I might also add, though it may seem cynical, and it wasn't something I'd bring up with Josephine, that loving someone, or even liking them, has never brought the slightest improvement to sexual pleasure. In fact, not liking the other, or actively disliking them – even hating them – could free up one's pleasure considerably. Think of the aggression – violence even – that a good fuck involves.

What, then, were the pleasures and who could guarantee them? Should I have been guiding the train of his desire towards the ultimate, if tyrannically ideal, destination, what Freud called, somewhat optimistically, 'full genital sexuality'? Or should I suggest he stop off at some of the other stations and sidings first? As the great Viennese satirist Karl Kraus noted – a man characterised as a 'mad halfwit' by Freud – it is the most tragic thing in the world for the fetishist who wants only a shoe but gets the whole woman.

One of the 'truths' about sex which Rafi would also discover – perhaps early on – would be how problematical sex is, and how much people hate it, as well as how much shame, embarrassment and rage it can encourage. Henry and his generation did a lot to educate us about the nature of desire, but however free we believe ourselves to be – liberated now from the horrors of religious morality – our bodies will always trouble us with their unusual desires and perverse refusals, as though they had a mind of their own, and there was a stranger within us.

Josephine liked to be flirted with, while pretending to ignore the subtext. For devoted parents there were opportunities for such fun. Many of our neighbours had strenuous shared lives organised around the school; lovers could meet at the gates twice a day. If the children were busy with one another, the parents were more so. As Josephine would come to learn, the school playground being an emotional minefield, with the Muslim parents keeping their kids away from white homes. In bed, in the days when we shared one, Josephine would give me the gossip. I was reminded of a book, Updike's *Couples*, that Dad had passed on to me and which seemed, at the time, deliciously corrupt in its banal everyday betrayals. As then, it was the betrayals – and the secrets they engendered – which were the most delectable transgressions.

Of all the perversions, the strangest was celibacy, the desire to cancel all desire, to hate it. Not that you could abolish it once and for all. Desire, like the dead, or an unpleasant meal, would keep returning – it was ultimately indigestible. Rafi's mother had insisted on, indeed clung to, her own innocence. The badness was always only in me. It was, from her point of view, a rational division of labour. What she didn't see was that the innocent have everything – integrity, respect, moral goodness – except pleasure. Pleasure: vortex and abyss – that which we desire and fear simultaneously. Pleasure implies dirtying your hands and mind, and being threatened; there is fear, disgust, self-loathing and moral failure. Pleasure was hard work; not everyone, perhaps not most people, could bear to find it.

The sex show was over. The boy threw his clothes down and went to bed. Through the open doors I could watch him sleep. He was wearing headphones and the music was loud enough for me to experience a familiarity with 50 Cent I could have forfeited. When Rafi's long lashes fluttered less and less, like a butterfly settling, I turned the music off.

I sat at my desk with part of my inheritance: Father's favourite and now mine, a glass of almost frozen vodka and a carton of Häagan Dazs vanilla ice cream. A slug and a slurp, and the cat sitting on my papers. I was all set. I would write with a fountain pen before typing everything into my new Apple G4. I could listen to music on it; when I was bored I would look at the photographs and pictures I was currently interested in. Unable to sleep and with bursts of obsessive energy – and this was a new thing with me – I had been thinking of the phrase Henry had quoted from Ibsen, 'We sail with a corpse in the cargo.'

For some reason it made me recall the line which had occurred to me earlier and which I kept hearing in my head: 'She was my first love but I was not hers.'

Oh Ajita, if you are still alive, where are you now? Do you ever think of me?

CHAPTER THREE

So, I must begin this story-within-a-story.

One day a door opened and a girl walked into the room.

It was the mid-1970s.

The first time I saw Ajita was in our college classroom, an airless dry box in the depths of a new building on the Strand, down the street from Trafalgar Square. I was at university in London, reading philosophy and psychology. Ajita was pretty late for the discussion on 'St Anselm's Arrow'; the class that day was nearly over; anyhow it had been going for two months. She must have had good reason for them to let her join the course at such a late stage.

It was as hot in those college classrooms as it was in any hospital, and Ajita's face was flushed and uneasy as she came in half an hour after the class had started, put down her car keys, cigarettes, lighter, and several glossy magazines, none of which had the word 'philosophy' in the title.

There were about twelve students in the class, mostly hippies, down-at-heel, hard-working academic types – the sort my son would refer to as 'geeks' – a Goth, and a couple of punks wearing safety pins and bondage trousers. The hip kids were turning punk; I'd been to school with some of them, and I'd still see them when I was out with my friend Valentin in the Water Rat or the Roebuck, and sometimes the Chelsea Potter in the King's Road. But I found them dirty and dispirited, thuggish and always spitting. The music was important, but no one would want to listen to it.

I'd always been a neat kid; talentlessness, to which the punks subscribed as a principle, didn't inspire me. I knew I was talented – at something or other – and my own look had become black suits and white shirts, which was both counter-hippie and too smooth to be punk, though it might have passed as New Wave. You wouldn't catch William Burroughs in beads or safety pins.

Now the Indian girl was at one of those chairs with a swivelling flat piece of wood attached, for writing on. She was pulling off her hat, removing her scarf and trying to lay them on the flat surface. They slid off. I picked them up and put them back; they fell off again. Soon we were smiling at all this. Her coat came off next, followed by her jumper. But where would she put them, and what would be next?

This performance, which was embarrassing her, seemed to go on for a long time, with everyone watching. How much clothing, perfume, hair, jewellery and other frills could there be on the relatively small surface of a girl? A lot.

Suddenly philosophy and the search for 'truth', which until that moment I had adored, seemed a dingy thing. The grimacing professor in a wrecked pullover and corduroy trousers, old to us (my age now, or perhaps younger) and in a Valium stupor, as he insisted on informing us, seemed like a clown. We smirked at one another whenever he said, with emphasis, 'Cunt!', which he assured us was the correct pronunciation for Immanuel Kant. And to think, only the other day the university was at the centre of intellectual ferment, dissent and even revolution!

Truth was one thing, but beauty, beside me now, was clearly another. Though this girl's arms were full, she wasn't carrying any accessory as routine as a notebook or a pencil. I had to lend her some writing paper and my pen. It was the only pen I had on me. I pretended I had more in my bag. I'd have given her all the pens and pencils I had, or, indeed, anything she asked for, including my body and soul, but that was to come later.

After the seminar she was sitting alone in the refectory. I needed to retrieve that pen, but did I dare speak to her? I've always preferred listening. Tahir, my first analyst, would say: people speak because there are things they don't want to hear; they listen because there are things they don't want to say. Not that I thought I had a talent for listening then, or realised you could make a profession of it. I was just worse at talking. I spoke all the time, of course, but only to myself. This was safe.

For years I perplexed women with my listening habit. Several of them were tired out by it, talking until they were shattered by the strain of trying to find the words which would do the trick. I remember one girl screaming I had listened to her all afternoon before she ran for the door: 'You've been ripping me off! I feel utterly stolen from!'

I didn't realise, until my first analyst told me, that it was my words rather than my ears they wanted. But with Ajita, I could not even sit down next to her and say, 'Can I listen to you?' I still find it difficult to sit down with strangers, unless I'm analysing them. People have such power, the force field of their bodies, and the wishes within them, can knock you all over the place.

Playing for time, and perhaps hoping she'd go away forever, I went to get some coffee. When I turned back I saw that my closest friend, the handsome tough guy, Valentin, had followed me in. He had gone to sit down right next to her with his coffee. God knows what the coffee tasted like in those days. It was probably instant, like the mashed potato and puddings we consumed: all you did was add water. There wouldn't have been much else about, but we always had water. My father liked to point out, having experienced British power as a child in occupied India, the war had been over for thirty years, but Britain still seemed to be recovering from an almost fatal illness – loss of power, depression and directionlessness. 'The sick man of Europe', our country was called. The end of empire was not even tragic now, but squalid.

It was lucky for me, and unusual for Valentin, to be there that morning. He didn't turn up much for lectures. They began too early for him, particularly if he'd been working in the casino the night before. He did come into college eventually, to meet girls and to see me, but mostly because the refectory food was cheap.

Valentin was Bulgarian. Often I asked him to describe his escape from Bulgaria, and he would tell me more details each time. I'd heard no other 'real life' story as exciting. He'd done National Service, and been in the Olympic cycling team; he could fence and box too. He'd conformed so well that he was able to become an air steward, one of the few jobs in the Eastern Bloc in which ordinary people were allowed to travel. He'd worked on the airline for a year, telling no one of his plans to escape. But someone had become suspicious. Intending to flee to America, his last trip was to be to London. As he and the rest of the crew were boarding the plane to Sofia he turned and fled, running wildly through the airport until he found a policeman. Various refugee organisations helped him. A woman who worked for one of these organisations was married to a philosophy professor to whose house he went, which was how he turned up in my college class.

Valentin could never return home, could never see his parents, siblings or friends again. The trauma rendered him incapable of the success he could have had. In England, where he was supposed to be studying, he was just hanging around, mostly with me and our German pal, Wolf, all of us trying to get into interesting trouble.

It was within my abilities to sit with Valentin and Ajita; and even to hear him boasting, as he liked to, about how close his room was to the college, how it only took him five minutes to get to a lecture. In comparison, I had to take a bus, an overground train and a tube. It took an hour and a half but, courtesy of British Rail, I did get to read *Philosophical Investigations* and *The Interpretation of Dreams*. It was during this time that I began to read properly for the first time, and it was like finding a satisfying lover you'd never part from.

With Valentin's assistance, Ajita and I had begun to talk. She was an Indian who, it turned out, didn't live far from Miriam, Mum and I, in the suburbs. Apparently Ajita's mother hadn't approved of England, which she considered a 'dirty place', sexually obsessed, corrupt, drug-ridden, the families broken. Six months ago she had packed her numerous trunks and gone to Bombay, my father's original home, leaving her husband and two children to be looked after by an aunt, the father's eldest sister. Ajita's mother didn't like living in the white suburbs without servants or friends. In Bombay she lived in her brother's house. He owned hotels; there were movie stars all around; help was cheap.

Ajita said, 'There it is like being on holiday all the time. But my father is a proud man. He could never live off others.' The mother had lovers, Ajita seemed to think, but would return, she implied, if circumstances were more to her liking. As a result, Ajita pitied her lonely father, who owned sweatshops somewhere in North London and was rarely at home.

After coffee, Ajita offered me a lift back to the suburbs. Although I wasn't intending to go home, indeed I'd just arrived in London and was intending to spend the rest of the day with Valentin and Wolf, I would have gone anywhere with her. This girl had many virtues: money, a car – a gold-coloured Capri, in which she played the latest funk – a big house and a rich father. When Valentin asked 'What does your boyfriend do?' she replied, 'But I don't have one, really.'

What more could anyone want?

'She's yours,' Valentin whispered, as I left.

'Thank you, my friend.'

He was generous like that. Or maybe it was because he had so many women buzzing around him, one more or less didn't matter. He took them for granted. Or perhaps he was indifferent to most human exchange. He could sit for hours, just staring, smoking, hardly moving, without any of the anxious shifting about and intermittent desiring that I, for instance, was prone to.

This stable attitude, I imagined, would be an asset. The other night I was talking with a screenwriter friend who is working on a 'tough guy' film, about why men like gangsters. Strong guys aren't exercised by the subtleties; they're not moved, or bothered by guilt. They're narcissists, in the end, and as ruthless about their rights as children. To me they were as self-sufficient, complete and impermeable as someone reading a book forever.

That was what I wanted then. Why? Perhaps it was because as a kid, when Miriam and I fought, or when she tickled me – she was heavier, rougher and altogether meaner than me; she liked to punch or hit me with sticks, something, now I think of it, which Josephine liked to do – I felt I was the girl and she the male. As so many others have discovered in their own case, my particular body didn't appear to quite coincide with my gender. As I was thin and slight with wide hips, I believed my form to be that of a small, weak, pre-sexual girl. Mother called me 'beautiful' rather than handsome. I suffered from extreme emotional states – screaming inside – which left me low, depleted, weeping on the bed. Often I dreamed I was Michelin Man, full of air rather than grandeur or gravity; one day I might float away, unanchored by male weight. What did 'men' do? They were gangsters, making their way in the world with decision and desire. With Ajita now, didn't I have that?

Ajita and I talked all the way through South London. The closer we came to my 'manor', as we called it then, the more anxious I became. I was delighted when she asked if I wanted to see her house.

'There it is,' she said a little later, turning off the engine.

If I always thought of Ajita's house as being American, it was because it was in a new Close and was the sort of thing you might see on *I Love Lucy*.

The building was low and light and open, with large areas of glass. To the side there was a wide garage, and, out front, a crew-cut lawn surrounded by a low picket fence. Inside, there were Indian carpets, wall-hangings and tapestries, wooden elephants, bowls, latticed furniture. Otherwise there wasn't much there. They might just as well have been renting it, complete with 'ethnic' fittings, though they had, in fact, bought the place four years before, after leaving Uganda with few possessions.

I liked her house and wanted to be there not only because of her, but because the houses in the suburbs I knew were old: the furniture was ancient, from before the war. It was heavy brown stuff, from which, as a child, I would scrape brown varnish with my fingernails. My maternal grandfather, who left his house to Mum, had owned a second-hand furniture shop, or junk shop as Miriam and I called it, from which we had filled our house. There were fireguards, clocks that ticked and chimed, ruched curtains, picture rails and pelmets, chamber pots and narrow beds, over which mother had begun to overlay, after she met Dad, dozens of Eastern pictures, swirly cloth and lacquered objects.

As a child and young man, I was left often in the care of my grandfather who wore, apart from a hat, which was conventional then, long white underwear, a tie, voluminous trousers held up by braces, and huge boots, which he cut into with razor blades to give his corns 'space'. He never tried to think of what I might be entertained by, but just took me along with him. When he had the shops, I'd play there all day, jamming screwdrivers into clocks. Later, I got to spend a lot of lunchtimes sitting with him in the pub – his club and office – as he 'studied form' in the newspaper, drank Guinness, smoked roll-ups and ate steak-and-kidney pie, usually at the same time.

For entertainment I would be handed the *Daily Express* or the *People*. My newspaper addiction has never diminished. But that wasn't all: we would go to Epsom for the races, to Catford for the dogs and to Brighton by 'charabanc' to see someone about a pigeon. On Saturdays we visited football grounds in the vicinity. The nearest was Crystal Palace, but Millwall – 'The Den' – was the most feared. As we walked about the neighbourhood, Grandad pointed out bombsites where his former schoolfriends had been killed, and bomb shelters where he'd hidden with Mum as a child.

Pubs, for me, particularly if they had a piano player, always had a Dickensian exaggeration: over-dressed perfumed landladies pinching your cheek and giving you crisps and lemonade; red-faced men in ties in the 'private' bars, and always a frisson between Grandad and some waiting woman, a subtle acknowledgement of available pleasure that made me wonder when it might be my turn.

You might consider my later penchant for the lowlife an affectation, but most days I've popped into some pub or other, hoping to find the characters from my childhood, the original white working class of London.

When I was with my grandfather I more or less passed for white. Sometimes people asked if I were 'Mediterranean'; otherwise, there were few Asian people where we lived. Most whites considered Asians to be 'inferior', less intelligent, less everything good. Not that we were called Asian then. Officially, as it were, we were called immigrants, I think. Later, for political reasons, we were 'blacks'. But we always considered ourselves to be Indians. In Britain we are still called Asians, though we're no more Asian than the English are European. It was a long time before we became known as Muslims, a new imprimatur, and then for political reasons.

Being so far the only dark-skinned student in the philosophy class, I thought Ajita and I would be a fine fit. She was thin and small, with a compact, boyish body not unlike mine. Her hair was long and dark, and she wore expensive clothes with jewellery, handbags and high heels. She might have been Indian but she dressed like an Italian girl, sprinkled with gold. She loved Fiorucci, whose shop was near Harrods. Every Saturday she went shopping with her female cousins.

Ajita was no wild girl, feminist, hippy or mod. I could imagine her running a business. But it didn't take me long to grasp from her sighs, helpless looks and moody pouts that she would have trouble with metaphysics. I thought I could help her with that, along with epistemology, ontology, hermeneutics, methodology, logic and, maybe, some other things, but not as much as I thought she could help me.

I was starting to become fond of money, too, having learned from the media what good use pop stars put it to. Ajita's family appeared wealthy to me, while we'd always struggled. If Mum bought us a present, we knew what an effort it represented, and we tried to use it for longer than its interest merited. Apparently my father, in Pakistan, had a driver, a cook, a guard. But he gave us nothing; it didn't occur to him.

Now Ajita went off to fetch some records and on this, my first day with her, I strolled about the spaces, trying them out, like I was about to buy the place and have it redecorated. Her father and brother were not there, but I could smell onions frying in oil and spices, and then I glimpsed a nose and a brown eye which must have belonged to her beaky aunt, who was side-on to an almost closed door.

Ajita said with sudden nervousness, as she put the music on, 'If anyone asks, say you're a friend of my brother. You've come to see him.'

'What is your brother's name?' Ajita muttered something. 'What?' I said, not catching it. 'What did you say?'

'He's called Mustaq. Some of us call him Mushy – or Mushy Peas. I think you're going to like each other a lot. You want to like him too, don't you? He is so much needing to be liked right now.'

'I'll do my best.'

'You don't have to whisper. She is not speaking English.'

'But my family is similar,' I said eagerly. 'Many of my aunts and cousins come to London in the summer. The rest have never left Pakistan.'

'Haven't you been there?'

'Dad has been inviting us, and Mum thinks Miriam and I should go. But Miriam can hardly get to the end of the street without tearing it up. You'll see, when you meet her. Ajita, can't you and I go to Pakistan together?'

'Not unless we're married.'

'Already?'

'They're very old-fashioned there. Anyway, my mother is busy finding me a husband in India. My brother takes the piss. "How is your lovely new hubby doing?" he asks. Come, Jamal, you want to step out with me, my new friend?'

We danced to her favourite disco records, watching one another's feet, holding hands and touching each other's hair. Later, after we'd kissed and I didn't know what to do next – it seemed too soon to go further, like eating all the chocolates at once – I said, 'Do you want to see *Last Tango in Paris* or go for a drive to Keston Ponds for a walk? Or we could go to my house. It's ten minutes away.'

'Your house.'

As we went, I hung out of the window, hoping people I knew would see me in the car with a girl. But they were at work, or at college or school. At least Ajita wanted to see my house; she wanted to know me. I needed Miriam, too, to know I had a real girlfriend, to see me as a grown-up, not a baby brother.

Yet I was nervous of them meeting. Not that I knew whether my sister was at home. Her bedroom door was always closed, and I was forbidden, on pain of having my berries come into unwilling contact with a cheese grater, to press against it in any way. Often, the only way to find out whether Miriam was in was to get down on your knees and try to smell roll-ups, dope or joss sticks drifting out from under her door. If I was feeling brave, after she'd left the house, I'd nip in, take a couple of records from their covers – *Blood on the Tracks* and *Blue* and *Split* were my favourites, but I liked Miles too – and listen to them in my room, over and over, until I believed I had them inside me.

You might also find in Miriam's room a college lecturer, a couple of neighbourhood boys, a pick-up or her latest girlfriend. If Miriam was indeed there, she'd be in bed until mother returned from work at five. Mother worked, at that time, in a bakery, wearing a kooky little white hat. We always had plenty to eat at home, even if it was a little stale.

That day Ajita and I didn't get as far as my house but stopped in a quiet street nearby, where we kissed in her car, something we liked a lot and were unable to stop doing, as though we were glued together.

It wasn't until the following morning that we drove to some woods not far away, near my old school, and made love for the first time, though her jeans and boots were so tight we thought for a while we'd never get them off without seeking help. Then we did it in the car in a secluded street near her house.

Something important had started. She was all mine, almost. She was not my first girlfriend, but she was my first love.

CHAPTER FOUR

My girl and I began to see one another all the time; mostly in London, at college or in Soho. Or we would meet at a bus stop near my house and drive into the city together.

I don't think I've ever stopped seeing London like a small boy. The London I liked was the city of exiles, refugees and immigrants, those for whom the metropolis was extraterrestrial and the English codes unbreakable, people who didn't have a place and didn't know who they were. The city from the point of view of my father.

My best friend Valentin was Bulgarian and his other best mate, Wolf, was German. Neither of them resembled the average student; they weren't overgrown public-school boys. Wolf was ten years older than me, and Valentin at least five. My father had numerous older brothers, who I idealised. I figured Dad always had someone to look after him, and that's what I wanted for myself.

Wolf, who was neither employed nor a student, was renting a room in the same house as Valentin. That's how they had met, and how I got to know him. Wolf wore a Bogart raincoat, black brogues and black leather gloves. The only time he seemed to take off his gloves was when he played tennis on the council courts on Brook Green, not far from where I live now, and where I take Rafi for his tennis lessons with a lithe South African.

Valentin and I would sit on benches outside the pub opposite and laugh as Wolf trounced someone. He didn't find himself, or the rest of the world, absurd and risible, as Valentin and I did. It would have been too much, had we all been like that.

We were amused by the fact Wolf carried a smart, smooth leather briefcase which he opened, with a key, against his chest so no one could see in. What did he keep in there? Guns, money, drugs, knives, paperclips? Having half-opened it, he then glanced about suspiciously, to ensure no one was watching, which they were, of course, now that he had engaged their curiosity.

Wolf and Valentin both had rooms in a dank boarding house on Gwendre Road, off North End Road in West London, owned by an old widow. Valentin, who read Kierkegaard and Simone Weil for what he described as 'pleasure', liked to say, winking towards the widow, 'Raskolnikov would have felt at home here.'

'Everyone feels at home here,' she'd reply, as we laughed.

We'd sit around the kitchen table to debate philosophy, talk about sport, drink beer and smoke weed. There was curling lino and the smell of gas and cat piss. There was an iron stove and oil-cloths on the spavined tables. The armchairs were greasy, the sofas seemingly bottomless. The toilets didn't always flush, the windows didn't close and it was usually cold; as the oil heaters smelled but didn't heat, we got used to wearing our coats indoors.

A favourite conversation with Valentin concerned moral absolutes and ideas he'd found in Balzac, Nietzsche, Turgenev and Dostoevsky about nihilism and murder, and how or when it might be legitimate to rid the world of the weak, stupid or evil in order that others might flourish. Who had the right to kill? It was, after all, only the most perversely pacifistic who could not accept killing in any circumstances. To supplement this speculation, Valentin and Wolf watched crime or Sylvester Stallone movies on TV; they'd never miss anything with Steve McQueen in it. 'Career guidance,' I called them. Ajita would lie around with us, before running away squealing, 'Too many electric chairs!'

'That's where he's going to be sitting,' I'd murmur to Valentin, nodding at Wolf, Valentin looking sharp in his dark suit, bow tie and shiny shoes, ready to go to the casino where he worked at night. That must have been where I got my black-suit style from, now I think about it. Val was Eastern European, educated to be a commie; he had good manners and was worldly, way beyond Western hippy frippery.

Wolf was an adventurer, and his stories – of spanking air hostesses and waitresses, and of fucking Playboy bunnies – never failed to pick me up. I admired his boys'-own style: smuggling diamonds out of South Africa up his arse; seeing Idi Amin and Kim Philby – together – in Tripoli, before being arrested, suspected of being American. Running drugs into Mexico, and being poisoned by a dirty needle when visiting a doctor; discussing the quality of brothels in Ipanema, Brazil. He was a man often suspected of not being a criminal, but worse, a cop!

Like a lot of gangsters, he had a smear – more than that, a large patch – of psychosis. He wasn't neurotic like me, or most people I knew, but supernormal, rational, intense, convincing, great at lying. He'd be up early in the morning making breakfast for everyone. Or we'd find him doing press-ups and lifting weights. Extra-organised: he loved making plans and getting everyone involved.

In contrast, Valentin liked to be amused. He was attractive; you'd say he was elegant or chic, particularly if he were wearing a dark polo-neck shirt and black jacket. But he was Kierkegaard dark; being so wounded, he lacked Wolf's endearing self-belief, boastfulness and earnestness.

How I loved being with the unassailable men. Me, the eager little kid, they would patronise as I tried to please them with jokes, tough talk and a swaggering walk. Often Wolf and Valentin spoke in French or German but so what, I was used to being surrounded by people whose language I didn't understand.

When Father was in London – he visited at least twice a year and stayed some weeks – it was only occasionally that he would see Miriam and I alone. His many male friends, his 'chumchas', speaking Urdu and Punjabi, in suits or salwar kameez, drinking and telling political jokes, were always with him, in the service flats near Marble Arch or Bayswater which Dad rented.

Sometimes he would take just us out to lunch, and talk politics. He was left-wing, probably a Communist, an anti-imperialist – naturally – and also a supporter of Mao, the Vietcong and students. In India, as a child, Father explained, being the son of a rich landowner, he had felt as alien-ated from the Indian masses in the villages as he did in any English vil-lage. But, having been bullied by *his* father, an army colonel, he'd always felt some identification with those who were called, in those days, the 'downtrodden'.

On the evenings of these visits, when Miriam and I would be thinking of returning to the suburbs on the train (or at least I would; she'd often go to parties in London, staying in the city for a couple of days), Dad's girl-friends, amazing beauties with brains, would turn up.

I was happy to see Father, whether he was alone or not, but Miriam, either on speed or trancs or both, could feel very disappointed. She had imagined the two of them sitting together for hours, exchanging their secrets and their despair. Her father would want to know her; how could he not be fascinated? His kind words would stop her 'acting out'. Not only had he not protected her from racism, it was he who had flung her into it, according to her.

So she waited for Dad to speak, to tell her how proud he was of her. But he was incapable of this kind of relationship with a girl. After leaving him, we'd drift down the King's Road together and I would ask her questions I already knew the answers to. 'What did Dad say?' 'Nothing.' 'Really?' 'Absolutely nothing.' 'Did you tell him you were pregnant?' 'Nope.' 'Did he ask what you were doing?' 'Yes.' 'What did you say?' 'Nothing much.'

My parents met when Dad was at the LSE, studying International Relations. A friend of Mum's, Billie, had taken her to a dance there, thinking mum would 'get along' better with an intellectual than she did with the local boys. They all went for a meal at the India Club in the Strand. Mum said she'd never met anyone who could talk like Dad, who could so enthral you with their stories.

She didn't talk often about him, but if you poked her hard enough at the right time, she might suddenly burst out with something like, 'Oh, Jamal, you're so much like him.' 'In what way?' 'Oh, you know. Dismissive. A man capable of jaw-dropping rudeness and imperious demands. A man used to having servants, or turning women into them. A man who could make you feel stupid and dull.' On other occasions she'd say, 'You'll never know what a fine man your father was when young and sober. Good looking and intelligent, he had that more-than-witty *thing*. What do they call it? Class. He had that: he had glamour.' Looking at me she said, 'You don't entirely lack his arrogance, as I'm sure people will tell you in the future. But unlike you, he absolutely knew he had it. And you know what, he didn't give a damn!'

'I was dazzled,' she said, making me wonder whether she still loved him. She added this wonderful thing, '*He was a like a light shining in your eyes.* Heaven knows why he was interested in me. I was a suburban girl and always felt sort of low voltage in front of him. When he wasn't kissing me, he'd take me to restaurants to meet his brothers and friends. I preferred Pakistanis to English people. I liked their food and their good manners. I was never one of those feminists, I couldn't afford to be, but I took exception when they expected me to cook and wash up, and stay in the kitchen. But my parents never said a bad word about your dad. I'd told them he was an Indian prince.'

While Dad was studying in London, his eight brothers removed the rest of the family from India to Pakistan, imagining the new country – brutally sliced from the old one like an afterthought, as the British vandal fled, taking a last swipe – would be a new beginning. During this time, although Dad was living in the London suburbs with the family he had made, he began to feel he had no home, as well as no vocation.

43

As Mum said, 'The suburbs weren't to be his place. We were living in my parents' house; we'd got engaged; we were married; we made babies. But he was still in transit. What was he doing? Sitting in the pub. Playing cricket out in Kent, wherever he could get a game.

'He would never stop talking to me about politics, sport, his family, while I was feeding you both. In the end I'd say to him "This is wasted on me, write it down! Put it in a column!" He did; he began to write for papers in India and Pakistan. He realised he had to be there, that he wanted to be involved. He was ready to work. He wanted to participate.'

So he went back to the subcontinent. There was no official parting but mum suspected 'something had upset him'.

At home, sitting in front of the TV eating Vesta curries, the closest we came to the subcontinent, we kept him with us by saying things like 'Dad wouldn't like you doing that' or 'Dad would laugh at that.' He became a made-up father, a collage assembled from bits of the real one. Each of us had our own notion or fantasy of him, while he stood in the shadows, like Orson Welles in the *Third Man*, always about to step into our lives – we hoped. If Mother referred to him as 'that man' or 'your damned father' this at least kept him in the network. But he could be used for unpleasant purposes.

One time, irate with Mother, Miriam said to her, 'You say Dad was an alcoholic and could be badly behaved, insulting and cutting, but he's had a successful life. Where did taking care ever get anyone?' 'I wouldn't call him successful,' Mum replied. 'Deserting your family isn't successful.' Then Miriam said, 'Dad had to leave you.' 'What do you mean?' 'Because you're so nasty, stupid and fascistic!' – which made mother put her hands around Miriam's throat. When they fought physically I would run out of the house and sit in the shed in the park, smoking, dreaming of the future and moaning to myself, 'There must be some way out of here . . .'

I had always been unsure of what job I'd get. Dad rarely gave us instructions or prohibitions. You could say he refused to give Miriam his ideas of how he wanted her to be. He gave me more, often pulling me to him and kissing my cheeks, ruffling my hair, physically demonstrating his adoration and telling me I worried too much about everything. I could persuade him to buy me clothes and books; I knew how to get round him. It was passionate and always tender, our love. I guess Miriam had our mother and sometimes I had Father, but I did feel guilty that he seemed to like me more.

There was another thing he gave me, for which I never thanked him. One time I went alone to Dad's hotel and, waiting for the lift at his floor, I saw a woman, small and plainly dressed, as if for an interview, in her mid-thirties – not one of the amazing ones. Dad's door hadn't yet shut and, pushing into the room, I saw he was asleep or passed out. The smell of her perfume remained.

I rushed downstairs and into the street, calling her. She hesitated before stopping. I thought she might flee but, although surprised by me, she didn't. Nervous and disappointed, chipped and gin-soaked, like a Jean Rhys heroine in worn-out shoes, I asked her to join me for a drink in the pub across the road where I asked her one question and then another, until I had her story, told in a low, croaky voice.

When the conversation ran down, I had the cheek to put an adolescent's direct enquiry: how much did she charge? She laughed and offered me a price. Naturally I had nothing like that kind of money on me, nor did I have anywhere to take her. I couldn't compete with Dad. Perhaps if I'd had more nerve, I might have enquired about a family discount. Nevertheless, I retained a passion for whores – as they say in the commercials, when in doubt use a professional – though, as with ordinary girls, you were always waiting for the right one, for the one you liked, or who liked you.

Father had once said to me that he'd wanted to be a doctor, like his own father, and wouldn't object if that's what I did. Unlike a lot of the early Freudians, who had been physicians, I had no aptitude for biology or chemistry, but I discovered that that didn't prevent me becoming a surgeon of the soul. 'Whatever you do,' Dad said in his backhandedly well-intentioned way, 'don't let me down and turn out to be a bloody fool.' I guess being an analyst solved a lot of problems for me, at least giving me the opportunity to spend time with people who made me think about what a human being was.

Ajita and I were able to see a lot of each other because her aunt had been told that college was a nine-to-five job, with occasional evening lectures. Her father was rarely home; he came back from his factory at ten at night and left early in the morning, six days a week. On Sunday the family visited relatives in Wembley, where Ajita danced with her cousins in their bedroom.

What a pleasant late adolescence it was. Being at university in those days was a mixture of extended holiday and finishing school. Unlike school, there was no bullying or cramming, and there was little of the concern about careers and money there is now. It didn't matter to me whether I got a Third or a Two-One; no one would ever ask me about it.

I read more then than I'd ever read before, and with a passion that was new and surprising to me. I was like someone previously sedentary discovering suddenly that they could run or jump. One of my lecturers said, 'Write about whatever interests you.' I worked on the first of my favourite Viennese thinkers, Wittgenstein, and the idea of 'private language'. The questions he asked were satisfyingly strange. It would be a while before I reached Freud properly.

When we were not at lectures, which was most of the time, I took Ajita to see Valentin and Wolf. She shopped and cooked us steak and chips. We were a little family. If I say she was my first love, I'd be saying she was the first woman I couldn't just pull away from; who stayed in my mind when I wasn't with her, and that I thought about continuously. When she was gone I minded very much.

We'd use Valentin's bed to make love while the guys smoked outside. 'Go on, lie down together,' Wolf would say. 'You two can't keep your fingers out of each other's pies.'

An odd sexual thing had begun to happen to me. There was no longer any discontinuity between orgasm and foreplay. The flutterings, surges, pulsations, were whole-body experiences, taking place inside me rather than only in my genitals, so that my orgasms were multiple. They didn't end with a bang, they didn't stop suddenly, but seemed almost continuous, like a series of diminishingly powerful shots.

What is a criminal? Someone pursued – wanted! – by the police. I wasn't wanted by the police, yet. Were my friends? I can't say I knew what 'crimes' Valentin and Wolf actually committed, if any. They would talk about fights, telling me how Romeo hit someone over the head with a chair. They would mention bent policemen and solicitors, and speak of how simple it was to bribe a judge or buy a passport.

There were numerous antique or junk shops in the area, which I would tour with Wolf. I was used to such places, and could help him find bargains. This was not easy because as soon as Wolf walked into one of these shops, he'd begin to distribute five-pound notes to the staff. They were certainly impressed, and moved about as if inspired, bringing him vases. Whether he was rewarded in any other way I doubted, prices would go up rather than down. The deference might have been enough for him. It was enough for me. At this stage, I still was intending to be an academic, doing the criminal stuff on the side. I liked the contrast. Plato the thief.

One time, though, something extreme did happen to Valentin. There was a guy he met in the Water Rat who wanted Valentin to fuck his wife while the guy beat off. Val needed the money and he got paid for doing this a couple of times. The wife seemed to find it moderately interesting, but what she really wanted was to see Val on his own, for dinner followed by the theatre. She'd pay him too. Then the guy came back to Valentin and said he'd pay him a lot more, a considerable amount, if he would tie the woman up, 'knock her about and slap her a bit'.

Valentin was sick, disgusted by the idea, though Wolf and I seemed to think that Valentin had a pretty good thing going there; the money available, he could have asked for more. What did happen was that when the man made this proposal to Valentin, Valentin hit him, knocking him down. Valentin was already depressed, liable to catatonic absences, and this made him worse. He didn't want to be a whore and he didn't want to be violent, why did these things happen to him? Oddly enough, I remember suggesting therapy to him, though I knew little about it, but he said that when he wanted to talk, he'd talk to me in the pub. A man could deal with it.

It came back to talking, then, the thing most people do a lot of. The whole family liked stories. My grandmother, who had lived with us before moving to a little flat nearby, read Agatha Christie and Catherine Cookson. There were piles of them, under the bed, in the corner, next to the toilet; my mother watched soaps, and Dad read Henry Miller on aeroplanes. I adored James Bond.

But the words in books weren't as hazardous as those that someone might suddenly say. Llike the words Ajita said to me one day, and I almost missed, but which stuck in my head, returning to me over and over, the devil's whisper.

She had turned up late to the philosophy lecture where I met her because although she was reading Law, she needed another 'module' to complete her course. She didn't love philosophy, as I'd hoped she would. She didn't see the point of it, though she was amused by my attempts to explain it to her.

'Isn't it about the wisdom of living, and about what is right and wrong?' she'd say.

'If only,' I'd reply. 'I guess you'll have to go to the psychology department for that, though you can't change courses now. For me philosophy is to do with Aristotle's idea that the desire for pleasure is at the centre of the human situation. But philosophy as it's taught is, I am afraid, about concepts. About how we know the world, for instance. Or about what knowing is – how we know what we know. Or about what we can say about knowing that makes sense.' Having nearly exhausted myself earning her bafflement, I went personal. 'I want to know you. Everything about you. But how will I ever know that I know everything about you?'

'You wouldn't want to know me inside out,' she said abruptly.

'Why's that?'

'It would put you off me.'

'How do you know?'

'It just would, I'm telling you.'

'You have secrets?' I said.

'Don't ask.'

'Now I have to ask. I'm bursting, Ajita.'

She was smiling at me. 'Curiosity killed the cat, didn't it?'

'But cats just have to know, don't they? It's their nature. If they don't shove their faces in that bag they will go crazy.'

'But it isn't being good for them, sweetie.'

I said, 'The good isn't always something you can decide in advance.'

'In this case it definitely is. Now stop it!'

I was looking at her hard, surprised by how defiant she was. She was almost always soft with me, kissing and caressing me as we spoke. We had this conversation behind her garage, where, unseen from the house, there was a little garden which no one used, with a decent patch of grass. When spring came and it got warm, we made it the secret place where we'd lie out listening to Radio One before driving to London for lunch.

Though we were dark-skinned enough to be regularly insulted around the neighbourhood, often from passing cars, we started to enjoying sunbathing naked, close to everything we needed – music, drinks, her aunt's food. Often Ajita would bring a bag of clothes out into the garden. Love through my eyes: she was teaching me the erotics of looking. She liked her own body then, and liked to show it, posing with her clothes pulled down or open, or with her ankles, throat or wrists lightly tied.

To me, the time we spent outside was a celebration. We'd survived the hard work of our childhood – parents, school, continuous obedience, terror – and this was our holiday before embarking on adulthood. We were still kids who behaved like kids. We'd chase and tickle one another, and pull each other's hair. We'd watch each other pee, have spaghetti-eating competitions, and egg-and-spoon races with our underwear around our ankles. Then we'd collapse laughing, and make love again. We had come through our childhood. Or had we?

Had Ajita's aunt been looking – and I often wondered whether she was, someone seemed to be watching us – she'd have seen Ajita lying there with her eyes closed and me on my knees, kissing her up and down her body, her lips parting in approval. All day I played in her skin, until I believed that blindfolded, I would know her flesh from that of a hundred women.

I did often wonder about Ajita's aunt, and the way she crept invisibly about the house with her head covered. I guess she'd have communicated with me in some way, had I been younger. As a child, when my Indian aunts had visited London, they'd pored over me, kissing and pulling me perpetually, certainly more than my mother. Who, though, did the aunt talk to properly? Certainly not Ajita or her brother. She washed and cooked for them, but didn't eat with them. Mostly she was alone in her room, more of a servant than a member of the family. I guess I believed, even then, in the necessity of conversation; believed, in fact, that she suffered for having no one to talk to.

There seemed to be no one else around. The neighbourhood appeared to be deserted, kids at school, adults at work. We'd have the radio on low, and occasionally we'd even glance at our college books. Otherwise all there was to look at was the sky and the house opposite. I observed that house and the couple who lived there, for days, without really seeing it, until it occurred to me that if my life in crime was to start – and I thought it should; with Wolf and Valentin I kept thinking I had to prove myself, to become tough like them – it could begin there.

Then I started to ask Ajita more questions. The things I wanted to know were the things she didn't want me to know. Where she had warned me off, I needed to go.

It was around this time, after we had been together a couple of months, that things began to get even stranger, and I began to feel I was in the middle of something I would never be able to understand.

Everyone has their heart torn apart, sometime.

CHAPTER FIVE

'A call for you, Dr Khan,' said Maria.

She was my sentry, and never normally called me to the phone at this time unless it was a potential suicide – every analyst's fear, and something many have had to deal with.

I would say that an analyst without a maid is no good to anyone; nor is an analyst without a shabby room. On the one occasion that he went to visit Freud, in 1921, André Breton, after circling Freud's building for days, was determinedly disappointed by the great man: by his building, by his antiquities, his office, his size. (Breton's colleague Tristan Tzara called Freud's profession 'psychobanalysis'.) Jacques Lacan's circumstances – the worn carpet, and the phallic driftwood on his waiting-room table – were often similarly disappointing to visitors. One expects to find a magician or magus, and finds merely a man. Analysis is at least an exercise in disillusionment.

We were having lunch: cold salmon, salad, bread and wine, a week after Rafi and I had been to Miriam's place. Henry had come over for talk and distraction.

Now Maria was holding out the telephone. 'Mr Bushy is outside.'

'I see. Thank you.' When I put the phone down I said to Henry, 'It's for you. Bushy's brought you the supplies you asked for.'

'Ah. Supplies. At last. What does Baudelaire call it? "The longing for the infinite . . ." Bring it on!'

There was considerable jangling in the hall, like someone pouring a bag full of coins down a metal chute. That wouldn't be Bushy. As an ex-burglar, he was a quiet man. It was Miriam herself, clearly wearing all her jewellery at once and up on both legs, too, without the sticks she sometimes used. In she came, removing her black crushed-velvet cloak and handing it to Maria, who gave her the respect she'd have accorded any queen I admired, male or female.

Miriam was wrapped in layers of flashing semi-psychedelic clothing along with a black, Goth, spider-web top. Her wild hair was freshly streaked with red and blue, her face-studs sparkling, a renovation which must have caused her considerable trouble.

'I was in a cage with the black wolf this morning,' she said as she swept in. 'Close to his spirit. He was looking away, to the East, worrying about those being blown up in the war. He said I should come here. Connections needed to be made. I had to bring this myself.'

'Right,' said Henry, looking at her eagerly. I have to say it surprised me to see Miriam come in by herself. Like any other celebrity, she didn't like to be seen alone, and because she was infirm she usually had a smaller person on each side of her, upon whom she could rest.

Henry seemed impressed. 'Absolutely.'

We leaned towards it. The 'infinite' was in the exquisite wooden box she held out in front of her. I recognised it. Our mother, with her passion for markets and antiques, had collected anything 'Eastern' and held on to it. 'It was only the husband who got away' was my response to her incessant dusting of various items of Chinoiserie.

She gave him the box. 'Here, Henry.'

'Miriam, darling, you are a good person.!'

'I am, I am – but only you appreciate it!'

You should have seen it – the two of them suddenly in each other's arms, long lost.

Miriam sat beside Henry, opened the box and unwrapped some grass. She offered it to his nose – a nose which had travelled the length and breadth of France in search of wine, with actor pals resilient enough to enjoy his monologues.

'Against death and authoritarianism there is only one thing,' he said once. 'Love?' I suggested. 'Culture, I was going to say,' he said. 'Far more important. Any clown can fall in love or have sex. But to write a play, paint a Rothko or discover the unconscious – aren't these extraordinary feats of imagination, the only negation of the human desire to murder?'

Now he swooned and his chins wobbled over the simplest thing.

'What d'you feel?' Miriam asked.

'Oh Miriam, it's your fingers I am admiring.'

'I know.'

'Where did you get the black nail varnish?'

'Wait, wait,' urged Miriam. 'Here.'

Henry leaned forward, her anxiety drawing him. 'What is it?'

Maria and I watched her place both hands on Henry's head. She shook her own head sorrowfully: Henry's discontent was vibrating in her finger-tips.

'What is it?' said Henry. 'Genius? Cancer? A jinn?'

'What sign are you?' she asked. This was not a good question to ask Henry, but she went on quickly, 'Have you seen a ghost recently?'

'A ghost?' he said. 'Of course!'

'How many?'

'You really want to know?'

'I can say you are definitely inhabited!' she said firmly.

'I always knew it,' he said. 'But only you recognise it!'

'But not possessed.'

'No? Not possessed?'

I could see that Maria, listening from the door, was about to panic. I took a last mouthful of food, glanced at my watch and said, 'I must go for my walk.'

Outside, Bushy was standing across the road leaning against his car, smoking. I waved and called out. Seeing me, he gathered himself together; his mouth began to work, no doubt a dream emerging from it.

'Want a lift?' he shouted. He was coming over, but I kept moving. He was beside me. ''Ere,' he said. 'You know all about it – I'm having more sex now than I've ever had! A man without his dick up someone is no good to no one.'

'I'm glad to hear it, Bushy,' I said, scuttling away.

When I returned from my walk, just before my first patient of the after-noon arrived, Henry and my sister had gone. Maria was clearing up. She said that Bushy had driven them down to the river at Hammersmith, where there was a pub, the Dove, that Henry knew. 'No doubt,' she said with some disapproval, 'they'll be spending the afternoon there.'

'Good,' I said, going into my room. 'Can you show the patient in, please.'

CHAPTER SIX

A man goes to an analyst and says, 'Please sir, I am desperate, if you cure me I will give you my fortune!' The analyst replies, 'I don't want your fortune, just fifty pounds a session.' The man says, 'Why so much?' To which the analyst answers, 'At least you know the price.'

My patients are businessmen, hookers, artists, teenagers, magazine editors, actors, PR people, a woman of eighty, a psychiatrist, a car mechanic, a footballer, and three children, amongst others. When I greet a patient at the door and follow them into my room, waiting while they prepare to either sit or lie on the couch – I prefer them to lie down; as Freud said: 'I don't like to be stared at for eight hours a day' – I am eager to hear what they have to say, and keen for it to go well between us.

As a therapist, what sort of knowledge do I have? What I do is old-fashioned, almost quaint, compared to the technological and scientific medicine now available. Though I do no examination and offer no drugs, I am like a traditional doctor in that I treat the whole person rather than only the illness. Indeed, I am the drug, and part of the cure. Not that most people want to be cured. Their illness provides them with more satisfaction than they can bear. Patients are unconscious artists of their own misery, and what they call their symptom is, in fact, their life, and they'd better love it!

Some people would rather be shot than speak. All I can do is let the subject speak for a long time; both of us taking their words seriously, knowing that even when they are speaking the truth they are lying, and that when they speak of someone else they are speaking of themselves.

I ask questions about the family, right back to the grandparents. Where can suffering people turn now for the disorders of desire?

In the end, what qualifies someone for analysis? Ultimately it is the most human thing, the recognition of inexplicable pain and some curiosity about one's inner life. How could analysis not be difficult? To have lived in a particular way for years, decades even, and then to try to undo it

53

through talking, is significant labour. Not that it always works; there is no guarantee, nor should there be. There is always risk.

Alas, to the surprise of many, psychoanalysis doesn't make people behave better, nor does it make them morally good. It may well make them more of a nuisance, more argumentative, more demanding, more aware of their desire and less likely to accept the dominion of others. In that sense it is subversive and emancipatory. But then there are few people who, when they are old, wish they'd lived a more virtuous life. From what I hear in my room, most people wish they'd sinned more. They also wish they'd taken better care of their teeth.

A smart, well-off, intelligent woman had asked to see me. She sat back neatly on the couch rather than on the edge, as other, more anxious patients tended to, and addressed me as though interviewing me for a job. She told me a little about her situation before saying she had come because her husband was 'having difficulties' with his work. Many people see analysts because of work-related problems; it is only later they reveal their emotional and sexual difficulties. However, she did not believe she had contributed anything to her husband's plight, but wanted to 'talk it over'. She was, she kept insisting, 'normal' or 'not abnormal at all.'

Later, on my walk, I wondered why I felt I had to be suspicious of 'normality'. The striking thing about the normal is that there is nothing normal about it: normality is the gentrification of ordinary madness – ask any Surrealist. In analysis 'the normal child' is often synonymous with the obedient good child, the one who only wants to please the parents and develops what Winnicott called 'a false self'. According to Henry, obedience is one of the problems of the world, not the solution, as so many have thought. But couldn't there be a definition of the normal which didn't equate it with the ordinary or uninspiring? Or which wasn't coercive or ridiculously prim?

It was, of course, in the nature of my work to spend time with 'nutters', as Miriam put it, just as medical doctors work with sick bodies. But, as Freud said, and as experience had taught me, my patients were not in a separate category to everyone else. It was those who didn't seek help who were most likely to be mad or dangerous. I was reminded of a story about Proust at the end of his life, wildly looking through the pages of *Remembrance of Things Past* in despair as he saw how eccentric, if not abnormal, all his characters were. As though one could make a novel, or indeed a society, out of the dull and merely conventional.

My work with the 'normal' woman would be to help turn her into a poet: she'd see what was puzzling but also fascinating in the experience she wanted to dismiss as 'normal', even as she attempted to convince both of us that the 'normal' was beyond inquiry.

Unlike the 'normal' woman, I have never stopped being amazed by the nature and variety of human pleasure, the most difficult problem of all. I am visited by a foot fetishist and compulsive masturbator who was about to lose his job, so much time did he spend in the toilet; a couple of men who dress as women; a powerful businessman who risked everything in order to secretly watch women through windows; a girl terrified of cats; a patient who had a breakdown on being informed for the first time, at the age of thirty, that her mother had always had a glass eye; the promiscuous, the frigid, the panicked, the vertiginous; abusers and the abused, cutters, starvers, vomiters, the trapped and the too free, the exhausted and the over-active, and those committed for life to their own foolishness. I hear from all of them. I am an autobiographer's assistant, midwife to my patients' fantasies, reopening their wounds, setting free their voices, making an erotics of speaking, unmasking their truths as illusions. Analysis makes the familiar strange, and makes us wonder where dreams end and reality begins, if, indeed, reality ever does begin.

I saw my first analyst, a Pakistani called Tahir Hussein, a few months after I'd left university and things had gone more than just weird with Ajita. I have to say – I was in great need.

Ajita and I had gone our separate ways without considering that we would never see each other again. We hadn't fallen out; our love had never become exhausted, but had been violently interrupted.

How I missed her adoration of me, her kisses, praise and encouragement, and the way she said 'thank you, thank you' when she came. Of all my women, she was the most memorably tender, vulnerable and uninhibited, like a Goya-esque Spanish beauty, her dark hair covering her face as she worked on my penis. She called me her pretty boy and said she loved my voice, loved what she called the 'timber' of it.

For months I had waited for her, thinking one day she'd turn up. I'd see her on the street, in departing trains, in dreams and in nightmares; I'd walk into a bar and there she'd be, waiting. I heard her calling me, her sweet Indian lilt in my ear, from when I woke up until bedtime.

At last, however, I got the real message, which was, after all, clear enough: she wasn't interested. She'd told me she loved me, but, in the end, she didn't want me. Her father was dead, the relationship was dead. Ajita was gone. I didn't want to get over it but I would have to. By now she'd be

with another man, married perhaps. I was already her history and, I supposed, was more or less forgotten.

In my early twenties I had left Mother too, having known for a while it
was time to get away from the house and the neighbourhood. If the suburbs
were the gentle solution to the question of how to live, I was out of there.

Through a university acquaintance, someone I'd directed in a female
production of *Waiting for Godot*, I had found a room in a house shared by a
group of white middle-class politicos. They were carpenters, teachers,
social workers, feminists and radical lawyers; two of whom later became
MPs, keen Blairites, often on TV defending the Iraq war. They had set up
several similar houses in streets nearby.

However, I wasn't able to move straight into the room I wanted. There
were other applicants and these politicos were democrats, from time to
time. I was to be interviewed, though I knew the lefties would offer me the
room as soon as I asked whether there were any black people in the house.
The guilt shuddered through them like a bout of food poisoning and I was
in, despite my pale skin and the queue of whites outside.

It wasn't exactly a commune; people had their own rooms and the cooking and chores weren't shared, though some tasks were. There were a lot
of meetings and mad talk, cycling and recycling. New posters – 'Protest
and Survive!', or a picture of a monkey being experimented on – along
with leaflets advertising meetings appeared in the hall every day, along
with piles of wood for 're-use'.

Often we cycled to the woods, with wine and dope in our baskets. One
time the others couldn't wait to get their clothes off and jump in some
filthy pond. Generally I was uptight, but this time I joined them.

Most weekends were taken up with some kind of anti-nuclear protest.
During the week there were Labour Party branch meetings held in draughty
halls on run-down estates. If I went, it was because everyone else went; I
wanted to know what was going on. It was serious work. The old guard, the
working-class stalwarts who smoked pipes and spoke interminably in difficult accents – and had many personal memories of Harold Wilson – along
with the eccentrics, the codgers, the plain crazies and those who had nowhere else to go in the evenings, were being replaced by the people I knew.

These were young, smart lawyers, housing officers, radicals from
provincial universities. A few of these 'activists' were actually Trots or
Commies, clinging to respectability and the possibility of real power;
others were channelling their ambition into conventional political careers.
The idea was to move the Party to the left by integrating radical elements

that had emerged during the mid-70s: gays, blacks, feminists. Michael Foot was elected leader of the Party, followed by Neil Kinnock. The Party was beginning to modernise but still wasn't electable. To become that, it was the left politics which had to go. How we all despised Thatcher, but she led the way.

I was amazed by the bitterness, viciousness and cruelty of small-time politics. Even here idealism was, as it always is, an excuse for quite extreme aggression. I leafleted local estates, and 'knocked-up' during local elections. Sometimes we were invited into the flats. I'd never seen such places before in the city and, I can tell you, it was an education.

In the house I didn't say much to anyone, staying in my room and reading. Usually there were political visitors. These were the days before the working class were considered to be consumerist trash in cheap clothes with writing on them, when they still retained the dignity of doing essential but unpleasant work.

Striking miners were popular with the gays; the Greenham women, in London for fundraisers, were favoured by the lesbians, though, apparently, they had to be bathed first; for the rest of us there were the Nicaraguans. (Several of our circle went to Managua to help out; I considered it myself, but heard it involved a lot of digging.) I liked the company, liked knowing there were people around. It was the first time I'd had a place of my own, somewhere I had to pay for.

Miriam and I had returned, not long before, from our 'roots' visit to father in Pakistan hating each other, hating everything. Not only did I not know what I was going to do, I was in bad mental trouble. I was beginning to realise that I'd thought, after the Ajita catastrophe, that the Pakistan trip would be a turning point. If I couldn't find Ajita there – how could I? – I would at least find my father, along with a sense of direction, some strength and my best self. What Miriam and I did in fact return with would take years to absorb.

I should have guessed I'd end up messing about with books. I found a monotonous but easy job in the British Library, where I was a sort of earthworm with arms, fetching books for readers from the miles of book-stacked tunnels under Bloomsbury. I spent my day in the intestines of the gloomy building, surrounded by rotting printed paper, emerging occasionally into the light and space of the magnificent Reading Room in the British Museum. 'I am a mole and I live in a hole!' I sang, or droned, as I worked.

My eyes, and those of my fellow workers, had become used to only low artificial light. We book-miners despised the readers, their self-importance, leisure and flirtatiousness with one another. Didn't they realise this was a library? Though we might be peculiar, freakish even – we were the foot-notes to the body of their text – didn't they ever think of what we did for them, how we kept them supplied? Bent-backed, I liked shoving along a trolley in the depths of the earth, in what Keats called 'dark passages'. Some of the people I worked with had laboured in the valley of books for thirty years, stifled and safe, nesting in forests of tomes. There was no bet-ter place to be buried alive.

One of the scholars working in the Reading Room – on Coleridge's *Notebooks* and the poet's love of *The Arabian Nights* – I had known at uni-versity. He had taught friends of mine. He walked on sticks and his body was shrunken and misshapen, as much by the steroids he took as by the ill-ness. Often we'd have lunch in cafés in Bloomsbury and one time he com-plimented me on my long, luxuriant hair. I said I wasn't growing it for reasons of fashion, but because I couldn't sit in a barber's chair, couldn't let myself be touched.

'Even by a woman?'

'Well . . . yes – especially by a woman.'

'You don't have a girlfriend?' he asked.

'I did. But she went away and she's not coming back. I thought she would. But it looks like she really isn't.'

'I'm sure women like you. If I looked like you, I wouldn't be sitting in the library all day. I sit down because I can't walk properly. My broken body is going to hell.'

'Libraries are sexual places,' I said. 'It's the quiet, the whispering. You readers don't see us watching you, but we know what's going on. We notice who leaves the building with who, and we gossip about it. Still, tell me what you would be doing instead.'

'Having it off, of course,' he said. 'As it is, the only people who touch me are prostitutes, something you don't need. I'm sure there are women who would pay you.' He talked about himself and his own problems, for a while. Then he said, 'Do you have any other symptoms?'

'Symptoms?'

'States of mind which prevent you leading a relatively rewarding life.'

I explained that I had begun to stop still in the street, unable to move at all, either backwards or forwards. Recently I had stood in the same place for an hour – suspended, paralysed, dead – reading and re-reading an advertisement, unable to get to work on time. If I was actually in motion, I found myself yelling at people in my mind. I wanted to fight them, wanted to get beaten up.

Mostly my mad stuff was inside me, but I would shove people on the bus; someone punched me in a pub. I wasn't far from becoming one of those lunatics who mutter and shout at themselves at bus stops. I had to leave work early in order to lock myself in my room because I believed, and didn't believe, that when I was outside others could hear my thoughts, that my head was transparent like a goldfish bowl.

In the evening, as you do, I'd catch glimpses of rats, birds and alligators from the corner of my eye. In my dreams bears would dance with me, buggering me from behind. Live chickens would be stuffed down the back of my shirt.

I found one day, soon after beginning the job, that I was unable to walk; a spinal disc was perforated. I had an operation, shared a hospital ward with the limbless, and learned to walk again. Living even at the most basic level was becoming more arduous.

The oddest thing was, I felt my experiences were not taking place in the world, but beyond it, in a void. There were no words for my suffering. Like the undead, the internal voices of hatred would knock on my door forever, seeking an impossible peace. If I was so ill, and getting worse, as I believed I was, how would I ever lead a useful life?

My friend said, 'From our talks, I am aware that the art you like is modernism, the exploration of extreme mind states, of neurosis and psychosis. I, too, have spent my life with such books, but reading Kafka or Bruno Schulz can only take you so far. You will find in books characters who are like you. But you will never find yourself in a book unless you write it yourself. It is the wrong place to search. To switch metaphors, you can't get out of a locked room without the right key.'

'What or where is the key?' I almost shouted. 'Have you got it in your pocket? Open the door!'

He said the key might be this fellow Tahir Hussein.

The next day he obtained Hussein's phone number for me, adding that he was much talked about. I said a lot of people were talking about me, but I was paranoid. I had no idea who was talking about Tahir Hussein. It was probably a small literary metropolitan elite all of whom had been at university together. That was how it worked in England. But I was sane enough to realise that without help I would fall into a black hole. For weeks I didn't call this man, continuing to believe I could survive alone and that my illness would disappear magically.

Another day: the morning, before work at the Library. I am standing on the street. People are bent forward; they look like tables, running. Everyone had purpose, somewhere to go. When they arrived, they would have plenty to say to each other. Didn't I too have plans? But – I almost said I had forgotten what they were. No. It was not that I had mislaid my plans in a far part of my mind. The future no longer had any force over me. I was too dizzy, with wild surges of mad feeling. My wish was to faint, to become unconscious. You cannot will a faint, I know that, any more than you can will a dream, a laugh or a fart. How I wanted some release from this suffering, to which even death seemed preferable. I wasn't driven towards suicide. I wanted only to be rid of this swirling whirring.

At that moment I saw ahead of me a red London phone booth, with a gap or trench open before it, into which I waded. I came up in the booth; I was surprised to find it working; surprised to find I had change; surprised to find it ringing and answered by Tahir himself. I was particularly surprised to be invited to see him.

He had said he would take me on. I could see him the next day. He gave me his address and said simply, 'Come tomorrow morning at eight and we will begin.'

If I'd had to wait more than a week I wouldn't have turned up. Waiting was another of my phobias. Surely I would die before the appointment? Also, I knew therapy would be expensive, exhausting most of my small income. But I couldn't see what else to do, and having nothing didn't hurt me; it was what I was worth.

But would I ever tell him the truth?

CHAPTER SEVEN

When I walked into that room where my life changed, although I'd studied some Freud at university and also when I was in Pakistan, I had little idea what an analysis involved, and there was no one I could ask.

In the lefty house where I lived, I kept *Civilisation and Its Discontents* under the bed, along with my favourite pornos *Game* and *Readers' Wives*, though with an E. P. Thompson paperback on top of them. This was because among the young intelligentsia, class was the paradigm. As a useful concept it was easier to deal with, and less dangerous than sexuality. The problems of the proletariat were not caused by being born a human being and living in families, but by class conflict. Once these were solved by social change, most problems would evaporate. Any difficulties left over could be solved by Maoist group discussions.

The Left could be puritanical: in the heaven of the far future there would be more than enough fucking, but right now the priority was that everyone pushed for change. Freud was reviled as a white bourgeois patriarchal pig and psychoanalysis was considered to be exhausted as a theory. What woman would admit to, or even accept the idea, of envying our little penises, though that, of course, was exactly what feminism was. As Adorno wrote, 'In Freudian psychoanalysis, nothing is more true than its exaggerations.'

Nonetheless, R. D. Laing – popularly known as 'the two Ronnies', after the television comedians – was still admired by students, mad behaviour was often idealised, and numerous therapies, a mixture of Vienna and California, were emerging. I knew Lennon and Ono had screamed and rolled around with Janov and that the great *Plastic Ono Band* album had been the result. But I didn't see what any of this could do for me. What of the quietly mad, the ordinary and unphotogenically disconcerted?

Tahir Hussein told me that not knowing anything about technique was the best way to approach analysis. To drive a car you didn't have to know what was under the bonnet.

'You're the mechanic of souls?' I said.

He invited me to lie down on the couch and say whatever came into my mind. I did this immediately, determined not to miss the full Freudian experience. His chair was behind my head but by his breathing I could tell he was leaning towards me, scratching his chin, waiting to hear. 'The thing is . . .' I said.

I began: hallucinations, panic attacks, inexplicable furies, frantic passions and dreams. It seemed only a minute before he said we had to finish. When I was outside, standing on the street knowing I would return in a couple of days, waves of terror tore through me, my body disassembled, exploding. To prevent myself collapsing, I had to hold onto a lamp post. I began to defecate uncontrollably. Shit ran down my legs and into my shoes. I began to weep; then I vomited – vomiting the past. My shirt was covered in sick. My insides were on the outside; everyone could see me. It wasn't pretty and I had ruined my suit, but something had started. I came to love my analyst more than my father. He gave me more; he saved my life; he made and re-made me.

After a few sessions, when I asked him how he thought I would pay for my analysis, he only said, 'You will get the money.'

This did concentrate my mind. I noticed that the man who had given me Tahir Hussein's phone number always studied the racing papers at lunchtime, but never bet on horses, even though, as he put it, he believed he could make a lot of money that way. I told him my situation so far with Tahir Hussein and asked again for his help. 'Easy,' he said, giving me a tip for the following day. I slung everything I had on the nag, about two hundred pounds, saved to pay my rent, and won over two thousand pounds, which I spent on my treatment. I went three mornings a week. It was serious and intense, the first time I'd taken myself seriously, as though normally what happened to me was not worth noting, and it wasn't a moment too soon.

My academic friend had told me that one of the virtues of psychoanalysis in England was that it had been developed not only by women, but by people of all nationalities, by which he meant European. Unusually for an analyst, Tahir Hussein was a Pakistani Muslim. Tahir had a smart flat at a smart address, in South Kensington. Even as I walked there, I felt rays of hatred emanating from passers-by.

Tahir's place was full of pots and rugs and furniture that had to be polished, paintings that had to be insured and sculpture that had to be plugged in. He was extravagant too. I'd almost expected a quiet guy in a suit and bow tie. But Tahir was something of a show-off, dressed in post-war ethnic gear. He'd wear salwar kameez, a kaftan, hippy trousers, even a fez, and those slippers which curled up at the toe. I'd say, at times, that he looked more like a magician at the end of a pier than a doctor.

Nevertheless, he had the complete exotic-doctor presence and charisma. Dark-skinned, with long greying hair, he was imperious, handsome, imposing. He must have been aware that he could seem ridiculous. Few would doubt he was arrogant, cruel, alcoholic, and more than a little narcissistic. But I guess he reserved the right to be himself, as much himself as he could be. For him, as for the other hip shrinks, it wasn't the work of analysis to make people respectable conformists but to let them be as mad as they wanted, living out and enjoying their conflicts – even if it meant suffering more – without being self-destructive. I caught on early when he quoted Pascal: 'Men are so fundamentally mad that not to be mad would amount to another form of madness.'

I fell in love with him, as I was supposed to, perhaps before I met him, and fantasised about his private life. I tried to seduce him, begging him to fuck me on the couch, while convinced that this was not something I really wanted; I took him small presents, coffee, pens, postcards, novels.

When it came to the important things, listening and interpretation, he was there, on the spot. He wasn't one of those analysts who terrify you with their silence, a sphinx identified with their own stillness. Once he asked if I thought he talked too much, but I said no. I loved the exchange. He said that silence was a powerful tool but that it could recreate the inaccessible parent and 'frantic child' scenario. So when he had something to say, he said it. Discussing Freudian theory was always considered a resistance, I knew that. But resist I would; the theory began to fascinate me.

Every time I saw him, I felt I'd moved forward in understanding; even as I rejoined the street I'd be asking myself new questions. Gossip had it that Tahir had had affairs with his patients; apparently he'd talked on the phone while seeing them, and even went to the opera with them. But he was nothing but focused with me. Occasionally, if I asked him what he was doing that night, he would speak of his friendships with painters, dancers, poets, knowing I liked to identify with him, that this was something I wanted for myself.

After sessions he'd watch me looking at his catalogues, at his poetry books. 'Take them,' he'd say. 'Take anything you need.' He knew I wanted to extend my mind, having by now a thirst for intellectual matters. When I said I wanted to understand Freud and analysis, he encouraged me to read Proust, Marx, Emerson, Keats, Dostoevsky, Whitman and Blake.

He said that in most of Shakespeare's plays there was at least one mad person, and in their madness they not only told you who they were, but they spoke important truths. He said that analysis was part of literary culture, but that literature was bigger than psychoanalysis, and swallowed it as a whale devoured a minnow. What great artist hasn't been aware of the unconscious, which was not discovered by Freud but only mapped by him?

Also, he'd say: My profession is not, and should not be considered, a straight science. It was impossible for Freud to say that he cured people by poetry. Yet observe the important figures and see how like poets they are, with their speculative jumps and metaphors: Jung, Ferenczi, Klein, Balint, Lacan, each singing their own developmental story, particular passion and aesthetic. Their differing views don't cancel each other out but exist side by side, like the works of Titian and Rembrandt.

Of course, at the beginning of the analysis there was something we both had to overcome, something sombre I had to talk about. But I wanted to know him a little, to know I could trust him, and myself, before I laid what I called my 'son of night' murder story on him.

His virtue, I discovered, was that he could speak deeply to me, that he seemed to understand me. He talked to the part of me that was like a baby. It was like being addressed by a kind father who could see all your fears and fantasies, and was entirely committed to your welfare. How did he have such knowledge of me? Where did it come from? I wanted to be like him, to have such an impressive effect on another human being. I still do.

I always thought of myself as a speedy person, uptight, impatient, getting anxious easily. With him I could let myself relax. What was I in love with? The quality of the silence between us. Sometimes fear makes no sound, I thought, as we sat there, combing through it all, Mother, Father, Sister, Ajita, Mustaq, Wolf, Valentin. Him leaning towards me, with just a side-light on, during those dismal wet London mornings, as people rushed to work. But this was a good loving silence, minutes long, supporting peace between people, not the sort of silence that made you unruly with anxiety.

'Was it a noisy house you grew up in?' he asked. 'But yes,' I said. When I did turn and look at him, he inevitably had a look of amusement on his face. Not that he found human suffering entertaining, even when it was self-inflicted, as he knew it mostly was. He was showing me he knew it went on. 'Illness is lack of inspiration,' he'd say.

Before I began analysis, I'd had a dream which had disturbed me for days. It was like a Surrealist painting. I was standing alone in an empty room with my arms by my side and scores of wasps in my hair, making a tremendous noise. Although I was standing by a door, a man with a head full of wasps cannot either move or much consider his emotional geography.

The 'wasps', of course, were White Anglo-Saxon Protestants, among other things, and once we began to discuss it, the image opened up numerous possibilities. Analysis didn't 'cure' my mind, then, of its furies and darkness, but it brought these effects into play, making them real questions for me, worth bothering with and part of my lived life, rather than something I hoped would just go away. For Tahir the wasps represented something. If I could find meaning there, I could increase my engagement with myself, and with the world. The wasps were asking useful questions, ones worth pursuing. Despite the tremendous grief of depression, Tahir spoke of the 'value' and 'opportunity' of the illness.

So it was, I found, that analysis creates interest, and makes life. I never left a session with nothing to think about. I'd sit in a café and make pages of notes, continuing to free-associate and work on my dreams.

I had already studied *The Interpretation of Dreams* and *Civilisation and Its Discontents* but now I began to read up on how Freud first began to listen to the words and stories of the mentally distressed, something that had never been done before. He found that if he concentrated on their self-accounts, the trail inevitably led back to their pleasure.

For Freud, as for any other poet, words, the patient's spoken words and those of the analyst, were magic; they brought about change. I was gripped. Fortunately, working in the Museum, I had access to all the books I wanted. If a reader requested a particular volume I was working on, I could say it had been lost. I'd sit on the floor in a far-away tunnel in the library and read; then I'd conceal the book until I returned. I re-read Freud's 'book of dreams' as a guide to the night, making going to bed the day's most worthwhile experience.

I adored the practice of two intelligent people sitting together for hours, days, weeks, maybe years, sifting through the minutiae of experience for significant dross, peering into the furthest corner of a dream for a coded truth. The concentration, the intensity: analysis was not a moment too soon for me. What compelled me was the depth of the everyday, how much there was in the most meaningless gesture or word. It was where a person's history met the common world. Like a novelist, this way I could make meaning and take interest from the mundane, from the stories I liked to hear.

It seemed to me that Tahir and I had both been talking a lot, working on a deep excavation. Miriam's understandable hatred of me as a child, her howling psychotic violence and her attempt to keep Mother away from me, for herself; the feeling I had of being alone, having been abandoned by both parents, Kafka's wounded beetle hiding under the bed.

But one day, after a long silence, Tahir said, 'Do you have something to tell me?'

That was it! I believed he was implying that he knew I was leaving out the most important thing.

I had lost my capacity for happiness. The truth was I had murdered a man. Not in fantasy, as so many have, but in reality, and not long ago. In the end I could only measure Tahir Hussein in terms of that: whether I could trust him, or whether I would go to jail. I had told no one my secret, though often I was tempted, in one of the putrid pubs I went to most nights after work, to unburden myself to some soak who'd forget my story by morning. But I was smart enough to know it wouldn't help me with my loss.

The murdered man wouldn't let me go that easily. He clung to me, his fingernails in my flesh. I would wake up staring into the flickering fright of his doomed eyes. The past rode on my back like a devil, poking me, covering my eyes and ears for its sport as I puffed along, continuously reminding me of its existence. The world is as it is: it's our fantasies which terrify; they are the Thing.

My mind had begun to feel like an alien object within my skull: I wanted to pluck it out and throw it from a bridge. Books couldn't help me; nor could drugs or alcohol. I couldn't free my mind by working on my mind with my mind. I thought: light the touch paper and see. Will it blow up my life or ignite a depth charge in my frozen history? Could I rely on another person?

Finally, I was forced to do the right thing. I would throw myself on his mercy and take the consequences. One morning, after making up my mind, I told Tahir Hussein the truth. How would the analysis ever work if I repressed such a momentous event? So Tahir heard about the physical symptoms, the shaking and paranoia. He heard about the dreams of the dying eyes staring at me. He heard about Wolf, Valentin, Ajita. He heard about the death.

'What do you think?' I asked.

He said, simply, straight away, that some people deserved a whack on the head. I'd done the world a service, offing this pig who was bad beyond belief. It didn't stop me being a human being. It was only a 'little' murder. He didn't seem to think I was going to make a habit of it, or go professional.

What a relief it was to have my secret safely hidden in the open! Tahir was worried about my temptation to confess and then be caught, my need to be punished, as well as the temptation to have everyone know me. To conceal is to reveal. Most murderers, he said, actively lead the police to the scene of the crime, so preoccupied are they with their victim. Raskol-nikov not only returns to the crime scene, but wishes to rent a room in the 'house of murder'.

Tahir was the only person I told. I was desperate at the time, and now Tahir is dead, along with the secret which will never be uncovered, the secret which had been turning my soul septic, until I couldn't proceed alone. After Tahir, with my two other analysts I kept it to myself. It wouldn't reflect well on my career prospects.

I had said to Tahir, a year after I'd started seeing him, that his profession was one I fancied for myself. How come? I was aware, from an early age, when I met people on the street with Mother, that I wanted to hear their gossip. This was the route, I saw later, to the deepest things about them. Not necessarily to their secrets, though this was part of it, but to what had formed and haunted them within the organisation of the family.

Soon, however, the everyday conversations that characterised life in the suburbs were not enough. I wanted the serious stuff, the 'depths'. I'd come to Nietszche and Freud through Schopenhauer, whose two-volume *The World as Will and Idea* had so entertained me at university. There I copied out the following passage: 'The sexual passion is the kernel of the will to live. Indeed, one might say man is concrete sexual desire; for his origin is an act of copulation and his wish of wishes is an act of copulation, and this tendency alone perpetuates and holds together his whole phenomenal existence. Sexual passion is the most perfect manifestation of the will to live.'

I had seen myself as someone who was always about to become an artist, a writer, movie director, photographer or even (fall-back position), an academic. I had written books, songs, poetry, but they never seemed to be *the* meaning I sought. Not that you could make a living writing haikus. I had always been impressed by people who knew a lot. The one thing Mother and I did do together was watch quiz shows on TV. *University Challenge* was our favourite, and she'd say, 'You should know all this. These people aren't as bright as you, and look at their clothes!'

None of the careers I'd considered excited me. Yet, unconsciously, something had been stirring within. Being with Dad in Pakistan, catastrophic and depressing as it had been in many ways, had instilled something like a public-school ethos in me. The sense of the family, of its history and achievement – my uncles had been journalists, sportsmen, army generals, doctors – along with the expectation of effortless success had, I was discovering now, been both exhilarating and intimidating. I wasn't only a 'Paki'. Suddenly, unlike Miriam, I had a name and a place, as well as the responsibility which went with it.

I began to see that not only was I intelligent, but that I had to find a way to use my mind. This was something to do with 'family honour', an idea which formerly I'd have found absurd. It was Tahir who brought everything together for me. It took me a long time to bring it up with him; I was afraid he'd think I wanted to take his place.

But at last I did. 'What do you think?' I said. 'Could I do it?'

'You'll be as excellent as any of us,' he said.

During the first year of my work with Tahir, I saw little of Mother and Miriam. I went to some trouble to avoid them. Both their arguments and their intimacy, without a father, I saw now, to desire them both in different ways, and to keep them apart, made me overwrought.

But when Miriam said we should go there for Christmas lunch, I wasn't able to disagree. Anyway, I wanted to see Miriam's first child, a cute baby provided by a cab driver whose fare, one night, she'd been unable to afford. By now she was living at the top of a council block with the child and another on the way, her only adult company being a violent man. She was stoned most of the time, with interludes on a psychiatric ward. Later she moved to the outskirts of London, arguing that she couldn't be high up, as the voices yelled 'Jump, jump!' 'But never quite loudly enough,' Mum remarked.

Over dessert they asked me if I was intending to remain at the Library, perhaps becoming an exhibit. I said 'not indefinitely'; I knew now what I wanted to do. I would become an analyst, a shrink, a head doctor. I floated this with as much seriousness as I could gather, but I had to bat away numerous irritating remarks. 'He *needs* a head doctor,' Miriam muttered. Mother: 'You're the one who needs it.' Miriam: 'Actually Mother, if you bothered to look within, you'd see it was you.' Mother: 'You look inside yourself, dear.' Miriam: 'After all, you made us . . .' On and on.

When this tailed off, I continued. While *The Devil's Dictionary* definition of a doctor is 'One upon whom we set our hopes when ill, and our dogs when well', the word 'doctor', as Josephine could have told you, inevitably went down well with most people. As I spoke, explaining the training, the theory, the practice, the income, the interest, the words, to my surprise, did seem to have authority. They were surprised, I guessed, partly by my determination and engagement. I knew they thought of me, I thought it myself, as passive and repressed, without much will or desire.

But now, rather than feeling only partly present, as I did before – my life as an interruption to them – I seemed to have some weight. I was able to be their equal and, to my dismay, it seemed to diminish them, render them a little pathetic even, as though I had been reducing my own stature all my life, to keep Mum and Miriam big. Unlike either of them, I seemed to know what I was about, where I was going. My crime was my spur. I would spend my life paying off that early debt. I was happy to do it.

'You will be doing good then?' Miriam said.

'Maybe a little.'

'That's nice.' She wasn't being sarcastic. Her other selves were almost always hidden beneath her aggression, her general *stroppiness*, which was a good, accurate word to describe her. 'You can help *me*, then, can't you?'

They were looking at me almost pleadingly. 'You both know,' I said, 'no doctor can treat a member of his own family.'

A year into my training, when I was beginning to work with juveniles, we heard that Father had died. After leaving Pakistan, Miriam and I didn't see him again. Did we mourn him? I'd have wanted him to know I'd found a vocation. Whether he'd have appreciated it, I doubted. However, I was strong enough by then to have ridden his disapproval. I was on my own, but I knew, at last, what I was doing.

That night, after I left the house, walking the familiar streets from which I thought I'd never escape, a boy semi-defeated by something he didn't understand, I was in a hurry to get back to my complete edition of Freud, the patients I would start seeing, the conferences I'd attend, the books I'd write. I wanted to be useful, to have done something.

Even then, at a moment of such hope, when the future was something I wanted, I would hear the dead man's words echoing in my ears: 'What do you want of me?'

CHAPTER EIGHT

Straight out I said to Miriam, 'You know I'm a gossip trollop and must have it immediately.'

'You and Henry sound so similar to one another,' she said. 'But he's like Tigger, and you were never so outgoing. Or have you changed?'

I said, 'Now it's you who is beginning to sound like him.'

'Oh God, we're all dissolving into one another!' she said.

Evening, and Miriam was in her kitchen when I arrived. Kids on bikes doing wheelies in the front yard. Other boys and girls distributed around the house with their friends; a teenage boy in front of the television at the other end of the room, his hand in a minger's chest, the other on the TV remote. Bushy perched barefoot on a chair, stuffing money into his socks before putting them on again. Then he threw his keys in the air, caught them, and went off to pick up a paying customer.

At her place Miriam seemed distracted or preoccupied, as she had been as a young woman, wishing she were elsewhere, wondering where the pleasure was. However, I noticed she was looking at me as I fiddled in her kitchen, preparing pasta for myself.

'So?' I said. 'How much did you enjoy seeing Henry? Did you stay long at my place?'

'Here it is,' she said. She had on her most serious, if not tragic face, which disconcerted me. But it was too late now. 'Did you set this up on purpose?'

'Henry asked me to get some dope for you. That's all I did.'

'Don't come in!' she screamed into the rest of the house, before shutting the kitchen door and jamming a chair under the handle, a rare cry for privacy. 'What happened? Henry wanted the dope but he doesn't even know how to make his own joints. While I was rolling a few, teaching him, he said, "It's the most useful thing I've learned for years." You know how he talks, for England and for his own benefit, as if he expects to be listened to. Even I had to shut up. That's authority for you. I get hot just thinking of it.'

'What did he say?'

'I was telling him from the off I was poor. I said I've never had nothing, not for want of trying. I'm no good at anything but the small stuff, so don't think I'm a catch, but I might inherit a bit.

'He said he lived with his wife Valerie, in luxury, for ten years. There were houses, cars, parties, holidays. They were friends with famous artists, politicians, actors who stayed in their houses, drank their champagne, swam in their pools. When she needed more money she'd sell a painting.'

'Henry did some excellent work during those years.'

'Without making much money, he claims. It was she who supported him. His nose was in her trough. Well, as he talked about it, he became more and more upset, calling it "an untrue life". I didn't know what to do. In his mind he's a crazy man. You spend the day with such people.'

'It was all talk?'

'I gave him the joint. It's special stuff. I knew it would draw out the subject for him.' Now Miriam came and sat next to me, lowering her voice. 'I'll tell you how he seduced me into love.'

'Love already?'

Henry had asked Bushy to drive them to his flat by the river at Hammersmith where he lived on the first floor. I often went there: the living room had a long window overlooking the Thames and the trees on the towpath opposite. The other three flats in the house were occupied by ageing theatre queens with whom Henry was always arguing, either about the dustbins or the number of rent boys, or, more likely, young actors, stamping up and down the stairs. Or they'd have long discussions on the landing about productions at the Royal Court in the mid-1960s.

Apart from the large living room, Henry's place was composed of a number of small and medium-sized rooms filled randomly with theatre memorabilia as well as the 'artworks' he'd begun to make himself in the last few years. Sitting on worn carpets were his 'sculptures' made of wire and plaster, or of egg-boxes mixed with Polyfilla; on the walls, among the broken mirrors, posters and sketches for costumes from numerous shows, were his drawings and watercolours.

Like a lot of people, he was prouder of his hobbies than he was of his work. His son Sam had told the Mule Woman, indeed any woman who passed through, that if you praised Henry's photography you were in with him, if that's what you wanted. In fact, the Mule Woman had been so in love with the idea of living near the river, which she watched constantly, that she attempted to dust a little, soon realising it would take a team of people several days to make an impression. Nevertheless, she'd honoured the pictures and received some kindness in return.

Henry had a large armchair by the window, and a radio on a table next to it. Here he read newspapers, poetry, plays and Dostoevsky, while watching the river. He liked to claim that at night he could see, among the trees, his gay friends participating in open-air orgies.

Miriam said, 'I liked the pad. The history of his life everywhere, awards, photographs of him with that famous French actress, Brigitte Bardot.'

'Jeanne Moreau.'

Miriam said, 'We wanted to get the sex done with straight away. Both of us were starving for physical love. He was like some mad woman, talking about how his body would disgust anyone who saw it. He wouldn't take his clothes off. He actually put his jumper on. You know I'm used to odd things, but it got bizarre, lying naked in bed with a completely dressed stranger who wouldn't stop telling me how frightened he was. Anyway, you don't need to hear about it.'

'Why not?'

'It might make you sad about yourself.' I laughed. At times she sounded as sentimental as Rafi, who would say, 'Oh Dad, I don't want you to feel sad.' Now she went on, 'Well, after the love, he got this book out. We were on the vodka, smoking another joint. He made me read to him. She was called Sonya.'

'From *Uncle Vanya*? The last speech?'

'He put a chair in the middle of the room and watched how I sat. He had the cheek to give me instructions.'

'What did he say?'

'He made me do it slower. He told me when to look at the book and when to look up. At the same time he wanted me to do it naturally, as if I were at home. The speech was about work and the angels and the heavens, full of emoting. Too much about work for my liking. He got very involved in it, dashing about here and there. I had no idea he could be so light on his feet.'

Now and again over the years, I'd sat in on Henry's rehearsals for both his modern and classical work. I'd particularly liked his workshops with ordinary people and his appreciation of what he called 'naive' acting which, he said, had its own beauty. 'Bring me only the worst actors. What could be more depressing than talent?' he'd say. 'I hope never to meet anyone talented again!'

If, when he was doing a production, there was an actor he couldn't get along with, he'd ask me to come in and have a look at them, and Henry and I would talk in the bar later. Henry was different at work; I'd heard he'd been a bully, particularly with women, but he seemed to have grown out of that. In the rehearsal room I was impressed by his assurance and intense concentration, by his concern for the actors and his interest in their ideas, as well his firmness when he wanted something. I saw that this was where he was meant to be, what he was alive for. But it also made me wonder why this self, so alert and vibrant, was separated from the anxious, daily self which I knew.

Miriam said, 'He told me he might record me saying the speech for television. Was he lying or just winding me up? I'm used to that stuff from men. Married men always adored me.'

'They did?'

'I swallowed everything.'

'Indeed.'

'I don't even mind him lying, but –'

'Henry wouldn't do that. He is supposed to be making a documentary about acting. If you're not careful he'll put you in it.'

'Really? I'll have to get my hair done and cover my tattoos. I wish I had some money.'

A few years back I introduced Henry to one of my ex-girlfriends, Karen Pearl, sometimes fondly referred to as 'the TV Bitch'. About eighteen months ago she had agreed to produce a documentary that Henry wanted to make. But instead of shooting it over a ten-day period, as most people would, Henry had decided he would make his film 'over a couple of years', with his own camera, while doing other things, like teaching, travelling and lecturing – his 'retirement' activity, though he hadn't retired, of course.

Karen wanted celebrities in the documentary, by which she meant soap stars, while Henry wanted talented, well-known actors with whom he'd worked before, as well as amateurs attempting pieces from the classical repertoire.

Henry had become annoyed with me for putting the two of them together in the first place, and Karen claimed his obduracy was helping to bankrupt her, though even he can't have been the sole cause. She'd invited me to one of her pop things recently, in a warehouse full of barely dressed and over-made-up semi-children. She'd turned into Hattie Jacques in the *Carry On* films: matronly, patronising, foolishly grand.

She was fond of the juice, and as furiously difficult in her persistence as Henry. One of the first to produce make-over programmes – gardens, houses, women – things hadn't gone her way for a while; everyone was doing it now. The company she had started had recently been fired from a series they were making. Therefore I didn't think Karen would be too pleased with Henry's new but touching idea to have his girlfriend recite Sonya's speech in its entirety on television. I could see many battles ahead.

Miriam said, 'Bushy got me home. I felt like I was lying on a cushion of air. It's been years since I've had any real love. I kept singing. I wanted to hear a song by Enya.'

'Oh, bad luck.' Before she could slap me, I said, 'Will you see him again?'

'Only if you tell me why he likes me.'

'You're likeable.'

She said, 'Why don't you have a lover? I know you miss Josephine.'

'I get lonely. But, as my first analyst used to say, "Don't worry about me, I've had my Sartori."'

She said, 'It was the one before Karen, Ajita, who was always your true love.'

'She was?'

'How many times did I meet her? Two or three? That was enough for me to tell. She was lovely, and uncomplicated. She gave me that jewellery too. Why didn't you stay together?'

'Things fell apart.'

'What really went on between you two? Maybe it will still work out. Why don't you search for her?'

'I'm not sure I want to.'

'Didn't someone get killed?'

'They did.'

'When will I hear the whole story?'

I said, 'She's been on my mind a lot. It's that time of year, the anniversary, when I saw her for the last time. I always sit and think of her, and feel damned dark, dark, dark.'

'Jamal, try and find her. She's probably living nearby. Like you, she will have been with other people, but I've got a feeling there's something between you.'

'What if there isn't? Wouldn't that be worse? To me it's Pandora's box.'

'You won't know until you find out.'

'Listen,' I went on, avoiding the subject. 'Miriam, you can go to Henry's when you want, but his son is sometimes there. I'll put my flat at your disposal. I will have two keys cut. Use the place when you want, when I am not working in the evenings, or at weekends. If Maria is there, send her out.'

I noticed that Bushy had come in; he was standing there, nodding at Miriam. Earlier I'd noticed, but not really taken in the fact, that she was wearing make-up as well as perfume.

'Jamal, I have to go. Henry is taking me to a club for a drink.'

'Excellent,' I said. She was passing her hand repeatedly over her face. 'What's wrong?'

'But I don't want this. I hate to go out. I have my people, the children, Bushy. Henry unsettles me. Perhaps he will ruin me and I have ruined my life too often. Do I have to go?'

'Yes.'

Behind us, Bushy cleared his throat. I said, 'Miriam, it is like the old days. You about to go out into the night and me about to go to bed.'

'I would invite you to come,' she said. 'But Henry wants to see me alone.'

'I am working on my book. It's the thing which interests me most now.'

In the last ten years I had published two books of case studies, *Six Characters in Search of a Cure* and *The Reader of Signs*. In each volume I took a number of individuals and discussed my sessions with them, musing, as the stories unfolded, on the nature of 'everyday illnesses' or symptoms: fears, obsessions, inhibitions, phobias, addictions. This was normal, every-day stuff any reader would recognise: symptoms around which whole lives are organised and on which, sometimes, they founder.

To my surprise, as well as that of the publishers, my books were suc-cessful and translated into five languages. As well as being an attempt to revive Freud's idea of the case study as a mixture of literature, specula-tion and theory, it was a way of explaining analysis to a new generation, a way of showing how it could succeed as well as fail. Therefore it was partly about how people hate the thought of giving up their symptoms – forfeiting one's illnesses is a big risk, since they work as cures for other conflicts.

I had avoided technical language and discovered that these accounts of distress naturally had the structure, organisation and narrative push of stories. They were, in fact, character studies, in which the subjects were collages of real patients, along with fragments of myself, and other parts which were invented. They were the closest I'd come, and it was pretty close, to writing fiction. It was a form, a relatively free one, unlike that of the academic article, where I could say what I needed to, musing on my daily work and on the thinking of others, poets, philosophers, analysts.

I wasn't inexperienced as a scribbler. I had a contract for another book, and it was my intention to write one: I needed the money. But this material about Ajita, which was emerging spontaneously and taking up most of my writing time, seemed different. I imagined my account of her, seemingly random and chaotic, would be not unlike that of a psychoanalytic session: a mixture of dreams, wishes, interruptions, disputes, fantasies, resistances, memories from different periods, and an attempt to find a way through it all. To what? I was trying to find out.

I walked around to the front of the house with Miriam. I noticed Bushy was carrying what looked like Miriam's overnight bag. Before getting in my own car, I kissed her and watched as Bushy opened the rear door for her, waiting as she struggled, suppressing various 'old woman' noises, to get herself comfortable.

Then, as she went to her pleasure, she waved and called out, 'See you later, brother.'

CHAPTER NINE

My lover was crying, shaking. I'd never seen her in such a state.

Ajita and I were putting our towels out, scanning the sky for clouds, when she broke down, weeping hard. It was some time before she admitted that something serious was bothering her. Her father was having trouble at his factory, the place he wanted her to run with him when she graduated. She had even hypothesised about whether she and I might manage it together, when her father retired.

There had been a television documentary about the factory which, as it happened, I had watched with Mum, not realising it was about her family.

A few months previously her father had been approached by a director who told him the putative 'doc' would be a sympathetic look at the lives of the Ugandan Asians, people who had come here with little but who were already pushing up, socially; a bright story about an immigrant's progress. Ajita's father had liked the director, with whom he had many talks about cricket, India and the politics of the Third World. However, it turned out that the director was a sort of double agent, as a lot of them were said to be. He was an upper-class, Cambridge-educated Communist, a clever, successful renegade who hated his own class and background.

In the documentary there were many shots inside the factory and interviews with the workers. Ajita's father had cooperated; he was flattered to be involved. But the Cambridge Communist had exposed Ajita's father as a merciless exploiter of his own people, as an arch capitalist and greedy villain. Ajita's father had tried to contact the man and remonstrate with him. But now the Commie wouldn't speak to him. Ajita's father couldn't understand how anyone could behave so perfidiously. It was 'typically English', from his point of view – as well as being what he described as 'Marxist colonialism'.

The factory workers had, of course, seen the programme and had become more difficult, complaining openly now and even threatening strike action. In Africa or India, of course, they'd have been fired or beaten up. Ajita said

77

to me, 'Why can't they just work? Surely in this political climate they're lucky to have jobs.' This must have been what her father had told her.

I made it clear to Ajita that when it came to such things I was on the side of the workers; that was my instinct and my belief, passed on to me by my own father. Somewhat self-righteously, I told her I was also a supporter of Rock against Racism, formed after Eric Clapton made a racist speech from the stage in Birmingham. 'Come on Eric,' went the original letter in the *Melody Maker*. 'Own up. Half your music's black. You're rock's biggest colonist.' But Ajita wasn't about to become a leftist. She said nothing; she wasn't taking anything in.

My hope was that despite our differences we would return to our indolent life, financed by the great exploiter, her father. The longer the old man was at work, harassed though we might be, the more time I had to eat his food, drink his beer and fuck his daughter. Other than when it concerned race, politics didn't fascinate me. People were always on strike in the 1970s; it was the only consolation for having to work. The lights crashed almost every week. You'd hear a huge ironic cheer going round the neighbourhood pubs and dance halls, before you could grab the girls and the candles came out. Or there were food or petrol shortages, along with some sort of national crisis with ministers resigning and governments surviving on the edge. Then there'd be an IRA bomb: among other things, they liked blowing up pubs, as well as Hammersmith Bridge, which was attacked twice. The wrong people were soon beaten, forced to confess, and locked up. We were used to it.

But this crisis at the factory was upsetting Ajita so much she didn't want to make love. 'Don't touch me, Jamal,' she said, turning away from me. 'I can't do this any more. I feel too bad.' It was the first time she'd refused me, the first shadow over our infatuation.

She wouldn't be comforted. To distract ourselves, we drove into college and were sitting quietly in the bar with Valentin. I liked being there, the men looking at her. She was a stand-out girl. I had my little gang now; I felt protected.

One of the most active student groups were the Iranian exiles. Every lunchtime they'd leaflet the bar with horrific pictures of the victims of the Shah's secret police, Savak, an organisation supported by the US, ever the dictator's friend and financier. I would speak to the young leftists who wanted our support; they claimed they would use the mosques to organise the people. Once the rebellion had started, the Left would take over.

The other active college group, always busy and looking for trouble, and related to the Anti-Nazi League, was the SWP, the Socialist Workers Party. A student in our philosophy class came over to hand us some of their leaflets. Like Marxism itself, he wasn't ready to go away, but drew up a stool and talked urgently to Valentin about a meeting.

The Trots were always trying to convert him, which was peculiar since he'd been brought up in a Communist state from which he'd gone to some trouble to flee, arguing that Marxist ideology had devastated his country. Despite the Trots' arguments that the system had 'gone wrong', after being hijacked by Stalinists, Valentin couldn't be convinced. He told me he found these guys amusing or 'almost mad', but he often listened to them, having nothing better to do.

Valentin seemed contemptuous of almost all human effort or enterprise, as if it were beneath him. Certainly, he considered me beneath him, which was perhaps why I was so keen to impress him. When once I asked him to help me with my logic, he just said, 'Oh, I mastered all this months ago.' Then, when we'd go to the King's Road on Friday and Saturday nights to pick up women, he'd usually score and I'd always have to get the last train home. I guess, when he 'gave' me Ajita, it was another patronising act.

I noticed that after glancing at the leaflet she had been given, Ajita then re-read it several times, which surprised me as she'd never been keen on either reading or politics.

The Trot jabbed at the leaflet. 'That factory owner there, the one we're concerned with . . .' He drew his finger across his throat and opened his mouth and rolled his eyes like a distressed figure in a Bacon painting.

'Right on, man,' I said dismissively.

A little panicked voice said, 'Jamal . . .' Ajita was whispering in my ear. She wanted to go for a walk along the river, at Embankment.

I grasped, through her sobs, that the factory referred to in the Trotskyite leaflet, where the students were asked to protest, was her father's.

For three years Ajita's family had had it good, the father building the business, the mother with the children, money to spend. The kids were set- tling in; they liked England. But it seemed now that England wouldn't admit them after all. Ajita's father was used to running things and to hav- ing power, but recently had become afraid of having it wrenched from him. Profits weren't great; he'd had to keep wages down. The whole business was in danger of collapse. He'd be left with enormous debts and then might be made bankrupt. What would they do then – go on the dole like everyone else in England?

The strike, which began soon after the documentary was broadcast, was led by a tiny Bengali woman. This brave, defiant figure had become a hero to other women, to the Left as a whole. She had everything going for her: race, gender, class, size. The numbers on the picket line were increasing every day. The factory wasn't far from London and was near a tube station. Actors from the RSC and the movies were supporting the picket before the workers went in the morning. A Labour minister had visited. The dispute was becoming a cause célèbre.

There were a few West Indian workers but mainly the employees were Asian: a mixture of Kenyan Indian, Pakistani and Bengali, older women, students and some men, overseen by white managers. Ajita told me that contrary to popular opinion, the workers were not peasants, but were educated and politicised. They wanted to start a union, but Ajita's father wouldn't negotiate with a union. The workers were Asian like him; he understood their family life, their religion, their food. He didn't see why they needed a white-led union pressurising him. He didn't pay well, but he didn't pay worse than anyone else.

Ajita's father had become furious and defensive. He'd fired several of the socialist jihadis and refused to reinstate them. Accused of attempting to bring the Third World to England, he replied that this was racism. According to Ajita, he was being picked on. 'Do you think I'm the only exploiter in this country?' he'd say. Britain wouldn't yield to him; he couldn't get his way. But there was nowhere else for him to go. All his money was in the factory. Not that he was unsupported: Conservative politicians talked of 'anarchy' and the 'rule of law'.

The afternoon after she cried in the pub we drove back to the suburbs. Ajita went home to study. Instead of joining her, I went to my house to read in my bedroom and listen to music. I went to bed around nine. Being a student, I wasn't used to getting up early: usually I caught the train to London after the rush hour, around ten.

But early the next morning, without telling Ajita, and while Mum and Miriam were still asleep, I went to the factory. Or, rather, to the demo.

Coming out of the tube station, the first thing I saw was a large banner saying '*Only Slaves Cannot Withdraw Their Labour*'. By eight o'clock the gathering at the gates was considerable. There must have been three hundred people, and they were noisy, almost riotously angry. The crowd seemed to be composed of sacked Asian workers from the factory, students from different radical groups and scores of other sympathisers, along with photographers and journalists. All of these people were surrounded by what looked like legions of police.

The besieged factory, as far as I could see from the gate, was made up of two long, low buildings which looked as though they'd been constructed from cardboard and asbestos. When I talked to the workers they complained that, amongst other things, the place was too hot in the summer and too cold in the winter.

I heard about the heavy stacks of cloth, for cutting, which the workers had to move around. The sewing machines were unsafe; the needles broke constantly, scoring the fingers of the employees. Bits of fabric seemed to fly through the air; everyone had blocked noses; no one breathed properly. There was an accident on the premises at least once a month. The workers were allowed only two weeks' holiday a year, but not in the summer, when there was more work to do. The washrooms and toilets were filthy; women were paid less than men; pregnant women were sacked; one woman said the white bosses forced the female workers to have sex with them.

The crowd increased in size and noise. I noticed that the protesters were carrying stones, bricks and lumps of wood. Then, suddenly, the bus carrying the scabs was coming through, its windows covered in chicken-wire. I was amazed to see it race recklessly through the crowd as a hail of missiles rained down on it. Using their truncheons, the police tried to shove us back, but people broke through to spit and thump at the bus.

Right behind the bus was an expensive car, and I noticed Ajita's father driving.

I recognised him because I'd seen him one time at the house, when he returned suddenly 'to find some papers' but really, it seemed to me, to watch a boxing match on TV. Looking at Ajita's face that day, as he opened the door and strode into the room where we were sitting with our feet up on the glass-topped coffee table, eating Smiths crisps and grooving to the Fatback Band. I realised she was scared of him. This wasn't just nerves; I thought she might faint.

Luckily Mustaq was at home, sitting in a corner peeping at me over the cover of *Young Americans* as usual, and Ajita was able, as planned, to introduce me as his friend. If only that had been enough. To show how consanguineous we really were, I had to spend the afternoon in Mustaq's bedroom. Ajita had often asked me to 'speak to' her brother, about whom she was worried. Their father was too 'distracted' to pay him much attention. He lacked fatherly guidance and example; he was girlish and knew nothing about football.

That day the kid was delighted to have me to himself. Did he make the most of it! He took my picture, before presenting his 'special' things: a train set, his *Peanuts* annual, his Snoopy stickers, a voodoo doll he'd carved himself from driftwood, complete with pins and numbers scrawled on it in black marker pen, his drum kit and acoustic guitar. There was also an ancient packet of condoms, a flick knife, and a picture of a female cousin in a bikini at the seaside.

Then he asked me to wrestle with him.

'Okay,' I said. 'Let's do it.'

Why would I agree to that? I thought it would shut him up. The blood drained from my head when slowly he began to remove all his clothes, apart from his pants.

I wasn't into the wrestling thing, particularly when I saw how up-for-it he was, jiggling and jogging on his toes and smacking one meaty fist into the palm of his other hand – bam, bam, bam! Although he had a lot of loose blubber on him, it didn't stop him looking like a tough, kicky little fucker.

He came at me like a bear, his teeth exposed, his arms out, and he embraced me straight away and held me. He threw me off the bed, picked me up and tossed me around the room, eventually sitting on me, tickling me and kissing my cheeks. When I tried to get up, he forced his hands down the front of my trousers. I couldn't shout out for fear of his father banging through the door with a shotgun. On top of me, Mustaq was wiggling his hips and coming on like a teenage trannie or vamp; he wanted to suck me off with his father and sister a few yards away.

It was a relief when he jumped across to the piano and started singing one of his own songs called, apparently, 'Everyone has their heart torn apart, sometime'.

'Listen, listen,' he said. 'Tell me what you think!'

'Great, great song, man,' I said. 'I like the "sometime".'

'You really think so?'

'You should record it, man, and send it in somewhere.'

In my haste to get away I stumbled over the edge of the bed and, being forced for a moment to look under it, noticed a sea of half-eaten chocolate bars, bright sweet wrappers and rotting Easter eggs.

I just about got out of there intact, cursing his whole family.

'Come back soon,' Mustaq whispered.

'Nice time?' said Ajita, smiling. 'I'm so happy you two really get on!'

I was so in love with her. The rest of the family I could have done away with.

I didn't tell Ajita what her brother had attempted with me, but next time

I took some books and magazines, mainly 'outlaw' American stuff that I thought he wouldn't have known about, Rechy, Himes, Algren, even Burroughs, all of which I handed over on condition he didn't fondle me. 'Fathers like boys who read,' I told him. 'They think books are only a good thing. They have no idea how dangerous they can be.'

To my surprise he read everything I gave him, talked about it and asked for more. I gave him *Tropic of Cancer* and *Quiet Days in Clichy* and he wrote me a note, saying he'd never before come across such Surreal poetry, madness and stupidity in one book. (Then he began to read Céline.) I gave Mustaq my own worn copy of Lou Reed's *Transformer* because I knew it too well, but continued to hear its dirty, decadent Bowie-sound every time I visited.

I liked to show off to him, to stir him up in an older-sibling know-it-all impressive way, as my sister did with me. If I'd wondered whether I could scandalise or even corrupt him, I soon saw he was more adventurous than me.

He did, from time to time, attempt a grope, and he was always changing his clothes in front of me – 'All I want is to know if you like me in stripes?' 'Only if they're embedded in your arse' – but he was a decent ally in the house, providing I talked to him. It was like having an annoying kid brother. He even stuck a photograph of me on the wall, besides boxers and actors and one of Bailey's early pictures of Jagger, when Mick looked like a surly teenage mod.

Every time I saw him, Mustaq invited me to a gig or movie. I always refused, until he hit on the irresistible thing: three tickets for the Stones at Earl's Court. We were sitting at the back and the tiny figures on stage resembled little puppets. It was like watching TV, except you couldn't turn over. Ajita and I snogged while Mustaq was enthralled, leaning forward in his Mick Jagger tee-shirt. At the end, he said, 'I want to be looked at like that. *I want to do that every day of my life!* Jamal, tell me, do you think I could achieve it?'

'Your father would be delighted,' I said.

The day their father came home early, he took no notice of me, but I did get a good look at him. He didn't return to work, but lay on the sofa with a huge whisky, staring at the television and smoking continuously. He was tall, thin, severe-looking and almost bald. His face was brown, creased and pock-marked, as if a bomb had exploded near him.

Even though the 60s were over and feminism had become assertive, the old men still had, and were expected to have, most of the power. Fathers were substantial men; they had too much authority to get on the floor with the children. They were remote; they scared you. This man laughed with Ajita a couple of times, but he didn't smile. He appeared to have no charm. I'd say he was terrifying. While I wanted Ajita to be my wife, I didn't want to be related to her father.

Standing in the picket line as the car rushed through the factory gates, I also glimspded Ajita in the back seat, crouching down, with her hands over her ears, or was it her head? What was she doing there? Why hadn't she told me?

I shouted out and waved, but it was no use. The spectacle didn't last long. People began to drift away.

'What an odd sight,' I said aloud.

'What do you mean?' said two students beside me, exhilarated by their activity.

'A handful of working-class Asians being abused by a bunch of white middle-class students.' I added, for good measure, 'I bet your fathers are all doctors.'

They looked at one another and at me. 'Whose side are you on?' they asked.

Later, Ajita came into college. We'd both been to the demonstration that morning, but neither of us mentioned it. I had a lot of questions. Do you love someone whatever they do, or does your love modify as your view of them changes, as you learn more about them? Love doesn't keep still, there are always things you have to take in. Bored at home, I had craved the unknown, an experimental life, and that's what I was getting, more than I could have imagined.

That night I was lying on my bed; Mother was downstairs watching TV; Miriam had gone to see Joan Armatrading at the Hammersmith Odeon. I was wondering what Ajita was doing at this exact moment. She must, I guessed, have been worrying about the strike. Then it occurred to me that this wasn't the only source of her troubled manner.

For the first time I thought: 'Ajita is being unfaithful to me.' Don't all lovers worry about this? If you want someone, isn't it obvious that someone else will want them too, as their desirability increases? But the second it occurred to me, the idea seemed more than a fantasy. What was puzzling me about her at the moment? I had intuited that she was hiding something from me. What was her strange mood about? Yes, concealment!

Soon the secret would not be concealed. I'd ask her about it when I saw her. I had to know everything.

CHAPTER TEN

Until recently Mother would go to Miriam's house for birthdays and Christmas. She would fall asleep in an armchair, wake up with a dog dribbling in her lap, and have Bushy take her home with her head 'banging'. But now she never visited. It was 'tiring', she said, to which Miriam retorted, 'Well, you'll have to watch me on television like everyone else.'

Although it was difficult to prise Miriam from her neighbourhood, and she didn't feel safe going far without some sort of entourage, Bushy and I insisted that every three months or so Miriam and I have lunch with Mother. It was usually at the Royal Academy in Piccadilly, where all elderly women went with their sons and which she considered 'her club'. Mother also enjoyed a sedate tea at Fortnum's, though Miriam had been turned away for being 'inappropriately dressed'. I guess they'd never seen so many tattoos on a woman before. Mother felt Miriam had embarrassed her, and Miriam had seethed and cursed, Mother having called her 'adolescent'.

Mum, after leaving the bakery, worked in the offices of a big company until she retired in her mid-fifties. She had been decently paid, and received a pension. Once Miriam and I had both left home, Mother's life continued in the same way for years. The old-woman walk to the shop trailing her wheeled basket; continuous TV soap operas, *Coronation Street* and *Emmerdale*: a stroll in the park if it wasn't too windy; a worrying doctor's appointment; a visit from a friend who'd only discuss her dead husband, the deaths of her nearby friends and neighbours, and their replacement by young noisy families.

She had always made it clear that her life was a sacrifice – to us. Without such a burden she would be kicking up her legs in Paris, as she sometimes put it. Like a true hysteric, she preferred death to sex, and often insisted she was 'waiting to die'. In fact, she'd add, with much sighing and many pathetic looks, she was 'pining' for death; she was 'ready'. As she'd spent her life hiding, or playing dead, Miriam and I can hardly be blamed for having taken our eyes off her. One day we realised that far from hurrying towards the grave in the hope of finding that which she'd lacked in the world, she had made a revolution in her life. Now, wherever she went, Billie was with her.

As far as I was aware, Mother had devoted little time or attention to sexual passion. After father, she never took up with another man. On a handful of occasions she stayed out all night, pretending to be with a friend. Miriam and I smirked and guessed she'd been with someone we called Mr Invisible. Sometimes we found programmes for dance shows or theatre plays, as well as catalogues for art shows, but no one ever came to the house.

I should have realised something was stirring in Mother when one day she said she wanted to go to the cinema, to 'a place called the ICA'. Did I know where it was? I had to admit I had spent some of my youth there, looking at shows, movies and girls in the bar. Mother could only admit how little she knew me or where I'd got to, but she was pleased I'd learned how to get about the city.

Now she wanted to see a film about a painter. When I looked it up in *Time Out*, it turned out to be *Andrei Rublev*. I had to warn her that a three-hour black-and-white film in Russian might be too much for us, but she was adamant. We were the only two in the cinema, and I thought how wonderful this city is that a man and his mother can sit in a building between Buckingham Palace and the Houses of Parliament, watching such a great work.

That was about three years ago. Since around that time, Mother had been living with Billie, a woman of the same age whom she'd known since she was eight. Mother had always seen a lot of Billie, and I'd talk to her when she came to the house. 'You prefer her to me,' mother said once. 'She lives more in the world,' was my reply, or something like it. What I couldn't say to mother was that as a teenager, and even younger, I'd fancied Billie. She was aware of her body; she moved well, she was sensual.

For years after Miriam and I had gone, Mother talked about selling the family house and buying a small 'granny' flat. It was what we expected her to do, as she liked to sit in the same place and do the same things every day, something I'd never understood until I read *Beyond the Pleasure Principle*, where Freud describes such repetition as 'daemonic' and characterises it, simply, as 'death'. And she did put the house on the market and she did, to our surprise, sell it.

Miriam refused to visit the house for the last time. It was painful to have to pick up our toys, school reports and books, and remove them to London. I had to throw a lot of things away (and I love to clear out) but each loss was a blow. I think mother Mother thought we'd be more senti-mental about the house itself; we'd grown up there, but for us it had no sentient life.

What mother Mother then did was go and live with Billie, telling us the flat she wanted wasn't 'ready'. Billie still lived in the house she'd grown up in, a huge place near the Common, a house I hadn't visited for years but one I remembered as being full of drawings, paintings, sculptures and cats. Billie was 'Mr Invisible'.

For thirty years Billie had taught at a studio for artists in a rough part part of South London, as well as organising photography, painting, draw-ing and sculpture courses for local people. Billie had had many boyfriends but never 'found love' or had children. She still wore black eye-shadow and gold sandals, had a Cleopatra haircut and dressed in some of the antique clothes and jewellery she'd always collected with Mum. She was intelligent and good to talk to. Now the two women got up early and went to the studio. They cooked, bought furniture and travelled, often spending their weekends in Brussels or Paris, or going there for lunch and an after-noon stroll. They were talking of renting an apartment in Venice or holi-daying in Barcelona.

Mother didn't want us to think her strange, individualistic or radical; she had just moved house. Whether they were lovers or not we didn't ask. Certain words were not promoted here; Mother referred to Billie as her 'friend'. Sometimes I called Billie her companion and she didn't object. It was the best relationship of Mother's life. Billie didn't seem in the least bothered by Mother's self-pity, anxiety and numerous fears, or her pen-chant for stasis. Mother didn't make Billie as anxious as she made us. Billie was too busy for that.

Unfortunately Mother, who had worried about Miriam all her life, now hardly concerned herself with her. Miriam felt abandoned, but I was more powerful now; I tried not to let her attack Mother.

At first, when Miriam and I saw Mum and Billie together, usually fresh from a pile-high book-buying spree at Hatchards, we couldn't avoid their absorption in one another; it was a revelation, particularly when they showed off the rings or haircuts they'd bought each other. Then, one time at lunch, Billie had asked whether Miriam 'had' anyone. Certainly Mother had never had a high opinion of any of Miriam's boyfriends; she considered them to be 'boys' – immature, not worth the space they inhabited – rather than men. Miriam could only answer, 'I am lucky enough to have several children to bring up.'

This time, when we met, Billie was polite to Miriam, but there was no doubt she considered her to be borderline cracked, which made sense in the circumstances. Like when Billie mentioned something 'marvellous' going on at the Tate Modern, Miriam's response was to say how stupid it was that the place was called Tate Modern rather than 'The Modern Tate', which, in her view, would have been less pretentious, more accurate. Billie said that would be like calling the Houses of Parliament the Parliament Houses.

As this tricky conversation developed, I could see that in such circumstances Miriam might easily revert to her teenage self, never far from the surface at the best of times, and I wondered whether she might seize some object and attempt to hurt the wall with it. As it was a cold day, the rising heat from her body almost warmed me, but the one thing I didn't want was for her to have a stand-up row with Billie. Mother sat there almost oblivious, like a tortoise in front of a street parade.

I had thought about whether Miriam might say she had 'met someone', whether she and Henry might become official. But Miriam was not thinking like that; she was already too angry. What infuriated her was that not only had the two women been travelling and buying pictures – some of them costing £3,000 – but that the women were designing an artist's studio for their garden, which they were intending to have built as soon as they found an architect they liked. Mother and Billie seemed to think they could do it 'for less than £15,000'.

Like everyone in Britain, Mother had made more money from property than she had from working. She had sold the house, paid off the mortgage and kept the rest of the cash, which she was now going through at a tremendous rate. 'If I spend it all before I die, I won't care,' she said to me. 'I'll borrow more, too, on my credit cards, if I need it.'

'Quite right,' I replied. Even more laudably, she gave none of her money to her children or grandchildren, even though Miriam complained with increasing volume that her house, which she had bought cheaply from the council, was falling apart. It hadn't been decorated for years and the roof was rotten. For some reason which Miriam couldn't fathom, Mother seemed to think her daughter should work for a living.

Miriam blamed Billie for being a 'bad influence', but Mother had changed too. When Miriam suggested the women might be too old to embark on such an adventurous building project, Billie refused to accept she was old.

'Old is over ninety,' she said defiantly. 'Soon people will be living to three hundred.' 'That's right,' said Mother. 'We're not too old to sit through an opera, as long as it's got two intervals and a nearby toilet.' She opened her bag and the two women grabbed a bunch of 'rejuvenating' pills, swallowed with rapid swigs of organic wine. 'No one calls me Grandma, either,' said Billie threateningly.

I wondered whether, on the phone, Miriam had said something to Mother about being a neglectful grandmother, because Billie then informed us that after marriage, domesticity was surely the lowest form of life. Certainly she abhorred anything which involved schools or bovine earth-mothers with their plastic bottles of milk and identical filthy-faced children all called Jack and Jill.

Now the two women were off to the hairdressers for the afternoon, followed by more shopping and a party given by a local artist. If the women had to be helped to the street and into the taxi, it wasn't because they were infirm but because they were so pissed and giggly.

On the way back in the car, Bushy was silent; me too. Miriam was sitting there trembling; we could hear her jewellery humming. She was tighter than a tuning fork. It had taken us a while to realise, but Mother was gone for good. She would always talk to us, but we were no longer at the centre of her life. She didn't appear to even like us much, as though we were old friends she'd fallen out with. She had discharged her duty and gone AWOL.

Miriam said at last, 'You sit there all Zen and beaming and I can't stand it.'

'What can't you stand about it?'

'You not saying anything! If you ever do that analyst's shit with me I'll wring your neck.'

'Maybe I was quiet but I was enjoying myself. What's wrong with you? Didn't you try out the "loving-a-girl" thing yourself?'

'You think I enjoyed it? Anyhow, those girls weren't in their seventies, they had bodies. Mother is pissing away the family money. A studio . . . Sculpture. A box at the opera. Jesus – mostly all they do is drink.'

'The money's hers,' I said. 'It's a pretty good thing those old girls have got going. What a decent way to go at the end, the two of them occupied and adoring one another.'

'Why doesn't she want to give us anything? I've got a new man to feed now! He will take it for granted I will look after him!'

'Did you tell her about Henry?'

'She will think he's the same as the others. To her they're all no-good scum. But what about the grandchildren she now ignores?'

'We're adults,' I said, tiring already of having to be the adult. 'Soon the children will be. They can make their own way.'

'You've always been down on me, you and Mother.'

I said, 'But I am the one with reason to complain, if you want to hear about it. When you were at home Mother was arguing with you. When you were out, you made sure she was worrying about you. What room was there for me?'

'I had awful problems,' she said. 'Made much worse by the fact you thought I'd lived a worthless life. You with your books and long-word talk, quoting poetry and pop songs, mocking me for my craziness. You do it less now, but you were always a sneery show off! In Pakistan you didn't back me up at all.'

'Fuck off.'

'Now you –'

She was holding my arm. I grabbed her other hand. I may be a talking specialist, but no one could argue with the fact that a cuff across the face would improve my sister's temper, except she seemed to think a punch would advance mine.

In the traffic Bushy slammed the brakes on and turned round. 'You two – stop! No fighting in the car. That's what I say to the children.'

Miriam was trying to hit me, but I'd grabbed her wrists, thereby increasing the danger that she'd head-butt me. After the cars behind us began to hoot, Bushy was driving with one hand and was in our faces yelling while trying to push us apart with the other.

'Any more of this and I'm going to stop the car right here and throw you both the fuck out! Jesus – you're worse than kids!'

To calm herself down, Miriam decided to stop off at Henry's flat. She wasn't intending to go in and 'bother' him, but stand outside and look up at his windows, 'to think about him being in there not patronising me – not treating me like shit – unlike you and Mother and her bitch girl-friend!'

I could see Bushy's eyes in the mirror. I shrugged; I'd long known it wasn't worth arguing with Miriam. He parked the car not far from the river, we walked to Henry's and, after watching Miriam stand there for a while, looking up, Bushy said, 'Go on Juliet, up you go! I'll come back later,' and off we went.

Maybe Mother's adventure had inspired her; maybe Mother was more of a model for Miriam than either of them could have admitted. Certainly in the next few weeks Miriam's relationship with Henry became more serious; and because of what happened I got to know more about it than I might have wanted.

CHAPTER ELEVEN

Miriam and Henry had begun to use my spare room for their assignations. About once a week they went to the theatre or cinema, but the room was where they ended up in the evening if I was out with friends, lecturing, or just walking about the city, thinking about my patients.

They had requested a cupboard they could lock, where they kept scarves, whips, other clothes, amyl nitrate, vibrators, videos, condoms, and two metal tea infusers. I wondered whether these last two were being used as nipple clamps, or did Henry and Miriam enjoy a cup of orange pekoe when they finished?

This new development was because there had been a crisis at Henry's place. He had been caught.

He and I have dinner at least once a week, always in Indian restaurants in the area, often ones we hadn't visited before. This was a passion not only for Indian cooking, but for the 'complete' restaurant decor of flocked wallpaper, illuminated pictures of waterfalls or the Taj Mahal, and the waiters in black suits and bow ties. Strolling about London I'd look out for such places which, like pubs, were gradually being replaced by swisher surroundings.

I had been expounding the idea that Indian restaurants (rarely owned by Indians, but by Bangladeshis) reproduced the colonial experience for the British masses. I informed Henry, as we sat down, 'This was what it was like for your forefathers, Henry, being served by deferential, respectful Indians dressed as servants. Here you can feel like a king, as indeed you do.'

He liked the theory but didn't want to be a colonialist when it came to his supper. His view didn't soften when I said the experience was 'Disneyfied', by which I meant that the real relations of production were concealed. The owners were not the white British, of course, but the Bangladeshis, from the world's poorest country. It also made him uneasy, but didn't disturb him as much, when I told him the waiters had deserted their own countries for the West. Henry said they were entitled to our riches after what their forefathers had been through during the colonial period.

In the restaurant he talked to the waiters of Tony Blair and Saddam Hussein, of the waiters' homesickness and their belief that God would save them, or at least calm them; their use of religion as therapy. He even said he was thinking of converting to Islam, except that the pleasure of blasphemy would be an intolerable temptation for him.

After we'd ordered, Henry said, 'To us it's these guys' faith rather than their social position which makes them appear infantile. But they're also lucky. These God stories really keep everything together. Surely they're better than antidepressants? There's more despair in godless societies than there is in the god-ridden ones. Don't you agree?'

'I don't know, I really don't.'

'You couldn't agree with that because unlike me you are a fortunate man.'

'I am?'

'You listen to women all day, for a living, as they idealise and adore you. I used to think of you as a "collector of sighs".'

He went on: 'I am, of course, at the age when my death demands I consider it constantly. I've noticed that living doesn't get any easier. But also, like a lot of old men, I think a lot about pleasure. Other people are always disturbing; that's the point of them. But if they're actors I can get them to play a part in my scenarios. Insofar as that is true, I've always been in flight from my passions. I thought I'd get addicted. I've tried to find substitutes. But I like to believe I am still capable of love.'

Henry had always admitted that he'd been afraid to enjoy a full sexual life. Almost phobic, he had kept away from it for a long time, partly out of guilt, after leaving the children, when he had finally realised how absurd it was to try to live with Valerie.

He said, 'I remember, years ago, an actress I was seeing said to me she'd been invited to visit an old man, someone distinguished. His wife was dying in the next room. He begged the actress to show him her breasts, to let him kiss them. We both thought this pretty low behaviour. Now I've become that man.

'The most significant post-war innovation, apart from the Rolling Stones and their ilk, was the pill, divorcing sex from reproduction, making sex the number-one form of entertainment. But – some irony here – you mustn't forget that in my heyday the women were not only hairy, they wore boots. They wore boiler suits. They had short spiky hair and big hooped earrings. They worked as roadsweepers and builders. It was said to be a historical phase, man. They were right. Those women now work for Blair.

'The young ones are minxes again. London throbs with them. In the summer you could weep because of the unattainable beautiful women in this city. But the hairy period terrified a lot of us, romantically speaking. Put your hand in the wrong place and you'd be considered a rapist, and already men were about as safe as an unpinned grenade. I became convinced that my body was repulsive to others, and others' bodies were certainly repulsive to me. We are dirt with desires. Oh, I am unbelievably fucked up.'

'But now you've got Miriam.'

He smiled. 'Yes, I have. And, much to my surprise, she continues to like me.'

Staring into the quicksand of his dhal, he told me that their love-making had mostly taken place at my flat, until the other night, when they didn't want to travel. Around eleven o'clock the door had opened on him and Miriam doing something with ropes, masks and a poetry anthology. Seconds later, Sam and the Mule Woman were standing over them.

They all looked at one another until Henry requested privacy, and that the kettle be put on. Miriam untied Henry and the two of them got dressed. Sam and the Mule Woman waited in the kitchen. Bushy took Miriam home. Everyone went to bed.

A year ago, when Henry's son had said he wanted to live with him, Henry had gone into a panic, caused mostly by exhilaration. Sam had always lived with his mother but eventually found it too embarrassing. He had a girlfriend who Valerie patronised. ('What lovely little clothes, did you make them yourself?')

Sam rented his own flat for the first time. Discovering that he not only had to pay rent but bills too, and even sometimes had to buy furniture, leaving little left over for drugs, music and clothes, Sam left the rented place for Henry's, saying, 'I can't believe this city's so expensive!'

Henry had laughed at his son's ignorance of the real world and even told his daughter Lisa about it. She-who-got-to-see-a-lot-of-reality said, 'And you're surprised I despise you!'

Henry, having left the family home before his children were teenagers, was ecstatically excited about having a family life again, before it was too late. After Sam had informed his father he was coming to live with him, Henry had stared into his spare room, which was full of dusty if not filthy and worthless junk, palpitating. Who would he get to clear it out?

As he couldn't think of anyone, he began, there and then, to do it him-self. He spent all night on his hands and knees, clearing the room and dumping the rubbish on the street around the corner beneath a sign saying 'Dump No Rubbish'. For the next week he was forced repeatedly to walk past his own broken chairs, pictures frames and rotting rugs.

I hadn't seen him so active for a long time. Being an obsessive, he was unstoppable, painting the walls of the spare room as well as over any dust that was there. He went to Habitat in King Street, Hammersmith, and bought a double bed, lamp, bookshelf and rug. In two exhausting days it was the cleanest, smartest room in the flat, indeed in the whole house.

Henry had been delighted to see, a day later, his tall son coming upstairs carrying a hold-all. How impressive the boy looked, so big, handsome and charismatic. How could he ever fail in the world? Henry was even more delighted when he saw, behind his son, a woman, whose name he would never want to remember, carrying even more bags, which contained main-ly shoes. She would stay when she was in London. He gave the two of them champagne, delighting in this opportunity to show himself as the paterfamilias he claimed he'd always wanted to be.

So badly did he not want to fuck it up, he could only fuck it up. In the morning Henry set his alarm early to make the couple breakfast. While their clothes were in the launderette, he went to the supermarket. For the next few nights, wearing a pinny which said on it 'British Meat', Henry cooked for 'his family', whether or not they wanted to eat. Having soon exhausted his limited number of dishes, he went out in the rain to fetch takeaways. He ordered Sky, and in the evenings watched TV with them, talking continuously throughout, informing his captive audience how awful and stupid the programmes were; perhaps they should read to each other from *Paradise Lost*?

Within a week the happy couple were claustrophobic and afraid to return to the flat where they knew Henry was waiting with another 'treat'. Sam rang his mother, who then rang Henry, ordering him to chill out. He abused her for her intervention, getting her message at the same time. He did chill out; for a while he and his son got along fine, and when the Mule Woman was there, or any of the son's other pick-ups, Henry no longer pursued them with his favours.

Now Henry said, 'Jamal, I can only thank you and say I never expected to be struck full-on by this passion for Miriam. Often I think of my roman-tic failures and the many missed opportunities, love being the only disas-trous area of my life, and so what? I've done other things. But I feel so tender towards her. I sit beside her when she sleeps because it calms her. I roll her joints.

'I've introduced her to my friends. She gets nervous, thinking she's no good at the social thing, everyone being so talky and her knowing nothing. But she's done brilliantly, she's brave, she can talk at anyone. We have revived one another's appetite.

'Then Sam and the Mule Woman walk out of a Woody Allen film – who would do that? – and catch Miriam and I at it on the floor.'

'What did Sam say?'

'Well, the next morning the woman's nowhere to be seen. Sam and I sit down for breakfast as usual, but he's sulking. I'm beginning to get angry that he won't discuss it when he says he's proposed to this girl and she has accepted. But now she has witnessed me on the floor engaged in over-whelmingly unusual acts.'

'So?'

'Sam says his fiancée will never be able to look at me again without thinking of me tied to a chair leg with a butt plug up my backside. I said that it was as good a memory of me as any. I wished I'd had a photograph. In fact I think I do, somewhere.'

After this, Sam's reproaches didn't get much further since Henry, provoked by this talk of marriage, told Sam he was too young to marry, as well as being too promiscuous. The boy liked women. He hadn't been committed to the Mule Woman. What was the point of binding himself to one girl at his age?

'I became aware,' said Henry, 'that I was going off on a rant. But I am the kid's father, and it's my right to give him advice until he dies of boredom. But what I needed to do was talk to the Mule Woman. I told Sam she should meet me and I would explain to her about the world, old men and the varieties of Jurassic sexual experience. Then I'd apologise and they could live their lives free of me.'

He went on: 'They want to cast me as the benign old grandad: impotent, repetitive, making no demands, sitting in the corner with nothing better to do than rub whisky in his gums. A position I can only spit at. My indignity is my only pride now.'

The Mule Woman had not returned to the flat since 'the incident'. Sam refused to let Henry talk to her, telling Henry she came from a 'good family'.

'Good family? Have you ever met one?' Henry replied.

Apparently the boy said, 'People respect you, Dad, as a director and even as a person. You're an artist and a big man in the world. Not many people are so talented. How can you let yourself down?'

'I let myself down exactly how I like,' Henry said.

'What about us?' Sam said.

'"I've never let *you* down that much,"' I said. 'But, Jamal, that wasn't the end of it. He accused me of looking at the Mule Woman lecherously, my eyes all over her like sticky fingers. More, he said that when his male friends came over I didn't bother with them at all, these boys, so lively, and with everything ahead of them. He called me a filthy old gobby fiend, saying I was envious of the young men.'

At this point Henry had the clever idea of calling the Mule Woman an exhibitionist. Didn't she want to attract his attention, walking about in insubstantial clothing like a 'bit of a tart'? 'And I like tarts, mind. I can hard-ly look at a woman these days without wondering how much she charges.'

Sam retorted it was Henry who was the exhibitionist with his 'mad talk-ing'. Henry lost control, yelled at the boy and, I gathered, attempted in a rather ramshackle way to whack the little shit upside his head. But Henry couldn't get a clear punch in, and the boy disappeared down the stairs, yelling abuse, calling his father 'perverted'.

'You've got this to look forward to,' he said to me now. 'Your children turning on you, their hatred total and inexplicable.'

Then, like the actress he could be when distressed, Henry had collapsed to the floor with his hand glued to his brow. Soon after, as when he had any kind of problem, he rang me, his wife Valerie, as well as various other former girlfriends he'd had years of indifferent – or no – sex with. Having separated from a woman years before was no reason, for Henry, not to communicate with her about the most personal things, daily – and, often, hourly.

After this, he retired to bed. It was then that Henry received a call from Lisa, who said she'd been 'grossed out' too. Not that she'd been any-where near the incident, having heard about it from her younger brother. Henry handled it pretty well, informing both kids it was none of their damned business. Did he tell them who they could fuck?

'"Grossed out",' he kept saying. '"Grossed out"! Is that the worst thing they've ever seen? What world are they living in?'

He was devastated that Sam had threatened to move out. Henry had refused to let him, saying he would go to wherever Sam was and drag him back physically, or he would lie down on the pavement outside wherever he was.

It had all gone wrong. I reminded Henry that now he had Miriam – with whom he was much absorbed – this would, inevitably, have something to do with Sam's animosity. Sam wouldn't want to feel he was letting his mother down by sitting around with Henry and his new girlfriend Miriam, the woman Henry really loved at last.

'Yes,' he said, 'I can see that.'

Henry seemed to have talked to everyone about being caught by his son in flagrante delicto, but he didn't tell Miriam about the response of Sam and Lisa. Not that Miriam asked: it didn't occur to her that Henry's cool middle-class children would be upset by such an innocuous episode.

Although the incident and its fall-out were causing confusion, I noticed that Henry didn't let it come between him and his pleasures, which were developing daily. Fascinated and appalled by his gay friends, Henry had always loved hearing of their adventures in clubs and bars and on the Heath, or even on the street. He wanted to ask to be taken along, 'to see', but had never had the courage to go. He'd always been curious whether any straight man would want to live in such a way.

A few days after our dinner, Henry was at Miriam's, and she was showing Henry her photographs: Mother and Father; she and I in Pakistan; her children when young; the men who'd beaten her up; her favourite tattoos.

'What's that?' He was pointing at an album secured with string.

'My black album?' she said. 'Filthy pictures. My first husband used to photograph me in a pose and would send them to pornos, *Readers' Wives* an' that. He'd get fifty quid for it. There's some of those in there, as well as stuff with the neighbours and pictures of orgies and parties we went to.' She began to untie it. 'If you look,' she said, 'you must promise not to be offended.'

Henry said to me: 'I looked at the obscene pictures, the cheap clothes and the wretched people, and I *was* offended that such things were going on in ordinary homes while I was reading. I was turned on. Yet only that morning I'd been thinking that I should be winding down. I'm playing the second half now, heading towards injury time. It should be painting, grandchildren, restful holidays with a book I'd always wanted to read, being interviewed on my life's work, giving my opinions on the past fifty years.

'The other day there was a party at a friend's. As I walked in I saw that everyone had grey or white hair. They were all old and done for, like me. I'd known them all my life.

'I thought I'd die of boredom, until I learned there was another way. The devil was calling me! At last I was getting his attention!'

Henry and my sister never had sex at Miriam's place, not with all the kids, the chaos and everyone sleeping anywhere.

'I was so hot after seeing the photos that I insisted she accompany me to the shed at the end of the garden where Bushy had the dope growing under lights. There was a well-used mattress. I couldn't believe that at my age I could feel such urgency. Sex is mad, mad, mad, Jamal.'

'You'd forgotten?'

'When we were pulling our pants up I said, "Why can't we do that stuff?"'

'So I got a Polaroid, the pervert's delight, and a little DV camera. I've made films, of course. But not like this.

'I guess I can't show them to you, it being your big sister. But when I shoot them I can't help turning them from pornos into little movies. I can cut them on my son's laptop! I've even put music on them, a few loose Brazilian tunes. They turn into little comedies.

'Then,' he said, 'things went further. We went to this place under the railway arches in South London.'

He described a nondescript doorway set in a railway arch. This was in a desolate stretch of South London. 'Ben Jonson would have recognised it.'

Bushy had been driving them back from a film screening and said they might 'fancy a look'. There was a couple he took there regularly. In fact, Bushy had been asked to play guitar at one of their 'parties'. He had rehearsed and got himself psyched up but, when it came to it, had been too nervous to go on. At the door it turned out Bushy had forgotten to tell them that to be admitted Miriam and Henry couldn't enter in 'civvies' but had to wear fetish gear: rubber, leather or uniform. The alternative was to go in naked.

Henry said, 'I was laughing. This was new to me. I've never been into any building naked before. Apparently Miriam had. It was cold, but nude sounded good to me. I've directed a naked *Lear*.'

'How could I forget? Even the daughters were naked.'

'Unfortunately for the public, old men can't wait to get their clothes off. I overcame my shame, and Miriam didn't bother with such needless sophistication. There I was, naked but for my shoes, my dick a shrivelled mushroom. But inside the fuckery it was warm and friendly. Everyone said hello. Soon I was enthralled.

'There were people on dog's leads, and lying in baths to be urinated on, others face down in a sling, queuing to be whipped. People lining up – rushing, indeed, to be in one another's bodies! I accompanied Miriam into a small room where she lay down and was satisfied.

'Then I met a twenty-three-year-old boy, a waiter, whose greatest pleasure is to lick people's boots clean. He knows what he wants and likes, even at that age. I'm telling you, Jamal, not since I was a socialist have I felt such a sense of community.'

I was laughing. 'Henry, you can't pretend you were at the Fabian Society.'

'The faces of people who are so close to their desire! Doesn't Nietzsche have something to say about it? How can you laugh? Surely, in your line of work, you've heard everything?'

'I'm not laughing at you, Henry, but at the idea that you have to give your behaviour a thorough intellectual grounding.'

He said, 'But in *The Birth of Tragedy*, Nietzsche writes of ecstatic states, of singing and dancing, of how someone becomes a work of art in themselves, rather than just an observer. It's all there, before Freud. No wonder Freud refused to read him properly. He knew the threat, the danger.'

Henry and Miriam had stayed at the sex party until the early morning, talking, drinking, looking at bodies. I asked him whether he suffered from jealousy, or whether defying jealousy was the point of it.

'Neither,' said Henry. 'When I see her with another man, I think of him as being devoted to her pleasures.'

'Are you sure it's something you both wanted?' I asked.

'Yes,' he said. 'We both wanted it. We want it again.'

CHAPTER TWELVE

I had observed and listened to Ajita for long enough. I needed to confront her with my suspicions. But when I saw her after the factory incident it was clear she had a lot on her mind.

'The strike is getting worse,' Ajita told me. 'Every day those people are trying harder to destroy us. I don't think they're going to stop. Dad is determined to defy them. But one side will have to give way.'

She wasn't reading, studying or eating as much pizza as she used to. I told her if she wasn't careful she'd never catch up with her work. I began to take her to the library; I'd sit with her, watching her eyes move across a page and helping her make notes, but she couldn't connect with philosophy in that state of mind. She'd fling notes across the table to me and burst out talking, and we'd have to go to a pub.

'I am scared, Jamal. The Commies have got a lot of determination and all the time my family is losing money.' I may have been on the other side, but she was my girlfriend. What could I say? 'If it continues like this we'll go bankrupt and will have to stay with relatives in India. The whole family will be ruined and shamed.'

Ajita's mother was still away. She rang and heard about the strike but had no intention of returning. She wanted the children to join her in India when they finished their studies for the summer, leaving the father to deal with the strike. This was bothering me. I didn't want Ajita to go away. I wanted us to be together all the time. Six weeks was an eternity.

Sometimes I glimpsed extreme anxiety on Ajita's face. We had been making love frequently in library toilets, cupboards or her car or house, but it rarely happened now unless I insisted. She was elsewhere. We had talked about marrying – somehow, some time – but the relationship had developed a slow puncture.

Because I was incapable of working out, and certainly of asking her about, the kind of infidelity she'd been involved in, I conceived the brilliant idea of telling her I'd been unfaithful. Almost as soon as it had occurred to me that Ajita was unfaithful, I had indeed been unfaithful myself, thinking a little equality would cure me of feeling betrayed. My concerns would be hers.

A week before, I had visited my former lover, Sheridan, to pick up a painting she had given me. We had gone to bed (as we often used to) in the afternoon. She was a thirty-five-year-old divorced book illustrator, whose children were at school. When they came home we'd get up and make their tea. Mostly I'd been in love with the idea of her as a pedagogical older woman, and she did take me to her club to play pool, where she introduced me to some prodigious and raddled drinkers, as well as Slim Galliard, by whom I was much impressed.

There can't have been many people alive with two pages devoted to them in *On the Road*, Kerouac describing how, in San Francisco, Slim free-associated – 'Great-all-oroonie, oroonirooni' – while almost imperceptibly stroking his bongos with his finger tips for two hours, as Dean Moriarty yelled 'Go!' and 'Yes!' from the back. Slim was still handsome and graceful, with a true gentleman's courtesy. Sheridan and I had dinner with him, but it was the ladies he liked – this was a man who'd known Little Richard and dated Ava Gardner, Lana Turner and Rita Hayworth.

But Ajita, when I told her about the brief return to Sheridan, seemed hardly concerned about my infidelity. If jealousy was the vindaloo of love, I'd imagined her tongue burning, and such a fire forcing her to spill her truth. But there was no noticeable heat. I could only suppose she had done the same as me. What I wanted were the details, to know where we both stood.

Wildly I was questioning her, asking her where she'd gained the experience she seemed to have, who else was she doing it with? Was it still going on?

'Well, you know,' she said. 'I've had other boyfriends, just as you've had other girlfriends. I know you don't really want to hear about it. It will upset you, Jamal,' she said, stroking my face.

'I know,' I said. 'But I'm upset anyway. Is it true that we've both been unfaithful recently?'

'In a way,' she said.

'Only in a way?'

'Yes,' she said.

'That's confirmation, then.' I said, 'So now I know. At last some truth! Thank God! Ajita, I guess that's evens.'

'Not really.'

'What d'you mean?'

She said nothing.

Why didn't she desire only me? What sort of infidelity had it been? How could she be with someone else when I was with her most of the time? When not with me she was with her numerous girlfriends or family. How had it happened?

The more she wouldn't tell me about it, the more I fretted. I had never felt this kind of vicious, penetrating unhappiness before. Certainly such cruelty had never been deliberately inflicted on me. I didn't expect it from the woman I had fallen in love with. What sort of self-protection was possible? When Valentin and Wolf told me how much weight I'd lost or how tired I looked, I admitted I was having trouble with Ajita, saying, 'I think she's going with someone else.'

They liked her; they didn't believe it, shrugging off my complaints as ordinary boy/girl stuff. They seemed to think I had been studying hard; and I had, indeed, begun to read a lot. But I wasn't able to concentrate on my work. Why didn't Ajita see how badly I was taking this? Where was her love for me?

When I begged her to tell me what was going on, she hardly paid any attention. She looked distracted. She certainly didn't look as though she'd been caught out in some unnecessary betrayal.

I persisted with my questions as this dismal secret increased in size and pressure in my mind. But she wouldn't tell me anything.

'It's nothing,' she said. 'Please understand that. I love you and will marry you, when you ask me properly. But there's so much else going on at the moment, you know that.'

It was a nothing which had become a big something between us. As this hurt was developing, and Ajita and I had less to say to one another, my criminal career took an upturn. Wolf had introduced me to cocaine and when I took it, talking and talking for the first time in my life, I fell into conversations which I shouldn't have had.

Valentin and Wolf had always been planning 'coups', as they called them. But whether they kept me out of them, or didn't tell me, or whether, as I suspected, they just didn't happen, I never saw a 'result'. One time, though, Wolf did turn up with a pink Cadillac, which he'd obtained in exchange for something or other. After a few embarrassing turns around the narrow West Kensington streets, it was 'disappeared'. Another time they obtained some money from a woman whose husband was about to be sentenced, having convinced her they'd pay off the judge. When they absconded with the money, she vowed to pursue them.

I was aware that Valentin was trying to pull a coup at the casino: Wolf would go in there and Valentin would ensure he won at blackjack, but it seemed like a lot of talk. Mostly they discussed what they'd do with the money when they had it, which part of the South of France they'd live in; maybe they'd get a boat, but which sort? They even talked of how they'd decorate their apartments and how the day would be spent reading papers, eating, swimming, having sex and fraternising with other criminals. Once, when I was sarcastic about their ability as crooks ('very, very small time,' I called them), Wolf asked me whether, if I thought I was so smart, I had any better ideas. I said I had.

One morning I took Valentin and Wolf to Ajita's. There, I pointed out the house which backed on to Ajita's, and explained how the couple went away on Thursdays and returned on Monday mornings.

A few days later, on a Friday, when Ajita was at college, her father at work, her brother at school and the aunt at the market, we broke into the house and took a lot of stuff. Oddly, Wolf had insisted on taking a dustpan and brush with him, in order to sweep up after. Valentin told me that a criminal they knew had informed Wolf that real villains are always careful. The loot was brought out of the back of the house, through Ajita's garden and into the garage. When Wolf and Valentin were ready and it was starting to get dark, they took off.

The victims were an old couple. We'd ripped off their life savings, tearing the heart out of their lives, for nothing really. It wasn't difficult; I was impressed by how easy it was. They didn't even have window locks. Wolf had been a builder; he knew how to take a window out. I was small, I could get through it and let the others in. I hated being in their house, violating them. Burglars aren't supposed to think of this, of what the people will think when they get home. To be a criminal, you have to lack imagination.

I wasn't sure exactly what swag they obtained from the house. There were several bags full of stuff: clocks, watches, ornaments, pictures, as well as jewellery and silver, I guessed. I suggested to Valentin and Wolf that we still had time to put the gear back, if they wanted. I can't have been a natural gangster if I felt this much guilt about my crimes.

It was to be a villain's carnival. They fenced the gear quickly and spent the day shopping for suits and shoes. They took me out to dinner before we went to the club, opposite the Natural History Museum, where

Valentin had worked as a bouncer. I had drunk a lot and wanted to crash through all the laws, knowing at last the excessive pleasures of cruelty and corruption.

In the club a woman (who I considered to be an 'older' woman, like a Colette heroine, because she must have been in her late twenties) came to sit beside me, slipping my hand up her skirt. At the end of the night, when I said I had to get the train back to the suburbs, she suggested we go back to the boarding house in West Kensington, where Wolf and Valentin would join us later. At the house she went into Wolf's bedroom, saying she had to 'get ready'. When she called me in, she was naked apart from an elbow-length velvet glove, and very willing to suck me off. Before she left, I asked if she wanted to see a movie the next afternoon. She said she couldn't; she had 'a client'.

I had already told Valentin and Wolf that things had been going wrong with Ajita, that she had been unfaithful to me and wouldn't tell me who it was. Despite the whore, they liked Ajita and told me I should try to work it out with her. On the other hand, they didn't like to see me getting hurt.

Ajita and I still made love when we met but it was unhappy love, the worst sort, increasing my loneliness. My nerves crackled and popped continuously. I wanted to believe my mind was under my control, that I could persuade it to go in the direction I required, but it became obvious that this was a false belief.

'Tell me who it is and we can sort it out,' I said once more, but she refused. I asked her what I lacked that made her go elsewhere?

'Lack?' she said. 'But you haven't failed me. You are everything I want.'

'I don't believe you,' I said. 'It's my fault. If it isn't,' I went on, 'tell me what qualities this other man has. The qualities he has that make you desire him.'

She said, 'What makes you think I desire him?'

'Can't you put me out of my misery?'

'Okay,' she said. 'I will. Are you ready, sweetie? Sit down and listen.'

She told me the truth.

For days after I walked around with this knowledge in my mind, trying to come to terms with it; because after she spoke, I thought I would – genuinely, and without possibility of return – go insane.

CHAPTER THIRTEEN

This is what she told me.

The summer break was approaching. We had been going out for eight months. The moment we saw the sun, we resumed our habit of lying on the blanket in her garden with our books, the radio, wine, cigarettes. I'd been rubbing and caressing her feet and ankles, and wondered if she was ready for love.

But I said, 'A few weeks ago I visited the factory.'

'You did?'

I explained that I had wanted to see the picket lines, the students, the whole hurly-burly. I said I had seen her going into the factory, half-concealed in the back of the car.

'It's no secret,' she said, touching my face tenderly. 'You never asked me about it.' She started to dress, or at least to cover herself up, as though she weren't wearing the appropriate clothes for what she wanted to say. 'For ages now you've been interrogating me with these questions about my lovers, as you call them.'

'Interrogating you? What about the truth cure? You have never once denied my suspicions.'

She said, 'I can't make you stop asking. You have to know everything and I like that about you. So, I will tell you and it will shut you up, oh yes.'

'It's Valentin isn't it?'

'What?'

'Wolf?'

'He is more likely.'

'Why?'

'He is insistent, and less concerned about deceiving you.'

'He came on to you?'

'They're your friends, and I wouldn't do that. Are you offering me to him?'

'No!'

'So how can you think such a thing about me?'

I was clutching my head. 'How can I know what to think unless you help me? My mind is going everywhere! Somehow the truth anchors us, I know that! Is there someone you love more than me? Am I only second best?'

'Come, rest here, in my arms. Listen carefully. I won't be able to say this again. The words are too heavy.' She said, 'Sometimes, after midnight, my father comes into my room and makes love to me.'

'He does?'

'Yes. He does, Jamal.'

I must have been nodding at her. I was empty, looking into her eyes. It occurred to me that I should know more. 'How long has this been happening?'

'What do you mean?'

'Is it before we met and fell in love, or after?'

Her eyes dropped. 'Before.'

'It was happening when we met?'

'It had just started.'

'Why didn't you tell me?'

'How could I? I was falling for you. Surely it would have put you off. Perhaps the news would have got round, and my father would have been arrested. Or his reputation would have been ruined.'

'His reputation?'

'The community means a lot to us here. We can't go against it without falling out of the circle.'

I said, 'Didn't you think you would have to tell me?'

'I don't know. What did I tell myself? Nothing. Perhaps I thought it would stop and somehow I would forget the whole thing. I have no experience of these matters. But do you not love me now? Am I filthy and disgusting to you?'

I kissed her on the mouth. 'Of course I do love you now. More, even.'

'Yes?' She said, 'Jamal, that was why I needed your protection so much, why I needed to feel loved. And I did receive that from you. My only darling, you have been good to me.'

'And you to me. You are my life. I want to marry you.'

'You do?' Her mouth twisted. 'Me too. But this isn't the right time for such talk.'

I said, 'How did all this start with your dad?'

'After my mother had gone to India, Dad came into my room one night and got into my bed. He kissed me, sexually, you know, with his tongue, and he rubbed himself against my stomach until he came off. Then he went away. He was in a sort of trance, like one of those Shakespeare ghosts, staring eyes, stiff movements, like someone hypnotised or sleep-walking . . .

'The next night I was terrified of him doing it again, so I stayed awake, with all the lights on and music playing –'

'What happened?'

'He did return. He opened my door. The music was roaring, all the lights were blazing like mad! Oh Jamal, you should have seen me in two pairs of pants, two pairs of trousers, a jumper, a coat. I was sweating and I must have looked strange. I even had a damn hat on, I don't know why. He took one look at me and went off. I got into bed with some relief, though I didn't sleep at all.

'He didn't come back for a few days. I thought I'd scared him off. Until it happened again.' She said it was still happening. 'If I wear a ton of clothes, he takes them off. That makes the whole thing go on longer. All I do is hold a tee-shirt over my face, so I don't have to see or smell him.'

'Ajita, why don't you lock your door?'

'There's no lock.'

'It's no trouble to get one fitted. Wolf and I would do it, today.'

'That's kind, but I can't do it,' she said. 'Lock out my own father? He'd kill himself.'

'What could be better?'

She screamed, 'No!'

'Do you have good reason to think he will do that?'

'He's threatened it before. He said that if things collapsed at the factory he would have to end it. He couldn't start his life again. If he failed his family, he couldn't face the shame.'

'Ajita, that is blackmail.'

'I have to look after him.'

'Only as a daughter. You're not his wife, for Christ's sake. He's a fascist and a bully.'

'You don't know him.'

'Every day he rapes you.'

'There's no force. Now please shut up. I can't bear this.'

To her dismay, I gathered my things and went away. I needed to take it all in. This wasn't something I could talk to Mum about; she'd panic. The only person who might have the experience to understand was Miriam. But her moods were unreliable, depending on what she was taking.

The next day Ajita brought up the subject herself, saying, 'You see, I do listen to you.' She couldn't lock her bedroom door, but she'd put a wedge under it. 'I heard him,' she said. 'I don't sleep much now. You say I look exhausted, but going to bed is a horror. Last night I heard his slippers outside as I always do. They sort of slap, you see, and you always know where he is going in the house. Then he was banging on the door.

'The harder he pushed, the more the wedge stuck. It went on for a long time, this pushing and shoving. Then it stopped. Later I heard snoring. He was asleep in the hall. I went out and covered him up. He was shivering. He could have died out there –'

'Don't be ridiculous.'

'He wants my warmth.'

'That's why he has a wife.'

'She doesn't want him. She is even thinking that he is a big fool.'

I asked, 'Your father never mentions what happens at night?'

'At breakfast he's always the same, hungover, curt, bad-tempered, in a hurry to leave for the factory, asking us if we're learning anything at college or whether we're wasting his money. Wanting to know when we're going to start earning a living.' She said, 'Jamal, you must never, ever, under any circumstances, tell another human being about this. Promise, promise on your mother's life.'

'I promise.'

In my own bed, I couldn't sleep. I'd lie there going over what Ajita had told me. I would imagine her father in a trance-like state walking along the corridor to her bedroom, opening the door, getting into bed, and forcing himself between her legs. Sometimes I wanted to masturbate, to rid myself of the image, remembering something she'd said: 'He's got such a large penis, it fills me up.'

'Does he make you come?' I asked her. When we made love she'd say: 'I love coming; make me come; I want to come all the time, I'm wet all the time I'm with you.'

'What a pathetic fool you are,' she said. 'But who could blame you, in such circumstances? I'm so sorry, so ashamed and lost.'

One night, so impossible was it to sleep, I did get up. I found myself getting dressed and leaving the house. I, too, was in a trance-like state, and the world seemed immobile, frozen.

Heading to Ajita's place, I climbed over the iron railings and into the park, and then legged it along the silent roads, past the cars and dark houses until I arrived at the familiar fence.

Now I had no idea what I wanted to do, but stood outside, looking up at the windows, wondering whether I'd see a ghost-like figure moving through the house.

But what if he were fucking my girlfriend at that moment, about to cry out in his orgasm? By ringing the bell or knocking on the door, I'd interrupt him at his terrible pleasure. The commotion might make him think it was the police, and he'd be startled from his reverie. I stood there with my fist over the door, ready to strike it and run, but I could not bring myself to crash into their lives.

Perhaps I was distracted by her brother's light, which was on. I became convinced he was peeping at me from behind the curtain. Terrified that he'd spotted me hanging around his house in the middle of the night, and would report me to his father who would have me beaten or arrested, I fled.

Over the next few days I went back three times, but was unable to act.

At college, sick with sleeplessness, I returned to Ajita, in the hope she'd become the person she was before and we'd have the same pleasures. But this stain couldn't be removed. We'd talk, make love, go out to the same places, but we'd lost our innocence. When we fucked I wondered if her father's face might be superimposed onto mine. Was I another male monster banging into this girl? Thinking this, I couldn't continue, and we'd lie there, side by side, lost.

There was no going back. But there was, I figured, a way to go forward. I was working on it, unconsciously, but wasn't yet ready to admit it to myself.

'Hitler', I called him. The man who would not stop. The man for whom 'everything' was not enough. The man who was turning me into a terrorist. Evil had stomped into my life like a mad mobster. It demanded to be dealt with. We would not be victims. It was either him or me.

What sort of man would I turn out to be?

CHAPTER FOURTEEN

I had been introduced to Henry through a writer friend of mine who had translated a version of a Genet play and wanted Henry to stage it. Having seen some of Henry's productions, I went along for the conversation, in the dark bar of a central London hotel, one of those hushed wood-panelled places that doesn't seem like it's in London at all. While Henry was trying to make up his mind whether the time was right for Genet to 're-enter our world' (he didn't think it was, just yet), he made me his friend.

I put it like this because it was sudden. When he fell for you there were no gaps in the friendship. It was passionate; he began to ring several times a day, or come around uninvited when he had something he needed to talk about. He'd ask me out two or three times a week.

As Josephine liked to point out if I remarked on her indolence, which I often had occasion to do, what people like Henry did most of the time in London was not work but talk about work, as they ate with one another. For them, known as the 'chattering classes', life was a round of breakfasts, brunches, lunches, teas, suppers, dinners and late suppers in the increasing number of new London restaurants. And very agreeable it was. Henry's activity delighted me; he had no desire for me to replicate him: we were complements.

I discovered that his wife Valerie, who he was separated from but constantly in touch with, was somewhere close to the centre of the numerous overlapping and intermarrying groups, circles, sets, families and dynasties of semi-bohemian West London. They were all constantly enlarging and moving together through a series of country weekends, parties, prize-givings, scandals, suicides and holidays. The children, too, at school and rehab together, married amongst themselves; others employed one another, and *their* children played together.

Valerie came from a family which had been rich and distinguished for a couple of hundred years. They were art collectors, professors, scholars, newspaper editors. Henry would sometimes say of some full-of-it reprobate, 'Oh yes, that's Valerie's second cousin by marriage. Better zip it, or you'll ruin someone's Christmas.'

He added, 'They're so everywhere, that family, I'd say they were over-extended.' Not only were they wealthy, they had a hoard of social capital. They were friends with, and had married into, numerous Guinnesses, Rothschilds and Freuds. The living room contained a Lucian Freud drawing, a Hockney portrait of Valerie and Henry, a Hirst spot painting, a Bruce McClean, a little thing by Anthony Gormley, as well as various old and interesting things that you could look at or pick up as you wondered about its history. The house was like a family museum, or body even, indented, scarred and marked everywhere by the years which each new generation was forced to carry with it.

Most nights his crowd went to drinks parties and then to dinner. It was expensive: the clothes, food, drugs, drink, taxis. Not that money was an issue for *them*. 'But it's like an Evelyn Waugh novel!' Lisa said, going to some trouble never to see any of them again. 'He's one of my favourite writers,' Henry replied. Anyhow, you couldn't accuse this group of artists, directors and producers, architects, therapists, pop stars and fashion designers of being either indolent or illiberal.

This was privilege, and Henry knew it was. The only way to pay for it was to work, which most of them did. Nor were they particularly dull. Henry just knew them too well. He claimed you could walk into a party in Marrakech or Rio and see the same faces and suffer the same claustro-phobia and déjà vu as when you holidayed or visited some art fair or film festival. So, if he was off to a dinner, to a party or opening, he'd want someone new to talk to in the cab or to leave with, after staying a few minutes and finding it dreary. I'd be dragged along, and I was curious too. Anyhow, I was interested to hear what he had to say.

Henry was twelve years older than me, and had been living and working in London all his life; he knew 'everyone'. He'd had analysis for two years when his marriage broke up, with a silent old-school stern guy who wasn't as intelligent as him. Henry was interested in therapy, claiming to be 'completely fucking messed up', but not enough to find another analyst. He used me to talk his problems through with, going into the most inti-mate and serious things right from the start. I liked that about him, but our friendship wasn't only that.

I'd started my work, of course, with only a few patients, and inadequate ones at that, who refused to let me cure them. I'd also learned from being with Karen that unless you had cachet, social progress in London could be slow, painful and futile. On occasions, out with Henry, it seemed that everyone else couldn't wait to kiss and effusively greet one another, while I'd stand in the corner in my best clothes, being ignored even by the waiters.

By now, with Tahir's words in my head, I was shameless enough to push into others' conversations; I wasn't as shy as I used to be, and I'd try to pick up a waitress: the staff were always more attractive than the party-goers and certainly dressed better. Dinner parties were the worst, when I'd be stuck beside the neglected wife of the deputy director of a publishing house while everyone else was tucked in satisfactorily next to their greatest friend or greatest fan.

Henry had worked in the theatre since leaving Cambridge, and had little experience of such serious condescension; in fact, he didn't believe it existed. On the other hand, there were others, like Angela Carter, who were not that way. They would remember your name after having met you only once before, and didn't consider London's social world to be like a violent version of snakes and ladders.

Henry's wife Valerie hardly noticed me when Henry and I first became friends, though I often went to the house. It was as though she couldn't quite work out who I was, or why I was there. She was renowned, and had been for a long time, for what was known in London as the 'enraptured gaze'. With one elbow on the table, and her chin resting on her fist, she would look directly at you forever, her eyes unblinking, as though you were the pinnacle of fascination. This was an opportunity, among the pompous or frightened, for many monologues, but it could induce, in the more insecure, total collapse or at least a catastrophe of self-doubt.

It wasn't until I received a good, prominent review in the *Observer* for *Six Characters in Search of a Cure*, my first published work, that her eyes enlarged when she saw me, and she came forward to seize my shoulders and slide her lips across my cheeks, leaving a faint pink trace, calling me, at last, her 'darling, darling, darling'. Gazed upon, I was in; now I wouldn't be ejected.

Not at all discombobulated by this abrupt switchback of emotional flow, I doubt whether Valerie troubled to pass her eyes over the book. She herself was on Prozac; for her, Freud's time had long gone, like Surrealism and the twelve-tone scale. But the book remained in a prime position on her living-room table for a few weeks.

Six Characters had sold well, 'considering what it was', as the publisher said, particularly in paperback. It was said to have even breached the self-help market. A big chunk of the reading population, it turned out, needed help. Apparently people wanted to develop their minds as they did their bodies; they saw the brain as just another muscle, and personal neuroses with a profound history as merely correctable mental dysfunctions.

I gave talks on this stupidity. I was asked to debate Freud's 'fraudulence', delighted he still had the ability to infuriate. I went on the radio several times, and once on TV, where I was expected to precis my work in a 'pithy' paragraph. I was flown to conferences abroad and gave 'keynote' speeches. Like a proper writer I visited bookshops to do signings. I was invited to literary festivals, where I read, was interviewed by Henry, and took questions in a half-empty windy tent. Shortlisted for a couple of prizes, nerve-racked, I had to wear a too-tight dinner jacket with a floppy tie, shine my shoes and attend terrible dinners.

It was worth it: I heard from my next ex, Karen Pearl, again. I'm not sure what image of myself I had created in her head, something of a lost cause I suspect, for she was surprised and intrigued by the 'hip young analyst' label. She phoned me and we began to meet for lunch. After her, at the end of the 80s, in a rush of libidinousness, there had been numerous others, some awkward, some fun, many embarrassing, before I found the unfortunate cure for my restlessness – Josephine. Karen and I had parted more than acrimoniously after two years together. But she had found someone and appeared almost happy.

As for Valerie, when Henry gave her a copy of my book and she saw the name on the cover and was able to say, 'I know him, he's always here', I became a real person for her, a name with social cachet, one she could pass on.

Valerie was intelligent and decent enough company if you didn't mind the steady name-dropping (unusually vulgar in someone of her background), as though she were filling your pockets with stones. Her tragedy was the fact that despite her fuck-you shoes and fuck-me tits, she was plain, and couldn't help disliking women younger and more beautiful, unless they were well known. But she had made her own way and had shown her worth by becoming a film producer, buying 'pleasant enough' novels, putting them with directors and raising the money to make the movie.

Her office was in the basement of the house, and she liked Sam being around so much that she bought him a plasma-screen TV in the hope of keeping him there for good. When he did return to live there, he told her that it was because he'd found Henry 'doing something disgusting with a tattooed woman'. Valerie, always content with the piece of Henry she currently was permitted, had said something like, 'At least it was a woman. How can you make a fuss? Dad's an artist and he does what he likes.

They're all like that, crazy as bees. Didn't you see that programme about Toulouse Lautrec the other day?'

She was smart enough not to complain about Miriam, who she referred to as 'Jamal's sister', my worth, such as it was, signifying hers. Not for a moment did Valerie believe she'd be replaced by another woman.

It took some time after my friendship with Henry began for me to be invited to her dinner parties, partly because I'd published a book but also to keep Henry company, as he felt alienated in what he referred to as 'Valerie's house'. For some years already he hadn't really lived there, working abroad for months or staying elsewhere, with friends or other women, keeping his clothes at Valerie's but returning to see the children, work in his room or just hang about. Valerie told herself and others that Henry required time and silence for his creativity. From this he learned how afraid she was of losing him, or, alternatively, how devoted she was to him, and that he could do whatever he liked and she would accept it, refusing to reveal her dissatisfaction to him, fearing he'd use it as a reason to turn away from her for good.

These famous parties had always been held in the big kitchen downstairs, with glass doors giving onto the garden outside, which would be lit with candles. She'd had numerous staff working from the early morning at the preparation, since sometimes there'd be thirty at the table, drinking champagne and expensive wine. There were legions of people in London richer than her but few as gracefully extravagant, or able to pull such hip people to her table. For some Londoners there were few occasions more terrifying than being invited to one of her dinners, some approached them as though they were walking into a PhD examination, and for other people there was nothing more dispiriting than realising you had been dropped.

Henry and Valerie had had a good divorce. They'd behaved reasonably, as the rich are able to do, sometimes. There were no lawyers or courts. It was as though they both knew that once the marriage ended their friendship would begin. Valerie might bore, nag and castigate Henry, but she kept his name and would never risk driving him away. As long as he took her calls, she didn't mind what he did. One day she would organise his funeral and speak first at his memorial service. She would reclaim him. Until then, she insisted on living a lot of her life side by side with him, whether he liked it or not, whether his girlfriends liked it or not, attending all previews of his work, speaking to his friends and monitoring his 'love life', confident it would remain as unfulfilled as always.

It had, after all, been she who'd helped him mould and extend his talent, even forcing him onto the social scene, telling him he was talented, he could meet whoever he wanted in London, as well as whoever she wanted. With him as her ticket, she had the mobility of the beautiful. She turned him from a long-haired, scruffy, bohemian, shy-angry kid into someone who socialised and had a country house with a swimming pool where friends visited.

During their marriage, he'd had affairs – which were mostly emotional – and eventually left. This caused her pain, but she swallowed her hatred, seeing it made little difference in the end. All she had to do was hang on. If he refused to take her calls, maybe he was on honeymoon, she waited for him to return. When he was hungry he went to her to eat; when he needed advice or an opinion he asked her; and, of course, they had the children.

Henry knew how pleased she was when Sam returned to live with her, particularly as the daughter, Lisa, had always been perverse and obstructive. She despised them for their wealth, privilege and social ease, claiming they knew only rich people, apart from their numerous employees: cleaners, builders, gardeners, nannies, au pairs. As a social worker, Lisa had seen the lower world and identified with it; she refused money from her mother, and hardly saw her. One time she even gave up social work to become a cleaner in small 'dole' hotels and bed-and-breakfasts, but was fired for complaining about the conditions and wages, and for trying to organise union activity.

Lisa's ambition had always been to go down, to be poor, the one thing it had never occurred to anyone in the family to be. Unlike the real poor, she was able to go to her mother and receive a cheque for ten thousand pounds, if necessary, and never have to pay it back. In fact, her parents would have been delighted that she had come to them, asking for help, and indeed a couple of years ago she did do this. The cheque, for at least five thousand pounds, she forwarded to a Palestinian refugee organisation, saying to her mother, 'But other people aren't given money! It separates me from others. Why are you afraid of equality?'

Henry and Lisa weren't speaking much at the moment. He was left-wing, and getting more so as London became more vulgarly wealthy, but she only sneered at him, saying it was 'superficial'. Henry had got himself into a bate about Sam leaving. He refused to admit the kid had gone for good; he wouldn't let him collect his things. Sam wanted his computer, his clothes and his iPod, but when he came to get them Henry had locked the stuff away, saying the kid could only have them if he lived in the house. The boy refused, not surprisingly, and threatened to come back and smash whatever it required to get his things. Henry didn't mind the boy's threats and the constant phone calls from his mother, since it meant he was still in contact with Sam.

I have to say I'm not sure why Henry was behaving like a spurned lover, since he was hardly at home. When I went to Miriam's now, Henry would often be there, cooking, washing up, sitting around, talking to Miriam's kids and their friends, who'd never seen or heard anything like him. At the moment, during the day, he had a group of film students he'd been working with, and he continued teaching whoever was around him. He was a good teacher, knowing more than enough about culture, politics and history, scattering ideas, names and movements. He did have a tendency to become irate at his students' ignorance, as though he thought they should know everything already. But although he was an egotist, he wasn't a narcissist.

When Henry had a new experience he became evangelical about it, as though no one had done such a thing before. He reiterated that the club he and Miriam attended was 'the most democratic place' he'd been. 'Fucking is a social event, after all. You can get to meet all types.'

'Like at the National Theatre?' I enquired.

He said, 'More so! Hairdressers go there, bank employees, shopkeepers, van drivers, people who live in cheap housing outside the city. From one point of view it is absurd and banal. From another, we all know that the highest and lowest people will risk their sanity, property, marriages and reputations for the satisfaction they require. We know, too, that this world of crazy desire is one our children will enter. How odd it is to think that such madness is at the centre of human life.'

He said he and Miriam weren't bored with one another, and they still made love normally. It wasn't as though they'd gone as far as they could with one another. Some men, when it came to sex, thought that there should be, ideally, another man present (usually a best friend) to satisfy the woman, if they were incapable of it. But I knew Miriam was one of those competent women who had learned how to ensure they were both satisfied.

One time they dressed up at my place, like a couple of teenagers preparing to go to a party: loud music by the Rolling Stones – 'Hey, shouldn't we go and see them, aren't they coming to town?' – and lots of water. I have to say it was an endearing sight: Henry in tight PVC trousers and an armless leather vest and heavy boots, Miriam in a short skirt, high heels and suspenders, a diaphanous baby-doll thing on top.

'This won't stay on for long,' she said.

I couldn't help myself, and said, 'I hope it's dark in there.'

'The fucking cure,' Henry had called it, as tmade their way to Bushy's cab.

'Why don't you come with us?' asked Miriam.

'Yes,' said Henry. 'I'm sure you won't meet any of your patients there. These people are having their therapy tonight!'

'I will come,' I said. 'Not tonight, but another time. Would that be okay?'

'Yes,' said Miriam, kissing me.

When they were gone I missed their noise and hope. The flat seemed empty. There I was, re-reading a book, hiding my penis between its covers!

I sat down to write. It was time for me to describe, to myself, what happened the night I could bear no more and finally decided to take action. I needed to go back there, as I knew I would always have to, over and over again.

CHAPTER FIFTEEN

Wolf, Valentin and I were sitting in a borrowed car, parked beside the garage.

I had become a void. Nothing spoke within me.

I may have wondered whether the clocks had stopped, but we had been there at least two hours that evening, suspended in the silence, not moving, hardly breathing, but smoking, sighing, whispering and twitching, and all the cocaine gone, as it always is.

The longer we waited, the more agitated I became. I was even hoping that Ajita's father wouldn't come home, that he'd be with his mistress, if he had one, rather than having to 'meet with' the three of us. Yes, it would be a grand night for him to visit this imaginary woman, since his son and daughter (my beloved) were staying with friends in Wembley.

Two nights previously Wolf had said to me, 'What's up, my friend? You're looking gloomy again.'

'So would you, if someone was fucking with your woman.'

'You believe it's still going on? Is it really true? But who could it be, man? When does she see him?'

'I can't tell you. She begged me not to talk about it. It's deadly serious, Wolf.'

'You do know who it is?'

'I do now. I found out, at last.'

'Yeah? You've got to tell us, your buddies, your pals,' Wolf said. 'She's a great girl. She comes to the house. She cooks for us. We really love her. If you weren't with her, I'd make a move on her – like that.' He snapped his fingers.

They persuaded me to go to the pub, where I recounted what she had told me.

'Jesus, that's serious,' said Wolf.

I said, 'I can't have her go through this one more night. We've got to do something. If this was a film we'd just go in and shoot him up. It would be a pleasure.'

'You're right. We should teach that father a lesson,' Wolf said. 'Give him a little polite warning. It's easy to do.'

'Why not?' I said. 'He doesn't know you guys. He's not going to go to the police and have all this come out. What do you say, Val?'

He was less keen, being a gentle creature with what seemed like a priest's desire for denial and suffering. But he wouldn't let his best friends down. After a time he said what we were doing was 'morally right'; apparently it was 'good' as Socrates understood 'the good'. Surely if it was good enough for Socrates, it was good enough for me.

My friends were set. The warning would be administered as soon as I gave the word. I waited for Ajita to tell me when she'd be out. I knew it would have to happen in the next few days, before we lost enthusiasm. The event would be straightforward enough if we knew the family's moves. When Ajita said she and Mustaq would be out, we planned 'the surprise' carefully.

We were almost asleep, or near-catatonic, when we heard a car. There was little traffic in that neighbourhood. I turned and looked.

'It's him,' I whispered.

'Let's go,' said Wolf. 'Calm. Only the business.'

We slipped down in our seats.

Once Ajita's father was there, everything began to happen quickly. The garage doors opened and he drove in. Now he was unable to see us. We crept out of our car and entered the garage by the side door he would exit from, a few feet from the kitchen.

We were in. I shut the door behind us. Valentin had brought a torch, which he switched on and rested on a bench. There was enough light for us to see our victim. We were standing around him as he got out of his car.

With his open hand, Wolf slapped the father twice on the side of his head, just to let him know we were there. Valentin stepped forward and punched him in the stomach, surprisingly hard.

Meanwhile I whispered fiercely, 'Leave her alone, your daughter, never touch her again, she's your child, you do not have sex with her, do you understand? We will cut your balls off.'

He tried to nod as he fought for breath. He was terrified, and his terror was so great it seemed to make him unaware of what I was saying or what we were doing there.

He did this strange thing. Valentin had knocked him against the car, where he was struggling with something. For a moment, I don't know why, I thought it might be a gun. Then I grasped that he had taken off his watch, which he gave to me with trembling hands. I slipped it into my pocket.

When I grabbed his lapels in order to elaborate my diatribe at closer quarters, he tried to give me his wallet.

'What do you want of me?' he repeated. 'I know you! I've seen you before! What's your name? What are you doing here? Help! Come, police!'

I couldn't take the wallet because by then I was determined he would stop yelling and hear me properly – I was pulling one of Mother's kitchen knives out of my jacket. It was intended to scare him into sense. It did scare him.

When he saw it, he started to hyperventilate, gasping so much he couldn't get any more words out. His hand was clutching my wrist; I had to prise his fingers from me.

He collapsed, shaking and clutching his arm and chest, making dreadful noises, begging for help as he fell to his knees, before toppling over onto his side.

I stepped back. I was ready to kick him in the head when Valentin said 'Enough!' and pulled me away.

We picked up the torch and got out.

Before I shut the door I could hear the father choking and gurgling. Or perhaps I imagined that. I'm sure Wolf said, 'It's done,' and shook my hand. 'That dirty bastard has taken it.'

'He learned his lesson,' Valentin said.

Wolf thumped one black leather glove into the other. 'We did him. The business.'

We drove away, none of us looking at the others. Not a word said. We were not exhilarated or high, but exhausted and frightened. At least the job was done. 'Only the business.'

Wolf and Valentin left for London, dropping me off on the way. I walked for a long time, often in circles and back on myself, stopping at various pubs for a half pint in each. I couldn't move normally; the different parts of my body seemed to have become disconnected.

At home, I washed the knife in the bathroom sink – there was no good reason for this – dried it, put it back in the drawer and turned to look at Mother, who had come into the small kitchen. Tonight I was glad to see her.

As always in the evening she was wearing, under her dressing gown, a pink bri-nylon nightie which crackled with static when she got up from watching TV. I didn't understand it then, how she could sit there, sober, her eyes bright, hour after hour, year after year, utterly absorbed by this passion for the flickering figures in front of her.

Before the nine o'clock news, she liked to eat cheese and pickle on cream crackers. I would, at least three evenings a week, sit in the house with her, listening to music, reading, but, ultimately, just keeping her company in her gloom.

Tonight, I became convinced she was looking at me with more attention than usual. I must have seemed wary; perhaps I blushed or my eyes flared.

'What are you doing?' she said.

'Coming to sit with you,' I said. 'What's on telly? Can I bring you a cup of tea?'

However unnatural this sounded, I didn't believe that Mum suspected I'd returned home after beating my girlfriend's father to the ground. Yet, unsurprisingly, my body kept reminding me something was awry. When I brought Mum the tea, I had to hold on to the cup, saucer and spoon with both hands, for fear of them vibrating.

The knife remained with Mum, of course. She kept it for years; perhaps she still has it.

Sitting there watching the adverts, I could feel the watch in my jeans pocket all that evening. Later, I hid it in my bedroom. After a few months I began to take it out and look at it, thinking over what had happened. I began to wear it in the house occasionally, telling Mum I'd liked the look of it and had swapped it for some records. I wore it outside a few times. I changed the strap. I took it with me to my new digs, hating it and needing it at the same time.

The morning after the attack I didn't know what to do. I had been walking about the house since five. At nine I went into the garden. At last I thought I'd go to college and see if Valentin was there.

I was leaving the house; the phone rang; I ran to pick it up.

'Dad is dead,' Ajita said. 'I'm at the hospital.'

'Who killed him?' I said.

'The strikers. They came to the house when we were away and scared him to death. His heart was weak already, he was having tests.'

There was a pause. I think I was expecting some kind of pleasure, or relief, in her voice. Hadn't I done her a favour?

'He looked,' she said, 'when Mustaq and I found him, not at all peaceful, as they say the dead do. But anguished, contorted, frightened, with bruises on his head and blood coming out of his nose. Why would anyone do that to a man?'

'Oh God,' I said.

'I'm going to wail now.' She was already sobbing. 'It'll be horrible, you don't want to hear it. I'll ring you again,' she said, putting the phone down.

I rang the boarding house and told Wolf and Valentin that the man was dead. I said nothing else, not wanting to give anything away on the phone. I would be in touch later.

The next time Ajita called, that evening, it was to say her father had been murdered by people from the trade union who had discovered his address and attacked him. She told me two people had been arrested. She called them 'racists', adding, 'Who else would do such a thing?'

'Burglars?'

'But nothing was stolen. His wallet was there on the floor, undisturbed.'

I had no way of knowing whether Wolf and Valentin had been arrested. I rang their place several times but there was either no reply or the landlady said they were out. When I called round, she said they'd left. 'Good riddance too. They owe me money.'

That night I received a reverse-charges call from a phone box on 'the coast'. Wolf, typically talking in a whisper, said they'd packed their things, left the boarding house, got into the old Porsche they'd bought with the money from the robbery and were heading for the South of France. It was a good idea, Wolf said, for them to 'lie low' for a while. They had been looking for an excuse to get away.

Their careers had hardly been prospering. So they ran and were not pursued, except by their consciences, if they had any. But from my point of view, they had disappeared for good.

'I cannot believe my papa is not coming back,' Ajita said when she called the next day.

'At least you'll be able to sleep at night now.'

'What are you meaning?'

'You know what I mean.'

'But I can't close my eyes at all! The racists are chasing behind us now, Jamal. We are all in great danger here.'

This was not only paranoia. We didn't know, in those days, which way the 'race question', as it was called, would go. My father had often said 'the persecution' might begin any day. When it did, he'd come and get us. 'Thanks, Dad,' I said.

'Where else can we possibly live?' I asked Ajita. 'Can't I come with you?'

123

'I'm being looked after by my uncle. Darling, I will be in touch.'

The next thing I heard from Ajita, ringing from the airport, was that she, Mustaq and the uncle, accompanied by the aunt who lived in the house, were taking their father's body to India for burial. The house would be put up for sale.

'Goodbye,' she said. Before I could ask her when she'd be back, she added, 'Wait for me, and never forget that I will love you forever,' and put the phone down.

I followed the case in the news, reading all the papers in the college library. Eventually, the charges against the so-called murderers were dropped. There was much speculative talk of a racist attack by white thugs, and the Left condemned the police for not taking racist attacks seriously. But there were no clues. Apart from the watch, we took nothing with us. There were no fingerprints or blood.

The factory was closed down; the pickets went away. I was amazed by the inability of the police to find me. I guess I'd have confessed pretty easily, but there was no evidence to connect me with the dead man.

The upshot of this nifty piece of criminality was that I never saw Ajita again. She had gone to India, where I didn't know where to find her. I waited, but she didn't contact me, though I told Mum that if she rang she was to take her number.

Ajita was gone; I hadn't realised she was saying goodbye for good. There was only silence, and I had lost my three closest friends.

I was in shock for another reason: I didn't kill the father with my bare hands, but without my assistance he'd be walking around, even now perhaps.

I had done for him, and called myself 'murderer'.

CHAPTER SIXTEEN

The plane must have touched down around three in the morning.

I had to slap and shake Miriam awake. She'd been living in a squat in Brixton and was eager to get away. The area had recently been torn apart by anti-police riots. Miriam had been up for a week throwing bricks and helping out at the Law Centre. The contemporary graffiti advised: 'Help the police – beat yourself up.'

Inevitably, Miriam had taken something to calm her nerves on the flight, cough syrup, I think, one of her favourites, which had pole-axed her. I helped her throw her stuff into her various hippy bags and shoved her out into the Third World. Lucky them.

It was still dark but warming up. In the chaos outside the airport scores of raggedy beggars pressed menacingly at us; the women fell at, and kissed, Miriam's red Dr Martens.

Wanting to escape, we got into the first car that offered a ride. I was nervous, not knowing how we'd find our way around this place, but Miriam closed her eyes again, refusing to take responsibility for anything. I'd have dumped her if it wouldn't have caused more problems than it solved.

We can't have been in Pakistan, the land of our forefathers, for more than an hour when the taxi driver pulled a gun on us. He and his companion, who looked about fourteen, wrapped in a grim blanket against the night cold, had been friendly until then, saying, as we took off from the airport to Papa's place with Bollywood music rattling the car windows, 'Good cassette? Good seat, comfortable eh? You try some paan? You want cushion?'

'Groovy,' murmured Miriam, shutting her eyes. 'I think I'm already on a cushion.'

This was the early 80s; I had graduated, Lennon had been murdered, and the revolution had come at last: Margaret Thatcher was its figurehead. Miriam and I were in an ancient Morris Minor with beads and bells strung across it. She must have thought we were approaching some sort of head idyll and would soon run into Mia Farrow, Donovan and George Harrison meditating in front of a murmuring Indian.

The driver had taken a sharp left off the road, through some trees and across a lot of dirt, where we came to a standstill. He dragged us out of the car and told us to follow him. We did. He was waving a gun at our faces. It was not Dad's house; it was the end. A sudden, violent death early in the morning for me – on day one in the fatherland. A death not unlike the one I had caused not long ago. That would be justice, wouldn't it? An honest and almost instant karma? I wondered whether we'd be in the newspapers back home, and if Mum would give them photographs of us.

Not that Miriam and I were alone. I could see people in the vicinity, living in tents and shacks, some of them squatting to watch us, others, skinny children and adults, just standing there. It looked like some kind of permanent pop festival: rotting ripped canvas and busted corrugated metal, fires, dogs, kids running about, the heat and light beginning to come up. No one was going to help us.

We considered the shooter. Oh, did we take it in! Sister and I were shouting, indeed jumping up and down and wildly yelling like crazies, which made the robber confused. He appeared to get the message that we didn't have any money. Then Miriam, who was accustomed to intense situations, had the stunning idea of giving him the corned beef.

She said, 'It's not sacred to them, is it?'

'Corned beef? I don't think so.'

She became very enthusiastic about it; she seemed to believe they should want corned beef, perhaps she thought they'd had a famine recently. They did indeed want corned beef. The robber grabbed the heavy bag and kept it without looking inside. Then the other man drove us back to the road and to Papa's place. Even robberies by taxi drivers are eccentric in Karachi.

'Papa won't be getting a brand-new bag then,' I said as we hit the main road. Miriam groaned as we swerved past donkey carts, BMWs, camels, a tank with Chinese markings, and crazy coloured buses with people hanging from the roofs like beads from a curtain.

Luckily, along with the reggae records Dad had requested, I'd put a couple of cans of corned beef in my own bag. Papa wasn't disappointed; it had been his request. Although, apparently, he had told Miriam that corned beef was the thing he missed most about Britain, I can't believe he'd have wanted a suitcase full of it. He *was* partial to the stuff, though, sitting at his typewriter eating it from the can and helping it down with vodka obtained from a police friend. 'It could be worse,' he'd say. 'The only other thing to eat is curried goat brain.'

Mother had wanted us to come here. She was sick of worrying about Miriam when she wasn't at home, and arguing with her when she went there to crash. Mother was also, at times, bitterly angry with father. She had found us hell to cope with, and she had no support. It would benefit all of us to spend time with him, getting to know how he lived and how he really felt about things. Even Miriam agreed.

Long before we got to Pakistan, like a lot of other 'ethnics' she'd been getting into the roots thing. She was a Pakistani, a minority in Britain, but there was this other place where she had a deep connection, which was spiritual, even Sufi. To prepare for the trip, she'd joined a group of whirling dervishes in Notting Hill. When she demonstrated the 'whirling' to me, at Heathrow, it was pretty gentle, a tea-dance version. Still, we'd see just how spiritual the place was. So far we'd had a gun at our heads.

Soon Papa's servant was making us tea and toast. Papa, not only as thin but as fragile as a Giacometti, yet dignified in his white salwar kameez and sandals, informed us we would not be staying with him but with our uncle, his older brother Yasir. To be honest, it was a relief.

'What the fuck is this, a squat?' Miriam said, when we were alone.

It turned out that Father, an aristocrat to those he left behind, was living in a crumbling flat, the walls peeling, the wires exposed, the busted furniture seeming to have been distributed at random, as though a place would be found for it later. Dust blew in through the windows, settling amongst the ragged piles of newspaper rustling on the floor and the packets of unused white paper already curling in the heat.

Later that morning, saying he had to write his column, Papa got his servant to drive us to Yasir's. It was a broad one-storey house that looked like a mansion in movies set in Beverly Hills, an empty swimming pool full of leaves at the front, and rats rushing through them.

Miriam was annoyed we weren't staying with dad, but I went along with the adventure. For a suburban kid with not very much, I like my luxuries. And luxuries there were at Yasir's, exactly how I liked them.

It was a house of doe-eyed beauties. There were at least four. 'The Raj Quartet', I called them. I was still mourning Ajita, of course, as well as assuming we could get back together when she eventually returned to London. I had never given up on her. When the time was right I would tell her what had happened to her father, and she would be shocked, but she'd forgive me, seeing that it had to be done. We would be closer than before; we would marry and have children.

Meanwhile, it occurred to me that this quartet of dark-skinned long-haired women staring at us from a doorway, Uncle Yasir's daughters, might help me bear my pain.

I was looking at the girls, confronting the anguish of choice, not unlike a cat being offered a box of captive mice, when there was a commotion. Apparently there was a rabid dog on the roof. We rushed out see it being chased by servants with long sticks. The servants got a few good cracks in, and the dog lay injured in the road outside, making God-awful noises. When we went out later, it was dead. 'You like our country?' said the house guard.

Miriam was told that she not only had to share a room with two of her cousins, but with a servant too, a couple of children and our grandmother, who was, apparently, a princess. This old woman spoke little English and washed her hands and clothes continuously; the rest of the time she spent either praying or studying the Koran.

It was a large house, but the women kept to their side of it and they were very close with one another. So Miriam and I were separated and each day we did different things, as we always had, at home. I liked to read the books I'd brought with me, while Miriam would go to the market with the women and then cook with them. In the evenings Dad and his friends would come over, or I'd go with him to their houses.

When Papa was writing his column, which he began early in the morning, I'd sit in his flat listening to the heroes of ska and blue beat while being shaved by his servant. Papa was working on a piece ostensibly about families called 'The Son-in-Law also Rises'. It was giving him difficulty because having written it straightforwardly, he then had to obscure it, turning it into a kind of poetic code, so the reader would understand it but not the authorities.

Dad's weekly column was on diverse subjects, all obliquely political. Why were there not more flowers bordering the main roads in Karachi? Surely the more colour there was – colour representing democracy – the more lively everything would be? His essay on the fact that people wash too often, and would have more personality if they were dirtier – thus expressing themselves more honestly – was about the water shortages. An essay ostensibly about the subtle beauty of darkness and the velvet folds of the night was about the daily electricity breakdowns. He'd hand them to me for my suggestions, and I even wrote a couple of paragraphs, my first published works.

This work having been done, at lunchtime we'd tour the city, visiting Dad's friends, mostly old men who'd lived through the history of Pakistan, and ending up at my father's club.

In the evening we'd go to parties where the men wore ties and jackets, and the women jewellery and pretty sandals. There were good manners, heavy drinking, and much competitive talk of favours, status and material possessions: cars, houses, clothes.

Far from being 'spiritual', as Miriam understood it, Karachi was the most materialistic place we had been. Deprivation was the spur. However, I might have considered my father's friends to be vulgar and shallow, but it was I who was made to feel shabby, like someone who'd stupidly missed a good opportunity in Britain. I was gently mocked by these provincial bourgeois, with my father watching me carefully to see how I coped. What sort of man, half here and half there, had I turned out to be? I was an oddity again, as I had been at school.

All the same, my father was educating me, telling me about the country, talking all the time about partition, Islam, liberalism, colonialism. I may have been a feisty little British kid with Trot acquaintances and a liking for the Jam, but I began to see how much Dad needed his liberal companions who approved of Reagan and Thatcher. This was anathema to me, but represented 'freedom' in this increasingly Islamised land. Dad's friends were, like him, already alienated in this relatively new country, and he believed their condition would get worse as the country became more theocratic. As Dad said, 'There are few honest men here. In fact, I may be the only one! No wonder there are those who wish to establish a republic of virtue.'

Many of my father's friends tried to impress on me that I, as a member of the 'coming-up' generation, had to do my best to keep freedom alive in Pakistan. 'We are dying out here, yaar. Please, you must help us.' The British had gone, there'd been a vacuum, and now the barbarians were taking over. Look what had happened in Iran: the 'spiritual' politics of the revolution had ended in a vicious God-kissed dictatorship with widespread amputations, stonings and executions. If the people there could remove a man as powerful as the Shah, what might happen in other Muslim countries?

I learned that Father was an impressive man, articulate, amusing and much admired for his writing. He'd almost gone to jail; only his 'connections' had kept him out. He had been defiant but never stupid. I read his pieces, collected at last, in a book published only in Pakistan. In such a corrupt place he represented some kind of independence, authority and integrity.

If he seemed to have the measure of life, it wasn't long before I had to put to him the question I was most afraid of. Why hadn't he stayed with us? What made him come here? Why had we never been a proper family?

He didn't shirk the question but went at it head-on, as if he'd been expecting it for years and had prepared. Apart from the 'difficulties' he had with mother – the usual stuff between a man and a woman, at which I nodded gravely, as though I understood – there had been an insult, he said. He had liked Mum. He still respected her, he said. It was odd to hear him speaking about her as a girlfriend he'd had years ago but now, clearly, was indifferent to.

I learned, though, that he had had, briefly, at the same time as Mum, another girlfriend, whose parents had invited him to dinner at their house in Surrey. They were eating when the mother said, 'Oh, you *can* eat with a knife and fork? I thought you people normally ate with your fingers.'

This was to a man who'd been brought up in a wealthy liberal Indian family in colonial Bombay. Among the many children, Father was the prince of the family, inheritor of the family talent. 'Isn't he a magnificent man?' Yasir had said to me. 'Your grandfather told me to look after him always.'

Dad had been educated in California, where he'd established himself on the college circuit as a champion debater and skilful seducer of women. He believed he had the talent and class to become a minister in the Indian government, ambassador to Paris or New York, a newspaper editor or a university chancellor. Dad told me he couldn't face more of this prejudice, as it was called then. He had 'got out', gone home to the country he had never known, to be part of its birth, to experience the adventure of being a 'pioneer'.

As we drove around Karachi – him tiny behind the wheel of the car – he began to weep, this clean man in his white salwar kameez and sandals, with an alcohol smell that I got used to and even came to like. He regretted it, he said, the fact that we as a family weren't together and he couldn't do his duty as a father. Mother wouldn't live in Pakistan and he was unable to live in England.

If he had left us in Britain it was, he added, as much for our sake as for his. It was obvious we would have more of a chance there. What should have happened, he said, was that his family should never have left India for Pakistan. India was where his heart was, where he'd belonged, where he and Yasir and his sisters and brothers had grown up, in Bombay and Delhi.

He now realised that Bombay, rather than Karachi, was the place where his ideals could have been met, crazy though it might be there. In Pakistan they had made a mess of things. He admitted it could have been predicted by a cursory reading of history. Any state based on a religious idea, on one God, was going to be a dictatorship. 'Voltaire could have foretold, boy. You only have to read anywhere there to realise.'

He went on: 'Liberals like me are marginal here. We are called the "high and dry" generation. We are, indeed, frequently high, but rarely dry. We wander around the city, looking for one another to talk to. The younger, bright ones all leave. Your cousins will never have a home, but will wander the world forever. Meanwhile, the mullahs will take over. That is why I'm making the library.'

Packages of books from Britain and the US arrived at Papa's flat a couple of times a week. Dad didn't unpack them all, and when he did, I noticed that some of them were volumes he already had, in new editions. With Yasir's money, Papa was building a library in the house of a wealthy lawyer. Such a darkness had fallen upon the country that the preservation of any kind of critical culture was crucial. A student or woman, as he put it, might want access to the little library, where he knew the books would be protected after his death.

Dad insisted I go to meet his older sister, a poet and university lecturer. She was in bed when we arrived, having had arthritis for the last ten years. 'I've been expecting you,' she said, pinching my cheek. 'This will be difficult, but there's something you need to see.'

We got her up and onto her walking frame, and accompanied her to the university, which she was determined to show me, though it was closed, due to 'disturbances'. She, Dad and I shuffled and banged our way through the corridors and open rooms, looking at the rows of wooden benches and undecorated, crumbling walls.

She taught English literature: Shakespeare, Austen, the Romantics. However, the place had been attacked frequently by radical Islamists, and no one had returned to classes. The books she taught were considered 'haram', forbidden. Meanwhile madrasas or 'bomb schools' were being established by President Zia. This was where many poor families sent their kids, the only places they would receive education and food.

When I wondered what it meant for my aunt to teach English literature in such a place, to people who had never been to England, she said,

'They've gone, the British. Colonialism restrained radical Islam, and the British at least left us their literature and their language. A language doesn't belong to anyone. Like the air, anyone can use it. But they left a political hole which others fill with stones. The Americans, the CIA, supported the Islamic revival to keep the Communists out of the Middle East. That is what we English teachers call an irony.' She went on: 'It is the women I fear for, the young women growing up here. No ideology hates women more than this one. These fanatics will undo all the good work done by women in the 60s and 70s.'

She would return to the university when the time was right, though she doubted that she'd live to see it. 'A student said to me, "We will kill 10,000 people, which will destroy this country's institutions and create a revolution. Then we could attack Afghanistan and go upwards . . . There will be the believers and there will be the dead. The West will defeat Communism but not Islam – because the people believe in Islam."'

Meanwhile my aunt was content to remain in her room and write poetry. She had published five volumes, paying for the printing costs herself, the Urdu on one page, the English on the other. She adored the Saint Lucia poet Derek Walcott, who was her light. 'His father, I'm sure, was a clerk in the colonial administration, like so many of our educated.' He had taught her that she could write from her position – 'cross-cultural', she called it – and make sense. Other local poets met at her house, to read their work and talk. They wouldn't be the first poets, nor the last, to have to work 'underground'.

'I envy the birds,' she said. 'They can sing. No one shuts their mouths or imprisons them. Only they are free here.'

Language; poetry; speaking; freedom. The country was wretched but some of the people were magnificent, forced into seriousness. Dad would have known the effect this would have on me.

Our lives had been so separate. Dad had never visited our schools or even our house when he was in Britain; there'd been no everyday affection. But as he drove about Karachi he did ask me, 'What is it you really do?' – as though he needed to know the secret I'd been keeping from the anxious enquirers at the dinner parties.

I didn't have much of a reply: I said I was going to do a PhD on the later work of Wittgenstein. I'd say this to anyone who enquired about my choice of career, and I did so to Papa. He could show me off or at least shut the questioners up. I had, after all, graduated with honours – whatever they are – in philosophy.

This was, though, only for the benefit of others and Dad knew it. When, in private, he called me a 'bum', which he did from time to time, often appending other words like 'useless' or 'lazy' or, when he was particularly drunk, 'fucking useless lazy stupid', I tried to defend myself. I was not bringing shame on the family. I did want to do some kind of intellectual work and had even considered doing an MA. But really I considered philosophy only as the basis of intellectual engagement, a critical tool, rather than anything that seemed worth pursing for itself. Who can name a living British philosopher of distinction? Later, psychoanalysis came to interest me more, being closer to the human.

This was all too vague for Papa, and the 'bum' taunts didn't stop. He'd say, 'Your other cousins, what are they doing? They're training to be doctors, lawyers, engineers. They'll be able to work anywhere in the world. Who the fuck wants a philosophy PhD? Yasir was like you, doing nothing, sitting in pubs. Then our father, who was in Britain, kicked his arse and he opened factories and hotels. So: you can consider your arse to be kicked!'

How could I put pleasure before duty? What could be more infuriatingly enviable than that? Papa had kicked my arse. Where had he kicked it to? I felt worthless, and glad he hadn't been around in London: one of us might have killed the other.

As I considered the serious side of Papa's attack, I drifted around Yasir's house wondering what to do with myself. I'd already learned how difficult it was to find solitude in this country. The price of an extended and strong family was that everyone scrutinised and overlooked one another continuously; every word or act was discussed, usually with disapproval.

One day I discovered that my uncle also had a library. Or at least there was a room called 'the library', which contained a wall of books, and a long table and several chairs. The room was musty but clean. No one ever used it, like front parlours in the suburbs.

I took in the books, which were hardbacks. Poetry, literature, a lot of left-wing politics, many published by Victor Gollancz. They'd been bought in London by one of my uncles and shipped to Pakistan. The uncle, who lived in Yasir's house but now 'roamed around all day', had developed schizophrenia. In his early twenties he'd been a brilliant student but his mind had deteriorated.

I sat at the library table and opened the first book, the contents crumbling and falling on the floor, as though I had opened a packet of flour upside down. I tried other volumes. In the end my reading schedule was determined by the digestion of the local worms. As it happened there was, by chance, one book less fancied by the worms than others. It was the Hogarth edition of *Civilisation and Its Discontents*, which I had never read before. It occurred to me, as I went at it, that it was more relevant to the society in which I was presently situated than to Britain. Whatever: I was gripped from the first sentence, which referred to 'what is truly valuable in life . . .'

What was truly valuable in life? Who wouldn't have wanted to know that? I could have ripped at those pages with my fingernails in order to get all of the material inside me. Of course, I was maddened by the fact that whole sentences had been devoured by the local wildlife. Indeed, one of the reasons I wanted to return to London was that I wanted to read it properly. In the end, the only way to satisfy my habit – if I didn't want to ask my father for books, which I didn't – was to read the same pages over and over.

Often, my only companion was my schizophrenic uncle, who would sit at the end of the table, babbling, often entertainingly, with a Joycean flow. The meaning, of course, was opaque to me, but I loved him and wanted to know him. There was no way in. I was as 'in' as I was going to get.

While I settled into a daily routine of carefully turning the medieval parchment pages of old books, I noticed a movement at the door. I said nothing but could see Najma, at twenty-one the youngest female cousin, watching me. She waited for me to finish, smiling and then hiding her face whenever I looked at her. I had played with her in London as a kid. We had met at least once a year, and I felt we had a connection.

'Take me to a hotel, please,' she said. 'This evening.'

I was mad with excitement. The bum also rises.

This advent of heterosexuality surprised me a little. I had already been made aware of the broad sensuality of Muslim societies. The women, for instance, who slept in the same room, were forever caressing and working one another's hair and bodies; and the boys always holding hands, dancing and giggling together in someone's bedroom, playing homo-erotically. They talked of how lecherous the older men were, particularly teachers of the Koran, and how, where possible, you had to mind your arse in their presence. Of course, many of my favourite writers had gone to Muslim countries to get laid. I recalled Flaubert's letters from Egypt. 'Those shaved cunts make a strange effect – the flesh is hard as bronze and my girl had a splendid arse.' 'At Esna in one day I fired five times and sucked three.' As for the boys, 'We have considered it our duty to indulge in this form of ejaculation.'

I had been introduced to young men of my age, and went out with them a few times, standing around brightly decorated hamburger and kebab stalls, talking about girls. But compared to these boys, after what happened with Ajita, I had little hope. They seemed too young, I was alienated, and had no idea where I belonged, if anywhere now. I would have to make a place. Or find someone to talk to.

It took Najma three hours to get ready. I'd never waited so long for a girl before and hope to never again. I was reminded, unfortunately, once more of Ajita, who was inevitably late for classes, giving the excellent excuse that she didn't want the lecturer to see her with bad hair.

Najma turned up aflame with colour, in a glittering salwar kameez with gold embroidery. On her wrists she had silver bangles; on her hands there was some sort of brown writing; her hair resembled a swinging black carpet, and she wore more make-up than I'd seen on anyone aside from a junkie transvestite friend of Miriam's. Najma didn't need the slap; she was young and her skin was like the surface of a good cup of coffee.

I assumed we were going to the hotel to fuck. I didn't realise that the Karachi hotels were the smartest places in town, where all the aspiring courting couples went. The radical Muslims were always threatening to bomb these hotels – and did occasionally – but as there were no bars and few restaurants in the city, there was nowhere else to go, apart from private houses.

Sitting there in my ragged black suit – I could scratch my crack through the gash in the behind – drinking nothing stronger than a salted lassi, all I did was worry about the size of the bill and feel as out of place as I did on the street. But in the car on the way home she asked if I'd let her suck me off. It sounded like a good idea, particularly as I doubted whether I'd be able to find my way through the complicated layers of clothes she seemed to be wearing. She pulled over somewhere. As I ran my fingers through Najma's black hair I thought it could have been Ajita who was satisfying me. At the end she said, 'I love you, my husband.'

Husband? I put this down to the poetic exaggerations of passion. Najma and I had a lot of time together and after our first love-making she made it clear she was in love with me. I liked that about her. I fall in love too easily myself. You see a face and the fantasies start, like tapping on the magic lantern.

She liked to deride the West for its 'corruption' and 'excess'. It was a dirty place, and she couldn't wait to move there, to escape the cul-de-sac which was Pakistan, the increasing violence, the power of the mullahs and the bent politicians. I would be her ticket.

I'd read and she'd lie with her head in my lap, talking. Other women who came to the house were training as doctors and airline pilots, but the Chekhovian women in my family only wanted to get away, to America or Britain – *Inglestan*, it was called – except that they couldn't do it without a sufficiently ambitious husband. The ones left behind, or waiting to leave, watched videos of Bollywood movies, visited friends and aunties, gossiped, went out for kebabs, but otherwise were forced into indolence, though their imaginations remained lush and hot.

I didn't want the sucking to stop. I liked it a lot, along with the spanking and other stuff I hadn't yet got round to. She liked – she was very fond of – the economics, too. Not a Merc, darling, I'd say, when she seemed to think that that was what we'd move around London in. I'd prefer a Jag. I've had Jags, even a Roller, a Bentley for a week, but I sent it back. I've had a lot of trouble with Mercs, they're always breaking down, the big ends go, Jesus.

Then I'd tell her New York wasn't enough for her. We would have to go out to LA, to Hollywood, where the swimming pools were top-class and maybe she could become an actress, she had the looks.

'Next week?' she said.

'Maybe,' I said, hastening to add that though I might seem a bit short of money at the moment, I'd had it before and soon would again, once I started back at work. It wouldn't take someone as smart as me long to make real money.

I have to say I didn't begin by wanting to deceive Najma with these spidery nonsense nets. She had taken it for granted that I was already wealthy, and would become even wealthier in the near future, like her male cousins. She'd been to Britain often, but had little idea of what it was really like. Most people, in fact, seemed to think that Miriam and I were rich. If we weren't we must have been stupid, or mentally weak. One time I saw a young servant of Yasir's wearing my shoes, then a pair of my suit trousers. When I remonstrated with him he just grinned.

'But you are rich,' he said in strange English.

'Get that stuff off,' I said, 'I'm going to tell Yasir.'

He acted like I'd hit him. 'Please, I beg you, no, no,' he pleaded. 'He sack me.'

Off he went in my gear. What could I do? He earned almost nothing. Miriam, being generous and ingenious, found a way to fund him while benefiting us. She got him to bring us joints which we'd smoke on the roof. Not long after, I discovered from Najma that Papa was referring to us as '*les enfants terribles*'. His own children!

Not that we weren't looking into him too, eager to get the low-down. I knew little about his romantic life, whether he had anyone or not. It seemed unlikely. He had his routine, his worries and his books.

There was, though, his second wife. Miriam and I went to her office, where she worked as the editor of a woman's magazine. She was very cool, small with fine features, polite, curious and intelligent. She had an English upper-class accent with the head-wagging Indian lilt I'd liked since meeting Ajita. I could see Miriam getting a crush on her. But she wasn't for a moment emotionally engaged with us. She didn't talk about Papa or our lives without him. After our visit, Miriam phoned a couple of times but was told she was away.

Things began to go bad. One time I was in the library and Najma was waiting outside as she always did. I went to her, checked for prying eyes, and kissed her shiny lips a little and begin to touch her, but she was cold and pushed me away. She was silent for a while, letting me take in her hurt, before beginning to abuse me in Urdu. Her father, in a rage, came in. They talked a lot in Urdu too. I got out of there. It was breaking down.

It turned out that Najma had gone to Miriam and confessed to her. We were in love, we were going to marry, we were off to London, New York, Hollywood, in a Merc, or was it a Jag?

Miriam calmly told her to forget it, Jamal was marrying no one. He's not even a student; he's got the degree but so does every bum and semi-fool in London Town. Forget the Jag, the fucker might be able to drive but he hasn't taken his test, they wouldn't let him on the road in England. If he's intending to marry, she finished off, he hasn't mentioned it to me, and he mentions everything to me, otherwise I slap him.

I was in a rage with Miriam. Why did she do this? She liked the girl, she said. She felt sorry for her being subjected to my lies and stupid stories. But what was she doing herself?

It was taken for granted that I'd accompany Papa during the day (I was learning a lot), just as he took it for granted that Miriam would stay at the house with the other women. But, apparently, she had stopped doing this. Instead, she had taken to driving off in Uncle Yasir's car, often with her head uncovered. When asked where she'd been, she'd reply, 'sightseeing'. I had some idea of what these sights might be when she told me that her favourite thing in Karachi was to go to the beach and there, under a palm tree, split open a coconut and pour half a bottle of gin into it.

Most of the sightseeing she did was from within the arms of one of our cousin's fiancés, an airline pilot, who had a beach hut. He and our cousin were to be married later that year, but the pilot was taking the opportunity to get to know the further reaches of the family. He and Miriam had also been meeting in rooms in the hotel I'd visited with Najma, where he knew the manager.

They'd been spotted. Gossip was one of the few things that moved urgently in Karachi. He'd taken it for granted that English girls were easy, and when he ran into Miriam he knew he was right. I'd been wondering how she knew so many little things about the country. Of course our cousin went crazy, and threatened to stab Miriam. Miriam was outnumbered; I refused to help her.

Miriam had thought we could live in Pakistan a while, get a job, save a bit, hang out on the beach and deal hash, and so on. But in little less than a month the whole thing had become impossible. We were too alien; there was no way we could fit in. There were American and British wives living there, but they had gone native, wearing the clothes, doing the accent, trying to learn the language in order to speak to the servants.

Outside, if Miriam wasn't covered she was jeered and hissed at. They even pinched her. She picked up fruit from stalls and threw it at people. I was terrified she'd get into a fist-fight or worse. I kept my head down but Miriam, being a modern woman of the most extreme kind, fucked them all up. Our grandmother, the Princess, had already gone to her, placed her hand on her forehead and said, 'I'm going to recite a small prayer which will drive out the devil and the evil spirits which posses you. Satan be off! Give us victory over those who disbelieve!' The following morning she had two sheep slaughtered. The meat was distributed among the poor, who were asked to pray for Miriam's quick recovery.

It all blew up at Papa's flat one morning when I heard a commotion in the sitting room. There were raised voices. Then I heard what sounded like a large object being thrown across the floor. I guessed the large object might be Papa. When I ran in, followed by the servant, Miriam was sitting on Papa, rather as she used to sit on me, screaming at him. He was trying to protect his face as well as trying to strike her. She was strong and difficult to pull off. There was something she wanted to tell him.

'He's been abusing me!' she said, as we held her, trying to pin her arms behind her back. Papa was dusting himself down. Then I saw she had spat at him, that her spittle was on his face. He took his handkerchief and cleaned himself.

She said, 'He says I kiss the arse of whitey! He calls me "a rotten girl" and a dirty slut who can't behave! Yet he left us there in London! He abandoned us! What could be worse than that!'

'Get out,' cried Papa in a weak voice. He went into another room and shut the door.

It was the last time we saw him.

Dad must have spoken to Yasir. When we got back to his house we were informed that we were leaving later, around one in the morning. We were not given any choice. The servants were already packing our bags. No one said goodbye or waved. We weren't allowed to say goodbye to the girls.

The funny thing was, we spotted Miriam's lover, the pilot, going through the crew lane in the airport. Later during the flight, he came to collect her. Apparently she 'guided the plane'. A packed 747 with Miriam at the wheel, sitting on the pilot's knee with, no doubt, her hand in his fly.

Mother had wanted us to see Father 'in his own environment'. She thought it would be informative. It was. We could no longer idealise him. In most ways he was worse off than us. He couldn't save us, nor us him. He couldn't be the father we had wanted him to be. If I wanted a father, I'd have to find a better one.

By the time we returned to London, Miriam and I weren't speaking. I hated her and didn't want to see her again. I didn't want to be the little brother any more. Usually I'm quite passive, if not evasive. I go along with things to see what's happening, not wanting to make things worse by tossing my chillies into the stew. But I had said to Miriam, as we left Papa's, that she had ruined the whole trip.

'No wonder Papa thinks you're an idiot and a bitch,' I explained. 'You can't control yourself for five minutes! These people have their own way of life and you just pissed all over it! There can be few people in this world who are more selfish than you!'

She was so sullen and freaked, traumatised, I supposed, that she couldn't even hit me. It occurred to me that she'd either damage herself in some way or go back on the smack.

We rode back into London on the tube. The little houses and neat gardens sitting there in the cold looked staid, cute, prim. Saying nothing, hating everything, we both had furious eyes. This was our land and it was where we had to live. All we could do now was get on with our lives – or not. At Victoria Station the two us parted without speaking. I went home to Mum and Miriam went to stay with someone who had a council flat in North Kensington.

*

I knew that whatever happened, I needed to get a job. Luckily, I had a friend from university who was working in the British Library, and he said he could get me something there.

The one person I didn't expect to see again was Najma, but she did turn up a year later in Britain and rang Mother, asking for me. For a moment, in my confusion and with Mum's lack of clarity – 'an Indian girl phoned' – I thought it was Ajita. I began to cry with relief. She hadn't forgotten me, she was coming back.

Najma had married a Pakistani who came here to study engineering, and the two of them were living in Watford with twins. I went out to see them a few times.

One kid had a fever, and the other was perhaps a little backward. The couple had been racially harassed, knew no one, and the husband was out all day. Najma would cook for me; she knew I loved her food, and we'd sit together, chastely, while she talked of everything she missed 'back home'. Exiled, she continued to curse the West for its immorality, while blaming it for failing to dispense its wealth to her family with the alacrity her fantasies demanded.

I took the husband out for a drink, and had to listen to him complaining about the excessive price of prostitutes in Britain.

I could only say that Britain might turn out to be more expensive than he thought.

CHAPTER SEVENTEEN

Henry had been getting into trouble, and the trouble was spreading, drawing us all in.

On my answering machine there was a message from his daughter Lisa. Soon there were two messages. She didn't want to see me, she *had* to see me. As insistent as the rest of her family, like them she expected to get her way. I was busy with patients and with Rafi but, being stupidly curious, I invited her for tea.

I'd always enjoyed hearing of her adventures from Henry, and over the years I'd run into her occasionally, usually with her brother. As a child she'd always been surrounded by artistic and political people, picketing the *Sunday Times* building at Wapping in 1986, and staying at Greenham Common at the weekends. She'd had an expensive education, before going to Sussex University to read sociology.

With such a pedigree, how could she do anything else but drop out just before her finals in order to live in a tree situated on the route of a proposed motorway? Henry could hardly object. Hadn't he taken her to march with E. P. Thompson and Bruce Kent against nuclear weapons? Nevertheless, when she did climb down from the tree, Henry took it for granted she'd return to 'ordinary' life. He or Valerie would ring one of their friends and her career would begin.

But she became a social worker at the lowest level, visiting mad old alcoholic men and women on her bicycle, refusing to 'section' people because it entailed forcibly taking them into psychiatric care. She left home to live on a druggie single-mother estate. Her flat was at the top of the block, with an extensive view over Richmond Park, and she filled it with Palestinians and other refugees. On occasions she threw paint at McDonalds or raided shops for pornography, filling up bags with the stuff. 'I hope it's going to the unemployed,' murmured Henry.

These actions weren't considered far-out among the bohemian young, for whom unconventional behaviour was compulsory. Henry considered her a successful extension of himself. But he did worry, saying, 'My daughter is still the sort of person who might seek a position as a human shield. How come she took the sins of the world on her shoulders? Where did this guilt and masochism come from? As long as her fury is directed at herself everyone's fine. When it's coming towards you, you better watch out!'

She showed up at my place on a bicycle, fresh from her allotment. Her hair was halfway down her back, and it was thick and dramatic, unkempt, of course, which spoke to me of a repudiated femininity. Not that I thought she was a lesbian, though she'd tried to be, I'd heard, and failed, as so many do.

She seemed to be carrying three rucksacks, and resembled a vertical snail. Her fingernails were dirty, her boots muddy and her all-natural clothing was coming apart. She wore no make-up or decoration. The veins in her face were broken from the harsh weather she liked to endure, and she looked weary, as though she'd been digging for weeks.

It didn't seem long ago, in February 2003, that she and I and Henry had walked together to Hyde Park on the anti-war march, attended by two million. Now, two years later, we were in the middle of a rotten, long conflict, which hadn't improved her temper, nor anyone's. While I made her a nettle tea, we agreed that we lived in a country led by a neurotic chained to an evangelical, imperialistic lunatic. She must have been the only Marxist left in the West, but I liked her passion. That seemed to be the last agreement we were to have.

She said, 'The other day I went to see Henry. It was about lunchtime. Sam was in a state because he'd had to move out. You know why.'

I was leaning forward. 'I heard the story.'

'And, childishly, Henry refused to give him his things back. The clothes Sam could do without, but the computer had his work on it. I said I'd fetch it for him, whatever it took. I wanted to see Henry.'

She had been let into Henry's house by one of the other tenants, who were scared of women like her. Henry left his flat unlocked, as the Mule Woman had discovered. To find him, she followed the fetid smell.

'He was more or less unconscious. He had been sick, the basin was full of it. He might have died. I found fetish clothes on the floor and other objects. There was a leather mask. I said to him, "What's this?"'

'And?'

'He said, "For the last few centuries these masks have been used for celebratory dances associated with major social rituals." I had to put my hand in my mouth and bite it to stop myself laughing. She said, 'Yes, another of his jokes, and I hate jokes now. He'd been clubbing. When I asked him what he'd been taking, he said E and Viagra – together!'

Henry was in no state to get up. He said Bushy would bring Miriam around later, and she'd help him.

Lisa said, 'Seeing him there groaning, I thought it would have been easier to raise the *Titanic* than get Henry up.' She looked at me reproachfully. 'I sat down next to the ruin of my father.'

'How ruined was he?'

Apparently Valerie had said Karen had been on to her, arguing that if Henry didn't finish the actor's documentary the project would be abandoned. Not only that but she, Karen, already in financial trouble herself, would be personally liable. Valerie told Lisa that Henry had been turning down other work too, apart from teaching, claiming that he had 'retired' and had 'nothing left to say'.

Lisa said, 'I asked if he wanted a doctor.'

'Was he really unwell?'

'When he was able to put some words together, he was in good spirits. Perhaps it was the drugs. I've never polluted my body with that shit, so I wouldn't know. Have you?' I said nothing. 'But,' she went on, 'you know he's had a heart attack. He almost died. How come your sister's letting him take amphetamines? Does she want to kill him?'

'I doubt it,' I said. 'Henry's stubborn, isn't he? He makes his own rules. We like that about him.'

She said, 'I think I've met your sister at some event or other. I've got nothing against her. But let me ask you this. What are they doing together?'

'Miriam is, of course, a Muslim single mother with a history of abuse. She has few taboos and she sees straight to the centre of things. Your dad – a free, single man – loves that about her.'

Lisa was sitting on the edge of my analytic couch, waiting for these banalities to pass, before she went into her rehearsed rap.

'We know better than anyone how to take care of him, while your family has been negligent.' She seemed to hesitate there but I knew she'd hardly started. 'But why would you worry about our little problems? I know you spend a lot of time thinking about the dreadful dilemmas of film stars and celebrities. Didn't they call you, in a newspaper, therapist to the stars?'

I said, 'You know it's not like that, though I have to admit that I've used my work to be with people who interest me. Just this morning I was wondering whether Kate Moss might like to see me. How could anyone not envy me that? Anyhow, I didn't see the thing in the newspaper. Did you?'

'Of course not.'

Over the years several sportsmen had approached me. Having gone to the trouble to learn about their bodies, they assumed their minds could also be trained to obedience. It was when this didn't work – when, as it were, they became curious about the mind-body relation – that they asked for help.

The incident Lisa was referring to involved a footballer I saw a few times. He had been followed to my place; photographs of him at my door, with half of Maria's head behind him, had appeared in the papers. His unhappiness was mocked all over. He was called mad.

She said, 'The little difficulties of the famous must be hell. But my father has stopped seeing his old friends. They bored him for years, apparently. These people are famous and high up in their field. But they are not pierced. He has resigned from two boards. As for those places he and Miriam go to together –'

'Places?'

'Fetish clubs. They are squalid and the people there riddled with disease. You think the women who go there want to be doing that? It's rape, their husbands forcing them to have sex with dozens of people.'

Which of Lear's daughters was she? I wondered how long I'd be able to resist the pleasure of giving her a little verbal slap.

'You're worrying about your father,' I said. 'He's changed a little. Everything will calm down.'

'Fuck that patronising analyst quackery.'

Her mother's tongue had been passed on like an heirloom.

I said, 'Quackery?'

She was looking at the postcard of Freud I kept on my desk, sent to me by an enthusiastic patient. 'Freud's been discredited over and over. Patient envy –' She stopped. 'Penis envy, I mean. Jesus.'

Despite herself, she laughed.

'What a lot of fallacious cock, you mean?' I said, laughing too.

'Jamal, my father loves you. He even listens to you. Valerie too. But my father is not in a good way, and you must take some responsibility.'

That word. Responsibility. When I watched Miriam on her TV 'agonies', it was the most-used word, apart from 'I'. Owning your acts. Seeing yourself as an actor rather than victim. I am all for responsibility; who wouldn't be? We are all responsible for our selves. But what are our selves? Where do they begin and how far do they extend?

'Yes,' I said. 'He is responsible for what he does. Not me. Certainly not you. Him. Just him. You and I,' I said, getting up and moving towards the door, 'are irrelevant here. We must be happy for them both and for the joy they give one another. Let's hope they marry – or at least live together.'

'Marry? Live together! Are you insane? Those two? Where did you get such an idea from? Is it likely?!'

I was being mischievous. She irritated me; I could only inflame her.

I said, 'I like to see others contented.'

She was already gathering her things. She asked me if I minded her taking something home. It was the teabag I'd used earlier, which she wanted to put in her 'compost' box. She squeezed it out, before dropping it in a pocket of her rucksack.

At the door she said, 'I will not let my father be destroyed.'

There was mud on the floor from her boots. She also 'forgot' one of her rucksacks. My patients often left umbrellas and coats, as well as change, lighters, condoms, Tampaxes and other stuff which dropped out of their pockets onto my couch. It was a form of payment as well of relationship. I knew Lisa would be back.

She returned two days later.

'Thank you for putting up with me,' she said, as though I'd had a choice. She sat on the couch, dragging her skirt up over her boots, another colourful thing, ethnic, like me. She was watching me looking at her legs and smiled. 'Did you know Valerie's got an Ingres drawing on her bedroom wall? It's lost in a mess of other stuff, some valuable things, family photographs and so on, but it's there. That's insouciance for you. You have any idea what it's worth?' I said nothing as she looked at me. 'Valerie says you're a sphinx without a secret. Aren't you the one who is "supposed to know"?' She paused. 'You nodded then, but tell me, how do you sustain that stillness, Jamal? The way you're just there. Did you learn it?'

'I don't think I ever did.'

'You never fidget, your hands don't fuss, your brown eyes are steady. They're soft but merciless. And that little Giaconda smile of yours, which seems to know everything as you hear everything . . . It's enough to convince a girl you could hear her soul murmuring. I bet all your patients want to be like you.' She was smiling at me. 'I could sit with you for a long time, surrounded by books, CDs and these lovely pictures.'

'They're all by friends.'

'The sketches?'

'My wife Josephine.'

'And your son's work too. So many photographs of him! Unlike my mother's friends, you're not showing off your wealth or power.' Silence. 'You're not supposed to give advice,' she said. 'You shamans don't even like to admit you can cure – if indeed you can.'

I said, 'The difference between therapy and analysis is that in therapy the therapist thinks he knows what's good for you. In analysis you discover that for yourself.'

'What would you say if you had a patient who was destroying themselves?'

'I would warn them.'

She said, 'Jamal, please, will you see me? As a patient, I mean.'

I told her there were good analysts I could recommend but I couldn't see her. I would phone her with suggestions. If she was in a hurry, I could find a couple of phone numbers right now.

She said, 'Why are you refusing to help me? I took your two books from mother's house and read them. I've studied your essays on the internet. Like all good artists, you make me believe you are writing for only me.' She went on: 'Will you answer this? What happens when you feel that the conversations you have are the wrong conversations with the wrong people?'

I noticed that while I was looking through my address book, finding a pen and paper, she had put her feet up on the couch and lain down.

'Lisa.'

'But I have to tell you what happened.'

'What happened when?'

'When I called Henry and we agreed to have dinner at that place near Riverside Studios. She was there when I arrived.'

'Who?'

'Your beloved sister. She's uninvited but never mind, she starts to talk. Capricorn rising or was it falling? Wizards she has known. Belly-dancing lessons. Posh Spice as a goldfish. Botox and how to get it cheap. *Big Brother*. On and on. A talking tabloid. He listens to every word. I think: how does he know what *Big Brother* is? She records it for him. How sweet! Then you know what he does?'

'What?'

'He shows me the tickets he's got for the Rolling Stones.'

'Did he say whether he got me one?'

'What is dad Dad doing – regressing to another adolescence? She has stolen him. He missed my childhood, having better people to be with. But in the past two years we were lunching once a week. Now he doesn't see me, doesn't need my advice. When I do get him to lunch that woman's there! He apologises, sees what I'm saying. He agrees to meet me. But he talks about her again, her arthritic hands, her agony. He says this awful thing: "But Miriam has liberated me from my horrible bourgeois upbringing. Almost everything I believed was stupid, wrong, sterile!"'

'There's no room for you?'

'I tell him, if you don't sort this out I'm going to do something!'

'Here,' I said, as she gathered her things to leave. 'Take this number. This therapist is a friend who writes well.'

She looked at the piece of paper, folded it and put it in her pocket. 'You have remarkable faith in these people.'

I said, 'The early analysts really thought about the structure of the human mind, about what it is to be a child, to be sexual, to be with others – to live in society or civilisation, as a gendered animal, and to have to die. They knew that every hour of the past, as Proust puts it, is inscribed on the body, indeed, makes the body. There's nothing more important or absorbing, is there?'

I picked up biographies of Melanie Klein and Anna Freud, and gave them to her. 'They are fascinating women, pioneers. Radical intellectuals.'

'Thank you,' she said. 'It's been a long time since anyone's given me direction. My parents just expected me to be successful.'

She went on: 'Before our "clients" see me, they visit their doctors, who prescribe medication which the patient may take for years.'

I said, 'Someone splits up with their girlfriend and they're given a pharmacological concoction, as though pain were unnatural.'

She said, 'Doctors haven't got time to take a history. They are with each patient for ten minutes. So I listen, but I am there all morning. Then I get into trouble for being slow.'

I said, 'Freud's revolution was in the fact he didn't drug people, hypnotise them or give them advice, which would have infantilised them. He listened. He wrote down their stories.'

The next time I saw Henry I told him that Lisa had been to see me.

'Don't you think I love to see Lisa too?' he said, worriedly. 'Now she calls me a deluded bastard. I am only a fool because I want them all to get along. I am, I know, ignoring basic human nature.'

We both wanted to talk of other things, and we did, but that was not the end of it. I didn't believe Lisa would see the therapist I'd recommended, but she was in a worse state than I'd thought.

The day after, Rafi and I went to visit Miriam. When Rafi was downloading ringtones with the other kids I looked over at Miriam – sitting at the table – and could see her hands were shaking.

'Who's bothering you, my love?'

'Lisa came over. She is a very naughty girl, that one. As she's Henry's daughter I take it easy with her.'

'How easy?' I said, uneasily.

I wanted to eat and to relax, but Miriam was giving me a mephitic vibe. At least she poured me a drink.

I said, 'Where is Lisa now?'

'In Casualty. I expect her parents are flapping around her.'

'How did she get there – Casualty?'

'How d'you think?' said Miriam. I got up to leave. She grabbed me. 'Please stay, brother. You know I need you tonight.'

After visiting me the second time, Lisa had rung Miriam and asked to see her. While Miriam was thinking over whether this was a good idea, as well as wondering whether she should talk to Henry first, Lisa walked in. She must have been on her bicycle in the street.

She came right into Miriam's kitchen and sat down. 'In my fucking face – right there!' Looking at Bushy and indicating the door, Lisa said the two of them needed to talk alone. So Bushy shuffled out to mess around with his car, but he was not far away, having an instinct.

Lisa started off by apologising for intruding and so on. But it wasn't long before she told Miriam to lay off her father. She begged. She wept. She mentioned the heart attack. Then she made her first serious mistake, offering Miriam money. She offered her two grand not to see him again.

Miriam asked why Lisa thought she needed her money.

Lisa – who visited the poor and dispossessed every day – looked around at the falling-down house, bursting with animals and children, with some disdain, as her mother might have done. I knew what Miriam meant. Hearing this, even I got an electric jolt of very bad karma, and the taste of vomit on my tongue.

Lisa was, by now, testing Miriam's patience, never a good idea. According to Miriam, Lisa was sweaty, hairy and probably dirty between her toes. 'I should have asked her to weed the garden.'

Certainly, Lisa was making a mistake with Miriam, thinking she was a pushover. Lisa went further: she said that Miriam was only interested in her father's fame and money. If Henry were nobody, Miriam would have no interest in him. She was implying that Miriam was a kind of groupie, a whore even.

Miriam was getting hot inside her head. But she loved Henry, she'd never adored a man so much. She didn't want things to get too mad; after all, Lisa was his flesh and blood and this fight would tear him apart. Just get the bitch out of here, she thought, that's all I have to do.

She ordered Lisa to leave the house. She said this in a loud voice, giving her one minute to get out, with the rider that she would set the dogs on her. They were barking outside already but Lisa tried to continue the conversation. However, Miriam isn't one of those middle-class talky bitches who'll go on and on until everyone's paralysed. Inside her broiling head, a limit had been reached.

Her fingers were creeping towards one of her numerous mobiles and before she knew it, it was airbound. She had flung it at Lisa's face, a lucky hit which cracked her lover's daughter's cheekbone. Then Miriam threw other things – pill bottles, videos, books on astrology – which smacked Lisa in different places about the head.

Lisa turned round and came back at her. She's strong: she rows, practises women's boxing. The kids were screaming. Miriam had lost it. Lisa was going mad, taking up postures, her fists flashing. Bushy jammed himself in there, stopping a cat-fight, throwing his body between them before the knives were out.

He hustled Lisa out before anything worse happened – threw her out into the street in the direction of her bicycle, which, it being a bad neighbourhood, now had no wheels or saddle, was the skeleton of a bicycle. Bushy then took hold of a piece of wood and held it up, defending the house! Behind him Miriam had come out with a knife and was threatening to rip up Lisa's smug middle-class face, reckoning she would look better with some ventilation!

I was twitching with agony over this when my mobile rang. It was Henry, whose calls I hadn't had time to take that day. I could hardly make out what he was saying. He was stressed out, stoned on dope and trancs, and, on top of this, somehow he'd mislaid his tickets for the Stones. He'd turned the flat upside down and didn't know what to do. Lisa had been ringing him, screaming that she was at the hospital and then at the police station making a statement. She was trying to get Miriam arrested for abuse, assault and attempted murder, and Henry was trying to get her to lay off.

I did work out that Lisa had said to Henry, 'You're killing me!'

'*I am killing you?*'

'Yes!' And she added, 'You wouldn't like it if you found me strung up by the neck one night!'

During the day Miriam had been telling Henry that it was too much for her too. She loved Henry, but would not see him until he chilled the daughter out. She was sorry that Henry had got caught between two women, but she felt at the moment that she wanted to separate. She couldn't have that madwoman coming round her house scaring the children and animals.

She knew, too, that she was ugly and stupid and rank and worthless, and no man could get his head around her, but she couldn't stomach any more rejection and she must not be insulted by Lisa again. After feeling loved for the first time in her life, she wasn't strong enough to survive Lisa's hatred.

At the other end of the phone Henry didn't know where he was, but he knew what he wanted, which was for her not to be hurt and for them to be together, continuing the life they had started. He started to weep and beg but he couldn't make himself clear and the phone line went dead.

A little later I was watching the Champions League on TV, as well as taking some of this in, while waiting for Rafi to find his shoes and re-prepare his hair, when Henry came in, looking wild, as though he'd got caught in a storm.

He was in Miriam's arms right away and they were sobbing, apologising, squeezing each other's buttocks and Henry wailing, 'But I will never reject you, never! You know that! You are my sweet, my soul, my sausage! For you I would become an outlaw from everyone – from my entire family! How could you think I would let you down when I want us to marry!'

'You're just trying to cheer me up –'

'No, no –'

Rafi came in and looked at them, amazed.

It wasn't long before the two of them were making phone calls, working out where they'd go that night to 'play'.

'By the way,' said Henry to me, patting his pockets as I was leaving, 'I found the tickets for the Stones. We're definitely going!'

CHAPTER EIGHTEEN

Despite my sympathy for Henry's suffering, I had to say, 'What could be more gratifying to a man than to have two women fighting over him? It would be worse if they got along!'

He was shocked. 'No pleasure without a price willingly paid? I hate to admit that you are right, but maybe you have a point,' he said, with some relief. 'And at my age! All Lotharios cause chaos. None of them make a smoother world! These are the knock-ons of desire! As long as the women don't go too far, how can I complain? Most people are far too well-behaved,' he said confidently. 'They go to their graves wondering whether they should have caused more harm to others, knowing they should. Jamal, thank you for your support! I'm sorry I brought such chaos to your sister's life.'

Even though she had taken him back, he had been devastated by Miriam's dismissal of him and was determined to bind her to him even more closely. That was why he wanted the Stones outing to be a success. Turned on by the Stones' decadence – only a quarter-century too late – Henry was more excited than I'd seen him for a while. He was ringing me all day. If I was with a patient he'd talk to Maria, though she barely understood a word. She liked Puccini.

Henry had obtained the tickets from a costume designer he knew, who was now working with the group. The band was due to play the Astoria in Tottenham Court Road. I had seen the Stones with Ajita and Mustaq, but I knew Henry had never seen them before, though he claimed to have been 'near' Hyde Park when Jagger wore an Ossie Clark dress, the first gig after Brian Jones died.

Marianne Faithfull had been in one of the productions he'd assisted on, as a young man in the late 60s, and they were still friends, difficult though she could be like any diva. But Henry had always been a little snobbish about rock'n'roll, unable to make up his mind whether it was tat or the revolution. He hated to dance, disliked anything too loud and was ambivalent about the joys of 'vulgarity', until now, when he knew Miriam would be impressed. She was.

Henry had mislaid the tickets, found them, lost them, and finally found them. At last, when the day came, Miriam and Henry spent the afternoon in Camden market, buying black clothes. We all had our most impressive gear on, with comfortable shoes. Bushy drove Henry, me and Miriam up there, dropping us off in Soho Square. Soho was always crowded now, but tonight it was rammed.

'At the risk of sounding like someone's aunt, can I say, do we really have to join that queue?' said Henry, as we approached the line. 'Don't we have good tickets? Isn't there a special entrance?'

'That *is* the special entrance.'

Crowds were already queuing around the block. Along the lines numerous touts were buying and selling tickets. The atmosphere was vital, almost violent and riotous, in a way that theatre or opera never is. As Henry noted, 'It's not like this at my shows!'

Even after so many years, audiences were mad for the Stones, the essential London group, playing at home in a small venue. Scores of photographers strained behind barriers, snapping at soap stars in blinding bling. Miriam had to point out these people to Henry, as well as identifying the children of rock'n'rollers we'd worshipped in the 60s, now comprising a new dynasty, and resembling in their 'social capital' the great noble families of the *ancien régime*.

Inside, on the way to the bar I ran into the Mule Woman. Accompanied by a good-looking boy, she was wearing little black-rimmed glasses, like a model who'd become a librarian. We kissed on the cheek and she asked about Henry. 'He's just the same,' I said. 'Would you like to have supper with the two of us next week?'

She agreed, but before we could arrange it there was a roar: the band was about to come on stage. People rushed to their places.

Although they had been doing those tunes for thirty years, the Stones didn't make their boredom obvious; they knew how to put on a good show, particularly Keef. Miriam's rapture was enough for Henry, who was entranced by the excitement and the audience as much as by the band. (In the theatre he liked to sit at the back, keeping an eye on the audience. He claimed the women caressed themselves – their arms, legs and faces – as they watched. 'How gentle they are with themselves,' he said. 'I wonder if this is how their mothers caressed them as babies.') At the Stones, the fact that he could sit down at a table at the front of the balcony was one of the main attractions. Despite the state of her knees, Miriam seemed temporarily resuscitated, and danced when they played 'Street Fighting Man'.

As we were leaving, and with Bushy parked up behind Centre Point, Henry's friend caught up with us and suggested we go to Claridge's, where Mick had a suite and was 'entertaining'. Tom Stoppard, an acquaintance of Henry's, had suggested Henry might enjoy Mick. Bushy drove us there.

As we got closer, Miriam's enthusiasm seemed to drain away; she started saying she'd be 'out of her depth'. Having never been in the same room as a 'knight of the realm' before – should she call him 'Sir'? – she tried to get Bushy to take her home.

'What a lot of nonsense you talk, Miriam,' said Henry. 'I won't put up with it. Once you get there, you will see that Mick's cool,' he said, as if he knew. 'He's a real person, like us. He's not like –'

'Who?'

'Ozzie Osbourne.'

Henry and I wouldn't go in without her, and we both said we'd do the talking. In the glittering lobby, PR girls and hangers-on clip-clopped about. Bushy had found a raggedy peaked cap in the boot of the car and insisted on accompanying us upstairs in the mirrored lift, putting on a deferential manner and nodding confidentially at Jagger's security, while tapping his nose as if he had a secret inside it that he was trying to draw attention to. Bushy wanted to be considered 'staff' in order to catch a glimpse of Mick, who he worshipped as a fellow bluesman.

There he was, Jagger, fit and lithe, and looking like a man who had seen everything and understood a lot of it. He had come out to greet his guests at the door, alongside his tall girlfriend. Inside, as we started to drink, Jagger ate, checked his email and looked at the newspapers, chatted to friends and to his daughter Jade. Henry was hungry by now and couldn't believe Jagger was sitting there eating without offering him anything. In the end Jagger cheerfully ordered Henry some sandwiches, which he scoffed gratefully.

Mick was glad to see Miriam's tattoos. She claimed to have been influenced by 'Tattoo You'. After, she was happy out on the balcony, looking across the city, chatting to a posh girl who turned out to be a Scientologist. While you could be sure that one of the things the wealthy and poor had in common was an interest in superstition, even Miriam couldn't bring herself to worship someone called Ron.

We sat in a small circle discussing Blair, Bush, Clinton, about which

Henry had much to say, though Jagger was more discreet. It was late for me, I told Jagger, who said he rarely went to bed before four but always had eight hours sleep. Jagger and Henry had a conversation about sleeping pills, Jagger being cautious about the whole thing, not wanting 'to get addicted'. People continued to come and go as though this was what smart London did, drift in and out of each other's apartments at one in the morning.

As one would with a rock god, I had an informative discussion with Jagger about good private schools in West London. When I decided to leave and was looking for my coat, a man I didn't quite recognise who'd come in towards the end of the evening, was brought across to me by Jagger.

'He wants to meet you,' said Mick, explaining that they were cricket pals, going to Test matches around the world together. George knew everything about Indian cricket.

I was close enough to the modern world to recognise that this fellow, George Cage, was a song-writer and performer. To me he looked kind of shiny, with the sheen of health, success and vacuity which comfort and sycophancy gives people. Miriam, who had by now come in, seemed to know who George was and was thrilled. 'My daughter likes you,' she told him cheerfully.

'That's good,' he said. 'Usually it's the mothers.'

I said I had to go, I'd get a cab on the street. I noticed that George kept looking at me and, at last, when I was fetching my coat, he came over and asked me to show him my arm.

'This might seem odd to you, but something is making me quite curious,' he said. 'Can I see that?'

He wanted to look at my watch.

I showed it to him. It was an old, heavy watch on a silver bracelet strap, with wide hands under thick, scratched glass. A watch with clear figures and the date, everything a man who needed to orient himself could require.

He bent over to study it. He wanted me to take it off so he could look at the back. I couldn't think of a reason to refuse.

He put his glasses on and studied it. When he returned it, he said, 'Can I ask where you got that?'

'I've had it a long time,' I said. 'Why do you ask?'

'My father had one similar.'

'I don't think they're expensive. What did he do?'

'He had a factory. He was a businessman. In South London.'

I held his gaze. 'Mustaq?' I said. He nodded. I said, 'Ajita's your sister?'

'That's right.'

'My God,' I said. 'Is she okay?'

'Oh yes. Did you think she wouldn't be? She is living in New York with her two children. Or at least one of them. The other is at college.' He took out his phone and looked at it. 'I'm going to ring her later. Would you like me to tell you I saw you?'

'Please.'

'A shock, eh?'

'Certainly.'

He said, 'I'm going out dancing. Nowhere smart – awful dives, mainly. Would you like to join me? Perhaps we could talk. My driver will take you home.'

I told him that my work meant I started early in the morning. Then I asked, 'Mustaq, how did the music stuff happen? Actually, I can remember you singing to me.'

'I am sorry. After my father died, when my sister and I were in India, in my uncle's house, I stayed indoors for two years, learning the drums, tabla, guitar, piano. Anything that made a noise. Anything that Dad would have disliked. That's how I was one of the first people to mix jazz, rock, Bollywood film tunes and Indian classical music.

'You know I'd always wanted to be a young American, and in New York I found other boys to perform with. I loved being on stage and was never afraid. But you must be too tired to talk now.'

As I listened to him I became aware that he was exactly as he had been, except that all his gestures were slightly exaggerated, as though he were a camp actor playing himself too seriously.

He said, taking out his Blackberry, 'Could I see you again? Would it be all right if I took your number?'

'Of course.'

Despite his graceful formality, before we left he took my arm once more, gently, as though he were going to stroke it, and put his face to the face of the watch, twice looking up quizzically at me. He may have amused me, but I recalled, from the time we wrestled, his tenacity.

On the way home in the car I said, 'It was uncanny seeing Mustaq – or George Cage, as he's called – again.'

'He was certainly giving you the eye,' said Henry. 'I'd say he was freaked. Did you two have a passion for each other?'

'I preferred his sister.'

155

Miriam murmured, 'He preferred you.'

'And still does,' Henry said, giggling.

I asked Miriam about George Cage. I'd heard of him, but he'd come to prominence when I was losing interest in pop and preferred the mid-period, chaotic, electric Miles.

'He and his boyfriend are always in the tabloids. How come you know him?' she asked.

'Miriam, his family lived close to us, across the park in Bickley. Have you forgotten I went out with his sister, Ajita?'

'Of course,' she said. 'I knew I'd met him before.'

'I don't think you did,' I said, recalling how ambivalent I felt about it at the time.

'Oh yes, I remember it – subliminally,' she insisted. 'I trust myself in that intuitive area.'

'Were you really glad to see him?' Henry asked. 'You both looked as though you'd been hit with bricks.'

'I will see him again, if he asks me. Will you come?'

Miriam turned and poked her finger at me, 'Didn't I instruct you, brother, to look for the Indian girl?'

'Not that I followed your advice.'

'Somewhere she knew, and heard you. You better watch out – long-lost love is coming in your direction.'

'She might be right,' said Henry.

As Henry and Miriam snogged in the back seat, Miriam saying what a great night it had been, I wondered about Mustaq and how strange it was not only to see him at Jagger's, but in this new incarnation.

Even as I wondered what he wanted from me, and what I was getting back into, I knew I was going where I had to go.

CHAPTER NINETEEN

I wasn't convinced, however, that I would hear from George Cage again. I imagined, that like most celebrities, his life had become a matter of keeping people away. Meanwhile, there were questions which had been going through my mind. Did Ajita want to see me? And did I want to see her?

George Cage had his secretary call me a week later, inviting me to a drinks party. Although it wouldn't just be the two of us, I realised George was trying to talk to me about the past. I could have refused to meet Mustaq – as I still thought of him – but I had been thinking about his father, whose face had appeared in several of my dreams recently. The dead man not only names his murderer, he whispers it throughout eternity, waiting to be heard.

Nor had Ajita disappeared from my life, as I'd thought she had. She was alive in the real world, existing outside my mind. Really, she was the one I wanted to connect with again. Once more it seemed pressing. I needed her brother's help in some way. Perhaps some sort of resolution might be possible.

I agreed to go over, asking if it was okay if I brought a friend. I'm happy going to places I haven't been before if Henry is with me.

George Cage's house in Soho was tall and narrow, in an alley off Wardour Street, sandwiched between a film-cutting studio and a walk-in brothel offering Russian, Oriental and black women. 'Even the brothels are multicultural now,' Henry noted.

Despite its location, George's house had a luxurious hush, as though it were soundproof. The decor was white; Oriental staff offered trays of drinks and sushi. Expensive dogs sniffed the guests' crotches. There were good prints on the walls. Be-ringed queens from the East End mingled with upper-class young men in priceless suits, pop stars, painters, Labour Party researchers and, to my surprise, a couple of black Premiership footballers – one in a white fur coat – who stirred more excitement than the pop stars.

George Cage introduced Henry and I to Alan, 'his future wife' and boyfriend of five years, the man he was intending to 'marry' when civil partnerships became legal. In his late forties, Alan was wearing a sleeveless tee-shirt and shorts, with white socks and sandals. He used one hand to carry, at all times, a glass of wine and a thin joint. He was muscly and wanted you to acknowledge it. He was good-looking, with a seductive decadence that stated there were few experiences he had eschewed.

I learned almost immediately that he'd been a fascist, a tube driver, a junkie alcoholic and drug dealer; he'd done his 'bird'. As a consequence, he seemed to suggest, he was suspicious of 'con-men' like us, who seemed to survive in a talky, false world whose violence was unacknowledged. When he told me where he was from, I was pleased to tell him I'd been brought up a couple of miles away. Miriam and I, as kids, would go on the bus to Ladywell Baths and spend all day there.

'What do you do, then?' he asked. 'You in the politics too?'

'I'm a therapist.'

'I got a therapist,' he said. 'An aromatherapist. Do you use scents?'

'Nope.'

'Not even vanilla candles?'

While I wondered whether Freud might have had a view on vanilla candles, Alan looked at me sceptically, as though he'd been about to recommend several people to me for therapy but was now thinking better of it.

He and Mustaq had met in a bar, he said. They still sometimes went to bed at ten and got up at two to trawl rough gay bars in the early hours. One place they'd gone to at four in the morning, only to be told they were 'too early'. Alan had always felt at home in these places, with what he considered to be his 'people', the aimless, lost, unfulfilled and 'perverted', and Mustaq had found a place there too.

There didn't seem to me to be any reason why Alan should feel alienated in Mustaq's world, but as more of Mustaq's friends came over, Alan would suddenly start into an upper-class accent, pinched, absurd, superior; a stoned Lady Bracknell. Mustaq seemed used to it, and no one else took any notice, aware perhaps that this was always the risk you ran with rough trade.

Mustaq said he was keen to introduce me to another of 'our people'. I wasn't sure what he meant; it turned out to be a plump Asian in a Prada suit with a lot to smile about. This was Omar Ali, the well-known owner of launderettes and dry-cleaners, who'd sold his flourishing business in the mid-90s to go into the media.

Now, as well as being a stalwart of the anti-racist industry, Omar Ali made television for, by and about minorities. The 'Pakis' had always been considered socially awkward, badly dressed, weirdly religious and repressed. But being gay, Omar Ali was smart enough to know how hip and fashionable minorities – or any outsiders – could become, with the right marketing, as they made their way up the social hierarchy.

After Blair was elected in 1997, Omar had become Lord Ali of Lewisham, which was the raw part of town he was from. His father, a radical Pakistani journalist who'd been critical of Bhutto's various deals with the mullahs – a man who had, it turned out, known my own father as a student in India – had drunk himself to death in a dingy room there. As is often the case in families, it had been the uncle who'd saved Omar in those Thatcherite times, letting him run one of his launderettes and telling him, despite his father's fatal integrity, to run out of the ghetto in pursuit of money, which had no colour or race.

Omar's lifelong penchant for skinheads, childhood friends who'd kicked him around, had got him into less trouble than it might have done at an earlier time. It was ironic to think of how Omar meshed with his times. His commendable anti-racism had made him into the ideal committee man. Now, as an Asian gay millionaire with an interest in a football club, he was perfect leadership material. He was disliked by Muslims for his support of the government's fondness for bombing Muslims, and hated by the Left and Right for good reasons I was unable to remember. But he was protected by a political ring-fence. No one could bring him down but himself.

If Lord Ali was smug it was because he had long been ahead of the game. He'd never had any scruples about combining cunning business practices with Labour Party socialism. Now, of course, many ex-leftists were turning – or trying to turn – towards business and the Thatcherite enterprise culture they had so despised. It had become acceptable to want more money than you could sensibly use, to enjoy your greed. With retirement coming up, the ex-leftists saw they had only a few years to make 'proper' money, as so many of their friends had done, mostly in film, television and, occasionally, the theatre.

'Still supporting the war?' Henry asked him. Henry had been drinking champagne quickly, as he did when he attended such functions. By the time we came to leave he'd be ready for a monologue. 'You must be the only one left.'

Omar was used to this. 'But of course. Removing dictators is a good thing. You want to argue with that?' He looked at me. 'I know who you are, though I find your stuff difficult to read.'

'Excellent.'

'We both have Muslim backgrounds, and wouldn't we agree that our brothers and sisters have to join the modern world or remain in the dark ages? Haven't we done the Iraqis a favour?' I could see Henry becoming annoyed, and so could Omar, who had a cheeky face and liked Henry's annoyance so much he went on: 'As a gay Muslim I believe other Muslims must have the opportunity to enjoy the liberalism we do. I won't be hypo-critical –'

Henry interrupted. 'So you urged Blair to kick the shit out of as many innocent Iraqis as he could?'

'Look, these Iraqis, they have no science, no literature, no decent insti-tutions and only one book. Can you imagine relying on just that? . . . We must give them these things, even if it means killing a lot of them. Nothing worthwhile was ever done without a few deaths. You know that. I told Tony, once you've done Baghdad, you can start on some of those other places. Like Bradford.' Omar made a camp gesture and said, 'I don't know why I'm saying all this. I'm a moderate, and I always have been.'

Alan, who was standing nearby, said, 'Only politically.'

'All I've ever wanted was to relieve the condition of the working class.'

'Oh yeah, that's all we need – someone who came up the hard way.'

Henry said, 'Blair's problem is self-deception. It doesn't help that he's surrounded by people like you who only tell him what a good guy he is.'

Omar said, 'You old Communist lefties, you can't let it go, can you?'

Later I would remind Henry that he hadn't always been as anti-Blair as he – and many of our friends – liked to make out. In fact Henry and Valerie had been invited to Chequers, the prime minister's country place, early on in his first term. It said 'casual' on the invitation, and Henry wore a suit and open-necked shirt. The other guests included a well-known but dull ex-footballer, a female newsreader, and either a runner or a rower, Henry wasn't sure. Blair, who to Henry's surprise told him he'd once con-sidered becoming an actor, was wearing what looked like over-tight Lee Cooper jeans and an unbuttoned purple shirt, with ruffles, and shiny black shoes. Henry expected a tribune of the working class, not a tribute to Brian May.

While Omar Ali and Henry were arguing, I noticed that Mustaq, the practised party host, was moving among the guests, introducing people, keeping an eye on things. Not that he had forgotten about me. I became aware that one of my purposes there was to be present when Mustaq told Alan – something I imagined he must have known already – that he and I had been brought up in the same neighbourhood, and that I'd known his father and sister.

Alan didn't seem fascinated and drifted away. But Mustaq told me he wanted to continue, leading me into a neat sitting room and shutting the door.

As he uncorked more champagne I said, 'Does Ajita ever come to London?'

'Would you like to see her?'

'I would.'

'I think she and her husband are planning to come later this year. What's that look – is it scepticism?'

I said, 'It means opening a door I tried to close a long time ago.'

'Why close it in the first place?'

'I was in love with your sister, but one day she went away for good.'

'I can see why you'd want to reject that,' he said. 'It was only recently that I was able to get interested in the past. Because of my "pop" name and fair skin I haven't been mistaken for a Paki for years – not unlike Freddie Mercury, another who "disappeared" into fame.

'I never talked about the factory and the strike, even when it was brought up by journalists. I didn't try to hide it, but I never advertised it. I just said it had been a "bad time" and anyhow I'd been young. Weren't all those pop boys, like Bowie, trying to reinvent themselves?'

I asked, 'Now you want to go back?'

'Did you ever see the factory while the strike was on?'

'I remember Ajita being taken inside – in the back of your father's car.'

'He made me do that, a few times. I would cry and shit myself before we set out. It was terrifying, the screams, bricks, lumps of wood flung at us.'

'Why did he do it?'

'We were supposed to take over the business when the time was right, so he wanted us to know what went on in the real world.' Mustaq got up. 'I want to talk more, but I must get back to the party.' I thought he was going to shake my hand, but he wanted to look at my wrist. 'You've taken the watch off.'

'I don't wear it all the time.'

'I'm not going to let this go,' he said.

'It is obviously important to you.'

'I'm thinking about my father a lot. I tried to be someone without a childhood. But there's something I need to get to the bottom of. He was murdered, after all, and no one was punished for it. Didn't you keep up with the case?'

'I tried to, but I wasn't aware of any outcome.'

'There was no closure. He was just another Paki, and the strike was causing a nuisance to the politicians.'

I said, 'I thought some men were arrested.'

'It was the wrong men, of course. The killers are still out there. But not for much longer.' He was leading me to the door, where Henry was waiting for me to join him for a curry. Mustaq said, 'The men who were picked up were nowhere near our house. So who was it? Why would they do it? What would be the motive?' Then he said, 'I have a place in Wiltshire. Not an English country house – my crib is comfortable and warm. Will you come? We will have time to talk.' He looked at Henry. 'Will you both come?'

'Yes,' said Henry. 'We will.'

I said, 'Mustaq, will you give Ajita my number?'

'Of course. But she will be as nervous of speaking to you as you are of her. Please – will you go easy on her?'

Part Two

CHAPTER TWENTY

'Oh my darling, Jamal, it's been so long, kiss me and kiss me again.'

'Better keep your hands on the wheel, Karen.'

'I can drive one-handed. You know there's a lot I can do one-handed.'

I said, 'I didn't know you were coming to George's this weekend.'

'You didn't? But I haven't been out for absolutely ages.'

'You've been hiding at home?'

She said, 'Things haven't been good. They've been bloody rotten and down on me. Can't we stop for a drink?'

'No.'

'Just a little one in a country pub?'

'It's a different decade now, I'm afraid.'

'Haven't we become too sensible?'

'The world has, but I'm sure *you* haven't. It's terrific to see you, Karen.'

'Is it? Is it really, Jamal?'

Karen was driving me to Mustaq's.

Miriam had become determined to live her own life, even though she still felt guilty about leaving the kids and the house. Nonetheless, she and Henry were looking for the opportunity to get away together. As there was a club they were reluctant to miss on Friday night, they would come to the country after lunch on Saturday morning. I could have waited for them or gone down on the train.

It was a surprise then, when my old girlfriend Karen Pearl, the 'TV Bitch', offered me a lift. I wasn't aware that she knew Mustaq, but it turned out that over the years he had appeared several times on her TV shows. Now and again she went to his house to recuperate from her life.

She turned up outside my place in a tiny red car, which roared when she pressed the accelerator. She'd asked her husband to buy it as compensation for leaving her, which he considered a more than fair exchange. If I was already anxious about seeing Mustaq and answering his inevitable questions, being squashed in a small space with Karen while being hurled down the motorway certainly made me breathe more rapidly.

'I am delighted and totally chuffed to be getting away,' she said. 'You?'

I felt unnaturally close to the road; Karen played loud music, mostly Abba, and, for my benefit, Gladys Knight as well as the Supremes, while smoking the entire time, as we always used to. Twice she opened the roof to demonstrate how it worked.

'Groovy top.'

'Isn't it? We're so old now, Jamal. My two girls are growing up,' she said. 'It's all slammed doors and lost mobile phones. But we have a grand girly time – like being back at boarding school. Otherwise, contrary to your corrupt view of me, I don't have much of a laugh these days. Tom' – her ex-husband – 'has taken the girls, along with his more-or-less teenage girlfriend, to Disneyland, Paris. As they are all of the same mental age, they'll have a great time.'

'You having anyone?'

'I'm an untouchable,' she said. 'This will make you laugh – I know exactly the kind of thing which will appeal to you.'

'Tell me.'

'Well, a few weeks ago I thought I'd give myself a treat. I tried it on with a potential toy boy. I'd heard that's what all the old girls were doing. I strong-armed this moody well-built kid into a ruinously expensive hotel room. There was champagne, drugs, and what you used to describe as my vast arse, in silk red panties, all ready. And the boy so fit and sweet –'

'Famous?'

'On his way there. At the moment, an extra – a speaking extra, mind, but words rather than sentences – from a soap opera. At some cost to the little dignity I have left I removed a good deal of my clothing, presenting said panties in what I considered to be a provocative way.'

'Oh wow.'

'He sat on the edge of the bed holding my hand looking, I think, at how withered it was. Either that or my nail varnish had hypnotised him. Within half an hour he was on the tube home. I sat there for a while crying –'

'Oh Karen –'

'Ready for my overdose, Mr DeMille. Then I went home and got into bed with the girls. Oh Jamal, think of all the nights you and I wasted not making love.'

'There were many,' I said. 'But I enjoyed every one of them with you.'

'You've got sweeter in your old age, Jamal. It's nice to talk to you again.

166

Why do you never call me now? Oh forget it, I'm going to think positive today. Isn't that what you psychologists tell us?'

'No.'

'What do you tell us, then?' After a while she said. 'Henry's coming down, isn't he? Will you put in a word for me?'

'You fancy Henry now? You two can't spend ten minutes together without falling out.'

'Darling, haven't you known desperation? He's a man, isn't he? At least below the waist, and he's free.'

'He just got occupied,' I said.

'Who grabbed the old fox?'

'My sister.'

'Isn't he trying to put her in the documentary?'

'Yes.'

'Fucking artists with their spontaneous ideas, I hate them. Remind me to kill him when I see him.' She said, 'Is your sister going to be around this weekend?'

'On Saturday.'

'They in love?'

'Yes.'

'I didn't think he'd last long on the open market. That's my hope accounted for, then. You still single?'

'There's nothing doing. These days there's rarely a twitch.'

She turned and looked down at my crotch. 'Yeah, right.'

I said, 'The idea of all that seems very far away from me. Josephine was hard work. Sometimes I think I miss being in love, or being loved. A little passion now and again would be a thrill.'

'You're too objective about love. You can see through it. I was thinking . . . you said this thing to me once. That you hated to fall in love, it was like being sucked down the plughole. You lost control, it was madness.'

'Did I say that?'

'Did you feel that about Josephine?'

'Sucked into some elemental state of need, over-idealising the other, drifting in illusion and then one day waking up and wondering how you got there? Yes . . . But –'

I didn't want to say it to her for fear of upsetting myself, but I had liked being in a family, liked having Rafi and Josephine around me, hearing their voices in the house, their shoes all over the hall.

I had met Josephine at a lecture I was giving, 'How to Forget'. She was a psychology student but was bored by the 'rats on drugs' approach. We had only been together for a few months when she fell pregnant. My father had died about eighteen months before, and I was keen to replace him with another father: myself. I was living in the flat where I saw patients, and beginning to make a decent living.

Josephine had her own place, which her mother had left her, and we bought a small house near what became my office. We hadn't been together long when I lost her almost immediately to another man, my son. Or, rather, we lost each other to him, and neither of us bothered to come back. Of course many relationships require a 'third object' to work: a child, house, cat; some sort of shared project. He was that, but also the wedge. Josephine knew how to be a mother; being a woman was far more difficult. She waited a long time before trying to find out what *that* might mean.

When he was little, I kissed Rafi continuously, licked his stomach, stuck my tongue in his ear, tickled him, squeezed him until he gasped, laughing at his beard of saliva, his bib looking like an Elizabethan ruff. I loved the intimacy: the boy's wet mouth, the smell of his hair, as I'd loved that of various women. 'Toys,' he called his mother's breasts. 'What is thinking?' he'd ask. 'Why do people have noses?'

Around the age of six, Rafi would wake up early, as I tended to, while Josephine slept. I'd sit at the table downstairs, making notes on my patients,; or I'd prepare a paper or lecture I was giving. He brought me his best pens to borrow, to help make my writing 'neater', as he put it. He'd sit with me – indeed, often, on me; or on the table – listening to music on my CD player, through headphones bigger than his cheeks. He liked Handel, and when he got excited he said, 'Daddy, I feel as if I've got people dancing in my tummy.'

We bought identical green coats from Gap, with fur-lined hoods, which we wore with sunglasses and trainers. Big Me and Pigmy, I'd call us, thinking we looked great. When he was smaller, I'd walk fast for miles across London, with him in his push-chair, stopping off at coffee shops to feed and change him. It's easy to speak to women if you have a baby with you. It was like being the companion of a celebrity. Strangers greeted him; people constantly gave and bought him things; women fed him, talked to him. He disappeared him into their midst like a rugby ball into a scrum, and returned reeking of numerous perfumes, his hair standing up and his eyes staring, his face covered in biscuit.

I liked playing Monopoly, and having paint, toys, videos and footballs over the floor; I liked eating fish-finger sandwiches, and the kid sneaking into our bed at night because he 'didn't have anyone to talk to', drinking hot chocolate in his bottle, stopping only to say, 'I want to kiss you lots of times.' I liked him holding on to my ear as he went to sleep; even liked the cat patting my face with his paw while I was napping. I liked reading to him in the bath, as he sat there talking to numerous plastic men attached by pegs to the washing line above his head.

Rafi was a desire machine, his favourite hobby being shopping. At school, when asked to name his favourite book, he chose the Argos catalogue, which he would pore over, ticking everything he wanted. Fortunately, like him, I enjoyed anything to do with Spiderman, the Incredible Hulk, Power Rangers and the Lion King. I liked kicking a football around with him in the street, and hearing him play Beethoven's Ninth on the harmonica. I liked arm-wrestling, chasing and fighting with him, and holding him upside down by the ankles, sometimes over the toilet. We liked, among many other things, jokes, swearing and hitting women on the arse.

We would spend whole weekends hanging around, eating pizza, swimming at Acton baths, kicking a ball to one another, watching *Star Wars* or *Indiana Jones* movies; the sort of days when, in the evening, if you asked yourself, did anything happen to me today? – and I did keep a diary of this sort at one time – the only answer could be no, nothing. Except we were enjoying one another's company, and no one could ask here, where is the meaning?

When it ended, and I had to go – I still don't know if it was the right thing to do – the loss seemed immeasurable; but all I could do was carry on living, as best as I could, seeing him every day, wondering what I'd missed of him. 'Are you another boy's daddy now?' he asked.

'I won't pity you,' Karen said, as we sped to Mustaq's. 'Tempting though it is. The chances are that a man as successful and well connected as you will find someone – and someone young too. But I will not. Maybe we should get back together – just for a bit?' All I could do was laugh. 'I'm sure you don't tell your patients you were a pornmonger. I know your secrets, and I still love you a little, you know,' she said. 'When we were together I felt all the time that you were too smashed up over Ajita to notice me much.'

'I'm always all smashed up over someone.'

'But you cared for me some, didn't you, although I was awful and stupid?'

She leant across and kissed me, brushing my crotch with the back of her hand.

'Oh God yes,' I said, sentimentally. 'Jesus, I've always loved you more than a little bit, Karen.'

'I always felt that you were just passing the time. You know, you're afraid of letting anyone near you. You want them, and then you disappear.'

She started to cry, which she did easily. She'd taken off her heels and was driving barefoot, her skirt riding up around her thighs. In her twenties she'd been sexy, but even then her weight went up and down and she called herself 'the potato'. Whatever size she was, she knew I still found her attractive; it was the familiarity, but not only that.

'It's not too late, Jamal. Can't we do it properly?'

I kissed her again, pressing my tongue against hers. Beyond the cigarettes, alcohol and perfume I could smell someone I knew and liked a lot.

CHAPTER TWENTY-ONE

I had been living with the lefties in Baron's Court Road, where the Piccadilly and District line trains ran alongside my room, rattling the windows. I first saw Karen upstairs, in the communal area, where I'd sit after returning from the Library, or in the morning, having breakfast, with some serious book – maybe *The Ego and the Id* or the *Ecrits* – propped up in front of me.

This was a vegan kitchen packed with pulses and gluten-free pasta, with chickpeas bubbling on the hob and the yeasty smell of wholemeal bread rising from underneath a tea towel. Imagine this level of earnestness and then, one Saturday morning, suddenly you see a young woman wearing nothing but lipstick, high heels and a Silk Cut, hunting about for something to throw on – which, in the end, was someone's old great-coat. It was like spotting a movie star getting out of a taxi in Bromley High Street. Of course, other people walked about the place naked, except that they (men and women alike) only wanted to exhibit their honesty.

A woman in the house had been at university with Karen, who had stayed over after a party. When one of the rancorous female lawyers referred to her as 'the TV Bitch' – a new genus, though I didn't know it then, but some clever cunt had intuited that Karen represented something about the future – it occurred to me that she and I might have something in common.

She stayed for the rest of the weekend and nobody since Ajita made me laugh like Karen. It cheered me that everyone else in the house disliked her on principle. When she was wasn't walking about talking into the phone, Karen watched soap operas with a pile of *Cosmopolitan* magazines in front of her, painting her nails. After all the shit I'd been through, her brashness, vulgarity and loudness gave me a kick. What she saw in me I have no idea, you'd have to ask her. How could it not have ended badly?

At one time girls wanted to be actresses, but in the 8os they wanted to be TV presenters. During that period Karen was a TV reporter on a local station outside London. I had to buy a television and carry it home in order that, if the aerial was facing in the right direction, I could see her talking about small-time politics, robberies, even the weather.

She didn't earn much but she knew she would. She was aware that she had entered, early on, an industry capable of inexhaustible expansion. If Britain was being de-industrialised – it no longer made cars, boats or clothes – what would people do for a living? Would they be waiters, make computers, sell tourism? Karen seemed to realise there would be little limit on how much TV the public would be able to tolerate in the future. We had four television channels; soon there would be hundreds.

For the numerous unemployed she had no sympathy. Taking good advice from her family, she put her salary into property near Canary Wharf and rented it. Meanwhile, as she had done as a student, she kept a room in a flat in Chelsea, where I stayed sometimes. All manner of girls Karen had been at school and university with would come by, often several at a times, but only those with names ending in 'a' – Lavinia, Davina, Delia, Nigella, Bella, Sabrina, Hannah – sitting on the carpet with their legs out, talking of what they would do now, the world having been opened to women like them. Would they make money in the City or be artists, before becoming mothers?

Most nights Karen took me out into the fast London she knew through her university set. We went to the new clubs, the Groucho in particular, room upon room and floor upon floor of grown-up decadence. It was the hippest place, full of writers, fashionable publishers, pop-promo directors, producers from *The Late Show* and the young movie people working at Channel Four, which had just started making low-budget movies. Often someone would lead us to Derek Jarman's place, a small flat in an old block on the Charing Cross Road. He liked to read from his hand-written journals, and I wanted to be like that, so self-absorbed, as people came and went.

There was, of course, the 'new' kind of shopping. Where my mother would make a list and return with the items on it (perhaps bringing home a treat like chocolate or biscuits), Karen would spend every Saturday shopping because she liked being in shop 'environments', returning with numerous artfully packaged objects she didn't know she needed. People were beginning to buy 'names' – brands – rather than things.

In the evenings there were other parties and new restaurants – with desirable names – where Karen drank ferociously until she staggered. She liked me to be there to help her out the door, into the cab, and into bed, where I'd sit beside her with a bowl awaiting the inevitable up-chuck and the sleep which would follow it.

'Tender is the night,' she'd moan, quoting neither Keats nor F. Scott Fitzgerald, but the pop song. She may have been out drinking until two in the morning but she'd be up for work early the next day, arriving at her desk at eight in the morning and staying there for twelve hours. Women had to 'prove' themselves then.

She didn't have a boyfriend, though I think she had quite a lot of bad sex with older men – the bosses – or with cameramen or others in the crew, as she was often travelling, spending about three nights a week out of London. I can see her now, idly throwing her legs open and looking away, out of the window or across the room, biting her nails and thinking of what she'd wear the next day. When she was away she worried that I was missing her, or lonely. If I spent the evening with someone else she'd ask if I'd had sex with them. If she and I were at a party, she'd tell me who was attractive and who was a likely conquest, and she'd even chat them up for me.

Although Karen and I were together as some sort of couple, it soon became a more or less celibate relationship. Like many people, she didn't really like sex, but would go through with it if she thought the other person badly wanted it. I find it odd now, but I did believe then – without, I admit, having much considered it – that the ideal of the exclusive couple was one which still compelled me, that this unchosen template suited everyone. Even when I was unfaithful to Karen, it seemed right I should experience the correct sum of guilt.

But perhaps our relationship was without passion because, after Ajita, I had no desire to suffer sexual jealousy again. I asked for no power over Karen; her life and body were her own. I wanted to be with a woman I didn't want. If love is the only intensity in town, what sort of love was that?

We did spend many nights together. In bed it would be me, her and an ashtray, the TV always on and her eating ice cream from the tub. We'd read the same magazines, both being interested in the same thing, women and how they became themselves. And we talked simultaneously, because she liked coke. With Karen there was no vulgar chopping with credit cards or snorting through rolled-up fivers from toilet seats. The gear she bought came in cute little bottles with a tiny spoon at the top. It was expensive but she and the other girls who went to her flat in Chelsea Manor Street had lived in a world – quite different to mine and Miriam's – in which there had always been money, and always would be.

I say we didn't touch or kiss. Maybe we were trying to forget about sex because there was too much of it around. As well as studying psychology, philosophy and psychoanalysis, I was developing into a pornographer.

I had left Mother and replaced her with books. At least in my work, I had discovered something I wanted. Whatever I did in life, I was usually bored, always feeeling insufficiently used or stretched. At this time I liked to study, I loved to read and I enjoyed my training, but it was expensive.

I was still seeing Tahir, as well as attending lectures on dreams, the Oedipus complex and the unconscious. I was reading Freud's early disciples, Ferenczi, Adler, Jung, Theodor Reik, and the later analysts, Klein, Winnicott, Lacan. It wasn't a long tradition, about a hundred years' worth, but there was a ton of it, and almost every word in abominable prose. This discourse, saturated in talk of pleasure, provided no enjoyment in itself. If the best thing to be said for reading is that you can do it lying down, Karen would lie with me, watching videos and reading fat shiny paperbacks about people shopping, waiting for her own face to appear on TV.

Then it started: I began to see my first patients, and I soon learned that listening to another person was almost the hardest task you could attempt. Tahir had taught me that the truth wasn't hidden behind a locked door in a dungeon called 'the unconscious', but that it was right there, in front of the patient and analyst, waiting to be heard. The lost object was the key to the language. Freud said one should attend to the unconscious with 'evenly suspended attention'. The therapist's unconscious was the useful tool here, along with the free play of his associations and fantasy. The interpretation, when it came, had to be like a surgeon's incision, in the right place at the right time.

Listening is not only a kind of love, it *is* love. But, sitting with my first analysands, trying to bear the anxiety of hearing someone unknown, whose dreams and ramblings I could not comprehend, I felt, at times, as though I were trying to decode *The Waste Land* at a first reading. I'd even hate the patients and my own clumsiness, as I became dragged into the vortex of their passion, of the spume and irruption of their unconscious. I'd want to flee the room, wondering who was more afraid, analysand or analyst. I was having to learn that this fear – on both sides – was part of the anxiety of hearing the new. It was patient work, learning patience, developing my analytic instinct, creating the time and space so the analysand could hear, or meet, herself. This was how, in the end, I trained myself.

I would go and talk to Tahir about it, and although he was drinking then, and often argumentative – he could be infuriated by the theories of other analysts, particularly Lacan, Freud's most significant heir – he had important and urgent things to pass on. Unintentionally, during a recent session, because I was tired, I found myself in more of a reverie than I was used to. Yet this hadn't made anything worse. Tahir said I'd hit on something useful: my unconscious was more closely in touch with that of the other if I didn't try too hard to understand. I had a tendency, he said, to over-theorise, and to decide too quickly what was going on.

He made me aware, too, that I was part of a tradition of listening. As Schoenberg had gone to Mahler for instruction and guidance, as T. S. Eliot had turned to Pound, so the analysts had handed down learning and procedure. Tahir had been trained by the great child-analyst Winnicott, who in his turn had been analysed by James Strachey and Joan Riviere, both of whom had been analysed by Freud. Having so little knowledge of my subcontinental family past – the Indian threads being severed by father's death – I had little sense of my connection to the past. Being an analyst joined me to another tradition, to another family which would 'hold' me during the insecurity of my training.

As my career started, Karen's faltered. It was a bad day for her when it became obvious she was no good on television, being too nervy. Her big eyes made her look homicidal. Even when she wasn't on cocaine, she was like someone on cocaine, about to burst out of the screen and bite into your windpipe. She was quick enough to know that power in the media rested with the producers, not the presenters, and began to work as an associate producer on a youth programme. I even went along to the studio a few times. What was happening to the world? Young presenters virtually naked, teenage bands, puerile jokes, pranks, interviews with idiots.

'Don't you like it?' she said. 'Perhaps you weren't stoned enough to relax.'

I'd used LSD in my teens, but found the effects of an acid inferno lasted too long, a horror movie you couldn't walk out of. I'd had more than enough adventures in my own head. But working on youth programmes, Karen heard of a new, less solipsistic drug being used in New York clubs, called Ecstasy or E. It took us a while to track some down, it was hard to get in London then. We started to hold Ecstasy parties in her flat, where she had a large circular bath. She liked the new pop: Sade, Tina Turner, The Police, Frankie Goes to Hollywood, Eurythmics. I didn't wake up wanting to hear a new record until later, when Massive Attack released *Blue Lines* – 'you're the book I have open' – during the first Gulf War.

Nights and nights on E, our pupils spinning in what I considered pure hedonism, with the guilt and anxiety it brought – for which I would compensate with days of heavy study – had me thinking about the uses and difficulties of pleasure, the whole question of *jouissance* in a person's life. Ecstasy connected me with others; it made me want to talk, as I disappeared into the dreadful voice of ultimate pleasure, a cheap ticket to the place mystics and psychotics have always headed for.

The music was loud, and the talk facile. Not only that, to prolong the buzz we'd take cocaine, which messed us up. Big new clubs were opening, with huge sound systems, run and owned by public-school boys who were turning the 'underground' into the Thatcherite market overnight. After a time I realised that Karen had more tolerance for these places than I did. Unlike most of the kids there, Karen wasn't committed to the project of unwinding and losing the self. She was at work: observing the clothes, the attitude, while going to the bathroom to note down the words being used. She wanted to turn it all into television.

We went to New York for 'meetings'. I stood on the roof of the hotel looking out at the glittering city for the first time. We began a frantic round of clubs, bars and the famous Knitting Factory. While I wanted to hunt through the numerous second-hand bookshops on the Upper West Side for obscure psychoanalytic books, she was buying us cocaine and trying to get us invited to parties with what she called 'atmosphere'. Londoners, being more cynical and knowing then, were less gullible when it came to celebrity. I began to dislike her; I felt dragged along, like a recalcitrant child and, back in London, made it clear I didn't want to live with her.

Karen was becoming tougher, someone you wouldn't want to work for, as she developed a flair for sacking people. 'Had to be done,' she'd say, as another loser limped out the door. For Karen, if anyone suffered it was their own fault; even if you were a persecuted black South African with no human rights, you had somehow brought the badness on yourself. After a while her callousness stopped bothering me because I saw how unbearable it was to her that anyone would hurt anyone else. For her, because it was unbearable it was untrue, and she didn't have to look at it.

The part of the day we most enjoyed together was breakfast, which we'd have in a Soho café, usually the Patisserie Valérie in Old Compton Street, after picking up the tabloids. The shameless *Sun* was in its prime – the royal family helpless before it – and the other papers imitated it. We'd read bits out to one another, screaming with laughter at the prose. This was before most people realised that the person who'd have the most influence over our time would be Rupert Murdoch – the author of the celebrity culture we inhabit, and clever enough to avoid it himself.

The newspapers were the first to turn wholeheartedly to trash. It hadn't yet reached TV, except through youth programming, where Karen and her pals encouraged nonentities to eat maggots – 'faggots gobbling maggots: what could be more entertaining?' – or share a bath with eels or – why not? – with animal and human faeces. The next day these newly minted celebs would appear in the newspapers, having spent the night with a soap star. Television was now watching us, rather than the other way round.

The papers would celebrate and then desecrate the new stars. I had never liked the punks, but this kind of anarchistic republican amorality appealed to me at times – I guess it was the lack of respect for authority, its destructiveness. At the same time it fitted with the liberal economics of Thatcher. Who could not be amused by the fact that the capitalism unleashed by the Conservatives under Thatcher was destroying the very social values the party espoused?

As we ate our croissants and drank a new thing in London, *caffe lattes*, Karen would fill her notebook with mad ideas for game shows, suitable for breakfast and daytime TV, which had just started. At that time daytime was a huge vacant space, soon to become even more vacant. Programmes were beginning to be made quickly and cheaply; cameras got smaller, and recording tape was of better quality. The contents were cut-price too, since the participants were not movie or even TV stars but 'real' people discovered by researchers, who could become enviable just by appearing on TV. To me it sounded like music hall: television versions of the mad variety shows my grandparents used to take Miriam and I to on our holidays. At the end of the pier at the seaside we'd watch jugglers, knife-throwers and fat comedians telling risqué jokes. After, we'd scoff 'hot sandwiches in gravy'.

For me all this was an amusement but for Karen it was a kind of calling, an opportunity that few people realised was there. I guess I realised the extent of her cultural terrorism when I suggested we might go to see a film which happened to be subtitled. 'No – never!' she cried. 'Not a foreign film you have to read! Are they in slow motion? Can't you feel yourself ageing?'

When I recommended the theatre or a gallery, it wasn't that she refused to go; it was not that attending such things made her feet ache – which wouldn't have surprised me, as she wore stilettos most of the time: even her slippers were four inches from the ground. It was that she considered art to be showing off, empty, worthless, an insult to the public and, if sub-sidised, a waste of public money. 'Tchaikovsky's Crime and Punishment, Chekhov's Last Symphony – yuck, fuck, muck!'

As a Thatcherite, she wanted to be rid of it. Here, at 'the end of history', the television ruling class, the old sensitive if not effete Oxbridge mob along with the monarchy and the Church, would be replaced by 'the people', by which she seemed to mean the ignorant and wildly coarse. I wasn't the only one killing fathers. In the 60s and 70s there was a cult of it, as patri-archy and the phallus were attacked. And what did we end up with, at the end of that iconoclastic decade? Thatcher: a fate worse than a man.

Now, of course, we live in Thatcher's psyche if not her anus, in the world she made, of competition, consumerism, celebrity and guilt's bas-tard son, charity: bingeing and debt. But then, these views were a novelty.

At least, with Karen, I learned to make no distinction between high and low art. I guess I'd been something of a snob before, wondering whether it was healthy to be so moved by Roy Orbison and Dusty Springfield. But Karen unintentionally showed me the futility of such distinctions.

Not that I could interest Karen much in what I was doing; although she left me alone to study, she considered analysis 'unconvincing' as a profes-sion, as though I'd decided to become an astral channeller or soothsayer. I realised this not only when she had difficulty – and showed considerable reluctance, if not embarrassment – in explaining to people what it was I did, but also when she decided, without asking me, that I'd be better off as a TV presenter.

There were few black or brown faces on TV; my fate was to correct this imbalance. I informed her it was hopeless, but she insisted I endure two auditions for the job of presenter on a new TV media show entitled *Television/Television*.

In front of a camera and wearing a borrowed Armani jacket, I had to sit at a desk (on a cushion, as it happened, being little), or on the desk itself. Then I would be instructed to walk around this desk, while saying repeatedly, 'Hallo, good evening and welcome to *Television/Television*. Tonight we have an exclusive interview with Sviatoslav Jarmusch, who claims that digitalisation is the future of this medium. To discuss this, we have in the studio . . .'

I guess I could have done it, and I'd be someone recognisable in TV now, but I fucked it up beautifully. I was bafflingly disappointing, like someone who'd never spoken before.

It wasn't, however, the end of my media career. Karen and I had talked of making porno films to earn money: her producing, me directing, neither of us starring. But she knew enough about the media to realise making such films took too much time; it wasn't a part-time job. It was less of a palaver to write the stuff. I had bought a fast electric typewriter – with a 'golf ball', which flew madly about like a bird caught in a chimney – and I liked writing. After becoming a murderer, was there nothing I considered beyond my talents?

At first I sent in stories to magazines at the low end of the market. When they were published, the editors started asking me to write more. Initially it was fun, trying to organise the story, the rise and fall of which represented coitus itself. I learned to write them quickly.

There's nothing more conventional than the sly prophylactic of pornography, with the end a foregone conclusion. Anna Freud, the eternal virgin, said that in fantasy you can have your eggs cooked anyway you like, except you can't eat them. Relying on fantasies is like trying to devour the menu rather than the meal. For those who want the same thing over and over, that is more than enough. Indeed, it was the same words: I made a list of them, the basic ingredients of word-porn, spicy and resonant – harder, harder, come, come! – and was sure to salt the text with them each time.

However, the magazines also let me work on semi-pornographic material, articles on de Sade, Beardsley, Hugh Hefner, the history of pornographic pictures, for which I enjoyed the reading.

One time I was sent to meet a sleazy guy in a dirty hotel who asked me to write short novels with titles like *The Disciplinarian*. It was big work – almost everything is, I was discovering – though if I got into the groove I could do a dirty book in a weekend. But not for long. If pornography is the junk food of love, I couldn't swallow any more. Being young, I was tempted to add, digress and generally express myself. What did the couples do after sex? Did they find it difficult, embarrassing, boring? What did they do at home? What did they say to their parents? They were barmaids, businessmen, hotel maids, people meeting casually for one reason only, a reason that wasn't compelling enough. The whole pornography scam collapsed when I wrote a novel about a couple married to other people who met only to talk.

'Talk! Anyone can talk! Where the fuck is the fucking fucking?' my man in the hotel yelled, rifling hopelessly through the manuscript and finally frisbeeing it across the room. 'What is this – Plato? It's certainly not *Plato's Retreat*!'

The line between literature and pornography was uncrossable. Breaking the porno spell was like that moment at a party when the lights came on and all you saw were haunted faces and debris. Now pornography is getting emotional, and straight movies more sexual.

It was a strange business, being in a celibate relationship while thinking of sex continuously. I'd discuss the stories with Karen and she'd suggest ideas, often from her own life. This was where our sexual relationship was, in this talk and in my work.

For me, everything was 'good enough' between Karen and I until she became pregnant. Such an event might seem awkward to achieve in a celibate relationship but not, as I discovered, impossible. Platonic love is a gun you don't know is loaded. At her place, going to bed drunk, as we did more often than I'd like to admit, we copulated in our sleep. I remembered enough to know it happened. We both took it for granted that she'd have an abortion. They knew her down at the clinic and I joked that she had an account there; one morning she set off with her overnight bag.

Karen was as tough as any artist with their vision. Occasionally she had to take a lot of contempt from artists and talented people, but it didn't stop her thinking of what they did as rubbish. But the abortion, used by most of her friends as a means of contraception, seemed to smash her.

I was waiting at her flat when she returned, ashen and unable to stand. For two days she lay on the sofa wrapped in a dressing gown. I knew she was ill because she didn't smoke or drink. I was blamed, but I sat it out with her, looking out of the window when I could, until she stood up and began to scream, telling me that I hadn't grasped what this meant to her.

'It was my only chance to have a child! Suppose I don't meet anyone else! Suppose I have to go it alone! And don't you realise I'll have to live with the murder of this child for the rest of my life?'

I was too immature to understand her. From my point of view, she was in her mid-twenties and had plenty of time to breed. I had taken it for granted that for her sex was a business transaction, or a way of spending time with her superiors. It hadn't occurred to me to think about children. As far as I was concerned I was still recovering from my childhood, and thought you might as well call adults recovering children.

She went on, 'The other day I thought: he only likes me because I'm silly, a kind of entertainment. Why would a man want that from a woman? Why were you with me?'

'It never occurred to me not to be with you. We always had a nice time.'

'Except you never loved me. You've been in love with Ajita all this time. You can't accept she's gone,' she said. 'Don't you understand the simplest things? Me, the woman, wants to be wanted – wanted more than other women! Without that there's nothing. You think we're friends?'

'Aren't we?'

'I have been in love with you.'

I apologised and I listened to her; at least I knew how to do that. But I sickened her, and my restlessness caused her to banish me. None of this pleased me. She'd wanted me to give her a baby but had no thought for what I wanted. Indeed, so little had I impressed my desire on her that I appeared to be hardly in the equation.

I wasn't doing well. Two relationships and two murders. I was on the way to becoming a serial killer. Karen had been an attempted treatment for the hurt I'd suffered with Ajita, which had made me phobic of romantic proximity. But I discovered that just because you don't love a woman it doesn't follow that she can't hurt you, that you won't suffer, particularly if you hurt her. Yet it was still a loss, and all losses, even when there are gains, leave their traces, reminding you of other losses, and all must be mourned, always incompletely.

After the split, I had wanted to remain friends with her, but for a long time we were rarely in touch. She began a relationship with, and later married, a TV producer who was envious of me, but we never entirely fell out.

'Wakey-wakey,' Karen was saying to me. 'We're nearly there.' We had been driving for miles through narrow lanes; at last we turned onto a rough, unmade road. 'I've got a feeling,' she said, 'one of us is going to get laid this weekend.'

'Goodie,' I said. 'Let's hope it's you.'

CHAPTER TWENTY-TWO

We had come to a high wall topped with barbed wire that we followed until we arrived at a big gate. Karen wound down the window and spoke into a grille beside the gate which, when it rolled slowly open, revealed a country house.

In the yard outside was standing Mustaq's boyfriend, Alan, not quite on both feet but successfully holding a joint and a glass of wine. He was giggling to himself and examining a large black iron cobweb with an iron spider – painted red – in the middle of it. 'I made that sculpture!' he shouted. 'That's art, that is! Hi guys! Welcome! Enjoy!'

Moments later Karen was in his arms. Soon, in the living room, Alan was opening a bottle, before asking a member of the staff – who I recognised from London – to show me to my room in the converted barn, which was where the guests stayed. 'Barn', of course, gave no clue to the luxury Mustaq could afford and liked to show his guests.

Karen and I had arrived early; we'd both wanted to get away from London. As I'd hoped, this gave me time to tramp across the fields which surrounded Mustaq's house. He'd told me, when he came in to meet us, 'As far as you can I see, I own it. Everything else belongs to Madonna. My fields are rented to local organic farmers, but please feel free to trudge through them as you wish.'

After two hours in the fields I returned to the house, where I looked at the luxuriant garden. This was Alan's domain: he did everything himself – flowers, herbs, grasses, ponds – and then put his iron sculptures out, dotted about the place like huge paperclips. He had become an artist; in London he would have a show in a major gallery; everyone would come, including Ron Wood of the Rolling Stones.

Mustaq had suggested I might like a swim after my walk. I had already noticed the pool, enclosed in a glass building to the side of the main house. Now, as I walked towards it, something I saw through the glass doors made me stop.

I had spotted a head above water, wearing a black swimming cap. I watched the woman climb from the pool and put on a dressing gown and flip-flops. For a moment she was looking towards me. Whether it was short-sightedness or because she didn't recognise me – so old or changed was I – she stared in my direction and I stared back. Neither of us made a gesture.

Not wanting her to think I'd turned away – if, indeed she had recognised me, which I doubted – I stood there, gazing at her indistinct outline through the thick glass beaded with moisture. Eventually she went down the steps towards the showers and changing rooms under the house. There it went, the body I had loved and wanted more than any other.

I was aware that Mustaq would want to have intense and fervent discussions. I needed to talk to him too. But I had not even guessed that the weekend was going to include Ajita. The moment I'd waited for had arrived. Soon we would be able to say everything we had yearned to say. But where would we begin, and where would the talk take us?

Nothing, now, would be as simple as it had been during those years when all I had to do was miss her.

I went to my room and sat at the window. In the courtyard, one of Mustaq's staff was brushing the tyres of his employer's Mustang. In the distance were fields bounded by a motorway, beyond which was the outline of the town. The clothes I'd driven down in, which I'd flung on the floor as I did at home, had been folded on a chair. The contents of my holdall had been hung up in closets, and my old trainers, not the most pristine, had been cleaned.

In an attempt to calm myself, to stop pacing, I lay down for a while, only to be woken by a loud disembodied voice. It wasn't paranoia: Mustaq had had speakers installed in the rooms, and I was being called to supper.

I showered and changed, thinking of Ajita's eyes on me at last. Regarding myself in the mirror – and the lines and flaws I had become indifferent to: now when I looked at myself, I saw nothing of interest – I wondered what she would see.

Crossing from the barn to the main house with Karen, who had been napping in the next room to me, I saw that the forecourt now resembled a car showroom. We were passing Alan's sculpture and I was beginning to tell Karen that one of Freud's disciples, Karl Abraham, had written a paper on the spider as symbol of the female genitalia: it represented the woman with a penis and therefore the possibility of castration. Naturally Karen didn't show much interest in this.

She did perk up when she noticed that the iron gates were closing once more. In the yard two self-regarding stars were now getting out of a sports car, looking around as though trying to make out where they were and how they'd got there. Karen slapped both hands to her face to make a 'Beatle scream'.

'Who is that?' I whispered. I learned that it was the Asian actor Karim Amir, fresh from a rehab near Richmond. I said, 'Isn't that Stephen Hero, getting out of the car after him?'

'Not Stephen Hero, for fuck's sake,' Karen said, striking me on the arm. 'Who the hell's that? It's Charlie Hero. Charlie. He's a Charlie and don't you forget it this evening or ever!'

I was delighted to see Karen had retained her integrity and was still capable of being impressed by the famous. Years ago she had, of course, been wildly impressed by anyone famous – indeed, by anyone who knew anyone famous – and still the celebrated had not disappointed her.

Karen led me into the kitchen for a glass of champagne and a cigarette.

'What's wrong? Are you nervous?' she said, brushing down my jacket.

'Terrified,' I said. 'I don't know why. You're the one who's good on these occasions.'

She was giggling. 'Are my breasts too on show?'

'You are virtually topless, and indeed,' I said, looking her over, 'virtually bottomless. The heels are great. Make the most of it, I say.'

'That's what I thought. Jamal, I'm glad you like it. A lot of the other men here will be short-sighted.' She held up a bottle. 'Let's not waste all this fucking drink – there's buckets of the juice here.'

'Pour me another.'

'Get it down you.' She was looking around the big kitchen. 'It is true, the rich are different. They don't have any clutter. They have people to throw things away for them, ruthlessly. I always thought I'd be rich,' she said. 'I took it for granted in the 80s. Didn't you?'

I said, 'I was too foolish to understand the real pleasure of money. You've done okay, though.'

'That's not enough. We've both let ourselves down, Jamal.'

We watched Mustaq's staff moving about quickly and silently, up and down the stairs, in their smart but casual uniforms. Not only did they not look at the guests, they lowered their heads as we passed.

Fifteen minutes later Karen and I entered the dining room together. At the end of the room was a grand piano; on the wall hung gold discs, photographs and guitars. Karen spotted Charlie and Karim immediately, and went over to sit with them.

I was holding back, hesitating until I knew for certain – until I could see it was true. Ajita was at supper.

She wore a black dress; her arms were bare, apart from a silver bracelet. I looked for her wedding ring, but was too far away to see. She'd always worn expensive clothes and still seemed to, with a hint of ostentation, looking like a woman you'd glance twice at in a Milan restaurant. Her hair was shining, black; it was unchanged, but her head was half-turned away from me, and she was laughing.

Karen was gesturing at me to come and sit down. I had my own excitement to deal with and stood where I was, wanting this moment to last, waiting for Ajita to look at me, knowing quite well that when she did there would certainly be trouble. Of which kind, I had no idea, but how could the world not trip a little, after such a sight?

When she did glance over, I saw her start suddenly and then take me in, her lips parting and her eyes widening. She watched me looking at her. I could feel the readjustment of perspective between us, as fantasy and reality crashed together and began to realign. Neither of us were students now; we were more than middle-aged.

She began to smile and so did I. She got up then. One of us had to do something. We were kissing and embracing, and swinging one another around until we were embarrassed.

When we were done her brother, not the only one watching but the most attentive, came and stood behind us, leaning down on both our shoulders as we dabbed at our eyes.

'My darling sweety sweets, I'm sorry I didn't tell either of you that you might meet tonight. I was afraid that one of you would change your mind. Was that wrong of me?'

'I don't know,' I said. 'But I think we'll be fine.'

'Yes,' said Ajita. She turned to me with a determined smile. 'So, how have you been? What's been going on?'

'Quite a lot, actually,' I said. 'There's years of it.'

'And with me too,' she said. 'Years of it.' We picked up our glasses and touched them together. She laughed, 'You always said "actually". I'm so glad you haven't changed.'

'How have you changed?'

'I guess you'll find out soon enough,' she replied, leaning over and kissing me on the cheek.

CHAPTER TWENTY-THREE

It was a long table; I guessed that thirty people could sit around it. There were half that number present, but more Londoners kept arriving, driving up for the evening or weekend and coming in to eat.

Karen was sitting opposite Ajita and she talked continuously, as she did when nervous. This didn't prevent her trying to get a good look at Ajita.

Omar Ali came and sat beside me. Charlie and Karim were further down the table, with people I didn't know. Knighthoods – that prosthetic for the middle-aged – were being discussed, and whether it was a good idea to accept one. Then the subject was whether Karim should appear on *I'm a Celebrity . . . Get me Out of Here!*

Charlie argued against it, saying Johnny Rotten had lost more than his mystique by appearing. But as Karim, after acting in British soaps, had been living in America for years, mostly playing either torturers or the tortured in bad movies, he didn't have any mystique to lose. Charlie had, of course, already said no, and was unsure whether to regret it or not.

Meanwhile, I turned to Ajita. When, years ago, Ajita was about to masturbate me – one of our favourite pastimes – she would rub her tongue on the palm of her hand as a preparation for the work ahead, a gesture I found unconscionably exciting. Later, when we were in a class together, we'd make the gesture to one another, and giggle. Now, when she turned to me, I repeated the sign. For a moment there was no recognition, before she began to laugh, and gave me her own demonstration of the long-lost lick of love.

After supper, but while most people were taking coffee and beginning on the brandy, Mustaq joined me. 'Come,' he said. 'Can we talk a little?'

He and I went upstairs to a large room with a long window overlooking Mustaq's land. While Mustaq gave instructions to the staff, I noticed that there were, on a side table, numerous photographs. Looking closer I realised they weren't what I expected: George with Elton John, George with Bill Clinton and Dolce and Gabbana, the stuff everyone had in their house. No, they were family photographs, pieces of frozen time which seemed, at that moment of the uncanny, to freeze me. As I picked one up, I noticed Mustaq looking at me.

'That's Mother.' He came over. 'Did you meet her?'

'She was in India when Ajita and I were together. I wish I had met her.'

'She's still alive, and still beautiful, though lashingly bad tempered,' he said. 'She's been here a couple of times.'

Less than a year after her first husband's murder, their mother had remarried in India, to the rich executive she'd been having an affair with. She often came to London, where they had a flat in Knightsbridge. She was one of those foreign women floating about Harrods and Harvey Nichols for consumables unavailable in the Third World. Did she ever go back to the house in Kent? No; she didn't like it the first time. She didn't suffer from nostalgia, either.

Another photograph: one I'd never expected to see again. It was me, in Mushy Pea's bedroom in the mid-70s, before our wrestle, I guessed. I had some kind of embarrassed smirk on my face, but at least I had plenty of dark hair. I supposed that Mustaq had displayed the photograph just for me.

'Yes, you,' he said. 'Fresh young meat, eh?'

'I wish I'd made more of it.'

He picked up another picture. 'Him – you cannot see.'

It was Ajita I noticed first in the photograph, a little younger than when I first met her; she was standing arm-in-arm with the father I had murdered, a massive dose of adrenalin in the heart stunning him.

I could feel Mustaq looking at me as I recalled that night in the garage, trying to picture the father's face and compare it to what I had in front of me. I had no photographs of Ajita, or of Wolf or Valentin. The only photograph I had was one of the father, cut from the newspaper, which I hadn't seen for years, and which must have been thrown out when Mother moved.

'Do you miss him?' I asked.

Mustaq replaced the picture. 'He would have hated all that I am. I can't imagine him having supper with Alan. But maybe he'd have appreciated my wealth and success.'

'That normally brings people around.'

'Are you pleased to see my sister?'

'Thank you Mustaq. Yes – delighted, though we haven't spoken much yet.'

'You've certainly been looking at one another.'

'Indeed. Is she with her husband and children?'

'I took them all to dinner in New York. When I told her I had seen you in London, and that you were coming to the country for the weekend, she came to life. She phoned me continuously, and began to move very quickly. Though she hates to leave the house, she brought no one with her. I suspect she might be ready for an encounter. Jamal, you lucky guy, you're all she's been waiting for.'

'I'd better not let her down.'

Mustaq lifted my wrist and looked at it, stroking my arm ironically. 'You've taken the watch off. What I want now is information. I know it was a long time ago, but how in God's name did you really get that thing?'

I reached into my pocket and drew out the watch. I couldn't look at it now without wishing I could wind it back until before the moment it was given to me. My attempted good deed had brought more hell into my life than I could handle. Mustaq's father was a ghost who still wouldn't take his hands from my throat and, I feared, never would. The one thing you can never kill is a name. I wanted to cry out, *Will the dead never leave us alone?*

I gave it to him and sighed. 'You can take it.'

He looked surprised. 'It's not mine really.'

'Nor mine, I guess. Please.'

He removed his own watch and replaced it with his father's. Tapping it, he said, 'Thank you. I have to ask you this. Why did you deny that it was my father's?'

'I wasn't able to say how I got it.'

'Why not?'

'It's a painful subject, Mustaq, going back a long time.'

'Painful for you or for me?'

'I will tell you. It may change your view of your father.'

'You don't know what my view is. *I* don't know what my view is. And I am almost an adult.'

'Okay.' I said. 'Now?'

'Yes, if you don't mind. Think how many years I've waited.'

The others were coming upstairs and quickly picking glasses of champagne from silver trays. Mustaq followed me across the room to a quieter spot, where we sat down together. The story took only a moment to make up.

I said, 'This was not long before he died. I was at your house with your sister when your father came home. I couldn't let on that I was her boyfriend, so I said I was waiting for you. He laughed and told me I was wasting time.'

'He said that a lot.'

'He wanted me to help him with a box of papers he couldn't carry himself. Upstairs in your bedroom, in that small dressing room just off it, full of suitcases, he took off the watch. He told me it was valuable, it was a gift, he was giving it to me. I said I didn't want it, but he insisted on stuffing it into my pocket. I noticed his trousers were open. He was touching himself. He took hold of me and forced me to caress him. Then we brought the box downstairs. That's all,' I said. 'I'm sorry I had to tell you.' While he was thinking, I said, 'Mustaq, did he touch you?'

'No! Me – never. Why are you saying that? He didn't go that way. He hated homos!' He stood up suddenly and stared out of the window. 'For fuck's sake – why are you telling me this! I have to consider it all now!' He was staring at me; his tone became absurdly gracious. 'And I have to apologise to you. On behalf of my family, I am sorry for what my father did to you.'

'Will you speak to Ajita about it?'

'She's fragile. She has a lot of depression, at least two weeks a month she is almost catatonic, and I really worry about her.' Then he said, 'Do you know whether he did this to anyone else?' I said nothing. 'Jamal, in your professional experience, do people who do these things do them to others?'

'My answer will be of no use to you. It depends on the subject's history. Often, people do it for a particular period in their lives, after a separation or when they are depressed, and never again. I think we're talking about a version of incest rather than paedophilia. They are different.'

He wasn't listening. 'The damned filthy man, with his bloody secrets. Do you hate him?'

'Me? No. It did disturb me. It shook me up. I guess it might have helped me in the direction I was going – to analysis. It spoiled my week but not my life.'

'Now I'm suffocating!,' he said. I noticed his hands were on his own throat, as though he was trying to strangle himself. 'I need to get out. I must walk freely for a bit.'

I watched him hurry out of the room. Alan went to him, but Mustaq brushed him aside. Alan looked at me and shrugged. I took another glass of champagne and wondered where Ajita was.

She wasn't outside. From the window I could see Mustaq in the illuminated grounds, pacing, his arms thrashing. After a while he seemed to make up his mind about something and disappeared into another part of the house.

'Look,' he said, when he reappeared. He was tapping his arm.

'What is it?'

'I've already had an allergic reaction to the watch. My wrist is red and a little swollen. There's a . . . throbbing!' I looked closely but could see nothing. He took the watch off and put it in his pocket. He said, 'I went to Ajita's room and opened up to her. I couldn't stop myself. I told her what you said about our father. I wanted her to know. I asked what she thought. You're lucky.'

'In what way?'

'She believed you, saying you were always a trustworthy person, with no reason to make up a story about our father.

He went on, 'The weird thing was: I thought it would devastate her, to learn father was like that. Wouldn't such knowledge do that to a person? To me it was an explosion. I watched her closely and she didn't seem shocked or even surprised.'

'Do you know why?'

'Sorry?'

I said, 'What sort of man was your father?'

'He was strict. I think I mean stern. There was always reason to be afraid of him. But he wasn't religious and never prayed. He'd have despised those mad mullahs and extreme Islam fascist wallahs. When Papa was alive, intelligent people thought superstition was dying out. Of course he hated the whites, particularly after his experience with the documentary. They were tricky and their racism was deep.

'But there was a barrier between him and me. Since before I was eleven I suspected I might be gay.'

'You did?'

'The other boys called me a fat Paki bummer. I guess that just about clarified everything. One of our cousins told Papa I wanted to be a dancer or hairdresser. Papa had already noticed I had a weak handshake. So his response – that fags should be killed – made it obvious that this was not only unacceptable but a crime.

'I expect you know it, but I was in love with you and couldn't wait for you to visit. I wondered what you wanted me to wear, what you wanted me to be. I read all those books thinking you might decide to test me on them. At the same time, whenever I was alone with Papa – only when we watched cricket or boxing together – I asked his advice about women. "How do you get a girl to be nice to you? Should you kiss her on the first date? What about marriage, should you bring it up sooner or later?" I knew he liked to talk about such things. The stupid indirect shit the straights have to go through. What's it laughably called – seduction? At least it made my father feel like a big man.'

'But never enough of one?'

'How could he be? All the time we lived in that house he was anxious about keeping the factory going. He said his only ambition outside work was to walk across Africa. But the strike made him so crazy he started to do weird stuff.'

'What sort?'

'I'd hear him walking about at night. Doors banging, groans, shouts even –'

'Do you know why?'

'He was drinking. Staggering around blotto. He'd drink half a bottle of Jack Daniels when he came home after work, and finish the rest by morning. When I opened my door in the morning, he'd be on the floor. I was scared to come out of my room. Ajita and I had to pull off his dressing gown and pyjamas and drag him into the shower. It was hard for her, she had to do everything.' He wiped his eyes. 'Did she tell you about it?'

'A little.'

'I'd throw the bottle away before I went to school. No wonder all I learned was how to masturbate. It was worse for Ajita.'

'Why do you say that?'

'Ajita adored her father, Jamal. I've never seen two closer people. As a girl she'd wait by the door for him to come home. In the evenings, while Mum was cooking, she'd oil and comb his hair, walk on his back, wash him in the bath. He'd tell her stories about India and Africa. I'm telling you, I *was* left out. When he was killed, I've never seen anyone more devastated. She hardly spoke for three months.'

'And your mother had already gone away.'

'Yes.'

'Had she left your father?'

He said, 'No one said that. But how could she be with him? She considered him a failure. He thought if he made enough money she'd come back. One day, according to Father, we'd be free of anxiety, because we'd be rich. Before then he had no time for anything else, for sport, culture, nature –

love, even. He didn't know what we were doing at school.' He leaned towards me. 'I had a voodoo doll – of father – which I stuck little nails into. I was convinced I'd killed him!'

'You wanted all the credit.'

'If he were alive today he would disapprove of everything about me. I have to be glad he's dead – which is difficult . . .'

I said, 'You remember when you asked me to go away with you?'

'Oh Jamal, I'm so embarrassed!'

'Why don't we run away?' Mustaq said to me the next time I went to the house. Last time we'd wrestled; now he told me there was something he just had to show me in his bedroom. 'What is it?' I asked. 'My haircut.' he replied. 'David Jones would be proud of you,' I said.

He was standing close to me, as he liked to, touching, if not rubbing, my arm. 'I know where my father keeps his money. He's got thick wads of it in an envelope under his socks.'

'What for?'

'He often says we may need to leave in a hurry again. The racists might come for us.'

'You're the one who wants to leave in a hurry. But why?'

'It's not much good here, is it?'

He said this with such sadness I'd have kissed him if I hadn't feared he'd kiss me.

'Why with me?' I asked.

'You're the most exciting person I've met.'

'Look,' I said, startled, 'let me give you something –'

I went to my college bag. Apart from books on philosophy, I was carrying music magazines, a couple of novels and an anthology of Beat poets. I gave them to him.

'Feed your head, man,' I said. 'I know you already have music, but I'll drop more books and mags off tomorrow. You know what you want to do when you grow up?'

'A fashion designer,' he said. 'But don't tell anyone.'

'Like who? Your sister?'

'She knows already.'

'Your father, then. I think I will tell him.'

I pretended to move off. He grabbed me, 'Don't do that. Keep quiet, please! I'll do anything for you –'

'Only joking,' I said. 'Why are you so afraid? Does he hurt you?'

In the weeks after this conversation I took a lot of stuff to Mustaq. He read so quickly and gratefully I was soon ransacking my bedroom for books I'd bought in London. It gave me a reason to visit Ajita, to sit around in her

always wore black. You looked smooth in suits, particularly with the baseball boots.

'But in my view, you looked best with nothing on and your lovely cock out. You were thin then, with a fine tanned body, and boy could you do it a lot – you guys were horny!' He went on, 'Other times I'd sit with you in the kitchen when Ajita was upstairs changing or on the phone. I loved it when you talked to me.

'But I couldn't have expected you to guide me. I should have been a doctor. That's what my father wanted.'

He was looking at me, smiling; I was trying to take all this in. Then he stood up, gave me a long look, as if wondering himself about the strangeness of our conversation, and excused himself, going to join the others, most of whom had now come into the room.

I watched Ajita with a friend of Mustaq's, laughing as she used to, putting her hand over her mouth as though she'd just said something outrageous, perching here and there to talk, helping her brother and Alan run the weekend.

When I rejoined the group, I discovered from Alan, who did a good imitation of him, that Omar had decided to drive into town 'to see who was around', adding, 'You see, I never lost the common touch!'

It turned out that Omar had rung to say he was 'stuck' in town and needed to be rescued. He wouldn't be able to make it back alone. Alan asked for volunteers 'to go in'. Apparently the town, a triumph of post-war socialist planning, was a sewer, full of tattooed beasts and violent zombies, with vomit and blood frothing in the gutters. I couldn't wait to see it.

There was a pub Omar liked to visit when he came up, where the local lost children, most of them junkies, listened to savagely loud music. At least one of these kids would be fuckable.

Omar was too drunk to return to Mustaq's and didn't want to leave his car behind. Of all his crimes, drunk driving might turn out to be the most viably punishable. Also, he had to get up early in the morning to fulfil one of his duties, which was to sit in a large black car surrounded by motorcycle outriders and greet some foreign dignitary at Heathrow on behalf of the Queen and the government, and then accompany this variety of murderers and torturers to their hotel while making small talk.

Omar said, 'I have to be quite careful. I'm always getting the words "dignitary" and "dictator" mixed up.' He was, apparently, often in bad shape for some of this 'meeting and greeting'.

Alan required one of us to drive Omar's car back. So, fancying a change,

I went into town with Karen, following Alan, who knew the pub. On the way out I said to Mustaq, 'Why don't you come with us?' He shook his head and smiled. As we got in the car Karen told me that the price Mustaq paid for his wealth was the fact that he couldn't walk on the street, go to the shop or pub without being mobbed, questioned, photographed.

We drove past a lurid building called the Hollywood Bowl, a multiplex featuring a drive-through McDonalds, security guards and hooded kids wandering around windswept, concrete spaces.

'Why so fast, Karen? We won't get lost. Are you drunk?'

'Yeah. You want to get out?' She said, 'I should have killed you five minutes ago.'

'What stopped you?'

'So that is Ajita. The one you really loved and were faithful to. The one you kept expecting to return. You would lie there, my darling, "thinking", with a book open on your chest, and you'd smile to yourself. I knew that's when you were with her in your mind. I absolutely totally *hated* you then.'

'Are you now pleasantly disappointed?'

'She's an ordinary woman of a certain age. The age of desperation. But I can see it,' she said, 'if I put my glasses on and look hard – what she had. The cuteness, the girlie voice, the desire to please. Unfortunately, I was supposed to feel sorry for her all that time. What sadness you moped about in, which I had to endure! Even to me she seemed mystically important. Wasn't her damned father murdered during a strike?'

'Something like that.'

'I only married the wrong person because of the whole mess. You made me feel second-best for so long I ended up with the first person who gave me their attention.'

'It would have to be my fault,' I said.

'Nothing cheered you up, even when you went to see that bloody analyst the whole time. After a session you'd spend hours writing it down. Didn't you ever see that analysis doesn't make people kinder or funnier or more intelligent? It makes them more self-absorbed. They start using all those awful words like "transfer" and "cathartic". Did I want to hear about your dreams, about your mother and sister, when we were in the middle of a disaster? Didn't that occur to you?'

'It was my vocation and it interested me more than anything.'

'I hate to say this, Jamal, but you are intelligent and you've done nothing with it but learn to say all those words which are no use to anyone.'

'Shit, you are in a bad mood.'

'I am now.'

I said, 'I'm definitely not going to fuck you tonight.'

'Bastard, it'll be the Indian girl, won't it? Why do you have to be so cruel, Jamal? Doesn't it matter to you, cunt-teaser?'

We discovered Lord Ali, with his jacket and shoes off and shirt half open, lying across several chairs in the back room of the pub, 'holding court'. This king-like position wasn't only due to his personal magnetism, or to curiosity among the poor about the Lord's work relieving the condition of the proletariat, but owed much to the fact he was buying drinks for everyone in the pub.

'Oh fucking Christ!' said Alan, as we approached. The Lord's eyes, as Alan put it, were like 'two pools of inky semen'.

We caught Omar telling the assembled drinkers, many of them already slumped, that he'd met the Queen on three occasions and sat in her carriage once. Last week he'd found himself alone in a room with her. She was concerned that Labour was going to attempt to ban shooting as well as hunting. '"We had a lovely shoot the other day,"' he said fruitily. Lord Omar said this several times, louder and louder, until it started to sound not only pornographic but an arrestable offence.

Alan was ready to pull him out of there before he said anything else that might turn up in the *News of the World*, or bring information about their weekends to the wider world, but Omar wasn't ready to leave. He hadn't managed any physical contact. Alan spoke to one of the kids and came away with some decent weed, and while the cock-drunk good Lord was satisfied in the toilet, Alan and Karen played pool.

I sat at the bar lining up vodka shots. The barman knew we were friends of George, and told me what spoiled, over-privileged rats we were 'up at the big house', compared to the people around here. 'What we need,' he said, as though it had never occurred to anyone before, 'is a revolution. Look at that,' he said, pointing at Lord Ali, who was emerging from the toilet with wet knees and a pasty-faced kid while murmuring 'Such, such were the boys . . .'

The barman went on: 'Some of these people work up there. We know how to get in. One day we'll all charge up there in a mob and pull it down and burn the lot of yer!'

'It's a good idea,' I said. 'But sadly, you're all too stoned to do anything like that.'

'Outta my pub, how dare you!' he said. 'Stoned? Who? You're barred for life!'

I had called the others, and was already stepping over someone in a move towards the door. Omar was being dragged along by Karen and Alan while singing 'Land of Hope and Glory' and yelling 'Thank you so much, my darling subjects, for a lovely shoot! A lovely shoot is all one wants!'

The landlord was spitting with fury and threatening us with the police.

Karen squashed Alan and the Lord into her car; I drove the Lord's motor back, tearing up the lanes.

At the house people were talking in the living room, but most had moved to what Alan referred to as the 'Brian Jones' pool. It was fashionable for rich people like Mustaq to buy art and photography. The corridor between the pool and the changing area was full of decent photographs, including one of a woman standing up to piss against a bridge.

Around the pool people were smoking; others were dancing, or swimming naked. Those vile bodies had cost a fortune to maintain and were made to be exhibited. Charlie Hero was in good shape; even his scars glowed and the slim bolt through his cock brought out its veiny contours.

Other friends of Alan and Mustaq had turned up by now, dancers, hairdressers, make-up artists, camp young black men, angelic boys, some in over-tight or shiny clothing, others keen to show-off their nipple clips. Some of these characters looked as though they hadn't seen daylight for some years. Few women would get laid tonight, I thought. This might be my chance to see whether I really was still uninterested, or whether I'd just been through a discouraging time.

Charlie had attached his iPod to the pool sound system, and suddenly a record came on from my youth, the Lovin' Spoonful's 'Do You Believe in Magic?', so full of musical sunshine and optimism that Karim and I both began to laugh, glancing at one another and laughing again. Like him, I'd been a little too young to be independently active at that time, but the mid-60s were where I was formed, and what did any of that love mean now, in these dirty days?

I swam a little, looking out for Ajita, but couldn't see her. While I dried off, Karim, his earnest brown eyes peering out from between the parentheses of his hair, offered me some coke. Although I fancied it, I wanted to sleep tonight. I smoked a joint, then someone gave me a double espresso and a chunk of chocolate. I took a diazepam and decided to go to bed, a relatively early night but with plenty to think about.

I was lying down, wondering what I'd listen to on my iPod – words can go so far, and then there is music – when there was a knock on the door.

'Hello,' I called.

'Can I come in?'

It was Ajita in a satin dressing gown. She came over and sat on the edge of the bed.

I took her hand. 'So you found me, then.'

'At last,' she said. 'Just you and me. Now we have some time together. All night, I hope. Will you stay awake? Do you want to hear me now?'

'Of course,' I replied. 'It's you I've been waiting for.'

CHAPTER TWENTY-FOUR

She took my hand. 'Earlier today, I believed I saw you from the pool. Then I thought no, it's a ghost and I've gone mad. In New York, Mustaq asked me if I wanted to see you again, but said he couldn't guarantee that you'd show up. But you did. Was that for me? Or shouldn't I ask?'

'Your American accent is charming.'

'Oh, don't say that. I've been trying to get rid of it and seem more Indian again, particularly since Indians have become so hip.'

'Yes, there can't be one of them who hasn't written a novel.'

'And it's embarrassing to be American when people my colour are under such constant suspicion. Going through airports is a nightmare for all of us, even for Mustaq. We all feel a step away from Guantánamo. Orange doesn't suit me.'

'Nor most people.'

'It's been so bad I'm thinking of staying in London for a while. I loved London, when you would take me about. I haven't been back since. I couldn't bear to see it again.' Her hand was on my shoulder. 'You don't need to get up, Jamal. Don't do anything. We don't need more light on. I'll pull the curtains.' She said, 'I know you're there and that's all I need. Mustaq told me what he knew of your story and I have read your books.'

'Did you tell him your story?'

'What d'you mean, mine?' I said nothing. She went on, 'Jamal, you're the person who really knows me. You were always my true love,' she said. 'Even my husband knew that. He used to say, "There is someone else stopping us from being close."' She leaned over me, kissing me on each cheek and on the lips, pressing her fingers through my hair. 'You've hardly changed. Your hair's grey, but it still stands on end, like a fluffy chick. You're a little lined and no longer all skin and bone. But you're distinguished looking, a man who's lived an important life.'

'Christ, no!'

She said, 'I was watching you at supper. You're even more good-looking than I remembered. What an attractive, smart man, he is, I thought. One who has been loved and wanted.'

'That is a kind thing to say. If it is true it means a lot. I will try to be more grateful.'

'I think you probably are.' She said, 'Who was the woman sitting opposite me? We were introduced but I didn't catch her name. She was observing you like a hawk, when she wasn't glaring at me. Was she one of your wives?'

'I have been married, but just the once, unusually. Not to her, though. I am still married – or rather, not yet divorced. But I did go out with the woman you're talking about – Karen – after you went away.'

'Was it a successful love?'

'Not from her point of view. I was still getting over you, I guess. It took a long time – probably because I always thought you'd be coming back in a little while.'

She was quiet. 'Jamal?'

'Yes?'

'Please don't say it's too late. We're not old. Or am I too far gone for you? Look.' She stood up and opened her dressing gown, then let it drop to the floor. 'This is me. Where I am.'

I looked at her, both familiar and unfamiliar now. 'What would your husband say?' I said quietly, before regretting it.

She put her gown on again and lay down on the bed. I stood up and took off my clothes.

While she looked at me, I said, 'I don't know what I want to happen between us. It's been a long time. All we can do is give it space.'

'There is still time, we have that. I will wait for you, as you waited for me.' She pulled the sheets over her. 'How I need to sleep with someone again. After years of trying to get my daughter out of my bed, she will no longer keep me company. My husband and I have our own rooms, in fact our own countries now. So to spend a night with a man . . . It moves me so.'

We lay there in the dark, not touching. Certainly people of our age, unless they are narcissists, wouldn't want anyone to see their bodies. I'd seen Ajita in the pool, of course. Her flesh hadn't aged badly, but she seemed to have shrunk into herself, as though she wanted to make herself smaller, like a younger actress playing the part of an older woman.

'Yes,' she said, 'I know I am like an old woman now. I could see that in your eyes. My sexual charm, beauty – all gone.'

'Mine, too. I was just thinking of how much we loved to sunbathe in your garden at the side of the house. You were almost black. Now no one does that. You remember how I had to pretend to be Mushy Pea's best friend?'

'What I want is that the four of us – you, me, Wolf and Valentin – meet again. Can you organise a reunion?'

'They disappeared soon after you did – to make their fortunes in France.'

'How did they do?'

'They didn't tell me.'

'What a shame.' She said, 'In New York I buy furniture, or clothes. I give something to charity every day, and I buy something new every day. It's a simple system – in and out.

'I walk in the park, visit friends, and when my brother's on tour or doing a TV show I design the costumes. It's a lot of work, a proper job. I do yoga, Kabala, anything that doesn't involve touching. If I don't feel fabulous within a few weeks, I try something else. All suicides kill others too, I am aware of that, so there is no way out for me. In the end my doctor gave me something –'

'An antidepressant?'

'Whatever. It keeps massive anxiety away. I want to feel normal.'

'It's more normal to experience anxiety than it is to be blank.'

'What I feel most of the time is dread,' she said. 'As though some catastrophe is about to befall me.'

'It has. Do you remember what you told me your father did to you?'

'Why shouldn't I remember that? I don't hate him. He was having a terrible time. It's not your family.'

'At college once you told me how much you loved him. "He's so tender," you said.'

She said, 'Is that so strange? He always kissed and petted me. He'd lose his temper and call us stupid, but he was never not a fond father.' She was lying back on the pillow. 'You wanted me to be a feminist and gave me those books. It was new then. You remember that woman – Fiona? She was one of the organisers against my father. I saw her on the picket line and then at college. She was hugely fat with her breasts wobbling everywhere, wearing dungarees and big earrings.'

'She was on TV last night, defending a bill to keep people without trial.'

'Is she thin? Jamal, did you want me to be a different kind of woman?'

I said, 'We were a dissenting generation. People like your father – we called them capitalists then – we hated on principle. In other European cities, people like us were kidnapping and killing capitalists.'

'You didn't want to do that. You couldn't kill anyone.'

I said, 'I was always furious with my parents, my father in particular. It seemed odd to me that you loved your parents without any hatred.'

We were silent; I thought she'd fallen asleep. 'Jamal,' she said, 'earlier this evening my brother told me what my father did to you. Why didn't you say anything to me? I told you everything but you didn't reciprocate.'

'How could I have added to your troubles?' I went on, 'When you were in India I was frantic missing you. My first thought in the morning was: will this be the day she rings? It was a terrible separation. For a while it broke me.'

She ran her hands over her face and through her hair. 'No, no, Jamal! You're saying I didn't think of you? I even wrote you letters – you remember those thin blue airmail letters? – which I never posted. I loved London, but how could I go back there after the strike?.

'My nightmares weren't about my father raping me night after night, but about that screaming mob outside the factory, students like us hurling lumps of wood and bricks. They reduced my dad to despair. He was a hard-working man expelled from Africa, trying to make everything all right for his family.' She went on: 'I went to America with Mustaq for a fresh start. I worked in fashion, designing clothes. That was my family trade.'

We lay there without speaking for a while. Occasionally, we heard laughter and voices in the yard; otherwise there was silence.

'I knew, Jamal, you didn't want to marry me. You were just beginning to move into the world; you were assured and energetic, keen to get on. In India I was going mad, I can't tell you how mad. What I needed was stability, a husband. I couldn't do that with you.'

'Did you get a husband?'

'I found a good man, probably too good. It was impossible to do him wrong without hurting. But Mustaq was keen on him, and paid for everything. He set him up in business.'

She spoke more of her children, work, daily life. I stayed awake for as long as I could, listening for her words, then her breath, thinking of Wolf, Valentin and our life together, and of what Ajita and I might want from each other tomorrow; and I thought of the presence standing between us, her father.

CHAPTER TWENTY-FIVE

It was late morning when I made it downstairs. Ajita had long left my bed.

Wearing a tracksuit, Mustaq was sitting at the table with his computer, eating strawberries and melon with his fingers. A couple of people sat at the other end of the table in silence, looking as though they'd just walked out of an explosion.

Mustaq poured me some juice. 'I won't speak too loudly,' he said. 'It was a good night for me too. I haven't been to bed. I called my trainer at four and got him to drive up for an early-morning session. Then I told my manager to prepare my studio. I haven't enjoyed playing music for years. You know, Dad hated me playing the piano. One time, when I was at school, he had my keyboards removed and dumped. Do you think that could have inhibited me later?'

'Very likely.'

'Our conversation yesterday turned me on, Jamal. I have a nutritionist and a life coach. Now I have you to inspire me.'

'You do?'

'The great new bands are British, and they sing in English. Help me to write again, friend, about my childhood and my father. There aren't that many rock stars whose fathers have been murdered. Where should I begin?'

'With whatever occurs to you.'

'Okay, thanks.' He began to type, saying, 'It begins with you – walking into our house one day, looking at my sister with extreme happiness and smiling across at shy me, as if you understood everything about me, and whatever I did was okay.'

I poured coffee inside me, but couldn't keep any food down. Leaving Mustaq to gesticulate and hum at the computer screen, I walked across the fields for an hour, and then waited for lunch.

Champagne was brought round. Repeatedly lifting a glass might well have exhausted the last of my strength, but there were many places to lie down. That dreamy afternoon it occurred to me, as my eyes flickered, that to lie on a chaise longue at Mustaq's, while others talked and drank, or played cards and listened to music, as gentle staff moved among you with trays of this and that, was the most perfect condition anyone could inhabit.

'Why hasn't this occurred to me before?' I said. 'That this is what money is for?' I had opened my eyes and noticed Henry standing above me, grinning. 'This is what we've been expostulating about for years, my friend. Capitalism unfurled. Here it is, and here we are. This is the life!'

He bent down to kiss me. 'Take it easy! Nothing's ever that good!'

'Don't say that!'

'Couldn't George have afforded anything cheaper?' This was Miriam, rattling over me, laughing and chattering. For a moment she lay down beside me, her face close to mine, whispering frantically in my ear, 'Oh thank you so much, brother, for bringing me here. You've changed my life completely and forever in the last year. You've been kinder to me than Father ever was. I had to let you know that and now you know it.'

She kissed me and went to join Ajita, who had just got up. Watching my sister cross the room, in a long-sleeved tee-shirt, tight embroidered jeans and high heels, I realised how much weight she'd lost, at least three stone. Her face was almost gaunt and heavily lined, but now it was no longer studded with nuts and bolts, her eyes appeared larger, and her face shone with enthusiasm. She seemed to have retired from motherhood to become a man's woman, or 'partner'. Adopting some of Valerie's grandiosity, she now liked to begin her sentences with phrases like, 'As the girlfriend of a leading theatrical producer . . .'

Henry sat with me. 'You didn't tell me Ajita would be so beautiful.'

'Is she the most beautiful of my girlfriends?'

'She might well turn out to be, but it's still early days for you. Why don't we go for a stroll?'

'I'm well embedded here.'

'I've got something to tell you,' he said. 'It isn't a secret I want to keep.' He put his arm around me. 'Show me where to go.'

I followed him. At the door of the kitchen we put on Wellington boots. Outside, I laughed as he stared at the sculptures. Before he could say anything I said, 'They're Alan's art.'

I noticed, beside another barn, a studio made of glass and new wood. The doors were open and I could see two drawing boards; on the floor there were pieces of cut and uncut metal, some of them painted – Alan's workshop.

'That looks good,' I said. 'Maybe I should suggest the architect to Mum and Billie. They're looking to get a studio built in their garden. Did they tell you?'

'Yes, I heard about it,' said Henry.

Miriam had taken him to lunch with Billie and Mum not long ago; and Henry had taken the two older women to the opera on another occasion, when he had been offered tickets. Far from being the anticipated and necessary wedge between parent and child, Henry, the new lover, characteristically failed Miriam – to her irritation. He not only liked Mum and Billie and shared their interest in the visual arts, he didn't take Miriam's complaints seriously. 'Oh, she's far better than most mothers,' he'd say. 'You can talk to her about anything! You should have met my mother, a woman whose hysteria and depression could have infected Europe!'

Now Henry said to me, 'I saw a woman last night, at Kama Sutra, a place we've started to go to. It was dark. She attracted me, I have to admit. But I couldn't stop thinking that I recognised her. She was wearing heels and a mask and some other skimpy stuff. She was thinner than I remembered, but it was her posture, her hair that reminded me of Josephine.'

I sighed. 'My Josephine?'

'Jamal, I had no idea what she was doing there, whether it was her first time or whether she was a regular.'

Josephine had always had a leisurely walk, day-dreaming as she went, swinging her arms. I had often wondered, how can anyone walk so slowly and still move forward? We would go separately to parties, so as not to have to walk at different speeds.

I said, 'It's quite a change for Josephine, to go to a place like that. But most of her friends are just people she feels sorry for, and her boyfriend dumped her. At least that's what I guessed. He was around for a while, then seemed to disappear. I asked Rafi, who said she found him boring.'

Henry said, 'I went into a bit of a panic. Miriam was busy. I lost my excitement. I knew it would be a big deal for you – for anyone. I followed her from room to room. She seemed completely distracted.'

'Did you talk to her?' He shook his head. 'Did she recognise you or Miriam?'

'God, no. Even I haven't spoken to anyone about it. I tell Miriam everything and hope for the same from her. But this was private.'

Like most people in the house, I'd been drinking since before lunch.

There had been coke too, brought around by the staff with drinks, which sobered me up briefly and enabled me to keep on drinking. The wind was fresh and the day was clear. I was beginning to take to the countryside. I had a joint in my pocket, which Henry and I smoked as we trod across the fields. By the time Henry had finished I was pretty gone, feeling as sad and empty as I had when Ajita, Valentin and Wolf all left me.

He said, 'I guess there's no going back now – if you ever thought about that. And I suspect you did.'

'Yes, I did. My wife still fascinates me.'

'Jamal, I'm worrying about you!'

'You're a good friend, but don't let it spoil your day. I guess I should be looking after her. It's what she always wanted, but she made sure I failed at it, over and over.'

'Will you say something to her?'

'I doubt it. All I heard was that she was speed-dating.'

He laughed, 'Thank Christ you never worked as a therapist with couples.'

'It's lucrative work, I hear. Plenty of demand.'

Henry said, 'Mind you, what am I saying? A cursory glance at the early analysts and their disciples and colleagues will show what a bunch of per-verts, suicides and nutters they were, apart from Freud. Completely human, then. But at least they knew one true thing.'

'What's that?'

'You either love or fall sick.'

That night most of us were too coked up to eat much, but Miriam and Henry were hungry, and I sat with them and Ajita at supper. Henry hard-ly noticed that he was being served by uniformed staff, but Miriam insist-ed on helping with the washing up.

That Saturday evening, in one of the barns a low stage had been con-structed. The staff set up lights and brought in numerous instruments. Crates of wine and beer as well as bottles of vodka and tequila were placed at the bottom of the stage. People sat around on chairs and those, like me, who found it difficult to stay upright lay on cushions on the floor.

However close to unconsciousness I might be, I didn't want to miss Charlie Hero playing an acoustic version of 'Kill for Dada', which he'd first recorded in the 70s with the Condemned.

Alan pushed Mustaq forward. There was much applause and excite-ment. Mustaq didn't want to play, but he would obey Alan. So Mustaq, now becoming George, sat at the piano. He was quiet for a moment and then began to doodle, waiting to see what might come. When the notes took shape, they became a terrifyingly honest and personal account of Neil Young's 'Helpless', as good as the version of that song I preferred, sung by k. d. lang. I was beginning to see why the former Mushy Peas was a famous pop star.

Ajita, now in a little denim skirt, joined him for the chorus with a tambourine, swaying and laughing. When she pulled me up to join her, even I couldn't resist. My dance moves hadn't evolved since the 70s. The difference between then and now was the ghost standing between us, her father.

Later, after Ajita and I had smooched – '"Smooch", my darling, is a word I haven't used for some time' – Karim and Charlie harmonised on 'Let's Dance', Karim playing some groovy bass, and Karen throwing her thong and then her Manolos at him. I think I saw her later with a servant, trying to retrieve a Manolo from a tangle of wires behind the stage.

Ajita had danced with Henry and Miriam and we shared a bottle of champagne on the lawn as we smoked and cooled down. Then we went back to hear Mustaq play 'Everyone has their heart torn apart, sometime', which he dedicated to me, its only begetter.

Don't ask me when, but the party turned into a rock'n'roll session with anyone who could play anything jamming, and Mustaq beating the piano like Jerry Lee Lewis. Henry couldn't wait to get naked, dancing as though swatting away killer bees, as if he'd wasted the 60s and needed to catch up. Miriam danced next to the speakers in bra and pants, wanting everyone to see her tattoos. She'd shown them to Ajita, explaining the idea and provenance of each one. Ajita, appalled and fascinated, had seemed to think, by the end, that her life would be improved by the addition of a 'tat'.

I can remember watching Mustaq help his sister out of the room and upstairs, and seeing a haunted, exhausted look on her face, one I'd never seen before. I cannot recall what time the staff carried me up to bed. Apparently, they were busy with bodies all night. I know I couldn't even spark up my lighter to hold it aloft.

'It was a major catastrophe,' Mustaq laughed, the next day.

I do remember getting up to pee an hour or so after I'd passed out, and seeing, as I walked past Karen's door, she and Karim Amir fucking. At least I thought it was Karen, and maybe it was Karim. Someone else was asleep on the floor at the end of the bed, or maybe they weren't asleep, because there was moaning from elsewhere in the room.

I stood there a moment, took a quick shower, cleaned my teeth and the blood out of my nose, and went in there with them, falling into a pit of bodies. I can remember sitting propped up against a wall naked, smoking and talking with Karim about South London and the Three Tuns in Beckenham High Street, which now apparently had a Bowie plaque but not a Charlie Hero one.

Charlie himself was going at someone, perhaps one of the waitresses from the town. I can even remember, with some gratitude, Charlie caressing my back from behind when it was my turn, though I'd rather he hadn't said, 'Go on, old fella, 'ave it', as I knew he was certainly posher than both Karim and me.

The next day, when Karen and I left for London, Ajita was standing in the yard, waving to us. She would stay in the country for a few more days before going to Mustaq's London house.

While Karen sat in the car, Ajita and I embraced and promised to phone each other later. Then she kissed me on the mouth; I could feel her tongue waiting for me. She pinched and tickled me, as she used to.

'Why are you laughing?'

'You,' she said. 'It can't only be a hangover. You look as though you've just seen a ghost. But then I guess you have.'

Karen was gunning the engine irritably and banging her hands on the steering wheel.

As soon as I got in she said, 'At least you have the decency to leave with me.'

'What?'

'I know how tricky you are. I sleep with the door open and I saw that woman sneaking out of your room, the first night. You were quick. Busy weekend, eh?'

'Karen, you are crazy.'

'You waited for her all that time and now don't you like her?'

'You can't go back.'

'And you don't want to go forward?'

'I wish we didn't have to leave this house.'

'You get any rest?'

'Rest?' I said. 'I'm ready for rehab.'

'Excellent.'

I asked her not to give me her account of the previous night; I didn't want to recall it. She said she'd pin her lips, which was unusual for her, but she giggled a little. 'Impotent, eh?'

Mostly, though, she was worrying about Karim and whether he would get in touch again. If he was going to appear on *I'm a Celebrity* . . . he'd be in demand from other females, and she wanted to make the most of him before this.

However much you dislike the country, you drive back into the city on a Sunday night after a weekend away and your heart sinks: the dirt, the roughness, the closeness of everyone and everything, so much so that you can almost believe you like leaving London.

CHAPTER TWENTY-SIX

On Sunday mornings most of the population of Britain, teenagers aside, can be found in the park, strolling, jogging, walking the dog. On Sundays Rafi and I played football with other fathers – actors, film directors, novelists – and their sons, ranging in age from five to twelve. The wives and girlfriends sat on benches on the touchline, drinking lattes, distracting their girls and helping the boys with their boots and laces.

The fathers didn't want to embarrass themselves by appearing to have made an effort, but the kids came dressed for the match even though the goal at one end was two trees and, at the other, bags and discarded tops. The pitch was muddy and broken, with a pool of water to one side, into which numerous children plunged, kicking out and usually falling over.

Rafi trotted across this in the full Christmas-present Manchester United kit, sweatbands on each wrist as well as a captain's armband, shin pads and immaculate Nike Total 90s in silver. Occasionally, he sported other shirts, those of Juventus or Barcelona, which I had picked up for him when attending conferences in Europe, but, apart from the unrepeated 'Arsenal incident', he would not wear the shirt of another British club. His hair was glued up like a stiff brush and he wouldn't head the ball for fear of mussing it. If he did score – which he often did, being quick, persistent and surprisingly strong – we relived it repeatedly, acting it out in the kitchen.

It's well known that you have to be wary when telling people you support the Red Devils. If you can't give a convincing reason, you risk being accused of merely following a successful and fashionable club. My reasons were impeccable, and nicely obscure. I'd liked football as a boy and played most days in the park, but lost interest as a teenager when I realised girls preferred music to football.

I became interested again only when Eric Cantona, a Frenchman then playing for Leeds, joined Manchester United in 1992, 'transforming the fortunes of the club', as they say on the sports pages. Man United began to win cups again. Cantona was the only footballer I'd heard of who'd had psychoanalysis; not only that, it was a Lacanian analysis. When he was playing for Nimes and was then transferred to Leeds, he suffered much anxiety at leaving his analyst. He said, 'When I am in analysis, it is like an oil change. I am in my best form, I play my best. Yes, I must start again. It is no longer a curiosity but a necessity. As a matter of fact, everyone should have the courage to have done one. Everyone should at the very least read Freud and Groddeck.'

A psychoanalysed midfielder who once inflicted, during a match, a vicious two-footed kung-fu kick on an abusive Crystal Palace supporter, as well as reading the crazy Groddeck – the 'wild' analyst who Freud admired, and one of the first to investigate psychosomatic medicine – was too much to resist. I was Man United for life and so would be my flesh and blood.

I had wondered whether I might have asked Ajita to join us in the park; she and I had been chatting on the phone every day, getting to know one another again. But she had invited Rafi and me to the country, where she had returned with Mustaq 'to relax', after only a brief visit to his house in Soho. I had considered returning to Mustaq's country place; although I was nervous of the relationship with Ajita going too fast, I did have plenty to say to her. But Rafi had refused, not wanting to spend the weekend with 'only lame grown-ups', even if one of them was a rock star.

All the fathers were enthusiastic about the Sunday-morning game, and competitive too. The other families socialised with each other, the kids in and out of each other's houses. Rafi and I didn't do that, but when I ran into any of the other fathers I was pleased to see them. It was hard to dis-like anyone you played football with, though all the boys would get upset or even feel rejected if no one passed to them. Like me, Rafi was a bad loser. As a younger boy he was the sort to pick up his ball and walk off if a goal was scored against him.

I was looking forward to getting back to my place, where I would sigh and sink down like an exhausted dog. Football was the only physical exer-cise I got or wanted; by the end, I felt as though I'd been rolled down the side of a hill in a barrel. Still, I considered a goal I'd headed from a corner taken by Rafi to be the second greatest moment of my life. (The first was his birth, of course.) I had lumbered in from outside the box, catching the ball on the forehead and briefly blinding myself. Light returned, with cheering. The ball had flown between the two trees, actors were ruffling my hair and Rafi had climbed onto my back.

After the match the adults and kids sat on benches outside the teahouse, eating crisps and drinking hot chocolate. Going into the public toilet, I dis-covered three semi-undressed Polish men having a stand-up wash. One perched on one leg with his foot out while another man soaped it. Scattered around, there were clothes and bags. Lots of Poles slept rough in the area; if they could survive for three years, they'd become entitled to state benefits. As I left, two policemen were rushing towards the toilets.

Outside, four pretty girls – two of them from Rafi's school – had appeared and gathered around the boy. Dressed in boots, miniskirts and numerous bits of bright bling, they stood close to one another, chattering about mobile phones. They were dressed a little extravagantly for the park, but one of them had rung Josephine earlier, who'd told them where Rafi was. He was a favourite among the girls at school. They'd come to see him play football.

'Did you see my goal?' he said.

He wasn't looking at them, but was aware, from the little amused smile on his face – which reminded me of my father – that they were looking at him. As they talked about his goal, he shook his head, as if at the daftness of all they had to say.

His pose was cool, his mussed hair looked good. His jewellery and clothes were always carefully chosen in H&M. The previous weekend we'd gone to the sales, where I'd been looking for clothes for myself, and returned with bags full of boy gear. He looked better than me in every way, more hip and stylish, and more handsome. That was how it had to be. Nevertheless, I couldn't help feel a pang of both bitterness and regret. Sometimes, all you wanted was to be fancied. Why had I always been less confident and far more anxious than he appeared to be? I couldn't resist envying him the years of pleasure with women he had ahead of him.

The girls wanted to leave; they were nervous, convinced a man was watching them through the trees. They arranged to meet up later with Rafi at the shopping centre, their favourite place, where they'd help him choose new trainers.

'I know how to be cool,' he said to me on the way home. 'And I don't even wear designer, apart from the D&G belt, unless I'm really in the mood.'

I rang the bell of Josephine's place, the house I'd lived in but never much liked. It was on three floors, with two rooms on each and a decent sized garden. At the back was the shed where Rafi played his drum kit and gui-tars, and where he held sleepovers. Regarding the place, I remembered one of my favourite jokes, which went: Why marry? Why not just find a woman you hate and give her your house?

'What are you giggling at, fat-old-man-now-out-of-breath?' Rafi asked.

'I can't tell you. Didn't I play well today?'

'You should be with the disabled.'

'Thank you.'

'You're losing your hair, too. When you bend over I can see your skull. It's pretty horrible, bringing deep shame on our family.'

Today, as we'd left the park he'd asked how much longer I thought he and I would be able to play football together, in the same team. The question surprised me: this sense of the future, of transience, seemed unusual in kids his age.

'You see, I'm twelve and have to start playing more seriously,' he told me. 'I want to join a proper team. You can drive me there, but you'll only be able to watch.' He adopted an American accent: 'Punk, will you be sorry for what you've done, and will you live to regret it?'

As he waited on the doorstep in his football socks, banging his muddy boots against the wall, eager to tell his mother about the volley and knock-in he'd scored, I decided to go into the house, if she didn't stop me, to see whether anything peculiar was happening with her.

Occasionally I wondered whether I might start liking her again, but it wasn't an idea I was enthusiastic about. The thought that occurred to me most regularly was that if it weren't for Rafi, we wouldn't need to see one another. Of course I hated myself for wishing the boy away, as I wondered who I'd be and what other mistakes I'd have made if he hadn't been born.

Josephine opened the door and I stepped into the hall and followed her down the stairs, into the basement. She turned to look at me, but said nothing.

Josephine and I had been arguing on the phone over Rafi's education and I have to admit I'd become a little agitated. He'd failed the entrance exams to two schools. These were highly academic places and, as Josephine said, the children there looked anaemic and stressed. I could only agree with Josephine that these schools were expensive machines for turning out smart-white-boy clone drones. All the same, I had cursed the kid. Josephine pointed out that I hadn't gone to such a place myself and refused to physically enter such schools. She also claimed I was being snobbish. I knew many parents whose kids had gone to those schools and couldn't believe my own son hadn't sauntered effortlessly through the gates. Apparently my competitiveness was making the boy rage and fume at home. He'd pulled his mother's hair and argued about everything.

Josephine was right to emphasise that this was about his future rather than my own self-esteem, adding that I seemed to have turned into my father, who hadn't been around and yet still expected us to be brilliant and successful. For my part, I had decided to stop my reproaches after asking Rafi rather aggressively, 'So, what are you the best at in your class?' He'd thought about this a while before replying, 'I'm the best looking.'

As a child he liked his food separated on his plate. The beans couldn't touch the potatoes, the potatoes couldn't touch the fish fingers. Now I saw how pleased he was to see his mother and I in the same room, as he watched us closely, eager to see what was going on – investigating a marriage.

I sat at the dining-room table; Josephine brought me some tea. When she went to sit down I noticed that Rafi had pulled her chair over, so that we were close together. He was making childish noises and gestures, as though pretending to be a baby for our benefit, to remind us that we were a family.

Josephine was a woman who said little; she had no small talk nor much big talk. As I was comfortable with silence, we might as well have been statues.

Her father the abuser: drunk, crazy, run over trying to cross a motor-way, some poor fucker carrying the memory of this madman rearing up in front of him. And the daughter, petrified for life, burning with anxiety, as though a car were coming at her forever.

Left with the exhibitionist mother, what Josephine liked – and hated in herself – was to be anonymous and silent, as though she'd never been able to grow out of the idea that the well-behaved are the most rewarded. Many of my friends forgot her name. Both of her therapists did that, and she'd angrily left therapy almost as soon as she'd started. It was inevitable that someone like Miriam, who Josephine liked to call an 'attention seeker', would make her annoyed. This, I liked to point out, was how she recognised how competitive the world was, and that by making yourself more attractive, or noisy, you might be able to arouse more curiosity in others.

I was looking at her, the silence standing in for all that we might say. As ever, her fingers were not silent but they drummed on the table, almost frantically, as though there was something inside herself she was trying to make dance.

Meanwhile, a mob of enquiring voices babbled in my head. Perhaps we had both hoped, as it ended, for some explanation, for a day when the knot of every misunderstanding would be combed out, strand by strand.

'Why don't you hold hands?' Rafi said, grinning.

'I don't want to drop my tea,' I said.

We were both anxious about him growing up. Me, because I wished I'd had more children and lived with them – I liked it when he brought his friends to my flat – and her because she feared his growing independence and sexuality, which she'd encouraged in him even as it programmed him to move away from us.

I asked her, 'Been going out? Seen anyone?'

If there was a pause before she answered, I knew she had taken a tranquilliser. Usually she took them in the evening with wine, reading the label aloud: 'Do not operate heavy machinery', 'Keep away from children.' 'That's good advice,' I'd say. Anything with 'pam' on the end, as in temazepam, lorazepam or diazepam, she liked. Polythene Pam, I called her. But as she didn't like to be dependent on anything or anyone, she had begun to ration herself.

'Not really,' she said eventually. 'I'm looking after Rafi, aren't I? You went to Ajita's brother's place. Rafi showed me George's autograph.'

'Yes, with Henry and Miriam.'

'They're together, are they? Good of you to help them.'

I said, 'If you need a babysitter in the evenings, I can always come over here and work. It would be a pleasure to see Rafi – and to see you, however briefly.'

'Yes? Thank you,' she said. 'That's kind.'

It wasn't long before I stood up.

'Let me make you another cup of tea,' said Rafi.

'That would be a first,' I said, kissing his head. 'But I have to go.'

As I was leaving he slipped a CD in my hand. 'For you, dad.' It was one he'd burned for me, of some of his current favourites, Sean Paul, Nelly, Lil John. What I had once done for him, he was now doing for me.

The door closed behind me like a gunshot. Unconsciousness on a Sunday afternoon was one of the few pleasures of middle age. When I began to see my first patients, I'd learned to sleep between appointments. I could lie on my back on the floor and sleep immediately, sometimes for twenty minutes, or even for ten.

But today I felt so moved and desperate after leaving Rafi and Josephine – him waving at me from the window, after holding me and saying, 'Daddy, don't die today. If you lived here you'd be safe' – that I went home, showered and made a phone call.

CHAPTER TWENTY-SEVEN

No other country has anything quite like a London basement. You turn sharply off the street and clamber down slippery and narrow steps into an echoey chamber, go through a door and find yourself separate from the clamour, underneath the city where everything is cooler. It is like crossing a border from a maelstrom into an easy country.

I was in a dark, narrow hallway with several doors off it. I said to Madame Jenny, who had let me in, 'I had a feeling that the Goddess might need help with her homework.'

'She does, dear, she does.' She took my coat. 'How are you, Doctor? We haven't seen you for a while. We even got you a Christmas card. Do you still want it?'

'I'd be delighted.'

The turbulent turn of the century – from the nineteenth to the twentieth – had been giving the Goddess some difficulty. In my view she spent too long on her essays and in the end got muddled and upset. Madame Jenny was proud of all her girls, and was chuffed when I called them 'intellectuals'. 'Yes,' she said, 'the girls in other places are not so bright as ours.'

'Nor as sexy.'

As I walked through the hallway Madame Jenny said, 'She's expecting you.' I had phoned earlier, of course; like me, they only worked by appointment. 'Otherwise it's a madhouse rather than a whorehouse.'

'Here she is, sir,' said Madame Jenny, leading me into the room.

It was fittingly dim, the walls painted maroon. I held the Goddess for a moment, kissing her blonde ringlets and stroking her face.

I paid her and said, 'I've been looking forward to seeing you, Goddess.'

'Where have you been? I hope you haven't been seeing any other tarts.'

'I wouldn't even dream of it.'

'How do you want me?' she asked, thrusting out a hip and showing me the end of her tongue.

I contemplated the wall, which was covered in costumes on hangers; on the other wall were the whips. I asked her to dress as an air hostess. My father, of course, had spent a lot of time on planes, which seemed exotic to me then. Once he gave me a BOAC shoulder bag.

She asked, 'Which airline?'

'British Airways, I think.'

'Patriotic as ever.'

She went off with the costume. Sex was niche marketing at its best. At least they didn't stick the prices on the wall, as they did in some establishments, on brightly coloured pieces of paper, charging separately for 'hand', 'oral', 'position', '69' and, my favourite, 'complete'. I recalled that apparently, in the old days, brothels liked to feature a one-legged woman. I did have, a while ago, a patient who masturbated over his mother's prosthetic leg. But I wasn't here to think about work.

I removed my Converse All-Stars, my trousers and my shorts. It was a little cold to take off my shirt. While I waited, hoping the Viagra and the painkillers were kicking in, I almost fell asleep, so contented did I feel, here where no one could reach me. I couldn't think of a better way to squander time and money.

She returned, telling me that for her MA she was 'doing' decadence and apocalypse, always a turn-of-the-century preoccupation, along with calls for a 'return to the family'. Unfortunately, this millennium, our fears had turned out to be realities. It had been worse than we imagined.

Not that I could take in everything she said, as she was trussing my balls with a stocking, the house speciality – 'tighter! tighter!' – and securing a vibrator to my dick with another one. No one could ever say she wasn't good at what she did. She knew that at my age I needed all the stimulation I could get. Then she secured me to the bed with handcuffs. In the corner of the room was a cross to which you could also be tied, but I preferred the bed. I was keen to try most perversions, provided you could sit down for them.

She sat on me, flinging her hair across my face. She showed me her breasts, of which she was proud. They were 'au naturel', as she put it, which was unusual here and had become, in contemporary sexual life, something of a boon. 'Enjoy them,' she said. 'They're yours.' She stood on the bed above me, bending forward, showing me her legs and butt, one of my favourite outlooks, I had to admit, along with the sight of the Thames from Hammersmith Bridge.

Untying me, she ordered me to kiss and lick her cunt and arsehole. I didn't require much encouragement. This was where I loved to be and felt at home, as it were, with my face in the posterior of a whore, 'a window on the world'. I wondered how many others had been in the same position with her today. Perhaps the only advantage of being older was that it took me a while to become aroused, and once so, it took me a long time to come.

Not that it mattered to me. I fucked her until I was tired, kissing her neck and ear and cheek, and she kissed the corners of my mouth. We adjusted easily to one another's rhythm; mercifully forgoing a show, she made the quiet and slightly surprised noises of normal love-making. When I did eventually come – it was hard work; I felt as if I'd shoved a heavy train through a long tunnel – she raked my back with her nails.

We lay together. The Goddess was kissing my neck, cheeks and lips with her own full lips. I stroked and kissed her, as she told me I was a gentleman. She lay on me; I liked to feel the weight of her body, wondering not about the anonymity or dehumanisation that Lisa had talked about, but the abstract tenderness, which was more disturbing. The bewildering thing about anonymous sex was, as a lot of adults knew, not the alienation but, on the contrary, the intimacy and strong feeling. I can remember Dad reading Harold Robbins's *Never Love a Stranger*. Only love strangers, more like . . . At least I had seen, a few years ago, that I was a naturally promiscuous person. I had realised this late, but not too late. Then something Paul Goodman had written came into my mind: 'There is no sex without love, or its refusal.'

I considered Josephine walking around the Kama Sutra club, like a figure from Dante's *Purgatory*. Ravenous, insatiable, perhaps bewildered, but pursuing something: the human desire to embody and manifest itself. *Even then she doesn't hurry. I still love her grace.* I thought of my sister and best friend playing with the bodies of anonymous others. I felt as mystified as ever about the multiplicity and importance of human desire, and of how destructive and fulfilling it could be, with, often, the destructiveness sponsoring the achievement.

Josephine's presence at Kama Sutra had surprised me: usually anxious and persecuted by unwanted thoughts, she kept away from extreme situations. Safety and stability suited her. She was ultra-hygienic, too, with a cat's narcissism, forever examining her body and rubbing unguents into it, like someone polishing the shell of a car with no engine. I had come to dread the trauma of sex with her. Her orders – *faster, slower, harder, softer, more, less, in between, up, down* – could only ever preclude abandonment. The need for love and its ultimate refusal – endless torment. I was angry with her anyway, as the relationship had successfully frustrated me for more time than I wanted to misuse. I put it to her once, 'Are you sure love is supposed to be this kind of work?' She had not realised, and perhaps never would, how funny sex could be. Ajita and I used to laugh and laugh.

Yet now something must have moved in Josephine. I was curious to know what it was, but it was probably too late for me to find out. I had always thought she would make some kind of progress, though not with me.

'You're not asleep?' asked the Goddess.

'Not quite.'

I thought: with a whore you pay for the right not to speak, not to have to give the most valuable thing – your words – to the woman.

She said, 'You're an eager, good little fucker – for an Englishman.'

'Thanks.' I murmured, mostly to myself. 'Wanna hear a joke?'

'Oh yes!'

Her bright face was near mine, listening. All I wanted was to make her laugh. It occurred to me that I wanted my wife to be a whore, and my whores to be my partners.

I said, 'A prostitute and a psychoanalyst spend the afternoon together. At the end each turns to the other and says, "That's £300, please!"'

She almost laughed. With the Goddess what was almost as moving as the sex was the way, at the end, she removed the condom and cleaned your prick with a Kleenex – the care she took. Most whores didn't bother with that; once you'd come, they wanted you out of there. It was a lazy Sunday, though, a quiet day for hookers. Any whore would tell you – and I saw two as patients – that Monday was their busiest day. After a weekend with their family, how many men couldn't wait to rejoin their favourite paid slut?

I kissed her goodbye and tipped Madam Jenny who was – as madams are everywhere in the world tonight – watching television while filling in a crossword. 'Here, darlin',' she said, handing me my Christmas card.

I swaggered out like a cowboy, sniffing my pussy fingers, full of laughter and disgrace.

I was also scared, but without knowing why.

Part Three

CHAPTER TWENTY-EIGHT

In the car, when he was driving me back home after lunch, Bushy said, 'Doctor, I hope you don't mind me saying this to yer now, but Bushy's got a funny feeling.'

'Is it affecting your driving?'

'Na. It's about you.'

'Me?'

'Sir, I have to tell you – you're being well looked at. Perceived. You know.'

'Perceived, you say. Perceived by whom?'

'A man.'

'A man? What sort of perceiving man? What are you talking about, Bushy?'

'I got this feeling – a freshness, a tingle – in me nose, which don't betray me.'

'Go on, tell me about it.' As he was about to open his mouth, I said, 'Hold on, Bushy. Are you absolutely certain I really need to know this stuff?'

Bushy was examining his nose in the mirror, running his nicotine finger down the centre of it. 'Nothing strange about me today is there, boss?' He turned round. 'Look into my face. At my . . . nose.'

I peered into a coarse landscape of blackheads, whiteheads, redheads, broken capillaries and holes. 'All in order.'

'Yeah, right.' He went on, 'I was saying, this guy who's perceiving you – I reckon he might be dangerous.'

'Dangerous?'

'Very, very much so,' Bushy said, with some relish.

I had been enjoying the journey. Bushy knew the route I preferred, knew I liked to see what was happening in the Harvey Nichols window, keeping left at the Knightsbridge junction and swinging past Harrods until the V&A came into view on the right, and I could see what the latest exhibition was. The V&A was a place I'd go to relax sometimes. Being in a building – perhaps in any beautiful building which wasn't a shop – where you could stroll about looking at art enabled me to have good thoughts, even if I had Josephine with me: we liked to go there often.

After the V&A there wasn't anything of much interest until we reached Gloucester Road. If I had the time, I'd get Bushy to drop me off outside the Gloucester Road bookshop, a second-hand place just up from the tube. I could spend half an hour in the basement there, and then go to Coffee Republic next door to read. My excitement and appetite for books – and the ideas they contained – hadn't modified over the years. My shoulder bag was always weighed down with the numerous volumes I couldn't wait to get inside me.

Like many taxi drivers, Bushy considered a journey an opportunity to express himself to a captured captive audience, but we'd been around enough together for him to know I wouldn't listen or reply.

He said, 'You're off on one, I know. But I think you need to know this stuff. A man without this knowledge inside him could suffer consequences.'

'Is that right?'

It was a while before I could turn my brain round to concentrate on what he was saying, if anything. I was still thinking of what Karen had said over lunch.

Almost first thing in the morning she had rung to invite me to the Ivy. There was some strange news she just had to give me. A reputation for listening to others can ruin your life. You can begin to feel like the village whore or, worse, a priest. But I hated to turn down an invitation to the Ivy.

Usually lunch there took too much time out of the day, as it was thirty-five minutes away by tube or car. However, on Mondays I had a patient who came to my door, gave me a cheque and shuffled away, head down, buying my time but not my presence. This gave me an extra hour. Bushy had turned out to be free; he drove me up to the Charing Cross Road and would pick me up later.

I was on time, and had a good nosy around the restaurant as I waited to be shown to the table. One of the assets of the Ivy was that the room was ideal: everyone could see everyone else without seeming intrusive. Today there was a good mixture of pop stars, actors, media executives, TV comedians and a couple of writers.

Karen had downed most of a bottle of wine by the time I arrived. I ordered a cappuccino and began to hear about Karen's husband Rob, their girls, and Rob's girlfriend Ruby, who had been to Disneyland while we were at Mustaq's.

'I think I might have told you they were all at Disneyland, Jamal, but you won't remember.'

'Won't I?'

'You were pretty much out of it at George's. I haven't seen you that way for years.'

'Oh Christ, I hope I didn't make a fool of myself. I don't much like to be drunk now.'

'Despite that, Jamal, you do tend to remember the details of a lot of things. They just cling to the underside of your sticky head.' She went on: 'Now, this girl Ruby is at the LSE doing political science. She plays in a women's football team, and makes documentaries about asylum-seekers in her spare time. She wants to be a film director. Maybe she will be. She's completely uninhibited and hip when it comes to sex. I asked him one time, what can she do that I can't? A stupid question, don't you think? Well, she takes her girlfriends along to join my husband in bed, a story which flustered me for days.'

'You wanted to be the friend?'

'How can I compete with this Ruby?'

'What else?'

'My youngest girl mentioned that Ruby was putting on weight. "I'm glad to hear it,"', I said. 'The other daughter then said, "It's not fat, it's a bump." Karen's eyes must have either narrowed or widened here, and rapidly. "A bump?" I asked. "A bump? Did you really say that? We're fucked. That's it. He's never coming back now. Give me a minute, I have to take two of my pills." Pour me a drink, darling Jamal.'

I emptied the bottle for her. She leaned across the table and said to me, 'The bastard's starting again. Maybe he didn't like it the first time. Now he's going to be happy. The girls and I, and the family life we had for years, means nothing to him. I have to admit that we imagined for ages that one day he'd walk back in through the door he went out of.'

'The girls are growing up,' I said. 'You'll have to find new things to do.'

She looked around the restaurant helplessly. 'There are no men available, you know that. I won't go with some urine-stained git on Viagra. And the girls, they're teenage trouble, seeing their first boyfriends, they're on the phone even more than me. They don't want to see me bringing some bastard his tea on a tray.'

Not having time to look at the menu, I had one glass of champagne and ordered my favourites, the potted shrimps to start, followed by the fish cakes with chips. I didn't notice what Karen was eating, but it wasn't much.

I mentioned Henrietta, an acquaintance of ours, who made no secret of her liking for men and sex. I said, 'Think how much pleasure she has. Far more than either of us. Men are in and out of her place all night, and she's got three daughters.'

Karen said, 'Henrietta? She's got a big house. There are still men walking around in there lost, unable to find the front door. Anyhow, the other day she was sleeping with some political fool. She woke up, went downstairs and looked at his phone. He had messages from eight other women. He was no Adonis, of course.'

'She makes sure she gets what she needs.'

'You know what she said to me the other day? She'd trade it all in for someone who just wants to be with her. Oh Jamal, what's wrong with an alpha female like me apart from the fact that I'm old, fat and alcoholic? Who's going to care for me, listen to me, make love to me?'

'You're humiliated, you poor thing.'

She was sobbing. 'Was I ever like Ruby? I was never that brilliant. There were always more intelligent and beautiful women in London.'

Karen had eaten little, but we did share a dessert. I despatched a double espresso. 'What about Karim?'

'I didn't hear from him, obviously. I called him a few times. He said he was busy preparing for his appearance on *I'm a Celebrity . . . Get Me Out of Here*.'

'Have you thought of getting a therapist?'

'Don't fucking say that to me!' she said wildly, as though we were still a couple. 'Can't we go to a hotel this afternoon? I'll do anything you want.'

I got up and kissed her. 'I have to work.'

She said, 'It's okay for you, you've got your girl back. Ajita,' she said slowly and with some scorn. 'Are you dating her again? George told me she's installed herself at his place. She came for a few days but now just refuses to go home. He doesn't know what to do with her. She's making him crazy.'

'Really?'

'Is that because of your influence?' She was holding my hand tightly. 'Jamal, don't you ever think about our son?'

'Sorry?'

'The one you wanted me to get rid of.'

She wouldn't let me extricate myself. 'Karen, please,' I said.

'What age would he be today, so big and strong and handsome?'

'I don't know,' I said. 'I have no idea.'

'He could be having lunch with us! The parents of a murdered child are still its parents. I am absolutely certain you would have wanted more children!'

I was late already. When I managed to get away from her she was looking around the restaurant for another table to join. Bushy was outside with the other drivers and we took off, the car fragrant with air freshener.

After all this, and the champagne, I wanted to nap, but hearing of Bushy's suspicions I said, 'Okay, let me have it. What's going on with this perceiving man?'

'Yesterday, right, I'm parked up the street waiting to pick Miriam up from lunch with you when I noticed this bloke nosin' yer from a car. An oldish man, kinda strange looking, well built. Your manor's full of weirdos, but when I came back he was still there. Then he followed us – I know because I took an odd route especially. He's been having a good look at you. You wouldn't mess with him –'

'Maybe it's one of my patients,' I said. 'Or a patient's spouse. When people start therapy they sometimes separate from their partners, and the therapist is blamed. I've had people throw bricks through my window.'

I didn't mention the fact that for a while Josephine would stand outside the flat when I was seeing patients, convinced I was having affairs with them. I could hear her yelling: 'You're not allowed to touch them, you know! You'll be reported and struck – if not struck off!' I did also have a psychotic therapist colleague – not a patient – but someone I'd attended conferences with who began, after the publication of my first book, to stand outside my door handing out a written statement to my patients, saying what a phoney I was.

'Maybe,' Bushy said. 'A man without a stalker is a nobody. But this one could be like that song – you know the one.'

'Which one? What are you saying?'

'"Psychokiller".'

He started to sing it. I said, 'Right, right. Because?'

'Because he's not spontaneous. We should check him out – now.'

'How can I check him out?'

Bushy told me what he required me to do, and then said, 'It would be to yer advantage.'

'Bushy, I have to see a patient now.'

'Shrinky, I'm insisting you better do what Bushy says.'

I did what he said. He dropped me at the corner of my street and I walked to my flat with him driving behind. My patient was waiting outside the building.

After she'd gone I phoned Bushy. 'So?'

'When you came along the street as per advised, our character hid – sliding down in the car. I think it's a rented motor. I'll check him out and let you know what's what.'

'You're going to a lot of trouble, Bushy.'

'I'm worried. Miriam ordered me to keep an eye on you.'

'I don't want her to know about this. She'll get in a flap and start casting spells.'

I woke at four in the morning, wondering who was out there watching me. I wondered whether Mustaq had employed someone to keep an eye on me. He was the only person who had the money, as well as the motive, to do that. But what would he hope to see? Occasionally I'd go to the window and look out, but I saw no one.

My first patient was at seven the next morning: an Old Etonian in his fifties whose relationships with women had been wretched. *Haunted by the idea that he will find the one who will complete him, therefore rejecting all others as wrong. The founding myth of heterosexuality: completion, the ultimate fulfilment.*

My second patient was at eight: a woman who had been phobic about drinking water since childhood, after hearing a story about a dead bird in a water tank. Reaching the stage when she was unable to drink anything she thought had contaminated water in it, her life was being gradually annulled, until it was almost impossible for her to be with others socially.

At nine I had some toast and made another pot of coffee. I rang Bushy. 'How's my stalker?'

'Boss, as I speculated, it is a rented car. I followed him all the way into Kent. I thought we were going to end up in dammed Dover. He kipped in a deserted street near a park.'

'Which part of Kent?'

He named the street and I knew it, though not well. Apart from the fact Kent was crammed with criminals – the county was close to the city and not far from the coast, as well as having plenty of the sort of houses favoured by criminals and pop stars – the street he mentioned was in the area where I'd grown up. That puzzled me. Why would he go there? Then it occurred to me that the street was closer to Ajita's than to my old house. If it was one of Mustaq's men, why would he sleep in a car there?

I asked, 'What should we do?'

'I can't bring him in and ask him questions meself,' he said. 'I'd have to get geezers. That would cost yer.'

'I don't want men,' I said. 'I can't afford it and I can't get involved in anything lunatic.'

He could only laugh at my naivety. 'You might already be up to the throat in the lunatic, Jamal. I reckons he'll make his moves in the next twenty-four hours. He can't hang around much longer. He's perceived what he wants to perceive.'

There was a silence, then I said, 'It sounds as though I'll have to start taking this seriously. What we need is a photo.'

'I can do that.'

Bushy borrowed my Polaroid camera and later dropped by with the picture he'd taken. It was difficult to make out who it was, as Bushy was no Richard Avedon. Someone was asleep in a car. I could see a shoulder and an ear, but had no notion who they might belong to.

'I can't wait any more,' I said to Bushy on the phone. 'I'm going to approach this guy. If I know him and he's not scary, I'll take him into the flat and try to talk to him. If I raise the blind, you come in.'

'Jesus no, there's no way I'd advise that!'

'Don't worry.'

Bushy said, 'You don't know what goes on half the time.'

'I don't?'

'You think you can X-ray people with your eyes, but you can't always.' He went on: 'When I see you on the street I always think: there goes the student.'

'Student?'

'With your worn jacket and uptight look, and always carryin' books, head down, as if you don't want to talk to no one . . .'

I put the phone down, a worried man with a worried mind, and went out of the house and approached the car.

The man was asleep, or at least his eyes were closed. I was about to knock on the window when he opened his eyes. He seemed to surge into life, and wound down the window.

'Ah, Jamal! At last! Did you know it was me?'

'Hello, Wolf. My eyes are open,' I said, looking up the street to where Bushy's car was parked.

'Can I come in?'

I said, 'Let's go to a café.'

'We have so much to talk about!'

'Why have you been hanging around out here?'

'I was afraid, nervous,' he said. 'It's been so long. But you do remember me?'

He was out of the car, embracing, kissing me and looking me over, as though wanting to see what remained after so many years.

He said, 'I thought this moment would never come. Hallo, and hallo again, my dear, my most missed, friend. What an important moment this is – for both of us! The moment I've been waiting years for!'

I was looking at him too, and said, 'Perhaps like me you look the same, apart from your hair. My son says I get more and more hairy, except on my head, where it counts.'

'Your son?' he said. 'I'm so glad for you. Is he here?'

'I hope he's at school.'

'I've got to hear all about him. Will you tell me everything? Aren't you going to invite me in?'

'Yes,' I said. 'I am. Come right in.'

'Thanks,' he said. 'This is beautiful. A beautiful moment.' He was looking up at my building. 'London is so great. It feels like I've come home. This is where I belong – here with you again, my dear friend! You know, I've got the feeling it's going to be like the old days again!'

CHAPTER TWENTY-NINE

Wolf refused a beer, and while I waited for the kettle to boil, he walked around taking everything in, 'with the concentration of a bailiff' I might have said.

'You've done well,' he said. Suddenly he had become serious. 'Since that night.'

'Which night, Wolf?'

'You've forgotten? I don't believe you have. But people can put these little things aside if they are busy.' I was staring at him. He said, 'The suburbs. We were in the Indian's garage with Val.'

'Right.'

'A girl's father.' His fist smashed into the palm of his other hand. 'Pow! We got him! He took it – right? – and went down begging and crying.'

'Yes, yes.'

'Do you think about it?'

'Not often now, no.'

'But you did once?'

'Yes,' I said. 'A lot.'

'What conclusion did you come to?'

'That it would be pointless to torment myself over it.'

'That's it? That is *all* you think about it?'

'There was no possible resolution. I quit the useless questions. They were a vice costing me time and money.'

He said, 'As a young man you were intelligent and sure of yourself. Now you're a doctor.'

I said, 'Only a talking one, I'm afraid.'

'I could do with some of that talking.'

'Why's that?'

He hung his head like an ashamed child. 'Jamal, I have come to you for a reason, and not only because of the depth of our friendship. Things have not gone well for me.'

'I'm sorry to hear that.'

'It was my first murder. It started me off. Since then I've been murdering others.'

'You liked it that much?'

He looked up at me and shook his head. His father had been a German cop, his mother was English. Brought up in Munich, he'd been living in London for five years when I met him, speaking English without an accent.

Now, a man almost worn out, he had the head of a middle-class respectable man but with a powerful, desperate, bitter aspect which I recognised from juvenile thieves I'd seen: those who were looking to take that which no one would give them. As he had the assassin's sunken eyes and the direct but confused look of a psychotic, I thought I should decide whether he would become violent. But Wolf had a cringing side which suggested he'd rather get something from me than hurt me.

Maria, who had come by to drop off the shopping, looked into the room. 'Maria, this is an old friend from my student days.' She nodded at him. She knew that if he were a patient I'd have shut the door.

'Who's that?' he asked. 'What is she doing?'

'She looks after me and the patients,' I said. 'She shops and washes too.'

'You're professional,' he said. 'Has she gone now?'

'I don't know. But carry on, please.'

'She's made me nervous. Is she watching us? Where did she get those eyes from?'

'Her mother.'

I sat down opposite him. It was a while before he began again. 'Okay,' he said at last.

He told me he had been living with a rich widow for years, a woman older than him who had become senile. A month ago her relatives had strong-arm guys remove him when he attempted to get his name on her properties, including small hotels, which she owned and he'd maintained, even rebuilding some of them. The family considered him a sponger, though he'd looked after her better than they had, doing everything for her. Since then he'd been living in a room in Berlin and was in a bad way.

'You must be furious.'

He said, 'I'm a man who's been robbed and left with nothing.'

'How did that come to be? You were always intelligent and resourceful. I liked your initiative.'

There was no doubt I'd long been fascinated by certain sorts of psychotic. I liked their focus and certainty, their lack of symptoms, the way they shrugged off the neurotic fears and terrors which made life so difficult for the rest of us. Psychotics appeared unworried; they could take a lot of criticism and made good politicians, leaders, generals. Unfortunately, their weakness was paranoia, which could become very severe.

And with someone like Wolf there was conversation; there was even fine intelligence. But, after a short time, about half an hour, you'd begin to feel restless, irritable, registering the fact that your emotional world is not really present to the other person. Not only that, they seem to be bearing down on you with demands you cannot answer. You begin to feel suffocated, assaulted even. You might want to run away.

Wolf told me that after 'the garage incident', he and Val had worked on boats in the South of France. Val had also worked in casinos. They had found that everyone there was rich, or wanted to be; it was expensive. The place was awash with criminals full of large ideas.

'We needed a big coup. Then we put all our money together. I went to Syria. I'm driving the car, it's full of hash – the pure stuff – which I'm going to smuggle into Europe in tins of pineapple, I know how to do that, when I'm arrested. When they say they think I'm an Israeli spy I know I'm fucked, and I am.'

'Why would they think you were a spy?'

'I had cameras and a Citizen's Band radio. Jamal, I can tell you, three years in a Syrian jail doesn't make anyone feel attractive.'

Sometimes he was kept in a hole in the ground, as well as in a small box. He was beaten and given electric shocks. He began to believe in God. He thought about grass and birds. He had a heart attack, murdered a Syrian in a fight over food (this, it turned out, was his only other murder) and, following pressure from the German government, was eventually released.

He went back to Germany, broken. During his rehabilitation he had taken up with different women. He said his one gift was to tell his story and induce sympathy. He had made the most of it.

Wolf and I had been talking for ninety minutes.

'Wolf,' I said, tapping my watch, 'I have to go and see my son.'

'London's the most expensive city in the world,' he said.

'Blame the government.'

He made no move to leave. He was restive. He wanted to stay. He said he'd sleep on the floor, he only needed a blanket, the car was cold and he had nowhere else to go. I said it wasn't possible. I didn't want to spend a night with him in the flat, not being convinced he'd leave the next day.

He was watching me. I couldn't help thinking: the present drags us back into the past, where all the trouble began, and which returns with its debt, wanting to be repaid. But who owes what to whom?

'Okay, my friend, if that's how you feel,' he said and, at last, got up. 'It's been good to see you again.'

As he was almost at the door, he put his hand on my arm and asked me for £50,000. I couldn't stop myself snorting loudly and saying, 'I wish I had that kind of money myself.' Then I asked, 'Why is it you want money so much?' He seemed confused by the question. 'Not that I'm trying to put you off.'

Suddenly he became angry and held my arm tightly, which was more painful than I'd have imagined. He said that if I didn't make at least a decent instalment – around £10,000 would be 'courteous' – he would see that 'the right people' learned about my murdering.

He emphasised that the amount wasn't random. He was intending to buy a derelict house, decorate it himself and rent out rooms. If I could only give him 'a start' he wouldn't ask for more, in fact he would then help me. Wolf may have had a strange mind, but he knew the housing market was where the money was.

I didn't know what to do or say, apart from, 'But that's ridiculous. Anyway, you won't get a house for £50,000. You'd be lucky to get a front door.'

'It will be a deposit. You know I'm not afraid to work. I could build a house from the dirt up if need be. All I ask is for that initial start.'

I shoved him away. I thought he was going to come back at me, but he stood there watching me.

I said, 'I haven't got any more time to discuss it. Never touch me again.'

'You're going to have to make time. This is important.' At the door he said, 'Why didn't you ask about Val?'

'Why, is he outside too, waiting to come in and ask for money?'

'You really want to know?'

'All right.'

He said, 'He did himself in.'

'He did?'

'While I was in jail. I found out about it from one of his women.'

'Was he depressed?'

'Always. The killing made him more so. He dwelled on it. He was more sensitive than us, and not so strong. He didn't blame you, but he might as well have. It was his turning point, sending him into hell.'

I said, 'I liked him. Lots of women liked him.'

'They couldn't save him.' Wolf was looking at me. 'The whole murder – I feel like my soul has been dyed black by it. Don't you?'

I realised I was whispering, though no one could overhear us. 'It was an accident. We wanted to scare him. We might have been young fools, but we were on the side of the angels.'

'The Hell's Angels?' He laughed bitterly. 'It doesn't matter. It comes back. No one told me that. I was naive, but made into a fool. Jamal, I need to get it out, you know. Better in than out.'

'Why invite punishment? You've been in jail. You liked it enough to go back?'

'What do they say over here? You can do the time if you've done the crime.'

I asked, 'Who have you told?'

My phone rang. It was Rafi. Wolf looked at me and smiled. 'You're afraid. I must have scared you. You're shaking.'

I could hear Rafi saying, 'Dad, Dad, you're coming, aren't you?'

I was watching Wolf while saying to my son, 'Yes, of course. I'm on my way.'

Rafi said, 'We've been working all day on this thing for you. I was thinking about it all night.'

'Rafi, I wouldn't miss it for anything.' I turned off the phone and said to Wolf, 'What we've been talking about – it's not something I'd want my son to know. It wouldn't help him to think of me that way.'

'As a murderer?'

'You see that, don't you?'

'You're lying to him.'

I said, 'He's not entitled to know everything about me. I don't consider myself to be a murderer.'

'In your heart you wanted to kill that man and you dragged me into it. You hated him and wanted him out of the way so you could have the daughter for yourself.'

I repeated, 'Who have you told?'

'Not many. Don't worry so much. A few women. You?'

'I have no desire to confess.'

'Not even to the mother of your son? What is her name?'

'Josephine.'

'You were with her more than ten years.'

I said, 'I've told her nothing.'

'Was that difficult?'

'Honesty is always a temptation. But no.'

'You must have thought you'd covered your tracks. Then I turn up, bringing it all back.' He said forcefully, 'Where's the girl now? Have you seen her? The Indian one?'

'Ajita?'

'Where does she live? Is she still alive? What does she think of it all?'

I was shaking my head. 'I haven't seen her since then. She went to India. I lost all of you. It was terrible for me. My mind wasn't my own for some time.'

He interrupted. 'But if you did see her, would you tell Ajita the truth, would you confess?'

'No.'

'But surely you believe you should, that it will release you?' He went on: 'We were a tight group, a little gang of four. In prison I thought about it often, to keep myself alive, reliving the good times in West London, the meals, the laughter, the drinks, the card games, the cinema, with everything ahead of us. Jamal, I want to see her again.'

'Why?'

'I tried to spend time with her alone, away from you. She came with me, twice. Don't worry, I didn't sleep with her. You were too young for her, and immature. You didn't understand how much she wanted you. You seemed to turn away. But she refused me. She loved you.'

I'd walked him to the door, but now he was back in the room, striding about as though looking for someone else to tell the story to. I picked up a pair of jeans from a pile on the floor; I found some money in my pocket, pulled it out and went to the front door with it, knowing he'd follow me.

As he was leaving, I gave him the jeans plus a hundred pounds I had received from a patient earlier, told him to find a cheap hotel, and asked him to phone me and arrange a time to come back.

I watched him drive away. I'd imagined he might calm down, and be easier deal with on another day. But now I wasn't so sure. As Eric Cantona memorably said, 'When the seagulls follow the trawler, it is because they think sardines will be thrown into the sea.'

I rang Bushy and asked him if he'd come over. He said, 'You sound panicked. Is he hurting you yet?'

'I need to talk tonight.'

He said he wouldn't be in my neighbourhood, but in his office and local, the Cross Keys, in Acton, attending to company matters. It was a bit of a walk for me, but I needed time to think.

I tucked my iPod into my shirt pocket; with my hood up, street robbers wouldn't be able to see the white wire or the tell-tale headphones.

First, however, I had to see Rafi. The boy had promised me a treat.

CHAPTER THIRTY

Rafi had decided to cook me a meal. When he and I had played football in the park a few days earlier, he had said, looking me over, 'Man, you don't look right. It's not that your hair's funny or your clothes more strange than usual. But you're lonely-looking and thin, and I've never said that about you before. Old man, you're not going to die are you?'

If his generosity surprised me, it was because I'd noticed he was about to become a teenager. He loved mirrors, as I once did. His upper lip was dark now, soon he'd be shaving. Whereas before he was happy to talk, indeed to chatter away interminably, now he kept his words sullenly to himself. But not all of them. He could be cruel, abusive even, trying to hurt, as though trying to make a space between us. How I'd been missing his younger self, when he'd let me read to him and kiss him, and he slept between us, taking up most of the bed. When he needed me more.

I arrived at the house in the early evening to find my prodigal hot, his face shining and luminous with enthusiasm. I could smell burning.

'Hello, old man. Still alive?' he said, leading me in. He was wearing a Hawaiian shirt under a pinny with the words 'The Mother' written on it. 'Did you know – you can sniff my hair if you want?'

'Thank you.'

'Don't disarray it. It's punked-up specially.'

I pressed my nose into the fragrant spikes. 'What is it?'

'Banana shampoo.'

'Yummy.'

'It doesn't mean I'm gay because I like fashion.'

'But you like pink too.'

'Not as much as I used to. Is that a sign of gayness too?'

'Yes.'

'Don't joke me, Dad. You know I kissed a girl.'

'Which girl?'

'You will never know that.'

Josephine had helped Rafi with the shopping and chopping before going for a run in the park. On a brightly patterned tablecloth a place was set for one, along with the best, heaviest cutlery.

I noticed a folded piece of paper with the word 'menu' written on it in wavy writing. I read: 'Omelette du jour (omelette of the day). Fresh tomato and courgette. Very good quality eggs and butter (fresh). Fresh avocado and potatoes. Shallot (fresh) and fresh good quality cooking oils.' Under 'pudding' he'd written 'pistachio ice cream'; under 'drinks' he was offering 'water, cider'. He'd signed it, or rather, autographed it, at the bottom.

I was supposed to be having a serious talk with him, and wondered if this was the right time for it. Recently Josephine and I had met in a nearby deli with long tables and the papers spread all over them, a place full of mothers who'd just dropped their kids off at school. After, she was off to be interviewed for a job in a college psychology department.

I'd got there early to read the papers and hear the women's voices. When I looked up and she was walking towards me, I was glad to see her; it was still her beauty and vulnerability I was drawn to, and the love in her eyes.

Though it was warm, I noticed she was wearing one of my scarves; she would always borrow my clothes, particularly the expensive ones – the raincoats she liked – though she was taller and thinner than me.

She wanted to talk because Rafi had been upsetting her, calling her, several times, 'a fucking bitch and a ho'. He'd pointed his fingers at her and threatened to 'blow her away' if she insisted he went to bed at a certain time.

She said, 'As if America hasn't done enough damage in the world! He takes these rap lyrics seriously. I hate all the aggressive gestures and shouting. What is it with boys and gangsters? You would say the boy has to move away from the mother. But why would they think that being a man is being a bastard?'

'It's cartoon. The bling and posing is no more real than a pantomime dame in costume.'

'Not all those kids can tell the difference. I've decided to throw his CDs out. That stuff is now banned from the house! I don't care that you hate censorship.'

I said. 'It's too late already. But I am sorry he spoke to you like that. Perhaps he's anxious about you going to work. He thinks you'll have less time for him.'

'Oh God,' she said, getting up and gathering her things. 'Perhaps that's it. I knew you'd make me feel worse. How did I ever waste ten years with you?'

Now, as I sat there looking at the evening newspaper, he came in and out of the kitchen. 'Are you looking forward to it, dude?'

'I can't wait.'

'It's cooking up beautifully. There's a lot of things I can cook now. Some of my dishes are legendary.'

'You're lucky to have a good mother who taught you. Miriam and I ate bread and dripping, and later, burgers, chips and cakes.'

'D'you feel a fool for leaving here?'

'Sometimes.'

'Come back then. Don't you love Mum?'

'I like her a lot. She's looked after you brilliantly.'

'That's not love.'

'It'll happen to you,' I said. 'Marriage, separation, kids here and there, the whole disintegrated thing. No one gets married at twenty-five and stays with their partner until they're seventy unless they are deficient in imagination. May you have many wives, son. And that's a curse!'

'Thanks, punk and role model.'

Eventually, like someone carefully carrying a birthday cake into a crowd, he brought the omelette out on a huge plate. He opened the napkin in my lap and gave me the knife and fork. He didn't sit at the table with me, but stood with his elbow on my shoulder.

'Start before it gets cold.' As I took each mouthful, he offered advice. 'Put some salad with it, dad.' 'Mix up the things more. Here's some bread.' 'Don't you like cucumber? Salad is good for you.'

The omelette was filled with melted cheese and a mixture of chopped tomatoes and cucumber. Thus supervised, I was taking my last mouthful when he ducked back into the kitchen and came out with a bowl of pistachio ice cream. As it was, I could barely move.

'Deep, eh?'

'Not only deep but heavy too,' I said.

'Have you ever had a better meal?'

'How could I have had?'

'You'll love this,' he said, putting the spoon in my hand. He went to a shelf, removed a bottle and poured me about half a glass of his mother's vodka. Catching a whiff of it he said, 'Smells like petrol. But this ice cream is your favourite. Mum and I had to go out specially to get it.'

When I was eating my ice cream and finishing the vodka, he sat down and ate his own omelette, pouring tomato ketchup over it until it was a red mess.

After the meal I lay down on the floor and slept briefly, while beside me Rafi sat cross-legged, attached to the TV by wires, clicking away like a widow at her knitting. Isolated figures murdered one another in what resembled the deserted Roman cityscapes of de Chirico.

I was woken up by his mother caressing my shoulder. 'Did you enjoy it?'

I got to my feet slowly. 'It was the best meal of my life.'

She and I still considered one another warily, like kids after a fight, both wondering which one will re-start the conflict. But our fury with one another was diminishing; I felt reluctant to leave right away.

My favourite thing had always been to watch her in the house as she walked about, sat, combed her hair, showered, dressed, read. All day she was different, her numerous moods transforming her look, and I followed them, indeed lived in them, as a child lived with its mother. At night, as she slept, I'd listen to her breathing and I would kiss her hair. We had our difficulties and disputes, but I believed at least she wanted to be here with me, that I was always everything to her.

I became a connoisseur of her body – transfixed, obsessed even; like a child, I needed her company, her reassurance and presence, and to escape into the world at the same time.

'Can I see what you've been doing?' I said. 'Your new work?'

She fetched her folder and spread her recent drawings on the floor. Friends often asked to buy them, but she rarely sold her work, preferring to give it away. I had one of her nudes, framed, in my consulting room. Next to it was André Brouillet's famous engraving of Charcot – the P. T. Barnum of hysteria – in the lecture hall at the Salpêtrière clinic in Paris, exhibiting one of his most famous hysterics, the somnambulist Blanche Wittman. Freud always had a copy in his office. It was in this hospital, years later, that the latest supermodel of hysteria, Princess Diana, died.

I padded among Josephine's drawings, telling her how much she continued to improve. She told me about her new day-long life class and about her art teacher, who was, inevitably, encouraging her to become a nude model as well as an artist. It was being an artist that she loved. She admired the ferociously weird and tender imagination of Paula Rego, particularly her prints.

Art was all Josephine wanted to do, but as well as not yet developing her own vision – as if she didn't know who she was – she felt guilty about it. Guilty that she didn't have a career and earned little money.

She felt herself to be a failure compared to other 'executive' women in their smart suits, with their computers and fast cars. I replied that unfortunately for these women, no man considered a woman to be more of a woman because she was successful. For some reason, that criteria applied only to men.

So I praised Josephine's art and her mothering, and watched her eyes for a gathering brightness, and then for an explosion of self-loathing. 'But I can be lazy, I don't work enough or earn enough. I still take to my bed for days, hugging the pillow . . .'

She interrupted herself by asking me if I were writing. I began to tell her about an idea which I was still uncertain about. Henry had never been a great reader of my work, seeing anything I said as an opportunity to entertain his own thoughts. Josephine read little, but her remarks were always pertinent.

I said I wanted to try to move analysis away from technical obscurity and 'scientism' – analysts writing for one another, and for students – to a more popular area, where it might become again, as it had been with Freud's lucid writing, about the stuff which concerns everyone: childhood, sexuality, illness, death, the problem of pleasure. Otherwise the public would be left with only self-help books and the authors putting 'PhD' on the cover, somehow a guarantee of stupidity.

'You're good at those little essays,' she said. 'Keep them odd and quirky. That's their uniqueness, their unconventionality. No one else can do it.' She was looking at me and said, 'Is something bothering you? You've got that sad, hurt face on.'

'I have?'

'Won't you tell me why? Are you in trouble? Is it a patient?'

I said, 'Will you look at what I've been writing? You know, sometimes I listen to you.'

She laughed suddenly and said, 'I had a thought the other day, we must not forget that people do most of their reading while defecating.'

'Indeed.'

'Oh Jammie, please, I don't want to be mean, bring it over and I'll make some suggestions. We could try lunch again.'

'Yes, let's do that,' I said. 'I like taking you out – if you're not being argumentative.'

She reached out to tweak my nose. 'If you're not being unkind . . .'

'If you're not playing the victim . . .'

We stopped; we were laughing. Silently, as if holding his breath, Rafi had been watching us. He'd only said, at one point, 'Well, of course, Plato is a great thinker,' and he'd imitated my voice, surprisingly deep, upper-middle-class at last, and pompous.

Now, as I was leaving – 'Was it really deep? Do you feel better? Will you come back?' – he pressed the menu into my hand and his nose into my sleeve. 'Booze, fags, piss. Your smell.'

'You'll never forget it.'

'I feel really close to you, Dad,' he said. 'We're almost like family.'

'Very funny. Kiss your beautiful mummy for me – lots.'

'Can't you do anything yourself?'

During the walk I stopped to look at the menu, which I would never throw away.

CHAPTER THIRTY-ONE

If you had the misfortune to pass the Cross Keys without being familiar with it, you'd think it was derelict. The windows were boarded over and graffitied. There was rusty scaffolding around the side of the pub, wreathed in barbed wire, but no other evidence of building work, which made me wonder whether the scaffolding was in fact holding everything up. Surely if it weren't soon knocked down it would fall down. Despite not even having a pub sign, the place was always busy and often heaving.

The Cross Keys stood on the corner of a desolate street lined with low-rise industrial buildings, the sort of places that would, in a more likely part of town, be converted into art galleries and lofts. Meanwhile the doorways were scattered with drug debris.

Dodging past a group of tall Africans on the street corner touting for minicab work, I shoved at the busted door. It had been a while since I'd been here, but nothing had changed. Just inside there was a small bar, and behind it a larger back room with a tiny stage, the windows blacked out. In here there were non-stop strippers, each undressing to one record.

There were pretty girls, pretty nasty ones, young and old, black, Indian, Chinese. It had been months since I'd last been to the Keys. I knew at least I was unlikely to run into any of my patients; or indeed into anyone I knew, apart from Bushy. A man could read the newspaper, have a pint and, from a distance of a few yards, stare between the legs of a high-heeled woman.

There could be commotions. Usually the two bars were composed of rough, loud men – or respectable men with briefcases and umbrellas soon turned into rough, loud men – and girls in flimsies trotting around with beer glasses, collecting change. The men gathered at the base of the tiny stage and, as the evenings progressed, were liable to collapse onto it, which was dangerous, as a springy Salome might be tempted to kick you in the head.

In the Cross Keys there were no bouncers or remixed music, no cameras, and, inevitably, there was broken glass on the floor of the toilets where, when you peed, the cistern dripped cold water onto your head. On the bar was a handwritten sign saying, 'Shirts must be worn at all times.'

This dive was overseen by a loud-mouthed harridan with whom no one messed, apart from Bushy. 'Leave my fucking dancers alone!' she'd yell, if anyone touched a girl. Oddly enough, the Czech barmaid, in her mid-twenties, was more beautifully angelic than the strippers, and would glance at the nude girls without emotion. It was ironic, of course, that she was the only person there you'd want to see undressed.

The Harridan was the woman Bushy had been 'going with' for a while, an upstairs room being used for their trysts. Now, while she was trying to persuade him to stay with her in her beach hut in Whitstable – 'Oh Bushy, dear, let's get far away from all this, I have a place by the sea!' – he wanted to let her know he was less wholehearted than his initial passion might have led her to believe.

The women who were waiting to perform sat inside a wooden pen beside the bar, doing their make-up, abusing or flirting with the men who leaned over the side to talk to them. Now, one of them was shaving her legs. I liked strippers of any age, the rougher the better. I could watch them for hours while wondering, each time, whether the outcome might be different, like watching the replay of a football match, where one had the strange experience of knowing more than the players. Such squalid privacy was dying out in London, particularly as, with the development of CCTV – encouraged by a blind home secretary – everyone now watched everyone else, as though the whole country were under suspicion.

I'd taken Henry to the Cross Keys a couple of times but he didn't like it. 'Even Christopher Marlowe would have given this greasy strip a miss,' he complained. 'Shit, I think I've got spit and spunk up to my ankles! Doesn't the zoo stink bother you? The only thing to be said for it is that one gets to learn something about contemporary fashions in pubic hair – who has, and has not, for instance, mown the lawn – an opportunity not to be sniffed at, as it were.'

The Cross Keys was a market where Bushy did many transactions, selling jackets, drugs, cigarettes, phones. I'd also seen him buying stuff. Various shuffling characters, some of them Korean or Chinese, would approach him, concealing something – usually bootleg DVDs – under their coats, or carrying suitcases.

'Wolf came into the flat. I talked to him.'

'What did he say? You don't look good, man,' said Bushy, sitting at his usual table. 'You ain't shaved a while. An' I got a sensitive nose. Is it the vodka you still on?'

'It was pressed on me by my son.'

'Jeez, and him such a decent bright kid too!'

I caught a glimpse of myself in one of the pub mirrors and gave myself a nod. I looked no worse than anyone else on the premises.

I said to Bushy, 'I know Wolf from the old days, when I was a student. He's come back because he wants to blackmail me.' I hesitated before saying, 'He's got something on me.'

'What sort of something?'

'I won't tell you.'

'One of those no-details things. Shit, it could be filthy.' I had impressed him at last. 'Bushy don't need to know whether you done a person or not. You're a man of integrity and dignity, and I don't care how many people you've offed. We're family, Jamal,' he said. 'I hate to see a good doctor like you in trouble. You're a gentleman and a scholar, but where will it get you these days, financially? Those books have put you in a dream world.'

'Have they really?'

I was wondering if he was right when he said, 'You know I can say something like that without meaning nothing by it.'

I said, 'Bushy, I've been thinking about this and don't know what to do. I can't go to the police. Wolf's after money and he has a lot of power over my good name, such as it is. The other day I was offered a weekly column on a national newspaper. Unlike a lot of people, I do, regrettably, need my reputation, otherwise I'd have few patients and no income. It's a big deal for me, and decent money. So, you see, I am inclined to give him some money.'

Across the bar, a young Indian woman squatted down and spread her legs, her genitalia looking as though they were pinned together by a silver ring. She turned over and showed three old men – unshaven toothless grotesques who occupied the same position all day most days – the shrivelled eye of her anus, the gentlemen leaning forward with their hands on the edge of the stage, as though to examine a rare object which had turned up after a long time.

Considering Wolf, I was reminded of that time at school when all through the lunch break the bully who used to be your best friend has been following you, and is now approaching. You're in the cloakroom; everyone else has returned to their classrooms; the school is temporarily quiet. He is stepping slowly towards you with a smile on his face, and what do you do? Fight and suffer more damage, or roll up in a ball and beg for mercy? I was tempted by the 'rolling up in a ball position' – to let Wolf speak, and allow everything to come down which could come down, at least for the pleasure of seeing where it fell.

To be punished, in other words. Wouldn't I be in a similar position to Ajita's father when his life was collapsing before he died, a man about to lose everything? Except that, unlike him, I would be playing with degrees of suicide. What gains would there be, except in fantasy? If I were one of my own patients, I'd recommend a longer-term strategy of silence and cunning. Perhaps the only way to not be eaten by a wolf is to cling to its back. But would it get me anywhere in the end?

Bushy said, 'Don't give him nothing. I'm sayin' you'll never escape it. Can you inform me of this, though, boss? The thing you didn't do but are in trouble about . . . Were there any other witnesses?'

'One. He's dead.'

'Good.'

I hadn't enjoyed hearing that Valentin had killed himself.

Bushy said, 'Is the dude coming to see you again?'

'Without a doubt.'

'Let's see what he say when you turn him down. If he gets nasty, I'll be right outside your house. Measure 'im artfully – otherwise we can't deal with him.' Then Bushy said to me, 'I'm not saying you might not have to off him. That's the only way to deal with some of these people. I can't do him myself, mind.' He shuddered. 'There's blokes here who might be able to manage the job.'

'How much might it cost?'

'I'll look into it for yer.'

I'd already lied to Mustaq about his father. Now this new matter was hurting me. I needed to discuss it. But I didn't want to worry Miriam, and it was a matter too explosively intimate for my present relationship with Josephine. The only other candidate was Henry, a gossip: there was little he'd keep from the general discourse. It wouldn't occur to him that I was in any real danger. With him, my secret would go no further than West London, which was too far for me.

I said, 'But maybe I can charm him.' Bushy raised his long eyebrow at me. 'Or offer him something else.'

'Like what?'

'I don't know. I'll let you know what he says.'

I finished my drink and was about to tell Bushy that I needed to get going when he put his hand on my arm and said, looking round the place, 'Boss, there's a little thing I want to ask you –'

'Yes?' I said. 'If there's anything I can do in return.'

'I wouldn't come to you for nothing, you're a professional man with ultra-high standards. But I been having these dreams. They keep coming back. They're tripartite.'

'Sorry?'

'In threes. You want me to sit down?'

'You're going to tell me the dream now?'

'Why not?'

'Okay,' I said. 'Do it wherever you feel comfortable. It's the words that count, not the seating.'

All societies, like all lives, are sewn together by the needle of exchange, and I was amused by the idea of being a dream-dealer, interpreting dreams in exchange for detective work, though under these conditions I'd have to say his work was probably of a higher standard than mine. I had never heard a dream – that daily dose of madness – in such peculiar circumstances. Though parts of it disappeared in the uproar of a dispute over whether a customer had put twenty pence or a pound coin in a stripper's beer glass, I was able to take his associations too, and attempt an interpretation.

'You think I've got a problem?' he said when I'd finished. Normally I would give an analytic grunt here, but I said, 'I think you need to play the guitar. You miss it more than you know.'

'Bushy can't do it sober.'

'I bet you weren't drunk when you learned to play the guitar.'

'I was a kid.'

'There you are. Miriam says you give a lot of pleasure to people when you play.'

'She said that?'

He was thinking about this and smiling to himself when Miriam herself phoned. Bushy had to leave. She and Henry were going out that night.

'One more thing,' said Bushy before we parted. 'Haven't you noticed nothing peculiar about me?'

He was standing directly in front of me, as though on parade. I looked him up and down. 'I haven't, no.'

'You sure?'

'*Is* there anything peculiar about you?'

'My nose. Can't you see, there's a groove in it.' He ran his finger down his nose. 'That's pretty deep, innit?'

'It's not an unusual feature, if that's what you mean. It doesn't stand out. You are a fine man, Bushy.'

'My nose is turning into a backside. That's not unusual – to have a pair of buttocks screwed to the front of your face?'

'Is it getting worse?'

'I'm telling you, soon I'll be shitting out of me nose. What can I do about it? Is there an operation I can have?'

'Like plastic surgery?'

'Kind of.'

'How much is it worrying you?'

'How much would it worry you,' he asked, 'if you had shit dribbling out yer face?'

'A lot,' I said, feeling as he intended me to, that I was either stupid or mad not to grasp such a simple truth.

'Don't mention the hooter to Henry,' he said. 'We likes each other. I wouldn't want him thinking I'm batty.'

I said, 'Bushy, you wouldn't want to be too sane. How dull is that? The sane are the only ones that can't be cured. My first analyst used to say, "Our work is to heal the well, too."'

The Harridan, who had been collecting glasses across the bar, trotted towards Bushy, pinched his gut, and kissed him on the cheek. 'Hallo, Bushy dear, you farting ol' pigmy dick, gonna come and have a drink and more with me?'

He almost turned his back on her. 'When I'm in a business meeting?'

'Oh dear,' she said. The Harridan succeeded in being tiny and voluminous at the same time. She didn't move – was she on castors rather than legs? – so much as *bustle*. 'You didn't used to be too busy for yer little yum-yum baby.'

'This man here's a high-flying doctor, one of the top men in the West.'

'Why's he in here?'

'To partake of your watered vodka!'

'Always nice to have a doctor in the house, just in case.' She made a face. 'Mind you, some of my girls could do with some looking into.'

'He's a head doctor!' said Bushy impatiently, tapping his forehead and circling his finger. 'A shrinker.'

'Even better!'

When she'd gone, I said, 'Let's see how the nose develops. We're going to keep talking anyway.'

'Will you keep an eye on it?'

'Sorry?'

'My nose?'

'I will,' I said. 'I will.'

'Thank God, boss, you saving me only life.'

One madman, Bushy, looking after another madman, Wolf. And neither of them heroes of desire, the sort of madmen that R. D. Laing idealised: their craziness not making an increase of life but, rather, consternation, despair, isolation. I felt as though I'd just stuck my tongue through the flimsy cigarette paper which separates sanity and madness.

Before we left, Bushy said, 'Thanks, boss, for hearing me. If I have any other dreams, will you have a look at them? There won't be too many – I can't sleep much.'

'Okay.'

'I like you, boss. Henry's a good geezer as well. Man, he can chat! Was he always like that?'

'Yes.'

'He won't let her down will he? It would destroy Miriam. You put them together – now she's a different person, really happy. An' she wildly pleased with you for taking care of her. She say you never did before. No one did. That's why she got such a close family round her.'

CHAPTER THIRTY-TWO

As I hurried home – thinking of myself bent forward, like a fleeing question mark – a section from Dante's Purgatory came to me: 'Accurst be thou,/ Inveterate wolf! whose gorge ingluts more prey,/ Than every beast beside, yet is not fill'd!/ So bottomless thy maw!'

I rang Ajita and arranged to see her. She was the person I wanted to see, the person I felt least anxious with at the moment. Then I thought how much I admired Bushy's curiosity about his inner world, and the fact that he realised the benefit of becoming acquainted with it, recognising, too, that he couldn't do this alone.

I'd been considering Ralph Waldo Emerson and his essay 'Circles', the first words of which are: 'The eye is the first circle.' For the next few days I could look at a door and imagine an eye at the keyhole – an eye followed by a head, by a body, a man. A man who had come to hunt me down, arrest me, condemn me. For what? For being a criminal; for committing the most monstrous crime of all. Things are always what they seem.

I suspected Wolf was watching me, but he didn't come to the flat. Perhaps he was only my dream. Echoes of echoes, and nothing known for sure.

Yet if I felt paranoid, it wasn't without reason. Murdering someone is no way to get rid of them. Speaking from experience for once, I'd say it's a guarantee of their repeated return. At the same time I was hoping that Wolf had decided that persecuting me was a futile idea, and had gone away. Not that I really believed or expected this. Our own wishes are no guide to reality. As far as I could work out, he had come to London only to find me and to remind to me, over and over, of my crime.

At lunchtime a few days later the door bell rang, and I knew I hadn't succeeded in keeping the Wolf from the door.

I asked, as he came in, 'By the way, how did you find me?'

'I'd been thrown out of my home. My clothes, my collection of antique swords, everything was gone. During the day, in the library where I'd keep warm, I saw a book by you, in German. It was a sign you were asking to see me. It wasn't difficult to get an address, don't forget my father was a cop. Now, I'm dirty.'

'Sorry?'

'Please, will you let me wash here?' He was unshaven and dishevelled. 'You cannot refuse a man a little water.'

He wanted me to cook him scrambled eggs while he took a shower and freshened up. At this point he was only asking for things it would be difficult to refuse. He was trying to make his way further into my life, and I was getting used to him again.

However, when he'd washed and eaten I told him, in my firmest voice, that financially I was on the run and always had been – every month I was one step ahead of what I owed. I had given Josephine my stake in the house, but she constantly requested more money. These days reparation for the crime of leaving your lover was limitless. Money had become the substitute for love. On top of that I had to pay for Rafi's education for another ten years. Henry blamed Thatcher; I blamed Blair for being unable to provide good state schools for the over-eleven.

I said, 'No one becomes an analyst for the money. There are scores of therapies and not enough sick people, if you can believe it. In London you fall over wealthy people everywhere, most of them without much natural intelligence or talent. It makes me crazy that I didn't think about my financial situation as a younger man, instead of walking around depressed and arguing with myself.'

'What you say makes me unhappy. Couldn't we do something?'

'It's too late.'

'Yes, why would you bother when you're all set? I am not. You know why.'

Everything bad which had happened to him since the night in the garage was my fault. If he hadn't volunteered – out of sincere goodness – to help a mate whose girlfriend was being mistreated, he wouldn't be in this position now: a man who had been persuaded into a murder that had stained his entire life.

He said, 'I had a drink with Ajita. Lovely house she's got there.'

'You went in?' He didn't reply. I said, 'How did you find her?'

He enjoyed watching me consider the question.

'I followed you,' he said.

The day before, she and I had met for lunch in a Moroccan place in South Kensington that I liked. Ajita was wearing a white trouser-suit and looked, in the modern style, more or less ageless. She was carrying numerous shopping bags, as well as books on psychology and Freud she'd picked up at Blackwells. She was eager to learn about my work and how I became involved in it. 'That whole chunk of your life, truly I know nothing of,' she said.

It wasn't transference, the unconscious or the Other that Ajita wanted to hear about. It was the guy who loved to shit himself in public, and wanted to do it more; the woman who stuck needles in her breasts and thighs until she bled, and orgasmed, and the man who covered his penis with insects and said he wanted literally to fuck my brain.

'But I'm normal, compared to this. Why am I so dull! I feel free in this city,' she went on. 'I want to stay here. America's at war. It's horrrible for people like us. I'd forgotten how wickedly realistic Londoners are.'

She wanted us to spend the afternoon together, but I had patients to see. Then she asked me to go away with her for a few days. 'We can shop, sleep, talk, walk.' I had wondered whether, if she was in the mood for a passion, it was a good idea. But now I was warming to the notion. I had good reason to want to get out of London, and perhaps in Venice Ajita and I might go further with each other. I had always been a cautious and nervous fellow; maybe it was time I changed.

What I didn't know was that Wolf had trailed me, and followed her home. How stupid of me not to have been more alert. When it came to crime, despite my efforts I'd always be an amateur; clearly, transgression was a calling that not anyone could assume.

I told him, 'She hasn't got any money. It's her brother's. He collects houses. He's got them all over the place.'

'He has? Where exactly?'

'I don't know. Wolf, he's tough like his father, and more powerful and brutal.'

'Thanks. I'll be careful.' He said, 'Ajita took me to a bar and ordered champagne. We drank two bottles, and ate oysters. Then we had smoked salmon and toast. She gave me a little something to help me settle into a lovely warm hotel, not far from her. I walked her back home. I didn't go in, though she asked me. I'm not one to impose.'

'No.'

'What makes you think I'm interested in her money? It's worse. I like her.'

'You told her your story – the time in jail?'

'It's all I have. I can tell she's been unhappy for a long time. Now she's looking for something.'

He went on, 'Oh, Jamal, she is still good-natured, kind and beautiful. I said to her, you are without doubt one of those women who will become more beautiful and attractive as you get older, with a sophistication younger women can only envy.' I recalled this as a recommended leg-opener of his, for use on any woman over forty. Its time had surely arrived. 'Jamal, you made us knock out her father and then you let her go. Why didn't you marry her?'

'She went away, like you and Valentin. The gang was broken up. I didn't see her again until recently.'

'You lied to me about that, too.'

'It was private.'

'Maybe. But didn't she want you?'

'She did, very much. She said she still liked me.'

'And you turned such a girl away?'

'I haven't said that. We get on well.'

'Is that all?'

I continued, 'From my point of view, when I met you you were already a criminal, Wolf. I was a kid whose father had left. I was easily impressed by tough guys.'

'You call me a criminal!' he shouted. 'I was never a murderer till I met you! Let the judge decide which of us was the ringleader – the one who gathered us together to commit the dirty work!'

'The judge? You'll go down too, you know.'

He shook his head and drew his finger across his throat. 'Valentin and I would be playing together in the great casino in the sky. I've got nothing to lose. You've got everything. Your wife, son, friends – everyone will be devastated by what you did. You will never escape the shame.' He then said suddenly, 'Is life worth living? Is it worth the trouble, the suffering?'

'I don't know.' I said, 'Listen, Wolfgang. We were good friends. We could still be friends. But you've got to drop the bullshit threats, okay?' He smiled. I carried on. 'It's important that Ajita doesn't hear about what happened to her father. I'm going to be upset, I may even get into trouble. But she will be more than devastated, particularly if it comes from you. She might want to hurt herself.'

'I can't worry about all of you when no one's worrying about me.'

'Why don't you go back to Berlin?'

'There's nothing there for me!'

'Your knees are bouncing. In a fury?'

He said, 'They'd taken Ulrike away to one of their houses, and then they came for me, three in the morning. Minutes later I was on the street with only the clothes I could carry. I'd considered barricading myself in and shooting at them. They were ahead of me in everything. So you see, Jamal, friend, I need a little help. I want to stay in London. I don't care if I have to sleep on the street. I've done it before.'

'I will try to stop that happening to you,' I said.

'How?'

I told him again I couldn't give him any money and that if he stopped frightening me I'd be in a better position to think about how to help him. Meanwhile, even as he had been following me, I had been trying to find him work.

Bushy had asked the Harridan to let Wolf work behind the bar at the Cross Keys. Wolf could sleep in the room upstairs where the strippers changed, the one he and Harridan used for their love-making; Wolf would, no doubt, be face down in the same fuck-stained sheets. At night there was no one there and, as local boys were always trying to break into the pub, he could keep an eye on it. If he was lucky he'd get to hurt someone, and with moral impunity, always the nicest way.

'What do you think of the job?' I waited while he wondered about it. He didn't seem delighted. 'Wolf, you know how to take your chances. I've got to go away for a few days and you can't stay here. Give it a try.'

'Sleeping in a bar – is that my worth?'

'Pretty much. There are many friendly girls and dozens of scams going down. Tonight you'll be in a better position than last night. You should leave Ajita alone.'

He laughed mirthlessly. 'Who said I was going to see her again? She and I said a lot to each other. She needed to talk, she couldn't stop. I think I was her therapy, but there's nothing else going on, don't worry.' He gave me his mobile number. 'When do I start?'

I was pleased to see I'd startled him when I said 'Right away'. I drew him a map, led him gently to the door and celebrated when I shut it behind him.

That evening I went to Miriam's for a drink. Bushy was out front, cleaning the car. 'It's working,' he said. 'Relieved?'

Wolf had successfully arrived at the Cross Keys; the Harridan had already pinched his arse and evaluated his muscles. I said I couldn't help wondering whether it was wretched for Wolf to work in such a place. Were we humiliating him? Would it make him more pissed off? On the other hand, the Wolf I remembered was interested in most people. He'd like the girls; he'd soon be sleeping with one of them and helping the others.

It had been Bushy's idea. He must have been hoping that the Harridan, being keen on men, would fancy Wolf, thus releasing Bushy, who'd be able to trade at the Cross Keys without harassment from her. At the same time Bushy would be able to 'have a look' at Wolf, sussing out how bad and desperate he might turn out to be.

'Good,' I said, 'let's park Wolf there for a while and see what happens. He might settle down. Thanks, Bushy, for sorting this out for me. I appreciate it. Do you have any more dreams? It's a fair exchange, I think.'

'Bushy don't want that,' he said, looking around as though to ensure we weren't being observed. 'Bushy want something else now.'

'What is it?'

'I bin getting itchy fingers. I'm going to play again,' he said. 'I got to do it sober, like I got to do everything sober now, otherwise Miriam will cut me off, she already threatened. I had a group, a few years ago, but we fighted on stage. One night they all walk off and only me left there. Since then I done just the one gig. What I want . . .'

'Yes?'

'Will you come with me? I get nervous, I sweat buckets, my nose starts to run. And you know what it means if that happens.'

'What?'

'With diarrhoea comin' out me nose? I'll 'ave to get outta there. I'll be so embarrassed I could hurt myself. But if you're there, doctor in the house, I'll be good.'

If he'd been my patient I'd have said no, it was something he had to get through himself. Since he wasn't, I could go and see him play guitar, while drinking and talking with Henry and Miriam.

'Sure,' I said.

'Now you've agreed, I'll arrange it for definite – at the Caramel Sootie.'

'The Kama Sutra?'

'They know me there personally. I never have to give my name: I helped them with their heating. You can imagine, they were grateful.'

'Can't it be a more ordinary venue? Why not the Cross Keys?'

'It's dark, innit, at the Sootie? They're screwing. They won't be interested in me.'

'Or your nose.'

'That's it. An' what's that Woody Allen joke Henry told me? If sex between two people is great, sex between five people is even better!'

'But what could be worse,' I replied, 'than to feel desire and have it satisfied immediately?'

'Shrinky, don't be alarmed up. It ain't compulsive to screw if you don't wanna. Meself, I wouldn't touch some of them people with asbestos gloves on. But Henry and Miriam rate it better than sex. There's this twenty-stone guy who lies there, and birds dressed as schoolgirls –'

'They've told me about the Sootie, thanks.'

'You'll do it?'

'I'll have to ask Henry and Miriam.'

'Let me embrace you, man.'

He held on to me, before saying, 'You knows you'll 'ave to look right, dress up an' all. The only other way they'll let you in is bollock naked and I can tell you, there's draughts in there which will cut you in two. Henry and Miriam will help you. I'm looking forward to it,' he said. 'My come-back and your come-out.'

'Indeed.'

He tapped the side of his nose. 'You an' me, eh – pals!'

CHAPTER THIRTY-THREE

Luckily, before this humiliation, I'd have a break. Ajita and I had finally decided to go away.

The holiday was Mustaq's birthday present to her. For a long time Ajita had wanted to go to Venice, and she asked me to accompany her. She was nervous about my response, imagining I would refuse her, that I was still angry about the way she deserted me after her father died. Or worse, that I was disappointed with her now she had reappeared. It was more likely, of course, that I had disappointed her.

I could only make three nights away, but I told her I would be delighted. She and I had been talking on the phone regularly – about her brother, my work, and what there was for her to see in London – but we'd met only once in the city since finding one another again. I was nervous. During the weekend we spent at Mustaq's I'd felt as though she were already interviewing me for a position as her lover, a situation I was incapable of fulfilling with her, or anyone, while Josephine was still on my mind. Perhaps Mustaq was keen to help Ajita find someone, for both their sakes. He often looked irritated with her.

Mustaq's secretary booked two rooms in the Danieli. Ajita came to the flat to pick me up on the way to the airport. There were two taxis, one for us and the other for her luggage. She made coffee while I finished packing. 'You know, I've never seen anywhere you've lived as an adult,' she said. 'Does it smell of toast all the time? It needs work, this flat, it's coming apart. If you don't do it, it'll lose value. I'll find a builder for you.'

She asked permission before opening drawers, looking in cupboards, picking up things and asking where I'd got them. She wanted to see Josephine's drawings, as well as photographs of her and of Rafi, which she looked at for a long time.

'A happy family, all of you quite pleased to be together,' she said. 'We seem to know each other, you and I, and yet we're strangers. Who are you really, Mr K?'

Now the shock of our meeting again had worn off, we were easier with each other. She was less of the care-laden older woman and more as she had been at university, laughing and enthusiastic, expecting the best of the world, despite everything. I, perhaps, was less suspicious.

Having tea in the Danieli is lovely; the view is one of the most calming I have seen. Arm in arm, Ajita and I went on boat trips, consulted guidebooks, visited the Lido and looked at Tiepolos and Tintorettos in deserted churches. It was cold; she wore a fur coat, fur hat and boots, but the sun was bright in the morning. It was the most peace I'd experienced in a long time.

Ajita insisted on buying me new clothes, dressing me up and parading me around expensive shops, informing me my wardrobe needed 'help'. We found watches with pictures, on the face, of Nixon meeting Elvis in 1970: Presley in his 'big collar' and 'huge belt' phase, with much bling. Ajita bought me one, as I had, as she put it, 'lost the last one'. It was true I hadn't obtained a new watch; I had the time on my phone, and in my consulting room there was a clock on the shelf above the couch. She got one for Mustaq too, more amused than I by our identical watches.

In the afternoon, when she napped, I wrote in her room and read Tanizaki for the first time, amazed by his view of the tenacity of desire, particularly in the old, whom it can still grasp by the throat, refusing to let them go.

Uncharacteristically, Ajita had brought some grass with her. Not wanting to get kicked out of the hotel, we smoked out of the windows of café toilets, like schoolkids.

'This is fun, Ajita.'

'Isn't it? As soon as I stopped leading a conventional life, I cheered up. At home, after a smoke, I dance like a madwoman.'

'You mean home in Soho?'

'Yes. My temporary new home in London. The place I've absconded to, like the teenage runaway I nearly became.'

We giggled about how well we got on, saying that if we'd stayed together we'd have married, divorced and become friends like this. I told her about Josephine, and how much there still was between us, saying that the furious disputes I had with her were the ones I preferred.

When I asked Ajita about Mark, her husband, she said he was a good man and a decent liberal American. I guessed his days were numbered.

She said, 'Mark and I married when Mustaq was worried about me, when his music career was starting. At the same time, Mark worked hard to build up the business. He manufactured clothes in the Far East, where

259

he spent a lot of time. I brought up the kids in a good apartment in Central Manhattan. One day they were gone. My husband was in LA, in our other place. I knew I had to return to London, which I'd avoided for years. There was too much there – it was an unhealed wound. But I had to re-start my life.'

On the last morning we were to have brunch in Harry's bar. Coming down to the lobby Ajita cried out: it was under a foot of greasy water. It was not a tsunami; the sea was slowly rising. This happened three times a month.

We were given galoshes and clambered out of the hotel. St Mark's was a trembling lake. Submerged tables and chairs stood in the street like objects in an installation, with drowned pigeons bobbing around them. Tourists squeezed past one another on trestles; shopkeepers attempted to pump out their premises. I looked out past the bursting waves towards the Lido, wondering how hobbling Byron swam so far. Even as a kid I wouldn't have been able to do half that distance.

We waded to Harry's and, after we'd downed too many Bellinis, I was about to reach across the table to take her hand. I wanted to tell Ajita how easy we seemed with each other. Perhaps something might develop between us. We had one night left; couldn't we try more kisses and conversation, and see where they took us?

'Ajita –'

'I don't want to interrupt,' she said, 'but I need to! I've been meaning to tell you – I've met someone.' She was laughing. 'I just knew it would happen in London, my lucky city. It's extremely early days.'

'I see.'

'He's tender and makes me feel beautiful. That's all I'm saying – certainly not his name. I can hardly say it to myself, let alone to you or my husband. It was you, though, Jamal, who gave me the confidence.'

Disappointment winded me. She had returned and I had let her go. At least age had taught me that the pain would not last, that I would even feel relieved.

'That's wonderful,' I said. 'What a great thing to happen.'

'Do you really think so?' She was watching me. 'We'll see. I can't tell you any more about it,' she said. 'It might be bad luck and I'll make a fool of myself. Don't think it's only pleasure.'

'Why not?'

'For the first time, I've been talking about Dad. He's interested, this man, in what happened to Papa.'

'That's good.'

'You know, Jamal, I noticed an odd thing.'

'Where?'

'Mustaq's people – who have been investigating the matter – found a press picture of Dad driving into his workplace the day he was murdered. We've studied it on a computer. We are almost certain he is wearing the watch you gave to Mustaq. Isn't that strange? What happened?'

'I wish I could remember,' I said. 'I was really knocked over by the abuse story. I do recall your dad coming to my house once, on his way home, asking if I wanted a lift to yours – to see Mustaq.'

'He touched you then?'

'I thought he liked me. A lot of people seemed to fancy me. I didn't know what to make of it.'

'I know it was a long time ago, but Mustaq and I aren't going to give up on trying to find out the truth about Dad.' She was looking at me. 'You okay?'

'It's still difficult for me to think about that time.'

She grasped my hand, which I'd omitted to withdraw properly, and kissed it. 'It was me! I made you so unhappy, Jamal! I was unfaithful! I haven't faced that properly.'

'How could you know what you were doing?'

'Can't you forgive me?'

'Yes.' I called the waiter. 'Let's just drink to you – to your return, and to your happiness.'

'Thank you, darling.'

I said, I hope without sarcasm, 'Your new man doesn't object to you going away with me?'

'He knows what a valuable friend you are now.'

'I can't wait to meet him. Can we get together with him when we're back home?'

'I'm not sure about that. We'll see. Don't make me go too fast.'

We drank a lot that day, and my hope increased that though I, the eternal vacillator, didn't feel capable of claiming her, she might claim me, by inviting me to her room. Then her boyfriend called. Her face seemed to open, and she laughed, hurrying outside the hotel to speak to him.

I left her to it, once more forfeiting love for a novel. Unable to concentrate, I called Rafi on his mobile. He was watching *The Simpsons* and was too busy to gossip. 'Phone back in a year,' he suggested.

I put my coat on and walked those lugubrious, echoing Venetian alleys, passages, bridges and archways for more than three hours.

CHAPTER THIRTY-FOUR

'So?' said my sister, almost as soon as I walked in the following night, on my way to visit Wolf at the Cross Keys. Kids and corpulent neighbours drifted in and out of the kitchen as usual, cats jumped out of windows, and there was always a stinking dribble-jawed dog farting on any chair you wanted to sit on.

'What so?'

'Don't fuck with me!' she said, suddenly attempting to throw me on the ground. The two of us struggled; I fought her off – no, I didn't, I couldn't – and the dogs barked.

'Bitch, maybe one day I'll be stronger than you,' I said, getting up. I wasn't too pleased about being attacked and thrown down by her. No one would want unnecessary contact with Miriam's floor.

We stood apart, out of breath, hair and laughter over her face. I was convinced she'd dislocated my shoulder again. For a while my differences with Miriam usually ended with my arm in a sling. Kids stepped around us disapprovingly, talking about eBay.

Miriam said, 'You and Ajita. Is it on?' In Venice I'd bought Miriam a black-and-white carnival mask to wear on 'the scene'. She kissed me and said, 'Henry and I have been frantic for it to work out between you two. He told me you were keen on her again.'

'Who's asking you two meddlers? You know these things take a lot of time with me.'

'Time? When you met her the Beatles were still together.'

'They weren't, actually.'

I took off my sweater and tee-shirt. She fetched a clean blanket, spreading it out on the sofa. I lay down, and she stroked, tickled and scratched my back, something she knew I loved. I turned round and she did the same on my stomach, her nails raking my bulging stomach, not as grand as Henry's 'waterbed' but heading that way.

I was drifting off when she said, 'You staying for supper? I'm making some dhal and Henry's coming by later. I've hardly seen him. There's a crisis: Valerie's been insisting that he go over there all the time.'

'He goes?'

'I guess you don't know this, but Lisa went into the house when there was no one home and stole a hand from her mother's bedroom wall.'

'A what?'

'I dunno. A *hand*.'

'What was a hand doing on the wall?'

'It's a picture, for fuck's sake. A famous drawing by some old guy. She's hidden it and won't give it back. Bushy's been trying to help Henry find it. But she's a cunnin' one.'

'What,' I sighed, 'is she intending to do with this hand?'

'Apart from trying to make her family crazy, you mean? Who knows. It's like a hostage.'

I was mystified by the story of the stolen hand but didn't want to hear any more about Lisa.

I said, 'Bushy wants me to come to the Sootie.'

'I noticed you two have become pretty close, talking together outside on the street rather than in my kitchen. Still, I've never seen him so excited. Is it true you're giving him the inspiration to play live again?'

'I may be the fuel but he has to be the rocket. I said I would have to ask you, but wouldn't it spoil your evening to have your brother hanging around that fuckery the Sootie as, you know, a spare prick?'

I got up and put my tee-shirt on.

She was laughing. 'Oh no, don't worry about me and Henry. We know how to take care of ourselves. Looks like you're going to have to come, bro.' She pinched my cheek and poked me in the stomach. 'I can't wait to see what you'll wear. You want me to help you choose something unsuitable?'

'No fear.'

'Have you done anything like this before?'

'Not even in the privacy of my own bedroom. There's no reason why you would have noticed, but analysts and therapists always dress oddly, the men looking uncomfortable in the sort of jackets that provincial academics wear while the women resemble wealthy hippies, in bolts of velvet with flowing scarves.'

'I can't wait to see you at the Sootie,' she said. 'I'm so going to laugh my big tits off. You've always been timid, a mincing little thing.'

'Thank you.'

'Actually you've got better,' she said. 'You were shy and quiet before, terrified of people, mooching in your room for days, not talking, miserable. In Karachi your nickname was Sad Sack. But you did change – when you went to live in that house in London.'

'I found my first analyst then, after we came back from Pakistan. You'd be reluctant to recall it, but I was in a mess.'

'We both were, thanks. You and Dad trotted off together like long-lost lovers, expecting me to spend every minute with the boring well-behaved women, like *I* was in purdah.'

'A position you rightly refused.'

'I was channelling Dad this afternoon and remembered that the last words he said to me were, "No one will ever marry a whore like you." Wasn't he right?'

'He didn't say no one would ever love you.' I said, 'My analyst was a Pakistani, you know, with a cute accent, like Dad's. I was lucky to meet him when I did. Otherwise I'd have ruined my life before it started.'

She said, 'I could have done with someone to save my life. Why didn't you send me there?'

'It was my thing.'

'He converted you?'

'Something like that. To a life of enquiry, perhaps.'

She said, 'Josephine used to wonder whether you were gay.'

'Thanks for reminding me.'

'She did come to me one time, at a family Christmas, got me in a corner and asked me if you were that way. My instinct was to give the cow a backhander – for being so unobservant. Then I nearly told her, "He's my brother, and a woman with your problems is enough to make Casanova gay." But I zipped it – for you.'

'Thank you, my dear.' I went on: 'She had this bizarre theory that because I liked her arse I was gay.'

'Even a sexual dyslexic like her can see you're not a boy-bummer.'

I said, 'No, I'm a married man with a married mind. There was a film premiere we went to, a few months ago, even though Josephine and I weren't together. Miriam, she looked great in her heels and black dress and red wrap, with bare legs. All evening I wanted to fuck her. For a while I wasn't bored.'

'She's a striking woman, being so tall.'

'Yes, I used to think one didn't so much go down on her as go up on her.'

'You can be sulky and moody, but you're also nervous and very evasive, Jamal.'

264

'Am I still?'

'Look at your bitten nails and the way your eyelashes flap.'

'They do?'

'But you got on by not throwing everything away like me. You knew there was a future.' She was tickling me. 'Now, you therapists are always talking about sex. Maybe you should see some for once. It'll be good for you to hang out at the Sootie.'

I said, 'I never knew whether you were glad Josephine and I separated?'

'I quite liked her, mainly because she liked you. *Loved* you, I mean. She never stopped loving you, Jamal, though you must have tested her hard.'

'Don't remind me of that, Miriam.'

We embraced; I told her I had to go. Wearily I walked to the Cross Keys to have a look at my parallel man, Wolf. While I was in Venice, Bushy had phoned to say he'd popped into the pub several times to see how Wolf was doing. Now I was wondering whether they might have been getting on too well.

Bushy was smoking at the bar. Wolf was in the cellar, changing the barrels. After my trip to Venice, the place looked less salubrious than I remembered it. Maybe it was time to find a new local.

Bushy indicated the Harridan. 'That's a smile on her gob. She's happy with 'im,' he said.

'How come?'

Wolf was physically strong and hard-working. When men tumbled onto the stage, or tried to dance with the girls, Wolf would pull them off and have them outside in seconds. The girls liked him, he involved himself in their problems, but he wasn't 'up an' all over 'em. He don't touch 'em. I think he's got someone.'

'One of the girls here?'

'No, he after something bigger. I'll find out soon as I can.'

Wolf came up out of the cellar and saw me. He wore a tight white tee-shirt and looked fit and toned, as though he'd been exercising. Unfortunately his jeans were too big, his belt just about holding them up.

He was subdued, and didn't shake my hand. Not that he appeared to be unhappy. He had requested one big thing and received a smaller thing – a job. It was, as Bushy put it, 'a hopeful opening' into which Wolf had moved.

Wolf said, 'Let's speak. Not here.' He added, 'What's with these jeans? Why are they so big?'

'They're knock-offs,' I said. 'Blame my sister.'

He took me up to the room in which he slept, a small dressing room for the girls containing a mirror and dressing table covered with discarded thongs and spangled bras. There was a single mattress under a rattling window covered with a soiled piece of net curtain. Through a tear in the curtain I could see, on the corner, tall Somalians, their busted Primeras lined up on the street outside the cab office.

He said, 'These African boys are busy up West all night. They take me with them. You've dumped me far out here.'

'What have you got going in town?'

He shrugged. 'Ventures.'

As we talked one of the girls – an Eastern European – came in to fix her hair. Before leaving she changed her thong: naked, she bent forward and dragged the cheeks of her backside open. 'Check me being clean, Wolfie, if that's good,' she said.

Having inspected her, he kissed her on the arse. 'Juicy as ever, Lucy.'

She looked at me. 'Punter here?'

'I'm a pal of Wolf's.'

'Sir, you like show?'

'I did the first time I saw it.'

'Next time I make it extra spicy for you special.'

After she'd gone, Wolf said, 'She likes you, didn't you notice? You still look decent for your age. But you wouldn't go for a girl like that, would you?' I shrugged. He said, 'You know that when I go to any city I want to be with the lowest, the whores, hustlers, criminals. To me these are the finest people. You and I are similar like that.'

'In what way?'

'You must have something like that in you, spending every day with the mentally diseased.'

'The sane are much worse. As you know, calling someone sane isn't much of a compliment.' I said, 'Wolf, I want to know about Val,' and sat down with the joint Miriam had given me as I left.

Wolf told me that he and Valentin had been looking for an excuse to leave London for a while. They even considered taking me with them, but decided I should finish at university. I wondered whether I might have been tempted to accompany them. Probably I would have.

In the South of France Valentin worked in casinos. He was well paid and respected enough to be trusted to train the new recruits. He considered this work to be worthless but he kept himself together, cycling for miles across the mountains on icy roads.

Wolf said, 'Back in his sparse room, he read those huge philosophical books, like a madman always with the Bible, trying to find the truth.' At night, when he left work, women, rich and poor, old and young, would be waiting for him. They wanted to sleep with him. Once they'd done that they wanted to help him. 'They wanted to send him to doctors, to find him a drug to make him well. But he refused. He wanted to be one of the lost ones. He never found a place. We should remember him a moment.'

Wolf bowed his head. I did so too, recalling Valentin earnestly advising me to take up his diet, which was Heinz tomato soup, two slices of bread with margarine spread on them, and an apple – twice a day. He'd sometimes walk five miles across London, wearing only tennis shoes, rather than taking the tube – an even more mephitic hole then – though most people used it for free, easily sneaking past the somnolent staff. Valentin's ambition had always been to reduce his desire to almost zero; there would be no excess of pleasure. But where did a lifetime of self-punishment get him?

I opened my eyes. Wolf had been looking at me. I got to my feet, not entirely sure where I was.

'But you must still sit down.'

His fists were clenched. But I was heading for the door, wherever that might be. God knows what Miriam had dropped into that joint. She liked a mixture of hash and grass and menthol tobacco, an unpredictable blend. Not only was I feeling paranoid, I seemed to be viewing Wolf down the wrong end of a telescope, an excellent way to shrink him.

He got up too, grasped me by the shoulders and pushed me down again. He drew his hand back, as if to strike me. He was easily more powerful than me, but not as angry. For a moment I thought I'd let him beat me up, as if that would be a solution.

'I haven't finished with you,' he said, sitting in a chair opposite me. 'There's an odour that chases me in my dreams, dragging me into that dirty night. What do garages smell of? Oil, petrol, wood, rubber. I can see how angry you were with that father. You were trembling.'

'I was afraid.'

'You didn't appear to be. We were there to give him a warning, and suddenly you had a knife. *What are you going to do with that? I keep thinking. Only the business, surely?* No one said anything about knives, not me, not Val. Where did you get that idea from? Why didn't you ask us first?'

'I was a young fool. Friend, you should have taken care of me a bit. I was like your little brother, and you let me go ahead with a wild and stupid scheme.'

'Are you going to cry? Will you kiss my feet and beg forgiveness? What you did made me see – right in front of my eyes – a dying man. If we'd been caught I'd have done a lot of time.' He went on, 'Now you say you regret it. If you could take back that night, you would. But there's one thing you have never said. One thing I want to hear you say.'

'What is that?'

He said, 'That you got it wrong and deserved to be punished. You thought it was noble to save the girl. You should have gone to the police. You should have talked with her more. I don't know what you should have done. You're the person who is supposed to know what to do in such situations.'

He was still staring steadily at me. I said, 'I didn't know how to listen. I misunderstood Ajita. I acted too soon and stole her initiative. But what can we do?'

'This,' he said. 'We could both apologise to the family. To the girl. So she knows what went on, so she can have – what's that stupid word they use? – closure, yes. You think about that.'

I said, 'I am not convinced that an apology will cause more good than harm.'

'I am,' he said. 'You consider it and get back to me. Otherwise I've been thinking it's something I should do myself – on your behalf.' He paused. 'Got something to say?'

'Yes.' I said, 'Unlike some famous procrastinators I could name, I took action and killed the man. You will only ever be a minor villain. What a shame you never did anything so brave or honourable. Any fucker can be innocent. I'm way ahead of you, man, and always will be. Have some fucking respect!'

'You're mad.'

I got up. He got up. I went downstairs. He followed me. Wolf returned to work at the other end of the bar and I stood with Bushy, who was passing over various items from inside his coat to some local characters. Wolf had turned up the music; I watched the naked grinders opening and closing their legs for the devoted regulars. Behind the stage the different coloured lights Wolf had rigged up were pulsating. I ordered a double vodka and drank it quickly. I ordered another.

When Bushy was alone I said, 'What news of the Hand?'

He shrugged. 'Lisa's a socialist worker with a lot of people to visit. My guess is the Hand's in one of their houses. What am I going to do – search everywhere for it?'

'Why should you?'

'Because I feel sorry for 'im, a good un, with that crazy daughter.'

I asked, 'How's the dreaming?'

'Dr Shrinky, my friend, your advice has been on my mind. I nearly ready to come out. I been rehearsing at Miriam's, in front of the kids. Your boy Rafi there one day thought I was deep and boom. Henry says I'm good enough for the Sootie. Miriam must have told you – it's next week.'

'No, but she has now.'

'Made up your mind 'bout what you wanna wear?' I shrugged. Another customer approached Bushy, who looked across towards Wolf; he, in his turn, nodded cooperatively. Bushy said, 'Wolfie's not so bad after all. He's just like us, on the hustle. He lets me sell what I like, as long as I give him a good bit.'

'I better go,' I said.

'See you at the Sootie, then,' said Bushy. 'I'll take you all there. Don't be nervous.'

The walk home was further than I could cope with in one go, so I popped into the Bush Hall, a small ballroom next to the mosque on the Uxbridge Road where Rafi, as a child, had appeared in a carol service. I wanted to catch the end of M. Ward's set. He was a sombre singer-song-writer Henry's son had recommended, whose melancholic version of Bowie's 'Let's Dance' never failed to move me. Ward was accompanied by a bass player, girl drummer and another guitarist. The place was only three quarters full; I hadn't had so much personal space at a concert in years.

I left, cheerful, after an exquisite version of Willie Dixon's 'Spoonful'.

CHAPTER THIRTY-FIVE

I had too much to think about. I was anxious and not sleeping. I had said I would visit the Sootie and it would be difficult to avoid; Miriam would insist. But there was no way I'd let her dress me.

At the end of the Shepherd's Bush Road, going towards Olympia, was a circus shop where I took Rafi to buy his bling. Next door there was a sex shop, with dummies in the window clothed in what looked like 70s punk gear, now worn by the middle-class at play, perversion as style. I went in and had a quick look around, but had no idea what was suitable dress for watching Bushy strum the banjo while others copulated.

I went outside. 'Goddess, can you come with me?' I pleaded on the phone.

'It's a strange request,' she said, between clients.

'You must have heard weirder. I'm a bit stuck here and a little embarrassed.'

'Oh, you poor dear. I'll have to ask Madame. We can't go behind her back.'

Madame seemed to think it was okay, as I was a 'good, clean, respectable customer'. The Goddess, who would offer her body but not the intimacy of her name to anyone, met me by the tube station and we walked along to the shop. I guessed she was wearing her college clothes: jeans, a black polo-neck sweater, black boots.

Asking her to help was a good idea. She went straight to the black guy who ran the place and he showed her the gear. Knowing that I didn't want anyone to see much of my body, and would only wear black and nothing too tight, she had me try on various items.

'Any silk or lace?'

'No thanks, Goddess. Think of me as a repressed Englishman.'

I posed around half-naked in a corner of the shop until I was well-covered up in rubber and some sort of sticky plastic. Apart from my face, the only part of my body anyone would see would be my arms.

We were coming out of the shop with the stuff in anonymous bags when the Goddess touched my arm. I was saying I wished the clothes were rentable, as they were expensive and I was broke. She was laughing, and telling me I'd like 'the scene' and would want to return, 'knowing your taste'.

She said, 'Someone's looking at you.'

'What?'

'Over there.' I assumed it was Wolf, the hell-hound on my trail, clearly getting madder. It wouldn't be long before the police picked him up, and then we'd both be done for. She said, 'There she is.'

It was one of my patients, hurrying away. She was very paranoid, often telling me she'd seen me in different parts of the country, places I'd never visited. Now that she'd actually seen me, and coming out of a sex shop too, what would it do to her?

I took the Goddess for a drink and she asked me what I did. I told her we both sold our time for money and were in the 'intimacy with strangers' business. In fact, I said, I had never counted the number of times I had been compared, by my patients, to a prostitute. 'Perhaps we are both rubbish dumps. People put into us what they don't want to understand. We're supposed to carry it for them.'

She was fascinated and horrified by what I did. 'Who wants to know what's in there?' she said, tapping her head. 'If you start poking about who knows what you'll find?'

'It comes out anyway,' I replied. 'You live it out, in your body, in your actions, in your choice . . . of career. What we all need, as my friend Henry says, are more words and less action.'

She seemed horrified. But when we parted, the Goddess gave me a plastic bag. 'Open it,' she said.

It contained a half-mask with gold eye sockets, made of turquoise, blue and purple feathers, with silver and blue stars sewn into it.

'It's beautiful,' I said.

'Yes, good luck!' She kissed me on the nose.

Having got the gear together, on the appointed night I went over to Henry's with the stuff in a bag. Miriam would get changed at home; Bushy would bring her over and then drive us all to the Caramel Sootie.

It took me ten minutes to get ready and another two minutes to fight hopelessly with my hair, while wondering that if everything that gives pleasure is unhealthy, immoral or forbidden, would the evening be enough of each?

Henry was in his boxers, having shaved his genitals, flinging things down and stamping drunkenly around in front of a mirror while listening to *Don Giovanni*.

I was happy sitting in his chair, drinking, and smoking one of the joints Miriam had made for him. But the joint tired me and I went to the bathroom for a little dab of speed to keep me going for the night. I was soon unaware of what I was wearing, but whenever Henry looked at me he giggled.

'If only your patients could see you,' he said. 'You look too good to have got that together yourself. Who helped you?'

'A friend.'

He was looking at me, 'How come I tell you everything and you tell me nothing?'

We might have a long evening ahead of us, but at least Henry and I could have a conversation before Bushy arrived. Henry philosophising about his desire always entertained me. I said to him, 'This orgy idea –'

'Yes, what about it? Hey – d'you think I should wear lipstick?'

'Only a little.' I went on: 'Isn't it a dream of merging? Of there being no differences between people? No one is left out. Sexually, it's a totalitarian idea. Isn't the orgy where people lose their individuality rather than find it?'

'I'm telling you this. You might feel a fool in those clothes, but who gives a fuck? This is an important and radical freedom.'

'At a time of harsh controls – indeed of terror – this represents liberation, man?'

'I am aware of your amusement, but all this bullshit about the conflict between civilisations, Islam and the West, is only another version of the same conflict between puritans and liberals, between those who hate the imagination and those who love it. It's the oldest conflict of all, between repression and freedom.' He was standing in front of me. 'How am I looking?'

'I can't begin to describe it.'

'A couple of generous words, my friend?'

'Only to confirm that make-up and facial hair don't go together.'

'They do now.' He went on, 'I like London being one of the great Muslim cities. It's the price of colonialism and its only virtue. At the same time London is full of people with their heads covered – either in hoods, like your son, or Muslim women. I have to say I hate that and even glare at the women, no doubt adding to their sense of persecution.'

I said, 'It shows that we are fascinated and disturbed by our bodies – covering, uncovering, the whole thing. We can never get it right, never be finished with this body business. Tattoos, weight, clothes . . .'

'You want to know why I'm listening to this opera? I'm trying to find something subversive and lubricious, a work that might speak to our condition. Want a Viagra?'

'Yeah, okay. Thanks.' He handed me the blue pill, and I swallowed it with vodka. 'You're going to stage *Don Giovanni*?'

'It's too puritanical for me. He goes to hell in the end.'

'Doesn't he refuse to recant? His is an ethical position, at least.'

I was aware of how powerful Henry's connection with his work still was when he tapped his watch and said, 'It's seven-fifteen. Every day at this time it occurs to me that all over this city, throughout the country in fact, there are actors preparing for a show tonight, sitting in dressing rooms, putting on their slap, doing warm-ups and vocal exercises, terrified and exhilarated. Performers. The people I have spent my life with – those who can do difficult things in front of people who have travelled to see them.'

A couple of weekends before, Miriam and Henry, accompanied by one of her own kids, had driven down to a pop festival in a borrowed caravan, with Bushy driving. Henry had insisted on accompanying them, not wanting to be alone. But he had become restless, hating the caravan and, after a couple of hours, hating the music. It was 'just white' and not as 'authentic' as the hip-hop he liked to discuss with Rafi. Miriam and the others had started to call him 'grandad'.

I was surprised, therefore, when, not long after, they started out on another short jaunt, this time to Paris, where Henry had been invited to a conference on culture. Naturally Henry despised 'official' culture, but saw the trip as an excuse to see his friends – gallery directors, producers, writers, actors.

While he and Miriam were eating well with Marianne Faithfull, Bushy's contacts in the Cross Keys had put him onto some Africans who hung around the Gare du Nord. Bushy also picked up some hot hip-hop in various African lingos for Rafi. On the way back they filled up the car with booze and fags to sell to neighbours and in the Cross Keys. If there was anything left over, Wolf could offload it 'up West'.

Henry had told me he'd been 'offered something' at the Comédie-Française, but had turned it down. He seemed both flattered and tempted. I wondered when he'd go back to work and how Miriam would react to not having him around.

He said, 'You say to me, why don't I think about working again? What have I accomplished anyway? I have staged the work of others, but I am not the originator. What value do I have? The actors I respect. What they do is dangerous. Have I achieved anything original or worthwhile myself? One time someone called me a facilitator and I nearly killed myself.'

'Aren't you just tormenting yourself?'

'Chekhov's characters are always going on about work. We must work, they repeat. I've never understood why he would consider work such a virtue.'

'Work is the price of guilt.'

He looked at me. 'Come on, we'd better go.'

Bushy had rung. He and Miriam were nearby, waiting in the car.

Watching Henry prepare for the evening, and envying his commitment to the far-out – 'To know sex,' he had said, 'you have to risk being destroyed by it' – I'd decided not to be so uptight. Along with the gear the Goddess had arranged for me, I was wearing lipstick, slap, a blond wig belonging to one of Sam's girlfriends – I hoped it was the Mule Woman – a black hat and dark glasses.

'Evenin', doctor, if it really is you,' said Bushy, as I opened the car door. 'Lookin' good, lookin' good. You made the right choices, the pukka decisions.'

'Thank you, Bushy, my friend,' I said. 'I can always rely on you for an accurate review. What do you think?' I asked Miriam, who was wearing a combination of black spider's webs in various materials, more or less her everyday look, apart from the miniskirt. 'Miriam?'

'I've lost the power of speech.'

'Put that camera down!' I said, trying to grab the phone she was holding up.

'Get off! Just one for the kitchen wall!'

'No – no!'

'Girls, girls!' cried Henry, as he got into the car. 'Save your excitement for later.'

CHAPTER THIRTY-SIX

Not far across the river at Vauxhall we came to a line of railway arches which were used as motor workshops. One of the doors was painted black, and there were a few people gathered around it. Pushing through three thick curtains, we were greeted inside by a middle-aged couple who had known Bushy when he worked in a warehouse nearby.

We helped Bushy unpack his stuff and carry it into the crepuscular Sootie. Henry found a way to light Bushy on a little raised stage at the back of the place. Miriam was attempting to powder his sweating face; Bushy was shy about having his nose over-illuminated. He was nervous and oblivious to the fact that everyone around him was dressed in unusual clothes, and even that they were beginning to kiss and caress one another.

The place was filling up. Bushy sat down in his position, tuned up and began to play a quiet blues. To encourage him, Henry and Miriam cheered and whistled as they did while watching trash TV. 'All I need is me guitar, an amp, a joint and my doctor,' Bushy said, pointing at me.

I donned my mask and walked through the numerous tunnels and rooms of the Sootie, wondering at the people and their lives.

I turned a corner and she walked past me. My wife was tall in the heels I'd bought her years ago, when I still believed in our love. Her legs were long and she looked good in her clothes. I was surprised to see her but not unhappy. Often, when we met outside the house, we found we got on. We wouldn't speak all day at home but then, in the evening, at a party, we'd ignore everyone else and begin talking as if we were friends who hadn't seen one another for a year. But tonight she seemed to be in a hurry, walking about alone, looking for something or someone, and I didn't want to follow her.

I could hear that Bushy had begun in earnest and I wanted to see him. By now his foot was bouncing, his muscles pulsing, his voice like dirty metal and Captain Beefheart.

He was competent in most styles, with great technique, but he couldn't complete a tune, as though he wanted to play everything at once, like some kind of psychotic jukebox. As he switched between complicated jazz chords, bits of blues and popular tunes, he talked or rambled. He had studied the blues-men and remembered the dates, saying this song was written in March 1932 or whenever. Sensing some interest, he'd give you more: did you know John Lee Hooker was a Jehovah's Witness? He'd do an impression of Hooker, almost a skit – the voice, the whole thing – coming to your house with his Bible, a copy of the *Watchtower* and a tune.

Bushy was compelling, keeping people from sex. What higher compliment could there be for an artist? Henry stood there proudly, leaning against a pillar. When a man approached to ask whether he was Bushy's manager, Henry said yes. The man gave Henry his card, took Henry's number and promised to get in touch. 'Bushy will always work now,' Henry said to me. 'I wish it had occurred to me before to represent talent for a living.'

Later, beyond a heaving pile of what looked like colourfully decorated slugs, I came upon a screen with slits and holes in it, and a chair behind it. I was looking through it as two men led her in. She seemed determined now in her search for the holy grail of pleasure, the paradigm of luxurious abandonment.

I sat to watch as Joesphine lay down, with her face turned towards me. I was so startled – it was as though she could see me. I thought for a moment that my ears might burst – I almost fled. I was more than tempted to lie in her arms again. To do it anonymously would be one of the oddest things I'd done.

I walked towards her as she lay there with her throat exposed, the other figures rising and falling in the mirrored wall, reminding me of how she liked sex in front of a mirror, with one leg up on a chair; little of me would be visible, just my dark hands moving over her fair skin as she watched herself.

I thought: in an opera, at this moment, someone would kill her. I was trembling, and wondered if I might fall down.

She was excited: her face appeared to be glowing. She lived in fear of blushing – 'an erection of the face, along with the desire to be looked at' – as someone described it, which, made her even more self-conscious. At times she didn't want to go out because of what she saw as her 'embarrassment'. Shame would have been the better word. When she became angry her face seemed to pulsate with blood pushing to the surface. 'An exploding strawberry,' I called her, helpfully.

Now it was my turn, she whispered in my ear, as though she knew me. 'Hallo,' she said, and 'Please' and 'Yes, yes.' I said nothing, smelling the other men on her, wondering if she'd know me by my flickering eyelashes, which she'd often commented on.

In the low light I was able to see, in her hair on the back of her neck, a mole I hadn't noticed before, which I kissed. Not far away Bushy was singing a Mavis Staples song, 'I'll take you there . . . I'll take you there . . .' I could almost have fallen in love with her again, as I thought: *a better man than me would announce himself, pick her up, cover her, and carry her out of here, to a cleaner place.* I wasn't sure any more what it was to love an adult, but looking at her familiar white limbs I knew I preferred her to anyone else.

I noticed Bushy was no longer playing. I was going to the bar when Henry found me.

'I've been looking all over for you,' he said, pulling anxiously at his beard. 'Bushy won't come out.' He pointed at the disabled toilet. 'The Security here can force him, but it would be easier if he heard your voice.'

I knocked on the door. 'Can I come in?'

'Git out!'

'Can I talk to you – about the music?'

There was a silence. The door opened and I entered the lighted box, Bushy locking the door behind us. The taps were running and the striplight was buzzing. The drier had jammed and sounded, in that space, like a motor mower. It was hot in there. Perhaps I was stoned: Bushy's body was almost anamorphotically distorted. I had interrupted this dirty Orpheus naked in front of the mirror, examining his scabrous hooter with a razor blade in his hand. His eyes, wide and unblinking, appeared in the strange light to be buried in one yellow socket and one that was lurid blue.

'Don't get the wrong idea.' He had suspended the blade over his nose, as though looking for the ideal spot. 'I'm not cutting it off. I'm going to nick into a section of it. I'm going to prune it – that way it won't toilet me no more.'

'You can't slash your snout. You'll get blood everywhere.'

'Why else would I be undressed?' He glanced at me and tapped his nose. 'You think this is the right place?'

'It's not the right place and this is not the right time. You'll make a mistake,' I said, coming up behind him with his clothes gathered up under one arm.

He said, 'Keep off!'

'I can't help it, friend, we're in a toilet together. People are backed up out there, waiting to pee.' I put my other hand out. 'Don't let everyone down now you've got them interested.'

He dropped the blade into my palm. He took the clothes and began to dress. 'You haven't said anything about the music.'

'It's heavy.'

'I'll give 'em my Latin.' He checked himself in the mirror and looked at me. 'Your wig's crooked.'

'Can you adjust it for me?'

'A pleasure, man of leisure. You're looking good, man, fully expressed. I told you I needed you here with me.'

Bushy went out before me, back to the stage area. Henry was waiting outside, with so much sweat coming off him I thought a pipe had burst over his head.

I showed him the blade before putting it in my pocket. 'A close shave.' Henry could see from my face that something bad had happened. 'I need a drink. Christ, Henry, some people are really crazy.'

Bushy's second appearance was indeed quieter, mostly Latin tunes accompanied by some gruff crooning. The music became so smooth and serious that people began to make love around him, on sofas and cushions; as they copulated, Bushy adjusted his time and rhythm. 'I was the illustrator of fuck,' he told me later. 'As their rhythm changed so did mine, in fuck-adjustment. Then I saw I could influence their fuck movement, making 'em do different fucking things.'

A couple lying on a sofa invited me to join them. I was left in no doubt, in such a place where other mundane norms were suspended, of how polite and courteous everyone was.

'He likes to watch,' she whispered. I just about managed to fuck the woman while the man looked on, idly stroking his flaccid penis, smiling and nodding at me as though I were doing him a great favour. After a time I felt I was. Occasionally, the woman attempted to suck him but otherwise he left all the love work to me. 'Thanks,' he said, as I rested breathlessly in his wife's arms. When I left we shook hands.

It was late when Bushy drove us back. Henry and Miriam were asleep in the back of the car. I wanted to shower.

'Thanks for my tune, Bushy,' I said.

'Pleasure,' he replied. 'Enjoyed it, sir.'

As an encore, and to thank me, Bushy had played Robert Johnson's 'Crossroads'. One time in the car, when he'd been humming it, I told him it was one of my favourite songs. It was, after all, at a place where three highways meet – a crossroads – where Oedipus kills his father the paedophile Laius, after which Jocasta, his wife and mother says, 'Have no more fear of sleeping with your mother./ How many men, in dreams, have lain with their mothers!/ No reasonable man is troubled by such things.' Bushy considered this founding myth a little soap-opera-like for his tastes. He replied by saying that Robert Johnson, who had bad eyesight and was rumoured to have sold his soul to the devil in exchange for his talent, was poisoned by a jealous husband in a bar called Three Forks.

Now Bushy said, 'People don't realise how difficult it is to play that song properly, using Johnson's fingering. But I learned it for you, because you helped me.'

'Thank you again, Bushy,' I said.

CHAPTER THIRTY-SEVEN

I found her washing up the next time I went to Miriam's house to watch the football. She didn't turn round to address me but said, over her shoulder, 'You've been keeping away from me.'

'I've had new patients. I've been asked to lecture. You know, I really enjoy my work.'

'So what? You didn't like the Sootie. You've told everyone but me.'

'Didn't I look funky in the wig? Even you admitted I made an effort.'

'You were taking the piss, calling them the clusterfuckers and stuff. You were acting superior that night and you know it.'

'Not only me.'

'Who?'

I said, 'Henry was like an officious parent commanding his children to enjoy their holiday. "You must like this or else!"' I added, 'It reminded me of our society's implausible commitment to optimism, and how much the depressed are hated.'

She turned and threw water at me. 'Snob knob! What did you actually say to Henry?'   .

'I told him it wasn't a real orgy. The real orgy is elsewhere.'

'Where?'

'Baghdad.' I went on: 'It suddenly became my job to calm Bushy down, while you sat with a group of women discussing animals and tattoos, just as you would at home. The men and their penises didn't appear to inject much zing into your ming.'

'I may have been quiet but I was having a lookout,' she said. 'There's a masked woman Henry always goes for.'

'Is she there often?'

Miriam shrugged. 'I'm not certain which one she is. People look similar with their clothes off, and I never wear my glasses in there.'

I raised the cat above my head. 'Of course not. Are you jealous?'

'He fucks the women, but he always comes in me. That's the rule. He's mine and he bloody well knows it, otherwise I'll tattoo my name onto his arse myself.' She said, 'Jamal, I'm warning you, if anyone annoys me today, I'm in one of my moods, they're gonna get it, okay? By the way, that cat's about to piss on you.'

Now I was laughing and she was shaking her head darkly. I knew that any dismissiveness of the Sootie was a sore subject for Miriam because she and Henry had recently been in deep dispute about 'the scene'.

After I had mentioned the Sootie to Karen – this was a while ago – Karen had gone to investigate with Miriam, wrapped in an acre of sticky plastic, looking not unlike a potato in clingfilm, as Henry put it. She had decided to make three programmes for TV about what she liked to describe, in 'tab-speak', as 'the underbelly – or potbelly, more like – of British suburban sexuality': swapping, dogging, fetishism and the like. She had already taken Miriam out to lunch to discuss it.

Miriam was excited not only by the idea of appearing on TV, but of working as an 'adviser'. Karen had suggested that Miriam would be the right person to persuade potential participants in the programme to take part. Miriam saw it as an 'opportunity'; it would make her 'a professional' in the media, like Henry's friends. Miriam had even said that Karen was planning to feature me on the programme, as a 'psychological expert.' 'She promised you'd get paid,' Miriam had added. 'What do you think?'

'Was Karen cheerful?'

'Oh yes. When I saw her, she was about to go out on a date with an American TV producer. I gave her great advice about what to wear.'

But when Miriam had put Karen's proposition to Henry as something they could do together, without any hesitation he trashed Karen and 'her ilk', delivering an intense monologue about 'the end of privacy'. If everyone could become a celebrity, and no celebrity could control how they were seen, there could be no more heroes or villains: we were living in a democracy of the mad, of the victim and exhibitionist. The media had become a freak show.

'What's the alternative?' asked Miriam, exasperated.

Henry argued that such intimacy, such a close-up of the individual, had always been the privilege of the novel and the drama. That was how, until recently, we examined the Other, through the imagination and intelligence of an artist like Ibsen or Proust. Now everyone revealed everything but no one understood anything. Being gawped at on television would not give him pleasure, nor would it provide one watt of illumination for the public.

Most of this Miriam characterised as 'over-brainy bollocks', but she understood Henry found her desire to work on the programmes as 'vulgar and idiotic'. It wasn't something she wanted to do alone, and it wasn't something he could participate in.

'I've never felt so different to him,' she said. 'We do everything together. Until he announces he's a super-elitist, too grand to go along with a ditch pig like me. The other day he said, "Miriam, how did you live so long and yet manage to pick up so little?"'

'What did you say?'

'"I haven't had fucking time! I've had five children and more abortions than you've had orgies! While you people were nancying around in theatres I was in a psychiatric hospital!"'

'That's no excuse,' Henry had replied blithely. 'So was Sylvia Plath.'

I said, 'Henry makes some people feel ignorant. But he doesn't want to do that to you.'

The odd thing was that, despite Henry's contempt for television, he wasn't too grand, after the night at the Sootie, to refer to Bushy as his 'client' while trying to set up another gig for him. 'I should have been a pimp,' Henry had told me. 'The perfect job for an artist. Even William Faulkner thought so. Failing that, I've become an agent.'

'For Chrissakes, Henry,' I said. 'What are you doing?'

He told me that after the Sootie gig, Bushy had had a few requests for private parties – straight and bent – which Henry was 'processing'. Henry said the odd thing was how 'being in management' wasn't any less compelling than anything else he'd done. But he had asked me this: 'Do you think Bushy's mental health will hold up?'

'You mean, do I think it could be like the last days of Edith Piaf? Or that you yourself could end up in a locked cage, screaming naked?'

'That's what I was wondering. But he's asked me to do this stuff. It's not me pushing him into it. I blame you entirely. You've given him the confidence.'

My guess was that Henry was becoming bored with his 'retirement'. He had been with Miriam for more than a year, and had spent a lot of time sitting around in her house, talking, cooking, walking the dogs in the grounds of Syon House or by the river, just being with his new love. One evening he had plunged into the chaos of the garden, digging, pulling weeds and planting. With his new predilection for exposing his body, he wore only gloves, boxer shorts and Wellington boots.

Whatever Henry did, of course, he'd do obsessively. To him it was all work – digging the garden, directing *Hamlet* in Prague – except that you didn't get abused in the newspapers for digging the garden. 'Nor do you get international recognition,' I pointed out.

Now Miriam came to sit with me on the sofa as I watched the match, taking my arm. I told her that Henry's fascination with Bushy's career was because he had always been intrigued by performance. Once the sexual side of 'the scene' had become exhausted – which, in my view, hadn't taken long – Henry had become interested in the images, metaphors and ideas that the Sootie inspired in him.

I said, 'I saw Henry watching the proceedings in the Sootie and he had his director's face on. He presses his fingertips together and looks over the top of them with huge concentration.' I made the gesture for her. 'I bet a good deal of what he's seen will eventually turn up in the production of *Don Giovanni* he's not planning. Bushy will be his Leporello. Fucking artists, that's what they do.'

There was some sort of trade-off with Bushy too, because in exchange for Henry helping him with his career Bushy was clearing out and rebuilding the shed at the end of Miriam's garden. This was where Henry was intending to work. Not only did he want to become a sculptor but, to prove it, he was determined to sell at least one of his works. This new direction had occurred to him after I'd taken Henry and Miriam to lunch with Billie and Mum.

The two women no longer wanted to lunch at the Royal Academy, which they considered too 'old women', so we went to a place they'd read about in the *Independent*, at the bottom of the Portobello Road, not far from the Travel Bookshop. Billie and Mum liked the nearby market, which was less crowded during the week. It might have been expensive, but they had no interest in saving money. Spending seemed to have become proof of their existence.

Over lunch Henry had conceived the idea that it would be a good idea for him to work seriously with clay. Billie would give him lessons, once the studio they were having built was ready.

During and after this lunch – Mum, Henry and Billie discussing their favourite sculptors, Miriam texting – Miriam had kept her temper, despite an early setback. On arrival, she had shown off her latest tattoo, a little dove on her foot, which failed to create the interest she'd anticipated. Indeed, Billie said, 'Apparently Freddie Ljungberg – the Arsenal football god, for those who know nothing – was poisoned by his tattoos.' 'He can't have been using Mike the artist,' said Miriam. 'Where's he based?' Billie asked. 'Hounslow,' Miriam replied.

Mother was gazing at Billie, smiling a little bit, which she did a lot of the time. Billie was smirking. This new bright side of mother – something dark had slowly been scraped off, or fallen away of its own accord – was independent, self-absorbed and dismissive of anything that didn't immediately concern her.

It can't have been a coincidence that a few days later, when Bushy began work on the sculpture shed, Miriam decided that Henry had to marry her. She had said this before but now she began to insist, saying that until she had a new rock on her finger she couldn't believe he loved her.

I had endured years of this whiney self-righteous side of Miriam and had grown no fonder of it, but Henry took it seriously, as he had to. The two of them spent the night together at least twice a week, either at his place or hers, but she still had children at home, at least some of the time. So it wasn't possible for them to live together, even if they wanted to. Though it would be an infinite regress of impossible confirmation, she required proof of his commitment, particularly now, when he was spending hours on the phone to Lisa and Valerie.

As far as Henry was concerned, he didn't want to marry *anyone* – 'Jesus, I don't want to get back into *that,* unless it's for a very good reason, like tax avoidance' – but Miriam interpreted this as rejection. Not only that but from her point of view he was still married to Valerie: it was she he considered to be his 'main' wife.

As I was leaving after the football, Miriam came after me. 'Brother, you've got to speak to him for me. I can feel myself getting wild. The other night I had a razor blade in my hand, ready to start cutting again. Help me, bro.'

The next day I met Henry for lunch. When he eventually turned up I said to him, 'Your hair's everywhere, you haven't shaved, there's dribble on your tee-shirt. You look a little manic, man, and my sister wants to marry you.'

'You'd be crazy, bro, in my circumstances,' he said. 'I think I need a dozen oysters. Will you have some?'

'I will indeed.' I said, 'Is there news of the famous Hand?'

He looked up from the wine list and removed his glasses. 'Jamal, I know Miriam's a mouth, but I am continuing to urge everyone to keep it zipped. I don't want this story carried around town – or in the newspapers.' He went on, 'It *is* amusing. Except the thing's worth a lot of money.'

'A Hand? Is this the Hand of God?'

He said, 'A fucking *Ingres*. It's a drawing. Brown crayon, a woman in pro-file. Valerie's room is so crammed with art I hated to go in there. Her father was a collector. The very rich are insouciant about such things.'

'I guess Lisa can keep it.'

'What the hell for? It's not insured and she can't sell it. Only a criminal would buy it, and she likes criminals even less than her own family. The stupid thing is, Valerie lives in such a fog of self-preoccupation that she didn't notice it was gone. Lisa must have been sitting in her digs waiting for her mother to explode.

'Lisa lost her temper and went round and jabbed at the bare patch. It's some sort of protest. Now Lisa's getting a lot of attention and so is Valerie, who makes me have lunch with her. Then she starts.' Henry enjoyed doing her brittle English accent, like a female radio announcer circa 1960. '"Christ Almighty Henry, we rip up masterpieces around here? Is that our relation to culture? I am on the board of the Tate Modern! They've asked me to help at the Hay Festival! I'm helping save all kinds of fucking art for the nation, fighting to keep culture alive in these dirty times, and our own daughter does this! If it gets in the papers we're going to look like fools." On and on. And you think I get the chance to say anything?'

'What does she want you to do?'

He leaned towards me. 'Valerie does have an idea. Don't scream – it involves you.'

Henry, I knew, rather sensibly liked to pass his problems on to others in order that he didn't have to think about unpleasant subjects. This was a good compromise with regard to Valerie, as there were many occasions when he needed her.

He said, 'You know she respects you, man.'

'She considers me an arse and a pretender. My social credit's flat. It's been too long since I've had a nice review, or any kind of review.'

'You are rather floundering about. Why don't you just publish some-thing?'

'Why don't *you*?'

He went on, 'But Valerie *is* respecting you right at this moment, because Lisa will listen to you. My daughter has a thing about your books, she underlines stuff in them for some reason, and knows what "abreaction" and "cathexis" means. I'm not asking you for a favour, I'm just saying the bitch has got a loft in New York where you can stay. Consider the West

Village before you say no. You know you like nosing around little book-shops and cafés there.'

'I attempt to take care of your daughter's mental health and in exchange I get free accommodation in New York?'

'As if I were the only one with woman problems. You know I was watching you in the Sootie.'

'You saw me watching my ex. What did you think?'

He said, 'I was wondering what such a sight would do to someone's head. I only hope you've been seeing Ajita.'

I told Henry that the last time I'd been to the house, to see Rafi, I'd stroked Josephine's hair in the kitchen. Not only because I wanted to, or because she had a headache, but because I'd been in search of the mole I'd seen in the Sootie. Of course I wasn't able to find it. Then I realised I'd been looking on the wrong side. But had it really been her there? Had it really been me?

Henry touched my hand. 'Old chap, I know she's an agony, but do what you can for my daughter. If I don't get that picture back, or if it gets damaged, I'm going to be hurting in the nuts.'

Not long after I'd said goodbye to Henry – he would stay in the bar, read the paper and finish the bottle – Valerie rang.

She was keen to invite me to dinner but, of course, wanted to talk about Lisa and the Hand. I could take some of her talk, but turned down the party – for which she had gathered a stellar cast of American film agents – as I suspected she'd use it as an opportunity to get me into one of her 'little rooms', where she'd go on more about Lisa.

Now she was saying to me, 'Of course, with Lisa, there's no reason for all that combing through the past you usually do. There just isn't time for that nonsense. This is an emergency situation, as she slips away from us into insanity.'

I told Valerie I would consider her request to help Lisa – help her *what?* – but added that I didn't believe there was much I could do personally. Not that I believed that saying no meant anything to this family.

Nevertheless, I didn't expect to hear from any of them quite so soon.

CHAPTER THIRTY-EIGHT

The doorbell rang.

That evening, when my last patient had gone, I was preparing to have dinner with Ajita. She had rung earlier and said she had a free evening; would I join her at the Red Fort in Dean Street? When I turned my phone on I saw she had texted me to say she was tired and was going to bed. I was disappointed: hadn't she dreamed and yearned for me tirelessly for years, as I had about her? Now, probably in response to my diffidence, she could hardly get out of bed for me.

Restless and horny, I was considering a visit to the Goddess; later, maybe I could go and find Henry and Bushy. I wanted, at least, to see whether Bushy had been able to perform without me.

So I thought it might be Wolf at the door. But it was Lisa standing there, holding her bicycle and – unusually for her – smiling.

'Ready?'

'Was I expecting you?'

She shrugged and continued to smile under her damp woolly hat. I wasn't ready for anything except for a walk, despite the rain. I didn't want to invite her in as, no doubt, she'd have stayed until Tuesday. I grabbed my coat and went out.

'You ride it,' she said, pushing the bicycle towards me. 'We're going on a journey.' Some of the way I rode the bike, which was big and heavy, particularly when she sat on the rack, this ungainly two-bodied burden heaving itself up the Fulham Palace Road. The rest of the way she trotted behind me.

'Where to?'

'Somewhere calming,' she said. 'You'll like it.'

Beside Bishop's Park we came to a locked gate – and, after opening it – to what appeared to be a field. There were lights in a couple of sheds, but otherwise it was dark in a way it rarely is in London.

'Come on,' said my tour guide.

What could I do but follow her across, trying to avoid puddles? It was hopeless; my feet sank into the mud and my beloved green Paul Smith loafers, which I'd got in a sale, were waterlogged. I was furious, but what was the point of stopping or complaining now?

At the end of the allotment, not far from the river, we came to a shed and she led me in, using a torch. She lit candles. We sat on wooden crates, and she rolled a cigarette. I noticed an old picture of her father pinned to the wall, ripped from a newspaper. Water dripped on our heads.

'I love to sit here,' she said. 'It's meditative. But it gets damp.' She was quiet for a bit. 'What do you think of me taking the Ingres?'

'It's your inheritance. What difference does it make whether it's today or another day?' Picking up a candle, I peered at the shelves. 'This is more interesting. What are these things?'

'Objects I picked out of the river mud and cleaned.'

Half-crushed Coke cans; shards of crockery; rusted keys; glass; a plastic bottle stuffed with mud; a shower-head; a length of metal pipe. Some had been cleaned; other pieces were enshrouded in a skin of grey mud. Here these broken pieces had some uncanny, compelling force, making you want to look more closely at them and wonder about their provenance.

'I'm impressed.'

'Anyone can do it. All you need is a bucket and a toothbrush. Oh, and a river.'

There were a pile of books: Plath, Sexton, Olds, Rich. 'You've been reading.'

For some reason I was thinking of the library my father had made in Pakistan, and wondering whether anyone used it now.

She said, 'My parents don't know I do it. They'd get too excited.'

'You're writing too.' I was looking at a pad with slanted writing on it.

'Don't tell. You understand why I don't want them to know?'

'Your secret is how much you resemble your parents,' I said. 'But you're entitled to your privacy. As they are to theirs. Did you see your father's piece in the paper?' She almost nodded. 'What did you think?'

Last weekend Henry had written an open letter to Blair, saying he was resigning from the Party he'd joined in the mid-60s because Labour had become dictatorial, corrupt and unrepresentative. Apart from the egregious lying, there had been insufficient debate over Iraq. Dissent was not encouraged in the Party, which was now run for television rather than with the aim of redistributing wealth and power. What had Blair achieved, apart from the minimum wage and the proposed extension of pub opening hours? For Henry, the Labour Party, along with other organisations, including corporations, had moved towards the condition of being cults, a project which not only claimed your loyalty but your inner freedom.

Henry had brought the piece round to me for discussion. It was strong polemical writing, penned in a fury, and was given half a page in a liberal Sunday paper by the editor, a friend of Valerie's. What surprised Henry was the number of friends and colleagues who rang to say how much they admired his stand and what he'd said.

After the piece appeared, he was asked onto *Newsnight*; he spoke on the radio and wrote again to the paper. He had plenty to say, and found that people considered him intelligent and eloquent. He'd taught, but he'd never much talked about politics, or even the theatre, in public, because he feared losing his temper and saying something insulting or crazy. I told him he was respected because he wasn't some penny-a-line hack or raddled politician. I hated to say the word, it had become so devalued by pomposity and contempt, but Henry was an 'intellectual', and doing what they were supposed to do.

I said to Lisa, 'A lot of people admire your father. If we're in a war, he's rebelling with his words.'

'Great, he's telling everyone he's against the war. How brave. He's leaving a Party he should never have joined.' She was speaking quickly. 'Why doesn't he actually support the insurgents in Iraq, and the bombers and resisters around the world? Why doesn't he accept the idea of the struggle moving to Britain? Everyone says – even the government – that the response is coming, that we're going to get it here, in London. Blair has brought retribution on himself and on us. Even one of your politicians, Robin Cook, said we'd have been better advised bringing peace to Palestine than war to Iraq.

'Why doesn't dad say that our corruption and materialism are so decadent that we have actively earned all that we have coming?' She was shaking her head, as though to clear her mind of fury. At last she said, 'I'm sick of what I have to say. Why don't you tell me what you are doing at the moment.'

'I was just writing, for months,' I said. 'About a girl. But going nowhere, you know.' She seemed to nod. 'Then I found a subject. It emerged. Or it was there all the time. Guilt.'

'Yes?'

'The notion of. How it works. Or what it does. The Greeks. Dostoevsky. Freud. Nietszche. "There is no feast without cruelty,"

Nietzsche writes. Guilt and responsibility. Conscience. All the important things.'

'Why such a subject? Do you have a lot on your mind?'

'Well, yes. It's difficult to escape. Among other things I had an argument with my son.'

I told her about it. The previous Sunday, Rafi had reluctantly come to spend the day with me. I was lying on the sofa reading the paper; we were listening to music; Rafi was on the floor, sitting at my feet. He'd been sitting there sullenly, playing with one of his lighted machines. Occasionally he gave me the finger or, if I was lucky, two fingers. When he walked past me he liked to give me a shove, pretending it was an accident. Was I like this? Probably. Miriam certainly was. Being a good parent means bearing this, up to a point.

Now he began to pinch me, hard. I was either ignoring him or paying him too much attention. I told him to stop, several times, but he was enjoying it, giggling and smirking. 'You can't take it, eh?' he said. 'Weak man. I'm never coming here again, you haven't even got Sky. We have to go to the pub or to your sister's to watch football. It's shit here. Can't you get a girlfriend?' Pinch, pinch.

I drew back my foot and kicked him on the top of his head, hard. He didn't make a sound, his head just dropped. He looked up at me, his brown eyes uncomprehending, as if he'd suffered the most tragic betrayal possible. 'My head is numb,' he said. He got up and screamed. 'I can't feel my head!'

He ran to lock himself in the bathroom. He was hurt, but not enough to forget his mobile. He phoned his mother many times. When I got him out of there he spent the rest of the day in a cupboard and I had to stand outside, begging him to come out, muttering to myself, 'Once, you little fucker, for years I gave up my sexuality to be with you, now be nice to me!'

In the end, I left him to it and went back to the newspapers. That evening, when he went home, I saw he'd pissed in the cupboard. He informed Josephine I'd stamped on his head, trying to kill him.

I rang Josephine to apologise and explain, anticipating a thrashing. I told her the boy had learned what fathers can do, what monsters they might turn into, when pushed. He had sought my limit and had found it. I said I was ashamed; at the same time I was defensive. She was sympathetic. Since she had been working – and she was sure this was the reason – he had attacked her on a few occasions, pulling her hair and frightening her. Other times he ran away into the street, not returning for an hour, giving her a fright. Now that he was becoming difficult we had to stand together. If she and I were to speak again – and we both wanted to, I was sure of it – he had to be the conduit; we could only love one another through him.

It gratified me, this solidarity. I had been rendered sleepless by hurting him. But he had a strong ego. He didn't bear grudges; he was too interested in the world. The next time I saw him he was trying to learn to play his electric guitar, which I had to tune for him. Meanwhile he wanted me to hear the new music he liked, which he played through his computer while giving me little glances to gauge my approval.

Lisa said, 'And here's me – still arguing with my father.'

I said, 'Lisa, why don't you cheer me up by reading to me?'

'Are you sure?'

'I want to hear the poem. Now you've dragged me all this fucking way in the rain you might as well do something for me.'

She spat out her cigarette, ground it into the floor and began to read without enthusiasm or emphasis; her face twitched and her tongue flicked. After about ten minutes she stopped.

I thanked her and said, 'Haven't you published before? I have some vague memory of you saying you had.'

At Oxford, I seemed to recall, she read English and wrote a thesis on 'Madness and Women's Poetry'.

'Yes, in student papers. No one noticed.'

I said, 'You want me to show these to someone?'

'Suppose they want to publish them? I can't be an artist.'

'You might be one already.'

'My parents are snobs. So-called artists came to the house all the time. I refuse to worm my way into Mummy and Daddy's affections that way.'

'Loving you has to be difficult?'

'Why not? They didn't even want me to become a social worker. And when I became one they took no interest, they never asked me about my cases.'

I said, 'Use a pseudonym.'

'For my cases?'

'I didn't mean that, but it's a good thought.' I sighed and stood up. 'I'm going.'

'I'm sorry,' she said. 'I've asked too much of you. I'm interested in what you think. I can't find anyone to talk to – someone who hears me right. I dream of the sea, over and over.'

'You want a child?'

'Shit, you foolish man, I hope not. You've gone too far.'

I was laughing and I could see she wanted to kiss me, and I let her, tasting this stranger standing in front of me with her tongue in the front of my mouth. When she pushed her body against mine and I reached for her breast, I wondered if I might respond, if there might be something there. She slid down my body. I let her blow me, which I considered some recompense for my doomed shoes.

She said, 'I didn't think the poem would be enough for you. We're both lonely. Sleep here, you can smell the river and hear the rain.'

'Not tonight.'

She got up. 'I'm not young or pretty enough for you.'

'And vice versa.'

She dropped the writing pad in a large plastic bag and gave it to me. I had opened the door when she said, 'Take this as well.' I guessed it was the Hand, wrapped in several layers of newspaper, still in its frame. I shoved it into the side of the bag.

The rain fell like nails. The sludge had thickened. Lisa's was the only shed now lighted, and it was a desolate place. I wondered whether the bag might be porous in some way, thus destroying the Hand.

With mud sucking at my feet and my trousers soaked up to the knee, I was trudging across a waterlogged allotment in the dark, hawking a masterpiece and some poems in a Tesco carrier. It was also the night Henry was accompanying Bushy to his second gig, a private party. A rich man was entertaining some business associates with a bunch of hookers. Henry had been afraid Bushy would play too much of the 'mad stuff', which he had been sure to warn him against.

Bushy wanted to do the gig without my help, but they'd suggested I join them. Earlier, I'd considered getting a cab and going over for a drink, but I would resemble a drowned jackass. By the time I'd walked home, I was exhausted.

I woke up at two. At three I unwrapped the Hand and looked at it, placing it here and there in the room. It wasn't large, about 14 by 16 inches, and on grey paper, luminous with intelligence, tenderness and beauty. Ingres, for one, hadn't been wasting his time. I placed it on the mantelpiece next to the whore's Christmas card.

Just before I went to bed, I checked my phone. There was a peculiar message from Bushy, who should have had better things to do that night. 'Info arrived,' it said.

Next morning Wolf came to collect his washing, which he'd put in my machine. He came in and out of my place as though we were close friends. I should have stopped it; but I'd thought he wouldn't return. He had said he didn't like to visit me since the first thing you saw, on entering the hall, was yourself, in the coffin of a full length mirror.

It wasn't until almost lunchtime, when I was in the middle of a particularly troublesome case – a woman had taken to punching herself, like the guy in *Fight Club* – that I realised the Hand had gone.

Wolf, of course, had some instinct for these things. He'd have known it was a good picture; how good, I'm not sure. I rang him and wondered whether he might be intending to return it anytime soon.

Even as I put the phone down he was cackling.

CHAPTER THIRTY-NINE

I had been intending to ring Henry to say I'd got the Hand for him. He would be relieved and we would continue with our friendship as normal. Now it was my duty to explain that I had indeed retrieved the picture – and had spent some time helping his daughter, at Valerie's request. Except that there had been a glitch.

I explained, 'The Hand has been taken from my flat by a psychotic patient.'

'Taken? You say taken?'

'Yes, taken. Sorry about that, pal.'

'Taken for good?'

'Maybe. How would I know? Do the mad explain their long-term intentions?'

'Taken by which madman, for God's sake?' He began to yell. 'Who was it?'

'That's confidential.'

'Are you serious? You are telling me there is a lunatic running about London with my wife's best Ingres stuffed in his backpack?'

'Exactly.'

'And you let them? Is this your rebellion – your hatred – of me? You've finally turned, have you?'

'Certainly the Hand has been severed.'

'Is it coming back?'

'Who knows? As Lenin might have said,' I added, 'one step forward, two steps back.'

The noises on the other end of the line were extraordinary. I turned off the phone.

After I'd finished for the day, Henry came by. We had argued often, and sulked and disputed vigorously, enjoying much of it, but not all. Both of us relished a good rumble, though we had never fallen out. Now I didn't want to hear another word about the Hand.

I must have come to the door with some leery belligerence, because he laid his hand on my shoulder and said quickly, 'Don't worry, cool it, I'm not going to bring it up. There are more important things than pencil marks on a piece of paper.'

We strolled past the line of busy pubs, with drinkers sitting outside in the sun, towards the bridge at Barnes and then back along the towpath towards Hammersmith Bridge. On the opposite side of the river path was a deserted bird sanctuary with a bench on a bank high above it. We sat there for a while.

'I wanted to see you. I'd have joined you last night,' I said, 'if I hadn't been dealing with your family.'

'I'm grateful for that,' he said. 'It was fun. There was a panic early on because the man holding the party phoned to call it off. As always in life, there weren't enough girls. But being in the agent business, I could be of assistance.'

'You?'

'Bushy called in at the Cross Keys and he came along to the party with three Eastern European grinders who were more than willing to have money put their way. But what do you know, they were accompanied by their manager – a Mr Wolf.'

'Big Bad?'

'You know him. Mr Wolf stayed for the evening, feeling his charges needed security. He was extremely pleased by the way it went.'

'In what way?'

'He had a briefcase full of charlie and there were plenty of takers. Soon the girls and the guys were lost in a blizzard of it. If I hadn't called a halt to the whole thing around three, I think we'd still be there.'

'How was Bushy?'

'He wasn't convinced he could play without you on hand. I had to tell him he was helping me out, that he was a staff member rather than a star. That seemed to do it.

'But he was – for reasons he wouldn't elaborate – wearing a white plaster on his nose, which made him resemble Jack Nicholson in *Chinatown*. At one point, his face turned red and his eyes started to pulsate. I don't think anyone noticed until he started shutting one eye and letting the other pop and bulge. One of the girls went into a hyperventilation and had to be taken out and slapped, but she was a write-off for the rest of the night.' Henry went on, 'Wolf's one of your oldest friends, if not the oldest, and I'd never met him before.'

295

'What did he say?'

'As the evening went on he told me about Valentin and Ajita and her father's factory. I'd forgotten that you'd been involved in that. I remember reading about it at the time. I'd say that Wolf's rather obsessed with you, isn't he? He wants to meet up with me to talk more. Would that be okay?'

'No.'

'I did hear about the unsolved murder and the whole three-years-in-a-Syrian jail thing. Don't look so worried, none of us is clean.'

Henry finished his drink. He was going to Miriam's. One of the dogs was sick; she needed him there. Miriam was on her own more than she liked to admit. The children, teenagers now, stayed where they could, often with friends. One of the sweeter boys, needing to escape, had even gone to stay with Mum and Billie in the suburbs.

I saw a lot of Miriam, particularly as she had the Sky football package I hadn't got round to renting, but I would never sleep under her roof. She was still more than capable of 'insane' behaviour: screaming, rolling around on the floor, punching the wall. At times, in her house, I could feel as though I'd been lobbed through the looking-glass and whirled back into my childhood.

I did think of accompanying Henry, but Bushy had called me earlier. 'I got the information,' he repeated. 'I'm waiting for you.'

I wondered whether it was a good idea for us to discuss this in Wolf's workplace. But Bushy wasn't concerned. He had other business on at the same time.

Henry and I parted, and I walked along to Hammersmith bus station and caught a bus inside the shopping centre. It was slow progress, particularly along the Uxbridge Road. The bus, low and long, was noisy with kids playing music on their phones. It stank, with every nation seemingly represented, and I wondered if anyone would have been able to identify the city just from the inhabitants of the bus.

Bushy, without a wrap on his nose, was at a table in the corner. Wolf, working tonight, was at the other end of the bar. The Harridan brought me over a vodka. She wanted to sit down but I told her Bushy and I were in a meeting.

I said, 'You and Wolf had a good night, I hear.'

'Shrinky, you're right,' Bushy said. 'That man jus' don't keep still.'

Bushy moved his chair closer to me, whispering; two old men in a pub, talking.

I asked, 'What information are you referring to?'

He glanced around and then at me. 'Don't yer know? I bin researching around for you. Listen.'

Bushy told me chucking-out time at the Cross Keys was still 10.30. It opened at midday and was always busy, particularly in the early evening, but it closed before most of the other local pubs. Like other dubious local businesses – minicab offices, porno shops, lap-dancing clubs, and corner shops which sold alcohol out of hours – the Harridan paid off the local police, but didn't want unruly behaviour to draw unnecessary attention. At closing time one of the Africans would drive Wolf up West.

I learned from Bushy that in Soho Wolf had been working as a doorman at a fashionable club, Sartori. As a natural hustler, in ten days he'd soon discovered that such work was lucrative, mainly because of the tips the door staff earned from the clamorous photographers who moved from club to club around the West End all night, earning top sums for the right picture. The photographers needed to know who was in the club – which footballer, soap star, pop singer or movie actor, the price of whose fame was a transparent life – and whether they were coked-up, drunk, copulating or all three.

This information was passed rapidly through the club's ecosystem, beginning with the bathroom attendants – the Africans whose night's work it was to clean the toilets, offer towels to the celebs, clean up their shit and pick up meagre tips. They appeared to be almost invisible, but were quite aware of who was smoking or snorting what. Above ground, the bar staff, security and managers were part of this chain of associates: every drink, pass or glance was intensively monitored by numerous unnoticed eyes. Wolf and his pals also had access to the club's CCTV system, selling the right piece of tape to the right Net dealer.

I said, 'What I've heard doesn't surprise me, Bushy. I think it's good for our friend over there to keep busy and make a living.'

'But do you know this? He pimping after something bigger. He cunnin' to the core. There's some rich Indian bird up West. After work he goes into her. She got a fine house in a quiet Soho street. You personally acquainted with the girl, Jamal?' He was prodding me on the arm. 'Are yer?'

'Yes, yes. Ajita.'

'That's the name, I think. You said it.'

'You know this for sure?'

Bushy tapped his nose. 'Everything go round the Cross Keys line. The drivers outside talk, all the girls natter. But it was me who put all them pieces together, like you do with a dream.'

'But Bushy, I'm getting confused as well as annoyed. You told me Wolf had started on something hot with the Harridan.'

'Look at her! It didn't last. You can see why. The Harridan guess Wolf goes to someone else. She don't like it but she don't want to lose him. He do the electrics, the plumbing, he can paint and all that. You know, I work for Miriam, not her. We're family. Harridan weren't ever my employer. I only did favours for her.'

'What are the rumours about Wolf and this girl?'

'He's risking it.'

'In what way?'

'If he want to get his name on the contract to the pub and all that, and be on the same level with Jenny Harridan, he shouldn't annoy her by going with other women.'

So Wolf had wanted to take over the Cross Keys; indeed, he had started work on the upstairs rooms, which the Harridan was keen to rent out for private functions. But the rumour was, and it seemed inevitable, that the Cross Keys would be sold and converted into a pub selling basil risotto and Spanish bottled beers with diced limes jammed in the top. It was the end for ordinary street-corner pubs, and certainly for rough and cheap places. The Cross Keys didn't seem the kind of hostelry that could survive. London was being decorated; perhaps the city would be rebranded 'Tesco's'.

I said, 'Wolf's more than a little crazy. If the Harridan refuses to let him run the place with her, or if she chucks him out altogether, he might go nuts. He's on the edge as it is.'

He said, 'Doctor, don't get me wrong, but have you thought, you might be the crazy one? Paranoias an' all that?'

'I don't know.'

'Wolf's getting laid at least. Sorry to tell you, but they're at it a lot, he's told the girls. He's going to be chilled.'

'Is he? Nothing helpful follows from that. It might be even worse. Crazies are always being let out of institutions because they're chilled. A week later they're sitting down to a plate of toasted balls.'

'You're the doc,' he said casually, making me wonder whether I was.

'About Ajita, I should have guessed,' I said. 'Perhaps I did, unconsciously. Now I can only worry about what he will tell her.'

'About yer dirty crime?'

'My dirty crime, yes.'

'Is it going round and round yer head?'

'At times.'

'I hate that,' he said.

I noticed Bushy was looking in a mirror at his nose and stroking it. I thanked him for the information, and went round to the side of the bar where the girls worked.

I ordered a drink from Wolf and said, 'Wolf, please. I need that picture back. You stole it from me, an old friend. How could you do that to me? What sort of man are you?'

'Don't raise your voice. I'm not a thief,' he said. He leaned across the bar. 'It was borrowed in lieu of other payments.'

'You're doing well,' I said. 'I set all this up for you. Isn't that recompense enough?'

'A job in a bar?' He looked as though he wanted to spit at me. 'You smoked my whole life like a cigarette, until it was ash.'

I was almost out of the door of the pub when I turned, nipped through a door marked 'Private' and ran upstairs to Wolf's room. His corner was characteristically neat: his jackets and trousers were on hangers, his shirts organised by colour, his shaving gear on a shelf above the sink. The rest of the room was such a mess of broken furniture, ripped curtains and cardboard boxes I wouldn't have known where to start searching for the Hand.

'Can you help me?'

One of the girls was behind me, half-dressed in pink high heels with a flimsy dressing gown over her shoulders, back-lit and looking like a woman in a Fassbinder movie, one of my favourite directors.

She said, 'You the psychiatrist and me you don't recognise.'

'Hello, Miss Lucy, how you doing?' She shrugged. I asked, 'Any chance of a quickie?'

'Quick? You think I that sort?' she said, approaching me. At least she grinned before she pretended to slap me. 'What you wanting up here?'

I said, 'I think Wolf might have something of mine.'

As she appeared not to grasp a word I said, I kissed her and held her hand. We were looking at one another curiously.

Wolf came in suddenly, looking annoyed and agitated, as though convinced he'd caught me at last, as he knew he would, and now would have to deal with me.

I said. 'Just looking for a G-string to floss with.'

'Hi, Lucy.' He winked at me and said, 'Up to your old tricks?' and went out.

'He was bad temper today,' she said.

I was laughing when I gave her my mobile number. I thought of Valentin and his charm and facility with women he didn't know: it was a rare man who wasn't afraid of women. How odd it was that I still identified with that part of him, after so many years.

I followed her downstairs and watched her for one dance. At the end I went over, kissed her and said, 'I can't wait to see you with your clothes on.'

CHAPTER FORTY

I rang Ajita that night but there was no reply. I decided to leave it a few days to see whether she called me. She didn't. The following week I rang and again asked if she had time to meet. She sounded sleepy but at least said she'd been thinking about me 'a lot'. We arranged lunch twice but she cancelled each time, saying she had a cold.

Finally I left a message with her saying I would be in the neighbourhood at the end of the week. I'd call by and see her, making sure it was early evening, when I knew Wolf would be working at the Cross Keys, a few hours before his evening excursions.

I wanted to see her, I was ready for it, and she, apparently, for me – at last. She had sent me a text saying there was 'something' she wanted me to look at as soon as possible. It was 'urgent'.

Before I could begin to think about what she might mean – whether she was going to tell me about Wolf, or about something he had told her – I received a frantic call from Miriam saying that Henry had disappeared.

'Where's he gone? What are you talking about?'

I managed to grasp that she had had one of the dogs put down, at home. During what she called 'the ceremony', Henry had walked out of the house. He had gone to his flat – or wherever – and stayed away for three days, not ringing once.

'Have you called him?' I said.

'I'm afraid to. Well, I did a few times but I turned the phone off when I heard his voice on the answering machine. I know he hates to talk on the phone. But what is he hiding – is it bad news, do you think? What if he's been blown up?'

'What? Why should he be?'

'If he goes on a train, like in the Madrid bombings! Two hundred people killed! It could happen here, couldn't it?'

'He probably has more chance of winning an Oscar.'

'What if he's left me? It would finish me off.'

'Has he said he's left you?'

'He only muttered something about not wanting to think about the Dalmatian.' I sighed. She began to cry. 'It was bad enough having to have it put down. But it's that daughter who has put him against me. You know where she lives? I'll get her address and I'll have her again – this time for good!'

On my way to visit Ajita later, I called around at Henry's, not really expecting him to be there. He might have taken off, as he did sometimes, to stroll around some foreign city, like Budapest or Helsinki, for a couple of days, sketching, reading and visiting museums.

But the window opened and his head popped out. He came down straight away, in his slippers, and was agreeable, indeed excited, not appearing to be in crisis.

'Was it the dog that did it?' I asked as we walked under Hammersmith Bridge, towards the station.

'It was a damn good dog. I walked it often. The "ceremony" was unusual.'

'It was?'

Miriam had invited some of the neighbours, the children, other friends, and of course Henry to be there when the vet injected the stricken dog with the fatal fluid.

Henry said, 'As I got down on my knees and took my place on the floor, lying there with my ear at the dying dog's heart – the dog that didn't know it was going to die – I enacted the goodbye with love, rolling about with all the shamelessness I could muster, even making appropriately agonising noises. No way can I be accused of shirking on my dog duties.'

'I can't wait to see the video.'

'But when the others took their turn, it occurred to me that I couldn't spend any more time with people who want to hug expiring mutts. The abyss of boredom is my phobia. I'm terrified of being enveloped and destroyed by it. I've never stopped running from it.'

'Or towards it.'

He was quiet, then said, 'Miriam and I had decided to go clubbing later to a new place, the Midnight Velvet.' I must have made a face; he said, 'You didn't like the Sootie?'

'Not at all, no. It made me feel wretchedly depressed, particularly seeing Josephine. I was annoyed that I allowed myself to be talked into going.'

'You blame me?'

'Partly, but mostly myself.'

'I'm really sorry, Jamal. I tend to agree with you now.' He said, 'For months I'd wanted to follow my desire to the limit, all along the razor's edge. But those places no longer haunt or attract me either. Didn't my own daughter call me a stupid, stoned fool? I hadn't faced up to its exhausted decadence. I felt unclean, repelled by myself. I had become that dying dog. And there was something in my old life I missed.

'I left Miriam without disturbing her – she was with her loved ones – and went home. The world of bloodied, shredded bodies under Bush-Blair had been making me angry and sicksick. I've been feeling more and more hopeless.

'But on the night of the dying dog I was up until dawn, reading poetry, Shakespeare, Dostoevsky, running from book to book while listening to Mahler, Bach. Isn't art the still point – a spot of sense – in a thrashing world? I wrote ideas down and emailed actors I wanted to use in the documentary. I outlined my ideas for *Don Giovanni*.'

I said, 'I'd been wondering recently whether you really are beyond one of the more useful male vanities – that of reputation,' I said.

'I do think about it. I want to have been of little harm,' he said. 'And of some use. I wouldn't want to have betrayed my intelligence or my talent, such as it is. Talent exists, you know, and is inexplicable. I used to write, in my end-of-year diary round up, "Thank God, nothing to be ashamed of." But this year I've done no work at all.'

I said, 'Why would it not be good for you to vegetate, to lie fallow for a while?'

'Like some Chekhov character who wants to work but doesn't know where to start, I believed my artistic ambition had run down. Now some sort of energy has come back.'

'Lucky you, with a surge of new life. Miriam will be pleased.'

'I'll see her, and try to find some clarity. Will you come by later?'

'I'm going to see Ajita.'

He said quietly, 'Is there any hope there?'

'My guess is we'll meet up for a bit tonight and then she'll go out.'

'Jesus, Jamal, how terrible. I know now you waited and waited for that woman and then – what? It just didn't work out?'

'Who said it won't, in time?'

'But there's something sad there, aren't I right?'

'Something impossible.'

We embraced; he went back to his flat. I got on the train, where at least

I had the chance to read. Like Henry, I still had some impulse to learn, to understand.

At Ajita's the housekeeper wore a crisp white uniform like a servant in the Edwardian children's novels I used to read to Rafi. She led me to Ajita's bedroom, right at the top of the house, knocked and said, 'Miss – your visitor.'

'Thank you,' said Ajita, coming out and kissing me. She almost knocked my ear off with a thin unmarked box. 'It's only a DVD. But it'll interest you, I think. I know how much you like to be interested in things.'

'Do I? But I thought you had something to tell me.'

'To show you,' she said. 'It'll certainly surprise you, I know that for sure.'

CHAPTER FORTY-ONE

The room took up the whole of the floor and had sloping attic windows which seemed Parisian to me. Visible were a range of Soho rooftops, aerials and chimneys; nearby, a waiter leaned out of a window, smoking.

At the end of Ajita's bed was a broad flat-screen television and a sound system playing an iPod. My ex-girlfriend was listening to some quiet girl funk, Lauryn Hill or some such, and dancing a little, good-humouredly, in her bare feet and dressing gown, with wet hair.

I asked, 'Are you in bed already?'

'Just getting up. I eat late. You know both Mushy and I do.'

'Is he here?'

'Is it him you want to see? He's gone back to America to try to find help for Alan, who is very ill.' I seemed to irritate her; perhaps she really hadn't wanted to see me. She said, 'Jamal, I'm sorry for being so flaky the last few days. I've been busy with lawyers.'

'How come?'

She hesitated. 'I've been talking to the children every day, and to my husband. I kept saying I was going back, but each time I almost bought the ticket I thought, what for?

'Mark is furious and wants me to come home. So I've told him I have decided to divorce. He's kind, he doesn't deserve it. But I have brought up our children and done my duty. Now there are other things.'

'What does Mustaq think?'

'Why the hell do you have to ask that? Of course, he's agitated. He was keen on the marriage. He keeps saying I have to be secure. But there are things I absolutely need to do here.'

'You've been in London a while.'

'Aren't you taking your turn now to make me feel rotten?'

'Your absence reminds me of your mother's absence when you and I started to go out. She was always not there, which was when your father first began to use you.' Unsurprisingly, she was furiously silent. I said,

'But you have good things to do here – with your lover. You told me in Venice.'

'Exactly.'

'Are you going to marry him?'

She snorted. 'It's not a relationship. It's an encounter – of some sort. He gives me . . . I can tell you this, can't I? For some reason I've always trusted you. And how could you be shocked? He . . . he –' I was watching her lips; she almost said his name. 'He adores me, ties me, worships me, hits me – but very nicely. And all the time we are talking about everything, about him, me, the past and the future, about our dreams and fantasies. He gets me, intuitively. Jamal, it's on a level, religious and spiritual, that I've never experienced before.'

'We should celebrate.'

'You mean it? Yes, why not? That hadn't occurred to me, party boy.'

She rang down; soon the housekeeper appeared with champagne and glasses. Then she brought in a selection of clothes. I helped Ajita dress for the evening, finishing the joint she'd left in the ashtray beside the bed.

I said, 'I hope all this is for me. Give me a hug.'

She wore a short black dress, high heels and a black choker at her throat; she put her hair up. She held me and kissed my face.

'You missed your chance, baby, you know you did. I haven't felt like this since I met you at college.' Then she said, 'Darling sweetie, I almost forgot. Before we split tonight, will you watch something.'

'But what is it?'

She went to the TV with the DVD, opened it and dropped the disc into the player. 'There you are,' she said. 'Watch to the end.'

'Won't you sit with me?'

'I'll be back.'

When she left the room, I thought I might just walk out. But I settled down in the cushions, still annoyed that although she'd invited me over, it was only to observe her preparing to go out with a man – whose name she couldn't say – who wanted to ruin my life.

If the joint she'd given me was strong, the DVD was stronger, as she had known.

I watched a good deal of the programme – the past, suddenly tangible, with its jumble of familiar faces unspooling in front of my eyes, a dream I couldn't crash out of. I became confused and then dizzy. If I saw any more the world might break apart entirely.

I stood up and made it across the floor. Soon my head was over the toilet.

I opened the windows and stuck my gasping mouth out into the roar of Soho.

I took a cool shower. Ajita returned as I was drying myself. She didn't seem surprised by my condition, but fetched me a dressing gown and some aspirin.

'Okay? So you saw it, then?'

'More than enough of it,' I said.'

'Hardcore?'

'Yes, very.'

'A revelation, even?' she said.

'Maybe.' I asked, 'Who else has looked at it?'

'Mustaq. He watched it on his own,' she said. 'Then he turned it off and went on one of his wild walks without saying anything, but flapping his arms, no doubt. Why should I give a flying fuck what he thinks?'

'Why do you say that?'

'He makes me angry, Jamal. He flies back to London for the weekend, sits me down and starts complaining about my life and what I do. He doesn't want me to be independent. I have to go to him like a teenager, and ask for a flat and for money to start a business with a friend.'

'Which friend? The man?'

'Now you start! Why does it matter which fucking friend? For years I helped and advised Mustaq and still he says to me, "Aren't you actually going to *do* anything serious, Ajita? Are you going to be a spoiled little rich girl exploited by any friend?"'

'What did you say?'

'I slapped him hard across the face – boy, I enjoyed that! – and told him I was going to leave. While I was packing he came into this room and threw my clothes out of my bag onto the floor, telling me I had to stay. Then he grabbed me and held me. I stamped on his foot. What are you going to do, I screamed at him, imprison me as Dad would?

'He let me go, but he was furious. He's got enough problems as it is. I agreed to stay, but one more word from him and I'm out of here.'

Outside, Ajita accompanied me to Dean Street, where the taxi she'd ordered would pick me up. She took my arm.

'Don't you miss the ridiculous mesmerism of love?' she said, coming close to me and pulling up her skirt to give me a final look at her legs. 'What do you think?' She was mocking me now. She knew I envied her; she was freer than me and more satisfied.

We embraced and I watched her walk away, towards Wolf. In the car I told the driver to take me home. After five minutes I decided to go to the Cross Keys. I could have a drink and a long think there without being alone. One of the Somalis could drop me at my flat later.

I shoved at the familiar door and walked through the bar. My blonde Slovakian Lucy was about to perform. She waved in my direction, the men turning to look at me. I watched her dance, watched the men watching her. At the end she came over and put her arms around me. Wolf had left a while ago. When she was done we went upstairs to his room.

'I like see you,' she said. 'I like when you come in.'

I lay down on the mattress and smoked, asking her to join me. She undressed, wearing nothing but a cross on a chain around her neck. Getting under a blanket, she kissed me on the mouth. 'I'm not prostitute,' she said. 'Just dancer. Next time I work with children, once I have money for English lesson.'

Semi-hard, I entered her and moved a little, shoving, it seemed to me, against a wall within me of indifference and deadness. She gave me enough encouragement, smiling and showing me her tongue.

In the end I pulled out and lay there with her, listening to her talk about her life in London, wondering whether this might be some sort of end for me. Had I seen through everything and now lacked passion, curiosity, interest? The fact we liked one another, and that she was kind, made it worse.

'Don't you like me?' she said.

'But I do,' I said. 'You are wonderful.'

I asked her about Communism, saying apologetically that many of my generation and older had more or less believed in it.

'But I am too young to remember anything like that. Only the lazy and the Jews liked it,' she said. 'Now we have market but still few people have money. We will stay in this country five years, or ten, until we can buy house there.'

We stroked one another; I began to relax, able, at last, to consider what I had seen earlier, and how Mustaq's people had obtained the television documentary in which Ajita's father had appeared, made in the mid-70s, just before the strike.

Tatty old buildings and old-fashioned cars on empty roads; workers with 70s layered and feathered hair, wearing wide-lapelled jackets and brown flares; everyone smoking, as people did then, on buses, trains, aeroplanes, even on television. A voice-over: the upper-class 'Communist' explaining the exploitation – 'As always it is the workers who bear the burden of others' ambition.'

There he was, the old man, Ajita's father, with his son's mouth, and looking younger than me, with darker hair, and with a touching enthusiasm and belief in the opportunities and equality here. A man talking about his family and wanting to do well in England.

In the background of one of the shots inside the factory, I could see Ajita and Mustaq – not yet twenty – talking with an employee. At one moment the father turned to the camera and seemed to gaze through it innocently, into my eyes, those of his killer – as if he already knew I was waiting for him with a knife.

The mousetrap had slammed down on me: the whole picture had darkened in front of my eyes until I believed there was a fault with the TV. But the weakness had been in me, and I couldn't take any more.

Lucy and I were almost asleep when the Harridan barged into the room. She recognised me and moderated her tone.

'But this ain't no knockin' shop,' she said, as we were hurried downstairs.

'No,' I said sleepily. 'At least there you'd know the price.'

Part Four

CHAPTER FORTY-TWO

'Why, what has happened?' I asked on the telephone. 'Is it serious?'

There had been a power surge, I was told by a patient who phoned to explain why she would be late. The Underground system had broken down; the buses had stopped anywhere. The city had come to a standstill. Outside, apparently, it was chaos.

Between patients I sat in front of the TV, waiting for news. The truth was slow to emerge, but we learned it later that day. Four explosives, hidden in plastic food containers in backpacks, had been set off by suicide bombers in central London, three on the tube and one on a bus in Tavistock Square. The number of dead and injured was yet to be counted.

That beautiful London square was where Ajita, Valentin and I had attended many philosophy lectures. We drank wine and ate sandwiches there, on the grass, discussing the idiosyncrasies of the lecturers. It was where Dickens wrote *Bleak House*, and Woolf *Three Guineas*; where Lenin stayed, and the Hogarth Press published James Strachey's Freud translations in the basement of number 52. There is also a plaque to commemorate conscientious objectors in the First World War, as well as another for the victims of Hiroshima, along with a statue of Gandhi.

My patients referred to the events as 'our 9/11'. The hospitals began to accept the legions of injured even as unspeakable infernos blazed beneath the city. That day and night we were haunted by TV images of sooty injured figures with bloodied faces, devastated in their blamelessness, being led through dark blasted tunnels under our pavements and roads, while others screamed. Who were they? Did we know any of them?

Two days later I learned that the Mule Woman – who Henry's son Sam still saw occasionally – had been killed in the King's Cross bomb.

Henry was on the phone continually. I didn't mention my little passion for the Mule Woman, but in my mind I went over the evening we'd spent together. Henry insisted we go together to 'the Cross' to lay flowers. 'Oh England, England,' he moaned. I had never heard him use those words unironically. He was very gloomy and agitated about the deaths, and also about the attitude of Lisa.

'I can't bear to hear what she has to say.'

'Like what?'

'"Why would a young articulate kid, from a decent family, well-educated and intelligent, with everything in front of him, become a zealot destroying thousands of lives? I'm thinking of Tony Blair, of course."' He went on: 'It must be the first joke she has made. Otherwise, she is almost triumphalist over the bombing. Not only does she claim to have predicted it, not only does she see it as just retribution, but she seems to think Bush-Blair will learn his lesson at last. And if he doesn't, there'll be more bombs.

'But I am different, Jamal. For years when we were young and not-so-young we worshipped revolutionaries, anyone who had the courage to act authentically. We weren't the only ones. Nietszche, Sartre and Foucault – who idealised the Iranian revolution – were our exemplars. But there's nothing glorious about any of it to me, now.

'For our convenience, wars are usually held far away. But remember the Falklands, and how foul this land was with jingoism – the pubs covered in flags, the landlords crowing? But this is worse. Like you, I am bitterly disillusioned and confused, Jamal. Didn't we grow up on radical Third World movements, from Africa and South America – and now the rebels, the oppressed, are killing us, from the far religious Right! Don't you ever feel you don't know what's going on in the world?

'How can I stop thinking about the horror of those bomb-blasted trains, the ruined bodies, the cries and moans and screams, which segue, in *my* head at least, into the diabolical killing of civilians in Baghdad – severed heads, blood underfoot, children eviscerated, limbs blown into trees. Could only Goya grasp it? Why are we making this happen?'

He wanted to *do* something. Henry and Miriam were planning to visit the Mule Woman's parents in the country, if Sam gave permission. 'We're going to weep with them,' Miriam informed me. 'Will you join us?'

'I'm already weeping.'

In the week after the attacks Henry insisted I join him on long walks about the chaotic, almost apocalyptic capital, taking pictures and looking at others who were also frightened, dismayed, angry. Police cars and ambulances rushed about; the sound of the sirens was abysmal. All day and night police helicopters thrashed above the damaged metropolis.

During those demon days it was difficult for me to work. Many tubes were closed and buses not running. Patients turned up late or not at all. It was tough and unpleasant to move about. Huge police in body-armour – looking like pumped-up characters from video games – cradled machine guns at railway stations and outside the tubes.

I was aware of others' eyes on me as I entered tube trains wearing a backpack. Opening it to take out my book was invariably entertaining. Dark-skinned people were searched at random; an innocent man was pursued through a tube station and shot – was it six, seven or eight times? – in the head at point-blank range, by our defenders. Everyone was frightened, the patients disturbed. If there was a bang outside they jumped on the couch.

Not that I saw any signs of hatred, or even of antagonism, myself. Mosques were not torched, though they were protected by the police; Muslims were not attacked. Nor were there any flags, as there would have been in the US. Being bombed didn't stimulate British patriotism. The city was neither united or disunited. Londoners were intelligently cynical and were quite aware – they always had been – that Blair's deadly passion for Bush would cost them. They would wait for Blair to go – after many more deaths – and then they would sweep the front step.

Henry was incensed that Blair refused to accept that his own 'massive acts of violence' had anything to do with the murderous response; another example, according to Henry, of Blair refusing to bear responsibility for what he had done. Henry called it 'moral childishness'.

Bush-Blair's efforts to prosecute a 'virtual' war, in which no one on our side was killed, had proved impossible, and the Mule Woman, along with many others, had died. Henry had been wanting to forget about politics and get back to work but, during this period, politics wouldn't forget about us. Everyone in our circle was speaking about difficult and abstract questions, arguing about religion, liberalism and integration.

Oddly, the person whose behaviour altered the most was Ajita.

Mustaq, who had returned to London, had had his secretary call me, saying he'd be grateful if I could come to visit him in Soho. He sent a car, which dropped me off in Dean Street, where he was waiting, which made me think he hadn't told Ajita we were meeting. He wanted to walk around Soho.

He had donned a baseball cap and dark glasses for the stroll there, saying how ironic it was that when young he'd wanted to be recognised and praised as a star, whereas having become older he yearned for his original anonymity, having realised that fame – a handful of snow – didn't bring you understanding from others but somehow rendered you abstract, even to yourself. Soon, he said, newspapers would be running 'Whatever happened to George?' pieces, though even those would stop eventually.

'Why is the British press so vile? I hate the version of me they present. But I wouldn't give the money back, of course,' he added. 'Though it was easy to make. I could hardly believe it when the dosh started dropping into my account – so much of it, and so often! But I should have been a doctor.'

'Are you sick?'

'Not me, no.' Mustaq told me, as he'd had to tell a lot of people, that he hadn't been in London much because Alan had been ill. Like many ex-junkies, Alan had hepatitis C and had been refused a liver transplant since his cancer had spread. 'Alan will die in the next year. I have to accompany him on this journey. That is my work. But I do envy you your work.'

'What about it do you envy?'

'Its seriousness. Fatuous limitless narcissism can't be what we homosexuals fought for. Can't we think about anything else but our hair?'

'You sound like your father.'

'He was a serious man.'

I said, 'So are you, and you are engaged in a great love. We heterosexuals are more frivolous – all we want is sex. You gays get married for life! The next step, of course, will be for a man legally to take three wives.'

'And a woman three husbands?'

'Equality is everything.' Then I said, 'What did you think of the documentary about the factory?'

'I missed him, my father, all over again. Whoever removed him did me a considerable disservice. And I kept thinking how much like him I was.' He went on, 'Ajita's been living here, as you know. I don't like it – this city is far too dangerous.'

'New York is safer?'

'From one point of view, yes. A man has started to visit her. He comes about four times a week, late at night, at five in the morning sometimes. Of course the house and the street are covered by cameras. You know this guy?'

'Late middle-aged, stocky, short hair, determined-looking?' When he nodded, I said, 'He was a friend of ours, from the time we were at university.'

'Is he reliable?'

'He lives and works in a bar in West London. He's hard-working and not a drunk or even a cokey. She likes him, but I wouldn't have thought he's trying to exploit her.'

'Are you sure? She tells me she wants to buy a little flat in London. She asked for money – about a million, if you can believe it! She wants to start an antiques business too, with a friend of hers, someone who knows how to do such things – she claims. Jamal, she's coming alive, at last, and how can I refuse her?'

He went on, 'God knows we're all strange, and it's not for me to judge or say anything about the kind of sex she likes. Passion is the only interesting thing, of course. I did think, though, that the two of you might make something together.'

'Sorry about that,' I said. 'My wife and I parted. I'm not ready to see anyone else yet.'

He went on, 'When we went back to India after Dad died, and she was mourning him, she had no one but me to take care of her. Blasted Mother was preoccupied with her boyfriend.

'Ajita went to the market, helped in the kitchen. She had groovy Bombay girlfriends called Boomi and Mooni. But she spent a lot of time alone, and then she started to disappear in the car. It was rumoured she was going with a lot of people. The aunties wanted her to marry. After the first few candidates, she said to me, "The only person I ever wanted to marry was Jamal."

'The aunties were closing in. She was thinking of marrying one of those eligible turkeys in dire ties. She didn't want to go back to London, though she talked about you a lot.'

'She did?'

'She'd say, "I want to know what he's doing at this exact moment!" She wondered whether you had a lot of girlfriends or just one. But so much time had passed, she couldn't come back and reclaim you.

'I took her to America and got her a job in the fashion business. She met Mark, who she now says she wants to divorce. He found her a handful but he stuck by her, and in my view she should be grateful. The guy's in pieces and I've begged her, but she refuses to comfort him.' He said, 'I found . . . I saw recently – I looked in her bag – I wish I hadn't, I regret it – that she is reading books about abuse.'

'A growing genre.'

'I've been wondering – do you think anything like that happened to her?'

'It's not impossible.'

He said, 'I'll take that to be a yes. How much did you know about it? Did you know then – or later?' I didn't reply. 'The poor girl. And I did nothing. We both stood by and did nothing, eh?

'I have to reinterpret my whole family history in the light of this. But Jamal, it must have been hard on you.' He was staring at me. 'Now I have to go to America to plan a tour. I want to make music again and play live. I will set up a music foundation somewhere in the Third World. Ajita can help me. I am nervous about leaving her alone in London with this guy.'

'On the other hand, you don't want to turn into a Muslim father.'

'You think I am?'

'When you said you resembled your father I thought you meant that you both have bullying natures.'

He went on, sharply, 'You see someone you love making a mistake and you don't warn them?'

I said, 'Who's to say she's making a mistake?'

He embraced me and said, 'Sorry, you're right. I'm too used to people doing what I say.'

We parted, Mustaq and I, as we always did, with some puzzlement and dissatisfaction, as if neither of us was quite sure we were friends.

CHAPTER FORTY-THREE

Mustaq went back to America and I arranged to see Ajita again.

A new Indian place had opened not far from my house, one of those contemporary restaurants where the waitresses were young Polish women studying English during the day. The food was made with fresh ingredients and was dry, not drowning in a pool of grease. The decor was disappointingly modern – no chains of undusted plastic flowers hanging from the ceiling.

The only relief from the eerie, suspended and scared atmosphere of the city was to be with people you liked. The bad thing had already happened; we were in recovery. However, a week later there was another, failed, attempt at a bombing. Everyone was tense and despairing. We felt threatened and angry but, I guess, not as threatened and angry as the Iraqi people. I saw patients and Rafi, or Miriam and Henry. I watched the TV news continuously. I preferred not to be alone.

I was curious, too, about what Ajita and Wolf were doing at this time, and in this place, central London. I suspected it wouldn't be long before Wolf told Ajita the truth about her father's death and everything came out. It didn't seem there was much I could do about it.

Ajita was late; I didn't mind. I had become used to writing in cafés, which London was full of now – Henry called London 'a city of waitresses'. Lately I had been reading everything about Islam, tearing articles out of the newspapers and keeping them in a file. Like many people, the entire time I had a debate going on in my head.

'You didn't recognise me,' said Ajita, when at last she turned up, dressed like all the girls in a summer dress and flip-flops with a bag. 'This might sound strange to you,' she said. 'But I've been wearing the burqa and sitting over there, watching you send texts and talking to Josephine so warmly.'

'That was you?'

'There's a verse in the Koran about it, which goes something like: "Tell thy wives and daughters to draw thy cloaks close around them."'

'And that's it?'

'It's enough for the Hairy Men. I've been walking about the city in the burqa. The West End, the East End, Islington. To see how people regard me.'

'And?'

'There has been some curiosity and many hostile looks, as though people wonder whether I'm carrying a bomb. A man even said, "Your bomb looks big in that."'

'Ha ha.'

'I am happy to be stopped by the police and searched, arrested even, like at the airport. I want to know what they think of us now. Don't you get harassed?'

'The last time I went through Heathrow the guy at passport control said his wife had loved my last book.'

She said, 'But this is what my father predicted. We would be victims, cattle, rounded up. We were never safe here. Now they have found good reason to hate us, to persecute us. I want to know what my people have to go through –'

'Your people?'

'Yes, the women you can't see. People stare at you, they grunt and sigh – women mostly. The men don't notice.'

I said, 'Ajita, I liked you partly because of your colour – because it was like mine. But I've never thought of you as a Muslim.'

'Miriam and I have been talking about it.'

'You have?'

Henry had been talking about Ajita, and Miriam wanted to know her better. With my encouragement, Miriam had rung her at Mustaq's and invited her for tea. I didn't go, but I guessed they'd had plenty to say to each other. Miriam had shooed away the children and neighbours, and the meeting went on late into the evening.

Miriam had attempted to talk about me. She had shown her photographs of Josephine and given Ajita an account of our trip to Pakistan. Being Miriam, she also tried to find out what was between Ajita and I, but Ajita had given her nothing.

Miriam had told Ajita what she had told me: that the area where she lived was becoming more racist, with the victims this time being the Muslims. 'Muslim' – or 'Mussie' – was a new insult, along with 'ham-head' and 'allahAllah-bomb'. In our youth it had been Paki, wog, curry-face, but religion had not been part of it.

320

'I like Miriam's,' Ajita said. 'The noise, the animals, the whole family thing. Why have I never been able to create anything so lively?' She went on: 'When we were together, you never talked to me about Miriam. You hardly mentioned her.'

When Miriam and Ajita had talked, Bushy drove her home. Apparently, on the way, Ajita wanted to see the Cross Keys. Bushy, being protective, refused to take her in. She yelled at him, resenting the fact that people wanted to save her from everything. She wasn't fragile, for God's sake: hadn't she already seen the 'worst things'! *I want to be included!* she said. 'Everyone protected me. Dad tried to keep me at home so I'd be safe, and look what happened to me there!'

Bushy agreed to park outside and fetch Wolf for her. When he came out the Harridan came out too, wiping her hands on her pinny, saying, apparently, 'I would never have employed *her*!' Out of Wolf's earshot, of course.

Now Ajita said to me, 'You know what I did to Miriam? I *tested* her. One afternoon I went across London on numerous public transports. You know,' she said with incredulity, 'they go so far!'

This diminutive covered woman, drifting through the dangerous city, watching carefully, while not being seen herself.

'I went to her house anonymously. It's awful wearing the bag on the tube. It is hot in there and it is difficult to see out. But Miriam came to the door and invited me in – before I revealed myself. She is the only person I can talk to now.' Then she said suddenly, 'I know why you didn't want me.'

'You do?'

She tapped her nose. 'I know where your heart is.' Then she put her finger across her lips. 'Miriam knows.'

'Miriam doesn't know everything,' I said. 'Ajita, you go across London, you wear the black bag, and what does it prove?'

'We were a secular family, Jamal. Father never went to the mosque or had a beard or moustache. What use would religion be to him? But I feel ignorant, Jamal. My parents deprived me of our family past. We know nothing of Muslim culture, of Western culture – which father ignored – or indeed of African culture. We were only rich trash, and probably still are.

'You acquired a culture for yourself, Jamal, through reading and study. At least you are connected to the history of psychology and all that.

'So now I am studying. There is an Algerian woman who comes to the house. Azma speaks good English and she's teaching me the Koran. She talks of her life, politics, the condition of our people, my brothers and sisters, the oppressed of Afghanistan, of Iraq, of Chechnya. I wouldn't blow up anyone myself, but this is a war.' She said, 'What did you think of the DVD I showed you?'

'I was moved and upset by it.'

'And?'

I said, 'What does Wolf think?'

'Wolf? Yes, okay, I see. Did he tell you?'

'No.'

'Mustaq then. He had no right to. Oh well, it was bound to come out. Maybe I should have told you straight away." She bit at her nails. 'Did you always know?'

'Why would it be a secret?'

'I thought you might feel left out.' She looked at me with some annoyance. 'But you're not even thinking about that, are you?'

'No, I have my own preoccupations.'

'About your wife?'

'I'm not sure she would call herself that now.'

'How come?'

When Ajita and I had finished our meal and were walking together, I told her that Josephine had been working as a secretary in a college department of psychology. It should have been obvious to me that she would be taken up by someone from there, particularly as I had so little time for psychologists. I had wondered if this new relationship might have unsettled Rafi; it was unsettling me. I had already guessed something was going on when I wanted to take Rafi to the pictures and discovered he'd already seen the film.

'You have?' I said. 'But it's one of your favourites, a black gangster picture featuring hair-trigger niggaz and ho's. Your mother would never watch that.'

'I saw it with Eliot.'

'Who?'

'Mum's friend.' His eyes narrowed. 'Mum said she never minded you going to bed with your clothes on, so you could get up and go out straight away, but she didn't like you wearing trainers in bed. She said you always had a musty smell.'

'She's a fussy woman.'

A little later I began to understand even more: I had to meet him.

Normally Rafi would come to my house on his bike, but as he couldn't carry his weekend bag too, I had to go fetch it. It wasn't only that he considered his parents to be his servants, but that at times he still wanted to be a baby, which he was, with adult gangster elements overlaid: one moment he'd be in tears and the next he'd be pumping his arse up and down on my head, wanting to 'burst' it because I was 'a bastard'.

To her credit, Josephine had warned me that her 'new man' would be at the house. Now Rafi opened the front door, saying nothing for once, but his eyes darted about nervously. His mother must have told him to keep quiet. This wasn't a meeting I welcomed, but I supposed that the reality of this guy – whatever it was – would keep my paranoia down.

I followed Rafi downstairs, whispering, 'Many are the trials of being an adult, my son.'

'But it's all your fault, Dad.'

Eliot was sitting at the table Josephine and I had bought on the Shepherd's Bush Road, before all the shops became estate agents and mobile-phone dealers. He was drinking from my Ryan Giggs mug and correcting my son's homework with a pencil.

Inevitably I had imagined a tall charismatic god, but Eliot had longish greying hair, an open-necked shirt, an old worn jacket, academic wear. He was boss-eyed too, looking in at least two directions at once, which must have amused Rafi, as well as being useful at parties.

He was a fuzzy, badly photocopied version of me, more or less the same age, width and height, except with more of a concerned 'hospital' look, though maybe I had that at times. A phrase occurred to me: 'sullen charm'. It took me a while to recognise its origin. Years ago I'd been so described by an interviewer, who might as well have added sulky, opinionated and self-absorbed.

I thought: the place of the dead is soon taken by identical others – as at some of the movie award ceremonies I'd had the misfortune to attend with Henry, where, if you left your seat, bow-tied students would steal into your place so as not to reveal an absence to the cameras. Eliot had stolen from me all I didn't want, and it felt like theft.

I was looking at Eliot and looking at her, wondering what there was between them. Maybe she had found what she wanted: a psychologist and, through him, twenty-four-hour care, like marrying a doctor.

I didn't want to hang around. I declined tea, extracted a shot of vodka I'd left in the fridge a few days earlier, asked about the university department where he worked, and shook his hand.

Leaving, I turned to see him wiping sweat from his upper lip with the back of his hand. My shadow would always darken his life; I would be his ghost. Wouldn't she always love me? My son's face could only remind him of me. What, he could only wonder, was he getting into?

'What do you think?' Rafi asked, as he accompanied me to the front gate.

'He's brave but I don't envy him,' I said. 'Being in your own family is hard enough. Joining someone else's is scary work.'

'Is he a different kind of psycho-thing to you?'

'He's only a psychologist. One of those people who says it's all biology, or all in the brain. I bet he talks about animals without realising you can find an animal to justify any intellectual position. What do you want? Snakes? Donkeys? Insects? Except that there is no animal capable of being grief-stricken, for years, like man.'

'They know nothing,' said Rafi supportively, adding for good measure, 'Fuckers. Don't worry about him, Dad. You should hear him talk. I'm snoring. He says all your stuff – it's only specu– . . . Specu–'

'Speculation?'

'Yes. Speculation,' he said in a Jamaican accent. 'An' it's all been dissed.'

'Yes?'

'Discredited. Years ago.'

I said, 'Probably the only true psychologists these days are advertisers.'

'I have to tell you, Dad, we're going on holiday together. To Malaysia.'

'You are?'

'Him, me, Mum, and his two daughters. I've got two new older sisters – even if we're not related and they're teenagers!'

'He's got money, has he?'

'You'll be paying quite a bit towards it, Mum says. Does that hurt you?'

'It's beginning to.'

'I'll tell Mum I don't want to go.'

'I'll be here when you get back, exactly the same. I have Miriam and Henry and other friends.'

'Mum says, when we go away, will you feed the cat? I hate it when you're sad,' he said, resting his head against my shoulder and nuzzling into me, as he did as a child. 'But Eliot does have an Arsenal season ticket.'

'This fucking boyfriend too? Is that what she advertises for?'

'It's very bad luck, Dad. T, those Gooners are everywhere.'

After I had told Ajita this, she said, 'I'm glad you've spoken to me. We thought we liked each other, but were really only interested in other people. Do you want to carry on seeing me?'

I said, yes, but like her, really wasn't sure about it.

I had no idea how soon it would be necessary for us urgently to talk.

CHAPTER FORTY-FOUR

It was when Rafi, Josephine and Eliot went on holiday that I rang Karen. I emailed her occasionally, but it had been a while since I'd heard from her. It turned out she was alone too. Her daughters had gone to stay with their father and Ruby, along with the twins Ruby had just given birth to.

We were in Sheekey's. She looked tired, and she was wearing a wrap on her head.

'You're not drinking,' I said.

'Order whatever you want,' she said. 'I'm paying and I don't care.'

'Antibiotics?' I said.

'You know,' she said, 'I was invited on a date. It must have been around the last time I saw you –'

'You were going to meet that guy.'

'Yes.'

'I went to meet him. Just before, getting ready, I was in the shower, luxuriating with my favourite French bath gel, Stendhal it's called. As my hand moved across my breast, I felt something that didn't move like the rest. I tried to find it again, but couldn't.

'We had supper at the Wolsey. He's talking, I'm talking. But all the time there's this other text running through my head. *Breasts change all the time. They're more fluid than people think. They get bigger, smaller, rounder by the hour depending on men's hands, babies, menstruation. But no one will ever touch me again.*

'I have my check-ups once a year. I worship my docto. He's South African, he likes women, our bodies, our breasts.

'At the end of the dinner the date and I take separate cabs, he's going somewhere else for drinks, he invites me but I'm too spaced to go. The last thing he wants to hear about is my lump. That's going to make him hard and wanting me, right?

'The next day my hand seems to hit it, sort of smack into it.

'I froze. It was the end of me being what I still hadn't become – desirable. Like Hepburn or Binoche. Just give me a chance, I'd think to myself, a moment, a week, a year, and I'll get there. In fact I'm more mature, smarter in every way. Less afraid of everything.'

'Why wouldn't it be a cyst?'

'Exactly. Why not? Mammograms are full of them and they mean nothing. The mammogrammists send you off for further tests – sonograms, nonograms. Then more doctors mash you with cold plates or warm, humming probes and peer into scopes and monitors – and it's nothing.

'Fool I might be, but I did the responsible thing and made an appointment with the doctor-hero. When he asked if I'd come for any reason, I said no, just a regular check-up. My man likes to see "his women" every six months but I managed to make it once a year. I didn't want to determine his observations, give him an agenda. If he found something during the usual routine, well, okay. If not, what is there to talk about?

'He did the right breast, then the left. Slender, cool fingers. His touch is elegant, not arousing. You feel like a piano being stroked by a genius. Do they study it?

'Both hands on my left breast. Suddenly I couldn't hear and I couldn't breathe. But it was important to act natural. If he wanted to get me into the cancer thing, then he'd have to do his own damn work.

'His hands were off my chest and he was pulling up the white disposable paper gown and saying, "Fine below and above, one of the lovelier uteruses, see you next time." I was free. I'd got through. "You mean," I said, "you didn't find anything?"

'I shouldn't have said that. He's stopped washing his hands, and turning round to look at me again. He says, "Why don't we just check again, to be sure? You think you've found something, don't you? Which one, right or left?"

'When he says "left" I blush and I feel my eyes widen to the size of the screen at the Sony Imax theatre. His hands are immediately on the left. He's watching me, my eyes. "Am I getting close? Going to give me a hint?"

'I don't say a thing. You went to medical school, you're on your own, pal.

'He finds it. "Aah." His fingers, both hands, passing and passing again over the thing, moving it, isolating it, angling it.

'He's not looking at me now. He's not my breezy, older, attractive, cool, flirty doctor any more. He's a lookout for the cancer team, and he's going to put me into the system, the system that finishes women. Once you're in, you're out. You're not a woman who counts in the world.

'How could I endure it – the obliteration, the ugliness, the havoc, of having no breasts or hair? I saw different doctors and they all had their disclaimers. It could be a cyst, a blocked duct or a tumour which wasn't cancerous. I believed every one. I can't even keep a husband. Who would look after me? I couldn't work. Who would look after the kids?

'I argued with the doctors. I tried to talk the breast surgeon out of insisting on the surgical biopsy. She was doing me a favour by scheduling it so quickly. But I felt I was being drawn into the hospital death trap. I met a woman at the hospital who was having a biopsy too. She was overjoyed. She wouldn't have the anxiety of not knowing.

'I was more dishonest. I didn't understand any of it until they told me in the hospital that I had a tumour of considerable mass.'

It had begun, my generation had begun to die. One by one we'd be picked off: illness, and then death. More funerals than weddings. Who would be next, I wondered?

The next death came sooner, and more suddenly, than I could have imagined.

At the end of supper I helped Karen into a cab. I walked for a while, looking at the city, aware of every person with a bag; every trip on the tube a potential death. Will it be now? Will he be a bomber? Will I be killed? Would I mind, or would it be a good way to exit – suddenly, plucked from the world? I thought of the Mule Woman's parents. What if it had been Rafi?

After Karen finally told me what had happened to her, I rang her most days. Even Henry was concerned, in his own way. He began to shoot more material for the actors' documentary which, on hearing that Karen was ill, he had decided to complete.

At the Riverside Studios, not far from his flat, he worked with Miriam on the Chekhov scenes. Despite the anxiety which caused her to call me incessantly, Miriam was ecstatic. In rehearsal he took her as seriously as he would any actor, listening to her, watching her, using what was there. 'Intuitively, underneath, I was always an actress,' she told me. 'Undiscovered, of course – until recently.'

Henry was directing the scene in several different styles, with different actors, before cutting the material together. He came over with his computer and showed it to me. He'd thought he was 'finished', but his energy was high and the work good. We were on better terms, too, over Lisa.

I had given her poems to a young Libyan acquaintance I met sometimes in a pub nearby. He was enterprising, with his own small-circulation magazine and a tiny publishing operation. He distributed the work himself, heaving the stuff around bookshops in a suitcase. He agreed to run three of her poems in his magazine. He asked her to write an essay on modern poetry.

She seemed a little put-out that the poems weren't going to be published in the *TLS*, but I thought she'd appreciate this young man and his efforts. She agreed to meet him and help him take stuff around the shops.

I resented the little time Lisa demanded of me. I was working hard. The practice was growing. I was being approached by more potential patients than I could possibly see. God knows, I needed the money. So the new ones I fitted in early.

It was one morning, in the often frantic ten minutes between sessions, that Maria came in looking more worried than usual, and without my coffee.

She said that Ajita had called to say Wolf had died during the night, in her house in Soho.

My first thought was: will this be my release or my condemnation?

CHAPTER FORTY-FIVE

Mustaq's office had located Wolf's sister in Germany and arranged for his body to be flown home. Ajita had informed Mustaq that Wolf had no family in Britain, and that she didn't want to go to the funeral. Neither of us did, for different reasons.

'Jesus, sweetie, you look more distressed than me,' she said when I turned up that evening. She was sitting on a sofa in a quiet little private club behind St Martin's Lane. 'Have something to calm you. This is an awful fucking business.'

'Ajita, tell me what happened.'

She said, 'We had finished making love. Wolf got up and was standing at the end of the bed in Mustaq's dressing gown. Suddenly I was struck by how much like my father he looked. A mixture of Mustaq and Dad.

'I never stopped talking to Wolf about myself, but I didn't really want to know *him*. We just did those intense things together. Sometimes I felt I was using him. Not that he would have seen it like that.

'A while ago outside the club where he was working, a man came at him with a knife and threatened to slash him. Wolf escaped, but he wept about it. I didn't want to see him like that, a child.' She said, 'What about you? Will you miss him at all?'

'I found him aggressive and needy this time round.'

'He didn't like me seeing you. He was pissed off that you hadn't been warm towards him, that you refused to recognise the friendship you once had.'

'I had too much else going on.'

'You shouldn't do that to people, Jamal,' she said. 'But who am I to talk? I was worse, always going on about myself. After he was attacked he complained of breathlessness and pains in his chest, but I thought they'd pass. How could it not have occurred to me to take him to the doctor?' She went on: 'When he was waiting for the ambulance, he asked me to forgive him. I said only God or a priest could do that.'

'To forgive him for what?' I asked. She shrugged. I thought she was going to say something else to me, but she looked away. I said, 'Shall we have supper here? Aren't there private rooms?'

To my surprise she said, 'Sorry, Jamal, I don't feel up to it. I need to go home. I hate you to see me like this,' was her explanation. She paid the bill and left me there.

Then I didn't hear from her. She didn't return my calls. When I went into Soho and knocked on the door there was either no reply or the staff, barely opening the door, informed me that no one was there.

Worrying about her, and not knowing what else to do, I rang Mustaq in America. Ajita had told him there was no need for him to return to London; she was 'okay'. She knew he was taken up with Alan; he didn't need any more deaths.

I asked Mustaq if Ajita was surviving and he told me, 'She's in the house, but in bed most of the time. She sees no one but the staff, and she doesn't talk to them. All they do is take her food. I'd be grateful if you could visit, Jamal.'

Mustaq informed the staff I was going to take her out. She was lying down but not unpleased to see me. She asked me to slip into bed beside her, to hold and cuddle her. She didn't want to be caressed but lay there still and heavy, in my arms.

I managed to get her to shower and dress, and walk to the end of the street, before she insisted on returning home.

The next day we walked further, but only a street or so, and she used an umbrella as a stick. She wore dark glasses, looking every inch the widow, in black. I guessed she must have been getting tranquillisers from some-where: doctors adored to prescribe them, and patients were disappointed if they left the surgery without a prescription. I liked walking slowly with Ajita, looking at the restaurants and at the people. We stopped to drink cof-fee and have cake, but she wouldn't eat.

It was not unusual for people to become depressed as they mourned. I wondered, too, whether Wolf's death reminded her of her father's death, and how these deaths were connected. However, we didn't speak much as we took another turn around Soho before she returned to bed.

We were approaching the house and passing an Indian restaurant. She asked, 'Did you help kill my father?'

I was silent but she waited for me. I asked, 'When did you know?'

'After you came to watch the documentary. You were upset. But how could I be sure? I went over and over it in my mind, wondering. Then

330

Wolf told me – after the heart attack, I guess he was dying. The ambulance took forever to come. They couldn't find the street. He said he wanted to "confess".'

'What did he say exactly?'

'He said it was his idea that you, he and Valentin should try to scare Dad so that he would leave me alone. Instead, my father passed away.' She was quiet, and then said, 'At least it wasn't Wolf alone. That would have fucked my head.'

'Does Mustaq know?'

'I have decided not to tell him. He gets so angry.'

'Will he get to know?'

'How would it make his life better to hear how I suffered then and what you went through? He'd just feel guilty. He likes you so much, Jamal. You helped him as a kid.'

'Will you tell him about your father and the abuse?'

'He seems to have guessed. But I'm not ready to go into it. I don't even *like* my brother right now.'

I said, 'I was a fool not to listen to you at the time. I just wanted to take action, to be a tough guy like the other tough guys.'

She said, 'I should have spoken to Mustaq.'

'Ajita, I doubt whether he could have taken on your father at his age, the kid brother.'

'I wish I had told you at the time of the abuse – Jamal, it was all so horrible – that I wanted to kill him myself. I thought all the time about how to do it. *Where do you buy poison? How much do you put in? Will it be detected?*'

She went on: 'Jamal, don't turn on yourself, when it was me. I killed him, my own father, by encouraging you to get rid of him. When he was raping me, I wished him dead a million times.

'At the time I wondered often if you had hurt him that night. But how could I ask you? I couldn't even think about it. You were young, and you risked your life for me. You were – what do they say? – chivalrous.

'I asked you once if only there was something you could do, if you would speak to him. But I did warn you that Dad was dangerous. Yet you went ahead and did it. You were brave, you were foolhardy, you were young. Do you regret it?'

'I don't know.'

'I do! I should have stopped Father by threatening him with the police. Or hitting him with something heavy. I shouldn't have put you in that position. I was a weakling but you took the action I couldn't take. I can't have you punished for risking your life to save me. Dad had been a wrestler, and he'd had people beaten up before. When I see pictures of Saddam Hussein in jail I think, that's Dad, what he'd have looked like now.'

'If I'd known that at the time, I'd have been more cautious.'

'Jamal, how can I ever apologise, or make it up to you? Can we be friends? You don't hate me, do you? You were so cool towards me when we met at my brother's after so many years. I was ecstatic to see you, but you were reserved.'

'I was nervous,' I said. 'I didn't know what you might mean to me.'

'You were relieved I meant so little to you, I could see that. Few things have hurt me so much, Jamal. I kept asking Wolf, "Why is he so cold?"'

I said, 'Isn't Mustaq left in limbo now? The only one who doesn't know, who will never know?'

'I didn't say he will never know. We'll see, won't we?' She said, 'You know what I wanted, all the time it was happening, Dad's abuse? I fantasised about us running away together. To take a train someplace and find a room there, and work in bars or bookshops or something. We'd never go back but get married and have kids. Would you have done it?'

'Yes,' I said.

But I was thinking: a murder is something it is not possible to recover from. It can never be worked through or forgotten; there will be no resolution.

By now we'd returned to the house. The staff were cleaning it. We went into a little sitting room downstairs where I noticed something familiar but so uncanny I couldn't place it.

'What?' she said, looking at me.

'There it is,' I said. It was the Hand, on a table, leaning against the wall. 'At last. How did it get here?'

'Why do you ask?'

'That wonderful picture belongs to Henry's wife – Valerie.'

'It was given to me,' she said. 'It was a present.'

'From Wolf?'

'Yes. I love it. I want it in front of me always. I move it around the house where I can see it.'

'It wasn't his to give, I'm afraid,' I said, picking it up and shoving it in my shoulder bag. It stuck out the top; I'd have to cover it with a plastic bag.

'The best thing he ever gave me was stolen?' she said. She came over and drew it from my bag. I could see she might be minded to smash it.

'Not a good idea,' I said, grasping it firmly, pulling it away from her and replacing it in the bag. I could see the two of us tearing the masterpiece apart.

'How can you do that?' she shouted from the front door. 'You're always taking things from me!'

In Dean Street I got into a taxi and went to Valerie's, where a uniformed maid opened the door. The hall was crowded with guests in smart clothes.

I put my bag down, took a glass of champagne from a tray and, with the Hand under the other arm, went upstairs to join the others. As far as I could see, the dinner consisted of film and literary people and politicians, with their wives and husbands. Valerie didn't seem surprised to see either me or the picture. When she took it from me, she put it under a side table and asked me to join everyone at supper.

Before I could sit down she said she needed to ask me something. I groaned inwardly but could see she was busy, surely it wouldn't take long.

She said, as we stood together in a corner of the kitchen, 'You saw Lisa. Does she need treatment?'

'For what?'

As always, Valerie looked like someone on the verge of a tantrum. 'For stealing my damn picture,' she said. 'I don't know. You're the doctor. But don't worry about it, there's something else.' She hesitated. I kept watching her but she didn't want to look at me. She said, 'Years ago, when Henry and I were going through our difficulties but were still together in some form or other, he said to me, "We'll spend our old age together. We'll get a place by the sea and we'll talk and eat and read and paint." It's what I've been looking forward to. It's the only thing I had in mind when I thought of the future, *our* future.'

'Right.'

'We're hardly young now,' she said. 'And he's taken up with this woman.'

'My sister Miriam.'

'Yes, yes. Charming though she is, I'm sure,' she said. 'Do you really think it is serious? Do you think it will last? You know him, he's your best friend. I couldn't ask anyone else.'

I said, 'You're asking me if Henry will return to you?' She nodded a fraction, as if she couldn't bear to show her hope. I went on, 'But he is with Miriam now. They've been together for more than a year. I believe they love one another.' She was studying me hard. 'It might be better to find someone new.' I almost said, 'You can never go back,' but didn't, considering it to be false.

'I knew I shouldn't have asked you,' she said. 'By the way, without Henry, you'd be nothing in London. You could be more grateful.' Her eyes dropped and she turned away.

The table was crowded; there was hardly room for all the chairs around it. I was glad to see Henry's son Sam, now going out with the barely dressed daughter of a rock star I'd adulated in the 70s. Sam took Rafi's mobile number. He and the girl, who apparently sang like Nico, wanted to rehearse some songs they'd written and needed a drummer. Sam had jammed with Rafi before, and rated him. Rafi would slot effortlessly into that world.

I found myself sitting with a group of women who, when they heard what I did, began to discuss their dreams. Unfortunately, in those circumstances I'm likely to feel like a doctor on holiday who finds that people insist on telling him their ailments.

Soon I tuned out and became aware of how bored and dissatisfied I felt. I didn't want to go home and be alone, nor could I cope with the chaos of Miriam's.

I considered visiting the Goddess, but wasn't in the mood. I was aware of how lonely I was, how far away I was from other people. And I thought I wanted to be in love again, once more, perhaps for the last time. To experience love, at this age, and to see how different it was to the other occasions. I wasn't ready yet, but I would be ready soon.

CHAPTER FORTY-SIX

To help him settle in, Rafi was accompanied by his mother on the first three days of his new secondary school, recommended by Mick Jagger. On the fourth day I took him. After that, aged twelve and determinedly moving away from us, he'd be on his own.

The two of us got on the bus at the end of my street. It was seven-thirty and a long time since I'd been out so early. He was anxious. 'Dad, Dad, take off the damn hood and shades! Don't speak!' he hissed.

The boy suddenly seemed taller, up to my chin now, his tie tight at his throat – I'd taught him to do a Windsor knot, as my father had taught me – his black shoes too big, his keys and phone on a coloured string around his neck, like everyone now.

Older boys, already bored, crumpled shirts hanging out of their trousers, slouched at the bus stop, smoking, listening to music on their headphones. Soon that would be my son, but now he was afraid, showing me his summer project on the bus, asking if it were okay, photographs of leaves and rocks, drawings of logs, and misspelled words scattered amongst it all.

We crossed Hammersmith Bridge, the river full, elegant and glittering in the early-morning sunshine, and up the bus lane to Barnes, past playing fields, wealthy houses and a conservation park. London was splendid in this late summer weather. The large grounds and Richmond Park nearby made Rafi's new school seem an idyllic ghetto.

At the gates we stopped. I told him I wish I'd attended such a place. My school had been rough and frequently violent, the teachers hopeless. But I wasn't sure I'd have rather been segregated from the harsher realities.

Rafi rushed away, fearing I might try to say something significant or, even worse, attempt to embrace or kiss him. 'Thanks, Dad, see you later.'

To pay for Rafi's education I was taking on new patients and beginning to make notes on my 'guilt' book. I was looking forward to researching it, not in the Reading Rroom of the British Museum which I remembered with such ambivalence, but in the new British Library in King's Cross.

I was no longer writing about Ajita; reality had alleviated my fantasies of her. But I did visit her one Saturday morning. She was still in bed, in a darkened room, and drinking champagne with whatever else it was she was taking. The champagne soothed her throat, she said. She could hardly speak, her throat was sore.

I said, 'Do you want to talk to someone? Is there something you need to say?'

'Of course,' she said. 'Why haven't you suggested it before? What have I got to lose?

She went on, 'It's almost impossible for me to go out. This house is becoming a bunker. On top of that, I have three men – you, my brother and my husband – trying to control me. I want to invite the children here for a few weeks. I want to see my husband too, and explain. But I cannot deal with them if I'm so weak, so feeble.'

'I know a very good woman analyst.'

'Don't I want a man?' she said.

'Not yet.'

'No, not some pompous peacock like you with those oh-so-calculated silences which drive you mad.'

I rang my analyst friend, and Mustaq's driver took Ajita to her first session. The analyst was Spanish, in her late sixties: thin, elegant, with hair that changed colour regularly. Her books were good, she was intelligent and cultured, a woman who you knew would hear you.

After the session Ajita called me from the car and said, 'You haven't seen Ana's room but it's marvellous. There are books and pictures, and a couch with a blanket on it. I sat on the couch – for a moment I did put my feet on it, and my head on the cushion. But I sat up again immediately, thinking if she couldn't see me, if I were passive and helpless, she wouldn't love me.

'Isn't it terrible, this kind of artificial love? After all, I know very well she doesn't love me as I love her.'

I said, 'Oddly enough, we say that the better the analyst, the more likely she is to fall in love with her patient.'

'What could be stranger than that?' said Ajita. 'To fall in love for a living. Like soul prostitution.' She went on: 'The whole thing is like being stirred inside by a huge spoon. I came out devastated, while feeling I've learned the most interesting and obvious things in the world.'

336

A few sessions later Ajita told me she had begun going five times a week, which was unusual these days. A daily analysis was still called 'classical', but Vienna in Freud's day was a small city; getting to Berggasse 19 wasn't a trouble for wealthy Viennese.

Ajita said, 'Ana was wearing a little cropped red jacket which I touched, saying goodbye and thank you to her. Jamal, it was mink.'

'Yes,' I said. 'She is a little different.'

'Ana is the woman I want to be, of course. Wise, educated, patient, experienced. A woman who can talk to anyone. I don't think of her having sex, though. Not that I think of myself having sex again.'

'At least you have a routine now,' I said.

'Yes, I get up early to see her, and then I write my diary of the whole experience. In the afternoons I can go to museums and galleries, or I read. I'm an ignorant fool, I've never understood why anyone would want to listen to me.'

'Wolf did.'

'Yes, he was wild about me, fascinated by me. He listened to everything, nothing was too dull for him. That was the real thing, wasn't it? And now it's gone again.'

I visited her often, sitting on the bed with her. Wearing black silk pyjamas, she'd play music and drink while I dozed. She was eager for information about the history of analysis. She asked many questions and liked me to sit with her even when she was reading.

'I had no education,' she said. 'Don't you remember that? Now, tell me, what exactly is the "angry breast"?' These sessions reminded me of the time we spent in her house as students, and I enjoyed them as much.

We could have begun to make love again. I had the feeling she might like that. I was no substitute for Wolf; she told me how much she liked his physical strength. But maybe I was better than nothing.

However, I was too inhibited to go in that direction and, as always, there was someone else on my mind, someone who wouldn't let go.

CHAPTER FORTY-SEVEN

'You said once, life is a series of losses,' said Karen. 'Let's say it again, there is the speed of death and how it flies at you like a missile, and before you've hardly glimpsed it – bang, you're gone.'

This time I was driving; Bromley revisited. After I'd passed on the details of Mustaq's architect to Mum and Billie, the garden studio was now finished. Today was the 'official opening', as Billie put it, with Mustaq as the special guest.

Rafi sat in the back of the car with his head down, listening to his iPod and playing with his PSP. The only way to reach him was to poke him, though it was dangerous to do so.

Still in chemo, and her girls with her husband's new love Ruby and their twins, Karen wanted to talk, her voice merely a whisper, as if she were speaking through a wall. She was cold and wore a big Farhi coat with a fur collar. Her wig was long and shiny, electric with static, rendering her eccentric, like someone deliberately failing to resemble a 40s movie star, or even mocking womanhood.

'I never saw the point of walking before, but now I like to do it, joining the stream of other slow people. They're on chemo too, exhausted from radiation, or off-balance because of vicodin. Then I drink coffee and I eat custard tarts and croissants until I can't cram in another one.

'You were right, I was being evasive with myself. It was not denial but self-destructiveness. You told me to talk to the oncologist but I hated to be inside the system, the machine. You insisted it worked, that it was the only way. Now he and I sit in the hospital café like two adults and I love him passionately while he shows me photographs of his wife and family. You said I should speak to these medics directly, as an equal. They wouldn't be afraid of my distress if they knew I'd seen my death.

'But facing reality, that's an art form. When I thought I was about to die, I wanted to ring everyone up and tell them – hey, didn't you know it, you're only playing at life!'

When we got to the house Mum opened the door, greeting us and smil-ing enthusiastically, offering her cheek to be kissed. Although she admitted to being nervous of Rafi and what she called his 'obnoxiousness' – though with her he was always polite – I was glad to see her. These days, though, when we met, it was like running into someone you knew well a long time ago but now had little in common with – indeed, felt awkward with – a feeling which had been reproduced with Josephine.

I said, 'You never much liked children, did you, Mum?'

'You give them everything,' she said. 'And when they're grown up they can't wait to tell their psychiatrist how much they hate you. Either way, they don't want you.'

'No.'

Mum said, 'But I thought you might have brought Josephine for me to talk to.'

'You did? I was just thinking of her. Why do you say that?'

'I like her.'

'Do you?' I said, as Mum led me into the house.

'She was the best of the lot. I'd like her to see the studio. Will you bring her?'

'She's with someone else.'

'Oh, don't worry about that. Tell him to go away.'

Miriam was there already and I was glad to see her, and she me. She was staring rather wildly around the place, as if she couldn't understand why her childhood had suddenly disappeared. She was still agitated and dis-turbed by Mum, as if Mum wanted to attack her for her crimes and mis-takes. But, nicely drunk, Mum only beamed at everyone with a sort of Zen perspicuity and benevolence, while Miriam clung to Henry's arm.

Recently Miriam had been spending more time at Henry's place; they were also talking of renting a country cottage. Henry was working again, with renewed persistence and concentration, trying to link *Don Giovanni* to consumer and celebrity culture, which he thought paralleled its vicious cyn-ical murderousness. He'd decided the only thing to be done was to remake the world, even as the politicians he'd supported were un-making it.

As we drifted out into the garden with glasses of champagne, I could see the fine new studio, made of pine and glass, set amongst trees and bushes. Alan was out there already, and Karen bent down to embrace him, to weep too.

In a wheelchair, Alan was frailer than even her, and wrapped in several blankets. He was exhausted, staying awake for days. Having been a druggie, he was convinced that his prescribed pills did not affect his corrupted body. He resembled someone staring into a universe of fog. 'London's full of ticking bombs,' he murmured, taking my hand. 'I'm one of them. Only a gay death for me.'

I wasn't surprised to see how gaunt Alan was, but Mustaq, usually sleek and manicured, seemed overweight, fretful and bedraggled, as if determined to walk all the way to death's door with his lover. If Alan didn't die first, they would marry in a few months' time, when the law changed to allow civil partnerships.

Mustaq touched, stroked and kissed Alan continuously. At other times, standing beside Alan, he seemed to stare at me, successfully locating my paranoia, while resembling someone in a dream. He only perked up when Rafi came out, asking the kid what music he was playing on the iPod.

As there were friends of Mum and Billie yet to arrive, I kissed Ajita and took her by the arm.

'Let's get out of here for a bit. I need to look at something with you.'

It was a short drive. We were standing outside the house Miriam and I had grown up in. Ajita had visited that house only twice, as far as I could recall, leaving Mum some of her aunt's 'special' dhal and aloo in plastic containers. The place was almost unrecognisable now, with many new rooms built on, and in the porch there were kids' bikes and toys. Then we drove the short distance to Ajita's old house, which she hadn't seen since the day she'd packed up a few things and left for India.

We arrived at the same time as the owner, who looked at us but said nothing. The layout of the place was the same. We got back into our car as the garage door opened like a mouth.

The space was tidy; just a few boxes. We watched as the man drove in. He got out of his car, glanced at us, and went into the house.

She was looking at me, I noticed, as I stared at the spot where her father fell. I wanted to make some kind of gesture – if I'd been a Catholic I'd have crossed myself – but didn't know what to do.

'Was it all true?' Ajita asked as we drove away. 'Did it really happen?'

'Who knows?'

I told Mustaq we had gone to the house and asked him if he wanted to see it again. He said irritably, 'Why do you ask me that? I dislike my father more and more. A man who didn't understand homosexuals, who would never have grasped this passionate love, who was incapable of such feeling.'

To our delight, when we all gathered round for the ceremony, Mustaq had decided to adopt the Queen's voice to open the studio, saying what a great thing it was and how fabulous the two old girls were. He smashed a bottle of champagne against the door and sang, along with everyone else, 'Vincent'.

Then, while we drank more champagne and ate from the tables laden with good food, a pissed opera singer, accompanied by someone on accordion, sang tunes from Puccini and Verdi. Some people danced; even Alan was persuaded from his wheelchair and tottered about in Mustaq's arms as the singer gave us 'I Love that Man' from *Porgy and Bess*.

As Mustaq and Alan kissed on the lips, Mother said, 'We're all shuffling towards the exit, one by one.'

'Yes,' said Billie. 'And some of us are singing!'

It was later, when we were having cake and sandwiches, that I saw the knife again, horrified as much by the way it had moved unnoticed through the years as by its history. Mustaq looked at me. 'What's up, Jamal? You look as though you've just seen a ghost.'

I could only walk away. I found Henry inside the studio, looking at Billie and my mother's work and using Miriam's camera-phone to photograph their tools. Through the window we could see Miriam with Rafi.

'Doesn't she look good?' Henry said.

'She's a little thin for me.'

'I like her like that. She seems more serious. We're not going on "the scene" for a while. But that's not the end of anything,' he added. 'I don't want to be Don Giovanni. Nor am I one of those who believes relationships become less libidinous as they continue, that intimacy is counter-erotic. In fact, sexual relationships between near-marrieds like us can become dangerously satisfying and deep. I guess they can feel incestuous, which is why people prefer strangers. What do you think?'

'When Josephine and I had sex, it was better than anything else.'

'You want to go back to her?' He was looking at me with concern. Then he started to laugh. 'You're joking. You're crazy.'

Karen slept in the car on the way back; she was saving her energy for later on, when she'd be watching Karim in *I'm a Celebrity . . . Get Me Out of Here*.

During the brief window while Rafi was searching through his pockets for his earphones, I was able to speak to him.

'Has Eliot been around?' I asked.

''Course.'

'What does he do?'

'What does he do when?'

341

'When he's in the house.'

'He sits around with Mum. Jealous?'

'Yes. But the torments of jealousy will not, I am glad to say, give you in particular a miss. Why should they?' I asked, 'But apart from that?'

Rafi said, 'He watches TV, eats pot noodles, reads the paper and sits in the garden and smokes.'

'Like everyone else, then.'

'What?' he said, as the music crashed in. 'What?' Then, for a moment, he took out his earplugs and said, 'Mustaq – that singer guy. He showed me some chords and told me about what he wants to do, stuff about Pakis and suiciders and paranoia, like Springsteen's doing in the US. He wants to invite me to his studio when he's recording, to show me how everything works. You'll take me there, won't you?'

The day had exhausted me. I dropped off Karen and then Rafi. But when Rafi rang the bell and Josephine opened the door she smiled at me and waved. I started to drive away.

But instead of going home, I parked the car and rang Ajita to get her thoughts on the day.

She was giggling. 'It was funny,' she said. 'I walked in the garden with Rafi. I have to tell you, he kept looking at me and he said, "You've got beautiful eyes. You're really nice-looking." He's got that twinkle, you know. He's going to be a dog like you.'

I was amused and proud, but irritated too and even envious. I left the car and went back to the house, where Rafi let me in before returning to the TV.

Josephine was coming out of the bathroom, pulling a towel around her lower half. She let me look at her – she'd kept her shape, there was nothing loose on her – before covering herself.

'You're back,' she said cheerfully.

I followed her downstairs. She fetched me a beer and cut me a slice of her homemade chocolate cake. Rafi scrutinised us before going into his room to play a game.

We were discussing her insomnia, aching neck, bad knees and bumpy skin, among other interesting things, when the doorbell rang.

'Hasn't he got a key?' I said.

'Not yet.'

I pulled her onto my knee. 'I'm never going to let you go,' I said, putting my hand between her legs.

'But you did.'

'I was a fool.' I kissed her mouth, and felt her respond. Her fingers were on my back. Once Josephine touched you, you stayed touched. 'Can we have lunch tomorrow?'

Eliot rang the bell again. Rafi, of course, wouldn't move a centimetre unless it was in his immediate interest. Josephine was beginning to panic. She said quickly, 'But it'll be rushed.'

'What can we do?'

'Will you take me to dinner?'

'Yes,' I said. 'I was going to ask you if you'd come with me to see Hussein Nassar.'

In my local Indian restaurant, as we ate our dhal and rice, an Indian Elvis impersonator, Hussein Nassar – known as the King's Jukebox – would be re-acting the whole of the 1968 NBC comeback special.

'We can't miss that,' I said. 'Don't think Muslims aren't making a significant contribution to cultural life here. And there is a lot I want to tell you.'

'Have you been surviving?'

'Only just.'

She said, 'Thanks for emailing me those pieces you've written.'

'I'm thinking of putting them together as a book.'

'It's about time you published another one.'

I said, 'Can we go through them?'

'I'd like that.' She said, 'I'll try to look smart for you.'

I said, 'Tomorrow, then.' I agreed to pick her up at seven-thirty. I kissed her again, I couldn't stop myself, and murmured, as the bell rang again and she pushed me away, 'It takes three to tango.'

Upstairs, Rafi's door was open and he was peering through, evidently amazed that not only were his parents speaking to one another but that they were intending, clandestinely, to go out together. When I went past he gave me a shy thumbs-up.

Eliot was waiting at the door, looking in the other direction. 'Hi,' he said.

'Hello, Eliot, how are you?'

'Fine, fine.'

'Good holiday?'

'Lovely.'

'Decent weather?'

'Warm but not hot.'

When he passed me and I turned back, I saw Rafi's face was at the window and we winked at each other and rolled our eyes.

*

Before going to see Miriam later, I walked up to the Cross Keys for the last time.

In a few weeks the Harridan would be gone – to the sea, no doubt. Though the lucifugous strip venue was usually full, it would be closed down and reopened as a gastro-pub. The girls were in a panic, not knowing if they'd find other work; they considered themselves to be 'dancers' – 'performers', even – and not whores. But they were too rough for the new lap-dancing clubs which were using only young Czech, Polish and Russian girls.

I sat at the bar with a newspaper, watching the intense delirium of the men who stared at Lucy. In her break we went upstairs to Wolf's old room, all his possessions having been removed by Bushy. To help Lucy with her English, I read to her, as I'd got into the habit of doing recently – but would do no more – passages from my favourite stuff: Elizabethan poetry, bits of *Civilisation and Its Discontents,* Dr Seuss.

Not that she grasped much of it, but it made us both laugh, lying there happily misunderstanding each other.

CHAPTER FORTY-EIGHT

I am no longer young, and not yet old. I have reached the age of wondering how I will live, and what I will do, with my remaining time and desire. I know at least that I need to work, that I want to read and think and write, and to eat and talk with friends and colleagues.

Rafi will soon be an adult; I want to travel with him and his mother – if I can raise their interest – to the places I have loved, showing them Italian churches, and having dinner in Rome. We could see Indian cities, bookshops in Paris, canals in Hertfordshire, waterfalls in Brazil, museums in Barcelona.

I am not, I feel certain, finished with love, either in its benign or disorderly form, nor it with me.

I shake myself and get up. I have been sitting dreamily in my chair for a long time. The bell has rung at least twice. Maria must have gone to the market.

I go to the door and let the patient in. He takes off his coat and shoes, and lies down on the couch. I sit just behind his head where I can hear him without being seen. For a while he says nothing.

I empty my mind, aware only of my breathing and of his, as we both wait for the stranger inside him to begin speaking.

·